FINAL
RESTING
PLACE

FINAL
RESTING
PLACE

A LINCOLN AND
SPEED MYSTERY

Jonathan F. Putnam

CROOKED
LANE

NEW YORK

Copyright © 2018 by Jonathan F. Putnam.

Published in the United States by Crooked Lane Books, an imprint of The Quick Brown Fox & Company LLC.

Crooked Lane Books and its logo are trademarks of The Quick Brown Fox & Company LLC.

Library of Congress Catalog-in-Publication data available upon request.

ISBN (hardcover): 978-1-68331-598-8
ISBN (ePub): 978-1-68331-599-5
ISBN (ePDF): 978-1-68331-600-8

Cover design by Melanie Sun.
Book design by Jennifer Canzone.

Printed in the United States.

www.crookedlanebooks.com

Crooked Lane Books
34 West 27th St., 10th Floor
New York, NY 10001

First Edition: July 2018

10 9 8 7 6 5 4 3 2 1

To my parents, Bob and Rosemary Putnam

PROLOGUE

The funeral service for my sister Ann took place at the Methodist Episcopal Church in Louisville. I sat between my parents—my mother convulsed in tears, my aging father staring straight ahead, unblinking—and half-listened to the words of comfort pronounced by the Rev. Dr. Humphrey. Nothing he said could lessen the pain of seeing Ann's small casket, wreathed by spring flowers, resting at the base of the pulpit.

Ann's birth had been a surprise gift for my father's 60th birthday. She had entered the world a decade after my parents' next-youngest child, and along with my nine other siblings I had doted on her from the moment she drew her first breath. So, when word reached us in Springfield, Illinois, where my sister Martha and I were living on the frontier, that Ann had contracted the dreaded smallpox from a playmate, we had leapt aboard the first eastbound stagecoach. Alas, by the time we'd reached Louisville, Ann breathed no more.

My elder brother James ascended the pulpit and thanked the Reverend Doctor for his fine Christian words. With our father's declining health, James now spoke for the Speed family. He gazed out on the congregation, packed with representatives of the other great families of Louisville, and took a deep breath.

"We are grieved," began James, "that the pattering of Ann's little feet has been stilled, that the music of her lisping tongue has been forever hushed. It is midnight for our blackened souls. Yet in time that midnight shall give way to the somber twilight that precedes the coming dawn. In time, we shall realize Ann is not gone but gone *before*, and that we may see her again one day, if we live our lives according to her example and His dictates."

A cry of grief rang out and I turned to look at the assemblage of a dozen of our house slaves, all dressed in mourning black, standing against the back wall of the sanctuary and listening intently to James's words. Martha and I had obtained special permission from the Rev. Dr. Humphrey allowing the Negro bondsmen to enter his church for the occasion. The wail had escaped from an old woman with long gray hair named Phillis, a midwife who'd helped birth Ann. Phillis's face was newly covered by the ugly scars of the pox, with which she'd been burdened during her tireless efforts to nurse Ann back to life.

"As I look out at this gathering," continued my brother, "I am reminded of the central role of family in our lives. As children grow . . . as parents age"—here, James could not help but glance at our father before continuing—"the bonds of family may weaken to the point where we become tempted to behold our own blood as indifferently as we behold the stranger. But the bonds of family are stronger than that, stronger than any earthly event, stronger even than death. The bonds of family may fray but, the Almighty willing, they shall never break."

Martha and I stayed at Farmington, our family's estate, for six weeks after Ann's funeral. I had time for several long conversations with my father, Judge Speed, conversations that reminded me of the great man he'd once been but, sadly, no longer was. Our time back home also reminded me of why I had been eager to leave and seek my own fortune by running a general store on the frontier. When the period of full mourning passed and half-mourning arrived, Martha and I agreed it was time to return to our new lives.

Martha wore a black traveling cloak over her unadorned gray dress for the long carriage ride back to Springfield. I had carefully wrapped a black crepe weeper around the hatband of my straw hat. And though custom dictated that I need not display my mourning on my sleeve for the death of a young sibling, such deaths being all too common, I had assured my family I'd wear a black armband for six more months.

"It's not fair, Joshua," said Martha after we had ridden for several hours, staring out silently at the thickly forested country-side. Martha was barely eighteen, six years my junior and the next-youngest Speed child to Ann. The death of our sister had affected her deeply.

"No, it isn't."

"She was so sweet, so innocent. Only eight years of age . . . Why would God take her from us?"

I raised my hands, palms facing the skies, and let them fall helplessly to my lap. Even now, what was there to say?

The ride back to Springfield lasted only six days, but it spanned a lifetime. Martha and I told and retold our favorite stories about Ann, and we cried until it seemed we were out of tears. Gradually, the tears gave way to laughter. Ann would never be far from our hearts, but as we neared home, both of us felt ready to resume something like our normal lives again. Our effervescent little sister would have wanted it that way.

Eventually we reached the vast prairie, awash with newly blooming flowers and freshly sprouted grasses, that surrounded Springfield. That evening we stopped at the Shelbyville crossroads. There were few other persons about at the inn, and Martha and I had the bed to ourselves. At least, we did until I found sleep.

Ann came to visit me that night—a tangible, achingly real vision of her. She was wearing her pea-green silk, with a garland of yellow and white flowers encircling her forehead. If possible, she was even more beautiful in death than she had been in life. She reached her small arms around my neck in an embrace and I smelled the honeysuckle in her hair.

"Come chase me, Joshua," she giggled.

And so, I raced her through the fields of Farmington, weaving around sage-green stalks of hemp that reached to my shoulders and up and down grassy meadows until we collapsed together on the steep banks of the small, clear stream that cut through our plantation.

I was awoken by a noise from the hallway. I could still feel Ann's soft touch as I stirred and could still hear the music of her tongue. As I opened my eyes, I saw her rising from the bed and waving good-bye.

"Ann! Don't leave!" I shouted, but it was to no avail.

Beside me in bed Martha startled into wakefulness, a strange, bewildered look on her face. I felt Martha's cool hand resting next to my warm skin.

"You dreamt of her, too?" said Martha. "Ann was in the school-house, in her yellow silk, and I was helping her learn her letters." She swallowed. "I suppose I never shall again."

I smiled a bittersweet smile. "In the next world, perhaps. For this one, we'll have to rely upon one another."

CHAPTER 1

The good citizens of Springfield had been waiting a long time for Old Man Evans to cross the great river to the next world, and in April, the week after Martha and I returned to town, he finally did. Evans had managed to outlive all of his nearby kin. Accordingly, there was no one around to take offense at the collective enthusiasm that accompanied his passing.

Many men pronounced themselves glad that they would no longer encounter Evans in one of Springfield's many grog shops, lest the old man say something in his drunken state that might provoke a brawl or, worse yet, a duel. Meanwhile, the townswomen breathed a sigh of relief that they no longer had to instruct their daughters to make a wide detour around Evans on the muddy streets, so as to avoid his lecherous tongue and leering eyes.

But without question the persons who welcomed Evans's death with the greatest excitement were the real estate speculators, a group that counted nearly all of the professional and political men in town among its number. Evans had been one of the original settlers of Springfield, and he owned the last vacant plot of land bordering the town square. With the state capital due to move to town next year—even now, the outlines of the grand new capitol building were starting to rise in the center of the square—Evans's prime property harbored untold riches.

Evans's land was auctioned off on the first Sunday in June at the old market house. I had secret hopes that I might emerge as the winning bidder. Other men in town had far greater experience with speculation, but I had what I thought might prove a decisive advantage: for the past year I had shared lodgings with the lawyer for Evans's estate, the man who would conduct the auction. His name was Abraham Lincoln.

"You realize I can't show favoritism towards you," Lincoln said as we dressed in our bedroom on the morning of the auction. Our chambers consisted of a narrow, second-floor room with two double beds perched atop my general store.

"Of course."

"The net proceeds from the sale are going to this Olson fellow, the second cousin I located in Boston. I'm duty-bound to get him the best price I can."

"I understand." I adjusted my tie in front of the looking glass nailed to the wall by the door. "But perhaps the final bids will prove even, and you'll go with the bidder whose credit you can trust."

Lincoln took his turn in front of the glass and settled his tall, black stovepipe hat on top of his head. The combined height of the man and his costume nearly scraped the low ceiling. He frowned at his reflection. "Perhaps," he said. "There's one way to find out. Let's be off."

The old market house was a two-story wooden building, topped by a square cupola, which stood on the edge of town. The ground floor consisted of a large, open hall, measuring some forty feet by eighty, interrupted only by thick, upright logs that acted as support columns. In normal times, it hosted farmers looking to sell produce, eggs, and firewood, as well as widows trafficking in gossip. When we arrived, it was overflowing with men and women, speculators and spectators. Everyone was dressed in their Sunday best and chattering with excitement.

Lincoln went up to the auctioneer stand that had been erected on the stage at one end of the room. Meanwhile, I spied the soft, oval face and light brown hair of my sister Martha, waiting beside one of the columns.

"You said it would be crowded," said Martha when I reached her and we exchanged kisses. "But I had no idea there'd be this much interest. There must be three hundred people here."

"It's by far the most attractive lot left anywhere near the square," I replied. "Everyone wants it."

Lincoln shouted for order and gradually the excited roar of the crowd died away. "When I was writing out his will," began Lincoln in a reedy voice that nonetheless carried throughout the hall, "I told Evans there was more appreciation for him in town than he realized. If only he could have seen this multitude."

"If he truly wanted to be popular, he should have died years ago," a man in the audience called out. Laughter and shouts of approval bounced around the great hall.

"Very true," said Lincoln, his lantern jaw lighting up with a crooked smile. "The lot in question is on Sixth Street, the east side of the square, between the apothecary and Smithson's dry goods. Mr. Enos"—Lincoln gestured to a sallow-faced man near the front of the room who was smoking a corncob pipe—"has been over the property twice with his compass and chain, and he assures me his survey can be relied upon. The title is clear.

"I've previously published in both the *Journal* and the *Democrat* the commercial terms the estate requires. One-third of the purchase price must be paid today in specie—gold or silver coin. I will accept notes written out and signed by men of good reputation for an additional one-third. And finally, the estate will accept one-third on credit, payable in twelve months.

"I'll start the bidding at twenty dollars. Do I hear twenty for the Evans plot?"

A vast forest of hands shot up. Lincoln inspected them and his eyes fixed on me. "By chance I saw Joshua Speed first," he said. An appreciative laugh spread through the crowd; everyone knew there was no chance about it. "Speed has it at twenty dollars. Do I hear thirty?"

It was to prove my only bid. In quick succession Lincoln heard thirty, forty, fifty, and every number up to five hundred. The number of active bidders dwindled from virtually the entire room to a dozen men, to seven, and then to three.

Each bid generated cheers from the crowd, but as the bidding rose higher and higher, the cheers turned to gasps. I heard a man next to me say that the previous town record for a lot this size was four hundred and twenty-five dollars, and when one of the remaining bidders shouted out "six fifty," the man gaped and shook his head with wonder.

After a half-hour of bidding, only two contestants remained. I knew them both well. One was the Democratic lawyer and politician Stephen Douglas. Word circulated through the room that Douglas was bidding on behalf of an unnamed benefactor, who in turn was sponsoring a new preacher and intended to build a church on the lot. My sister had taken to rooting for Douglas, and every time he uttered a new number in his distinctive baritone rumble, she gave an excited "Hooray!"

The other bidder was the apothecary Henry Owens, a jovial fellow with a carefully trimmed beard and eyeglasses perched on the end of his nose. He was a prosperous man but hardly wealthy, and his continued presence in the bidding produced a great deal of whispered supposition that leapt around the room like wildfire. Eventually a rough consensus formed on the idea that Owens was bidding on behalf of a syndicate of some sort, but whether this was true and who comprised the moneyed aspect of the group continued to be fervently debated.

Prodded by Lincoln, Douglas and Owens went back and forth, higher and higher. Men in the audience turned to their neighbors and placed side wagers on which bidder would ultimately prevail and at what price. Seven fifty. Eight hundred. Eight fifty! The crowd was in a frenzy of delirium. At the sound of "eight seventy" from Owens's mouth, a cheer arose so loud that I feared the roof of the market house might fall down on top of us.

Near Lincoln on the stage was a broad-shouldered fellow with muttonchop whiskers and a head full of loose blond curls. He was watching the proceedings with a smile that seemed to grow wider in direct proportion to the latest bid—and for good reason. The man was Joseph Early, the registrar of the Springfield land office. He would have to formally record the transaction, and by federal statute he was entitled to pocket six percent of the purchase price for every land sale registered. It was already an excellent day for Early, and it was only getting better.

"The bid is eight hundred and seventy dollars," repeated Lincoln. "Your response, Mr. Douglas?"

The whole crowd turned to Douglas. Many stood on tiptoe to try to get a view of the man. Douglas had arrived from the East several years ago, and he had been in a hurry to make a name for himself ever since. Unlike the apothecary, Douglas's participation in the final bidding surprised no one.

Douglas considered. The room was suddenly dead silent with anticipation. I could hear my sister's breathing. There was a muffled jingle, as if Douglas was sorting through his coin purse. "We bid," he began, as the crowd sucked in its collective breath, "eight hundred and eighty-one dollars and—" A scream of excitement drowned out his words, but I managed to catch "five cents."

"Hooray! Hooray!" cried my sister, throwing her arms around my neck. "He did it! Stephen won!"

I was no friend to Douglas, nor he to me. I pried my sister's arms off. "Not yet, he didn't. Let's see what Owens does."

Lincoln turned to the apothecary. "Mr. Owens?"

This time the roiling crowd couldn't keep quiet. Owens's eyes darted around the room, seemingly catching the gaze of several other men, and a swell of whispers raced about, renewed speculation on the nature of his mysterious syndicate. Owens turned back to the stage.

"Why not make it an even nine hundred, Mr. Lincoln," called Owens. Douglas threw up his arms, turned on his heels, and walked from the hall. And bedlam reigned.

Twenty minutes later I stood beside Lincoln and watched him count out the coins and scrutinize the notes proffered by Owens. After lengthy, deliberate consideration, Lincoln pronounced himself satisfied, and he handed a bill of sale and promissory note to Owens to read and sign.

As the apothecary reviewed the papers, Lincoln doled out emol-
uments from the coins that had been handed over: fifty-four dollars
to Early, the registrar; ten to the surveyor, Enos; five dollars to the
owner of the market house; and so on.

"You should take something yourself, Lincoln," I said, "for
getting such an outstanding price."

"Evans paid me my standard fee of three dollars for drawing up
the will. And he proposed to stand me for an ale at Torrey's, though
I declined the offer. The fee was mine to keep, whether I sold the
property or not. The second cousin gets the rest." Lincoln shrugged
and turned back to the apothecary. "How are you coming on the
papers, Owens?"

As I waited for my roommate to finish his scrivening, I looked
out at the hall, by now nearly empty. My eye was caught by a man
leaning against one of the support columns. He had not moved to
disperse with the crowd after the auction ended, and he was intently
watching the transaction on stage with his arms folded in front of
him.

The man was short and trim, and he had the appearance of
a dandy. But it was the look in the man's eye that caught my attention—
and held it. There was something *ravenous* about his expression. It
was a look I would not soon forget.

CHAPTER 2

I took out my pocket watch and was aggrieved to learn that only five minutes had passed since the last time I consulted it. I cursed under my breath. Lincoln was late. I knew he was consumed by politicking and electioneering, but I was too tired from a long day behind the store counter to wait for an audience with my own roommate, even if he was a politician in the midst of a hard-fought campaign.

It was several weeks after the tumultuous auction at the market house, and I was in the gentlemen's smoking room of Colonel Spotswood's Rural Hotel. Spotswood's was the most fashionable hotel in town, though it was soon to be overtaken by the grand American House, now rising to a fourth floor—the first building in town to reach such heights—on the southwest corner of the public square.

A dozen other men were scattered about the smoking room with me, and the conversation had been dominated by the ongoing political season. The year was 1838, an election year, and voting would take place soon, on the first Monday in August. The men and women of Springfield could talk of little else.

The race attracting the most attention was the battle for U.S. congressman from Illinois's Third District, a huge tract of mostly unpopulated land stretching all the way up to the border with the Wisconsin Territory. Lincoln's law partner, John Todd Stuart, was the candidate of the Whig Party for the seat; his opponent from the

Democratic Party was the Eastern newcomer who had come in second at the market house auction: the peculiar, some said remarkable, Stephen Douglas.

The smoking room this evening was filled by the competing arguments of the Whig and Democratic men in attendance about how best to rescue the country from the lingering economic problems caused by the banking Panic of '37. The various arguments espoused and debated involved such arcane matters as the "sub-Treasury Scheme," the "Specie Circular," and the "Loco-foco Rebellion."

For all of the passionate arguments, however, there was precious little chance any votes would be swayed tonight. Every man present was a dedicated supporter of one party or the other and one candidate or the other. But the essence of politics on the frontier sometimes appeared to be the insistent repetition of one's viewpoint as both the speaker and his listeners became increasingly intoxicated. It was hard to tell if the ultimate objective was to persuade men to change their views or rather to incapacitate one's opponents through drink and therefore drive down their numbers on election day.

For myself, I tried to get along with men on both sides of the partisan divide. While I was, like my roommate Lincoln, a committed Whig, I was mindful of my own commercial interests. As I had explained to Lincoln, Democrats purchased as many dry goods and patent medicines from my general store as did Whigs. Especially in these uncertain economic times, I was in no position to refuse the patronage of half of the two thousand residents of our frontier town.

"Care for another, Speed?" came a hearty voice from beside me. Looking up, I saw the broad form of Jacob Early, the land office registrar and another devoted Whig.

"Most obliged," I replied, handing him my empty ale glass.

My eyes followed Early as he lumbered over to the open cask sitting in the corner of the room. A pipe carved of yellow ivory was clenched between his teeth.

"Waiting for Lincoln to appear?" Early asked as he returned with two slopping glasses and handed one to me.

I nodded. "He told me he'd be here an hour ago."

Early consulted his own pocket watch and loosed a low growl. "He told me the same. I know he's focused on Stuart's race against Douglas, like most of them are"—Early indicated the men spread about the smoking room with a sweep of his burly arm—"but he should pay attention to his own race as well. It's no good to tend to the fields if your barn falls down behind you."

In addition to the Stuart–Douglas match, there were a dozen other races on the ballot. The one of most interest involved Lincoln seeking reelection to his seat in the state legislature. Early himself had placed Lincoln's name into nomination at a meeting of Sangamon County's Whigs earlier in the year.

"He'll arrive soon, I should think."

"I hope so. I've brought him intelligence from New Salem on the actions of his adversaries from that part of the county. And I need his counsel on another matter as well."

Something about the way Early said this final sentence made me turn. "What other matter?" I asked.

Early glanced around to make sure no one else was within earshot, then said in a low voice, "Something I've discovered looking through the files of my predecessor. An *official* land office matter. Best kept for Lincoln's ears at present. You understand."

Lincoln had ensured Early's appointment as registrar after the Whig successes in the last election. Not least among the reasons for the avid interest in politics on the frontier was the wealth of plum patronage jobs that went to the winners. And there were few patronage jobs plummier than registrar of one of the federal land offices sprinkled throughout the West.

The speculative buying and selling of real estate sometimes seemed to be the official pastime of the frontier, as the national government worked as fast as it could to sell into private hands the land it had appropriated from the native tribes and men thereafter traded property deeds like playing cards. The registrar stood directly at the intersection of the twin obsessions of real estate speculation and politics. And as Early's enormous share of the auction proceeds demonstrated—fifty-four dollars was enough to feed a large family for several months—the registrar was practically guaranteed to become a wealthy man.

"Have you heard of this damned fellow Henry Truett?" Early added.

"Who?"

"A right son of a bitch," he muttered, shaking his head and spitting onto the sawdust-covered floor. "Wants to be appointed to replace me at the land office if the Democrats win in August. It'd be a disaster, and not just for my purse. The man has no idea how to—"

Early interrupted himself, his jaw falling open. He needed to catch his pipe before it fell to his lap, and he swore out loud. At the same moment the entire room fell silent and then erupted into an even louder cacophony. Lincoln and another man had walked into the room at the same time. I hurriedly took leave of Early.

"Here I am," I said, extending my hand and giving Lincoln's a firm squeeze.

"Sorry I'm late," he said, gripping my shoulder.

I stepped back and contemplated my roommate. He was now just shy of thirty years of age. Even with the slight stoop in his shoulders, he was the tallest man in town, standing nearly six and a half feet. He wore a black frockcoat, black vest, and black trousers. His dark hair emerged beneath his stovepipe hat and curled down around his ears. He had a high-peaked forehead, wide-set gray eyes, and a prominent jaw. I sometimes thought him the homeliest man in town, but I always found him the most compelling.

"This blasted campaign," Lincoln continued. "I can't hardly wait until it's done and gone. I've spent all evening plotting with Stuart. He and Douglas are neck and neck. If we all do our duty, I think we shall succeed in the end. But if we relax an iota, we shall be beaten."

"And your own campaign?"

"I'll be fine, as long as I don't attract any controversy before election day," he said with a laugh. "That's why I'm spending most of my time trying to help Stuart take down Douglas."

"Get out!" This shout came from the other side of the room.

Early was standing behind an upholstered armchair and gesturing angrily at the person who had accompanied Lincoln into the room. I looked at him now and, with a start, realized he was the very same man I had seen at the market house, watching the final transaction with hungering eyes.

"Who's that?" I asked Lincoln.

"Fellow named Henry Truett. An old acquaintance of mine, in point of fact. From back before I moved to Springfield."

"Early was just telling me about his rivalry with Truett. I've never seen Early so agitated."

Lincoln sighed. "It's not only the voters I need to worry about at this season. It's the office-holders and office-seekers as well. I've already given Early my assurance that his job is secure if we Whigs prevail."

I looked at Truett again. He was a compact figure, dandified almost to the point of parody. He wore a red velvet coat, cinched tight over a ruffled white shirt, and checkerboard trousers. The fine gold chain of a watch dangled from his pocket. His cravat, tied smartly around his neck, was a silky lime green, and his black top hat was tall and shiny. He wouldn't have been out of place in the retinue of King Louis Philippe on a drive around the Tuileries. Looking at the expression of hatred spread across Early's face, I thought it could be no coincidence Truett had appeared here in such extravagant fashion.

"What business have you?" growled Early.

"Does a man need business to enter a public room in this town?" returned Truett. "I think not."

"You should leave at once, if you know what's good for you."

"I wonder," said Truett, "if you saw the pamphlet circulated at the Democratic Convention in Peoria last month. The one accusing me of being unfit to run the land office."

"Of course I saw it." Early's strong jaw was set and his eyes glinted. "Everyone at the convention did."

Truett nodded. A hint of a red flush began to creep into his temples. "I was told you were the author. Do you deny it?"

"Who told you that?"

"A friend. I'm not at liberty to reveal his name."

"Then I'm not at liberty to answer your question." Early clenched the wings of the armchair.

"You're a damned scoundrel is what you are," said Truett. "A damned scoundrel and a damned rascal."

A murmur went up from the other men present, all of whom were watching the argument in rapt attention. A few more verbal rounds like this and one of the rivals was likely to challenge the other to a duel. The antipathy between them was even greater than I had imagined.

Early hoisted the armchair high off the ground. The chair brushed against the candelabra hanging in the center of the room, and for a moment I feared the chair might be set ablaze by one of the swaying candles. Early shook the chair back and forth in front of Truett. In his hulking arms, it was easy to imagine the object as a deadly projectile.

Shouts of concern arose from all corners of the room. "Stand down, Early," commanded Lincoln. "We must concentrate our fight on the campaign. After we've prevailed at the polls, there'll be plenty of time for figuring out the spoils. And plenty of spoils to go around."

"I'll stand down once he leaves," said Early, shaking his chair in Truett's direction.

"I refuse," said Truett. "I was libeled and I deserve to know by whom. Just admit you wrote the pamphlet, Early. All I want is the satisfaction of hearing you confess what you've done."

"It's not libel if it's the truth," said Early.

"Then we'll do it your way," said Truett. He reached underneath the flared folds of his frockcoat and drew out a compact belt pistol, about six inches long, with a walnut stock and polished silver barrel.

All hell broke loose.

The man standing closest to Truett leapt at him and knocked the pistol out of his hand. The two men fell to the floor. At the same moment, Early hurled the chair at Truett, but it missed its target and crashed down onto the floorboards, breaking apart into several large pieces. Swearing, Early dove at Truett on the floor. Men rushed toward them from all directions. Cries flew and punches landed. It was impossible to tell the peacemakers from the trouble-makers. Lincoln charged into the melee and began pulling men from the seething, squirming pile.

I was about to join him when my eye was caught by a sudden movement from the side of the smoking room. Two new men, one older and one younger, were walking through the door. They hesitated, sizing up the situation, and then the older man made a direct line for Lincoln. From the twisted look of malevolence on his face and his tensed fists, his ill intentions were clear.

The older man reached Lincoln just before I did, seized Lincoln's arm, and spun him around. Lincoln's face contorted with surprise. I grabbed Lincoln's assailant from behind by both arms and tried to pull him away, but the old man was barrel-chested and surprisingly strong. Inches from him, I could smell the telltale odor of a man well acquainted with the whiskey bottle.

"Step away," I shouted, "or I'll—"

"Wait, Speed!" cried Lincoln, his voice cracking.

I froze. Lincoln and the older man gazed at each other in silence as the melee continued behind us. Something passed between them. Lincoln's face twitched. After a moment, the old man relaxed his grip on my friend and spoke in a hoarse voice.

"They said we'd find you here. It's good to see you again, my son."

CHAPTER 3

An hour later I sat in a chair by the fireplace in the back room of the Globe Tavern and contemplated Thomas Lincoln, the father Lincoln had almost never mentioned during the fifteen months we'd shared living quarters.

He was a thick, stocky man of sixty years. He had a full shock of white hair above a proud face, with prominent cheekbones, a very large nose, and a high forehead. The more I stared at father and son, the more I thought the forehead was the principal feature of resemblance. But lower down on the face the similarities ended. Where Lincoln's mouth was always active, always ready for a broad smile, his father's was limp and tired. He had a weak chin and sagging skin around his neck.

Thomas Lincoln wore an old frockcoat, nearly threadbare and badly faded from exposure to the sun. As I'd noticed in our initial encounter, the coat carried the whiff of whiskey. The white of his shirt underneath was uneven, as if a vigorous application of the washing board had not been completely successful at removing the many stains of the wearer's life. His pants carried a similar fade, as did his coat, and his boots were caked with mud. Encountering him alone on the street, I would have guessed him an itinerant peddler of books or perhaps of quack remedies.

Now he slouched on a chair and stared at his son through rheumy eyes. The son ignored the gaze, staring instead at the blackened bricks of the quiet fireplace. And there was a fourth man present, too—the younger man who had entered Spotswood's at Thomas Lincoln's side. While no one had bothered to introduce us and the man himself had not once deigned to look either me or Lincoln squarely in the eye, I gathered from the conversation that his name was John Johnston and that he was Thomas Lincoln's stepson. In our time together, Lincoln had never once mentioned having a stepbrother.

After we'd ensured that order was restored at Spotswood's without permanent bodily injury being sustained by anyone—although I feared we hadn't seen the last of the feud between Early and Truett—we'd gone out on the dark streets. Thomas Lincoln and John Johnston had pronounced themselves hungry after a long day's journey, so Lincoln had led us to the Globe. The innkeeper, Saunders, now came in with two bowls of stew for the travelers. Both men grasped the bowls and started drinking eagerly. Casting surreptitious glances at the newcomers and then at Lincoln, whose face was taut, Saunders withdrew.

"I still don't understand why you didn't write to advise me of your intention to visit," said Lincoln to his father.

"Don't think we had the intention," said Thomas Lincoln, looking up from his bowl. "Until we arrived, that is. Do you always know what you *intend* to do the next week, or the next day, for that matter?"

"Yes," said Lincoln, stiffly.

"Well, we ain't," said John Johnston. He loosed an enthusiastic belch and grinned with pride.

"Not every time, we don't," said Thomas Lincoln. "But I wouldn't think that too important. Intention or not, we're here. So how we doing, Abe?"

"Very well, thank you."

"It seems to be so," said his father, nodding rapidly. "It seems to be so. When we arrived here in town and asked that fella"—he gestured to where Saunders had been standing a minute earlier—"where we could find tall Abe Lincoln, we expected him to say, 'Who? Abe who?' Didn't we, Johnnie?"

"We sure did."

"We sure did. But instead he said something very different." Thomas Lincoln affected a rich voice unlike either his own hoarse rasp or Saunders's guttural growl. " 'You're looking for the esteemed Abraham Lincoln? Abraham Lincoln, Esquire? Why, at this hour you'll be likely to find him over at Spotswood's smoking room, the finest establishment in town, where gentlemen of the fine character of Abraham Lincoln, Esquire, are given to lounge in repose at this time of evening.' "

"I very much doubt those were his exact words," said Lincoln.

"Exact words? Or course not. How am I supposed to remember his exact words? But that sure was the impression he gave us. Wasn't it, Johnnie? 'The esteemed Abraham Lincoln, Esquire.' "

"Sure was," said Johnston. " 'Course, those weren't his *exact words*, right?" He guffawed and elbowed his stepfather in the ribs.

Lincoln's facial muscles were frozen in place. I could tell he would have given anything to be anywhere other than here, now. I tried to come to his rescue.

"Where are you two men traveling from?" I asked.

"Let's see," said Thomas Lincoln, still slurping at his bowl. "Yesterday we was in Athens. And the day before that we was in Bloomington."

"And tomorrow?" asked Lincoln.

"Tomorrow? Why, I think we'll be in Springfield tomorrow, most likely—"

"At least, that's our *intention*," broke in John Johnston, turning to his stepfather with an eager grin.

"Don't be a bore, Johnnie. We've all left that one behind. We'll be here in Springfield tomorrow. Be here for several days, I should think. We're hoping you'll conduct us around town, Abe. Show us the sights. Introduce us to your friends. That is, in addition to Mr. . . . what'd you say your name was?"

"Speed. Joshua Fry Speed." I'd told him twice previously.

"In addition to Mr. Joshua Fry Speed. I'm sure you've got quite a few other friends for us to meet, knowing how much you like to chatter about. Now, where are you from, Mr. Speed?"

"Louisville. I moved here four years ago—"

"Kentucky? Why, we're from Kentucky, too—me and Abe and Johnnie. Not a fancy town like Louisville, mind you. Little speck of spit called Sinking Spring. Course, these boys did most of their growing up across the border in Indiana, along Pigeon Creek."

"So Abraham's told me," I said, trying to keep from smiling.

"You should of seen Abe in Indiana, Mr. Speed. What a rascal! The smartest boy for miles around. But a goddamned troublemaker, I'll tell you." Thomas Lincoln's face was lit up by a grin now—not unlike his son's face as he warmed to a story, I considered—and he gave Lincoln a hearty slap on the back.

"You should of seen him in Pigeon Creek. You remember the time with your dear mother and the whitewashed ceiling? Remember that one, Abe?"

"I do," said Lincoln, his expression still tense and drawn.

"Remember it, Johnnie?" continued Thomas Lincoln.

"I do," said John Johnston, with a lack of enthusiasm matching his stepbrother's.

Thomas Lincoln turned to me. "Let me tell you what happened, Mr. Joshua Fry Speed. Abe and Johnnie's mother, Sarah—this is my second wife, Johnnie's blood mother. Technically Abe's stepmother, but no blood mother ever loved her son more than my Sarah loves my Abraham. Isn't that so, Abe?"

"It is," said Lincoln quietly. I looked back and forth between him and John Johnston. The starkly contrasting expressions on the faces of the two sons, one by blood, the other by marriage, pointed to the same conclusion: Thomas Lincoln had just uttered a deep truth.

"Anyhow," continued Thomas Lincoln. He stopped and shook his head. "I'm losing my own story. My mind ain't what it was. Where was I?"

"Whitewashed ceiling," I suggested. Lincoln shot me an aggrieved glance, which I ignored. Even if Lincoln couldn't, I could see Thomas Lincoln had real feeling for his son. It seemed unkind to deprive him of his reminiscence.

"Exactly! Whitewashed ceiling. See, my wife Sarah, she was mighty proud of her nice whitewashed rafters. They was about the only part of her house she could keep clean, what with all them kids underfoot. Now as Abe grew and grew, she was always on him about keeping his head washed. Because he got to be so tall that any dirt on his hair rubbed against her rafters and caused them to lose their shine.

"Now what do you suppose this goddamned Abe did? He agreed to keep his head washed, all right. But one morning after it rained, he gathered three little boys from the neighborhood. He must of been—what? How old was you when this happened, Abraham?"

"Fourteen."

"Sixteen, I think it was. He must of been sixteen. And he got three boys, ages seven or nine, something of the sort. And he told 'em he'd give 'em a penny each if they walked through a mud puddle. Well, that was the dumbest thing he'd done in his whole life, god-dammit! You don't got to pay 'em a penny! Ain't been a nine-year-old boy born yet who wouldn't walk through a mud puddle for free." Thomas Lincoln roared with laughter and slapped his son on the back again.

"Anyhow, after he'd paid 'em a penny each and they'd walked through the mud, one at a time he picked 'em up, held 'em upside down, and carried 'em into our house. And he told 'em to walk their muddy feet up and down my Sarah's whitewashed rafters. And of course they did it—you ain't got to pay 'em a penny to walk through the mud, Abe!—and a little bit later my Sarah comes home and opens her door and screams. Every inch of her precious white-washed rafters is covered with muddy footprints.

"Now what do you suppose my dear wife did next, Mr. Joshua Fry Speed?"

"Whipped him?"

"Nah. He was too big for that. More important, he was too loved. Too goddamned loved! After Sarah got done screaming, she started laughing. And she laughed and she laughed until tears ran down her face. And then she called for Abe and they looked at the footprints on the rafters together, arms around each other's waists, and they laughed together. You should of seen it! 'Course, then she ordered him to scrub up her ceiling till it was like new, and 'course he agreed, being the good son he was."

Thomas Lincoln reached up and ran his aged hand through Lincoln's hair. With a great, almost tangible, effort, Lincoln did not pull away. John Johnston glowered.

Throughout his stepfather's story, Johnston's irritation had been visibly building. He was about the same age as Lincoln, maybe a year or two younger, but that was the extent of the similarities between the stepbrothers. Johnston was slight and blond-headed, with a wispy beard and a delicate nose. His clothes carried a sheen that suggested a studied attempt to obscure the poverty of the wearer. As Thomas Lincoln's story came to its end, what remained of Johnston's self-control gave way.

"Tell 'em about what happened the other night, Papa," he said eagerly.

"What other night?" Thomas Lincoln was still staring at Lincoln and shaking his head at the wonder of those muddy footprints all up and down his wife's whitewashed rafters.

"The other night in Bloomington, when we fooled that barkeep into giving us a second pour of whiskey for nothing."

"You go ahead and tell 'em if you like, Johnnie."

Johnston's face fell further. He hesitated. "Maybe another time. Can't give away all our tricks, can we?" He fiddled with one of the buttons on his coat. "So, Abe, how're you making out with the womenfolk of Springfield?"

Lincoln turned toward his stepbrother. "Fine, I suppose, John."

"'Fine?' Just 'fine?'" Johnston looked directly at me for the first time. "Did Abe ever tell you, Mr. Speed, what went on with him and the fairer sex back when he was living in New Salem?"

"I'm not sure I consider it any of my—"

"He must not of. I'm going to tell you. There was this girl he had a fancy for. Name of Ann. Ann Winkhouse . . . Rutland. Something along them lines."

"Johnnie—" began Thomas Lincoln, but Johnston waved him aside and continued his story. Johnston thrust his chest forward, mimicking, whether consciously or not, the posture his stepfather had assumed during his tale.

"Anyway, this Ann happens to be betrothed to another man.

Our Abe is too proper, too honest, to make a play for her, even though it's obvious to everyone he wants to. What's more, this beau fellow of Ann's is off in the wilds somewhere, so Abe's stuck. He's got no one to fight for Ann's hand.

"Now, as time passes, Ann falls for our Abe. How could you not, just looking at him?" Johnston laughed; Lincoln's eyes were diverted to the ground. "But her beau's still nowhere to be found. So they keep on waiting. And then it turns out this other fellow's a fraud, a trickster. Turns out Abe knew this other fellow all along, only he knew him by a different name than the one he'd given Ann. He was a trickster, and he was playing Ann for a sucker. Playing Abe for one too, if you think about it."

Johnston paused for a breath and finally took notice of the look of censure on Thomas Lincoln's face. Johnston opened and closed his mouth, then opened it again and said to me, "That's about the extent of the tale, if you ain't heard that one before."

Turning to Lincoln, he added, "Whatever happened to Ann Rutland? You don't talk much about her no more."

"Ann Rutledge," said Lincoln in a voice so low it was hard to hear. "She died of brain fever. Not quite three years ago."

"Oh." There was a long pause. I could hear Saunders banging a pot around in the kitchen next to us. "Sorry, Abe. I didn't realize—I didn't mean to . . . I guess you didn't ever bother to tell me about it."

Thomas Lincoln struggled to his feet. "You'll have to excuse John's lack of common sense this evening, Mr. Speed," he said. "We've had a long day on the trail and we're both in need of a good night's sleep. Let's go, Johnnie. We'll find a tree in the fields to sleep under."

"I'm afraid our room is too crowded as it is, but I can arrange a berth for you upstairs here at the Globe," said Lincoln. He was on his feet as well.

"No need for that," said the elder Lincoln. "We'll be fine in the fields, won't we Johnnie? On a beautiful summer's night like tonight? Couldn't be finer, just us and the heavens. Besides, we don't want to bother you any more than we have already. My esteemed Abraham Lincoln, Esquire."

He took a step toward Lincoln, his hands outstretched, but Lincoln shrank back and Thomas Lincoln ended up patting his son awkwardly on the wrist. Then he grabbed his stepson by the coat collar and pulled him roughly to his feet. Without another word, the two men walked from the room.

CHAPTER 4

The next morning Lincoln and I were back at the Globe, sitting amid a dozen other men at the common table in the public room, waiting for Saunders to bring us breakfast. The Globe had once been the embodiment of progress in the frontier town, but now it was showing its age: its walls peeling, its ceiling cracked, and the odors of the stables out back seeping in through grimy window-panes. Its location right around the corner from our lodgings was about all that still recommended it for breakfast.

Around us, conversation buzzed about the confrontation between Early and Truett. Though only one or two of our break-fast companions had been present at Spotswood's, every man not only was well versed in the particulars of the dispute but also had formed a definite opinion about which combatant was to blame.

"Attempted assassination . . . right in the middle of the gentle-men's smoking room, can you believe it?" said one man.

"Truett came in looking for trouble," said another. "Otherwise, why would he have concealed his pistol under his coat?"

"Early's at fault for being a busybody," said a third. "He runs the land office like he's got a warrant to look into the affairs of every man who walks through his doors."

"He's not a busybody," interjected Lincoln, coming to the defense of his ally. "He's merely attempting to do a professional job. A wel-come change from the way the land office has been run in the past."

"Won't be his job for long, once the Democrats prevail at the ballot," rejoined the man. "As they will when your man Stuart falls flat on his face, Lincoln." He punched my friend good-naturedly in the shoulder.

"I deny it," said Lincoln, smiling, "but I will admit public brawling is bad for the town of Springfield. It's not the impression we want to project, not with the state capital arriving."

"I think it's very *good* for business," came a new voice. "Mine, at least." Looking up, I saw the distinctive, egg-shaped figure of the newspaperman Simeon Francis, publisher of the *Sangamo Journal*, settling himself into a chair opposite us. The rotund publisher was in his shirtsleeves, the white cloth dotted by splotches of printer's ink. Several days' irregular growth of whiskers clung to his weak, receding chin.

"You can't sell enough papers merely covering the election, Simeon?" I asked.

"People tire rapidly," the newspaperman said with an assured wave of his short arms, "of reading about politicians discussing politics. There's only so much artifice, so much deep contrivance, a man can take with his porridge. But attempted murder? A man'll stay interested in that, week after week. And his wife will, too."

The men around us nodded with strenuous agreement. Simeon let out a contented sigh. Then he added, "Speaking of deep contrivance, Lincoln, there's an item in today's *Democrat* that's intended for you, I should think."

The newspaperman slid a copy of the *Illinois Democrat* across the table. It was the other newspaper in town, as reliably supporting the Democratic political position as Simeon's *Journal* supported the Whig cause. "Look at the bottom of page two, on the right," he added. "The letter from 'S.G.'"

I looked over Lincoln's shoulder at the sheet. There was a notice offering a reward for the return of "a runaway Negro man who calls himself Newton, about fifteen years old, with light skin and an impertinent manner, who fled from his owners at Roman Hall under false pretenses." Further down the page was a short report on the camp meeting of religious revival that had been going on in the small forest west of town all spring, a gathering that had occasioned controversy in equal measure to the number of souls who had professed to have experienced justification by faith in atonement of their sins.

In between these two items appeared the following letter:

July 1, 1838
Lost Township, Ill.

To the Editor of the Democrat:

Every right-minded man living in Sangamon County must support the Democrats in the upcoming election. The Democrats have solutions for our turbulent, uncertain times, solutions for the problems the hapless Whigs have foist upon all of us. The Whigs have only ideas that created the Panic and Depression in the first place. And they are led by a certain person (I ignore the term 'gentleman', for it fits not) of great height and low intellect, who has tried a variety of occupations, both here and elsewhere, before coming to the Legislature. He has Failed and Failed in all of them. This person is hereby Warned that his remaining days are Numbered. Judgment is coming.

S.G.

"Why do you assume, Simeon," Lincoln asked, a grin spread across his face, "I am the man of 'great height and low intellect' in question? Surely there are others around who answer that description."

"Others of some height, perhaps," replied the newspaperman, amusement lurking around his fleshy eyes. "But great height *combined* with spectacularly low intellect? You're the only one it could possibly be."

Lincoln and several of the other men sitting near us laughed heartily. Simeon added, "Besides, you're the only target big enough to be worthy of such a challenge."

Lincoln remained jovial, but I felt my heart beating as I read the letter a second time. "Who do you suppose this S.G. fellow is?" I asked. "And it sounds like a threat to me. One you should take seriously."

"It's not a threat, it's a compliment," said Lincoln. "No one but my political opponents is after me. And all they want is my seat in the legislature."

"There must have been two or three anonymous letters in every issue of the *Democrat* over the past month," added Simeon, nodding. "In my *Journal*, too. This time of the election season, everyone thinks they've got a message to deliver, whether it makes any sense or not. And the less sense it makes, the more likely they are to conceal their identity."

"As for 'S.G.' . . ." Lincoln looked up and down the common table at our fellow diners, each of whom had examined the letter for himself by now. "Any guesses?" There was a low murmur of conversation, followed by a chorus of shaking heads. "Me neither. I can't think of a single man in the county with those initials. Though I'm sure one will come to me."

Saunders appeared with scalding coffee and a steaming plate of buckwheat cakes. Thirty minutes later Lincoln and I finished eating and walked out together into the bright sunshine.

"Can you spare a minute?" Lincoln asked. "I'm making a call, and I'd value your company."

"Sure. Are we going to visit your father and stepbrother?"

He made a face. "Later, I'll have to. Alone. To try to hustle them out of town at once. I'm sorry you had to meet them last night."

"Don't be foolish. I enjoyed them."

"They were—are—an embarrassment."

From the expression on Lincoln's face, I felt certain that the unexpected arrival in town of his unwelcome relations during the election season was far more concerning to him than the anonymous letter from S.G.

"Not to me, they weren't," I said. "Besides, name me one man who doesn't get embarrassed by his own family at least once a week."

Lincoln muttered to himself and shook his head. We started walking toward the town square. "It's not them we're going to see. There's someone . . . I'd like you to meet her. Properly, that is."

"*Her?*" I repeated, my interest piqued. "Has something at long last sparked for our homely honest Abe?"

"Perhaps." There was a hint of a sly grin on his face.

"Don't be coy. Who's the unlucky girl?"

"Margaret Owens."

"Really." I tried to keep my voice as neutral as possible.

"You don't approve?"

"Of course I do." Miss Owens was a pleasant girl with a round face and straight black hair hanging nearly to her waist. She lived with her older brother, the apothecary. She was occasionally sickly and sometimes disappeared from public view for weeks at a time, presumably battling her illness. If she had uttered five words in her life, I hadn't heard them. She seemed an odd choice for my garrulous friend.

"It sounds as if you don't like her." Lincoln's expression was falling fast.

"I don't know her, is more like it. Barely had the pleasure of her acquaintance. But if you'll be keeping company with her, then I look forward to knowing her better. Starting with this morning."

"Maybe the whole thing's a folly," said Lincoln, his face now pale. "I haven't let myself have feelings for anyone since I lost Ann, you know. But I was over at Henry Owens's store, looking for a remedy for a sore tooth, and Margaret was helping out behind the counter, and—well, she has a nice way about her. And she smells like lavender."

I laughed out loud at this last sentence as we came to a halt. We had arrived at the entrance to the Owens apothecary, which stood opposite my general store on the other side of the town square.

"Fantastic. Truly, Lincoln, you should know better than to take my advice on matters of women and the heart. Not that I have any advice to give as regards Miss Owens. Now let's greet the woman."

We pushed open the door, and Henry Owens looked up from his counter. The apothecary wore shirtsleeves, a black vest, and a reassuring expression. The walls of his store were lined with wooden shelves, each holding hundreds of colorful bottles and small glass vials. Restoration awaited! One could not help but feel more healthful after merely walking into the establishment.

"What brings you gentlemen in?" asked Owens. "Don't tell me that toothache has recurred, Lincoln?"

We looked around the shop, but Miss Owens was not in evidence. "The tooth is fine," said Lincoln. "But I thought, perhaps . . . your sister . . ." He tailed off into awkward silence.

Owens gave him a knowing smile. "She's out, I'm afraid. Be back this afternoon. I'll tell her you called."

"Er—yes—thank you," stammered Lincoln, turning to leave.

"Before you go," called Owens, "there's a question I've been meaning to put to you. I've been tending to my investments in real estate lately and I've found this fellow Early, the registrar, difficult to deal with."

"I'm sorry to hear it," replied Lincoln patiently. This wasn't the first time I'd heard him take complaints about some public official. Many local residents seemed to view it as part of his job as a state representative.

"So I've been wondering," continued Owens, "whether there's someone else I can take my land office business to."

"Just Early, I'm afraid. He's a good man. You tell him I said to treat you fairly."

"Thank you, Lincoln. I shall." The apothecary seemed mollified.

"It's all I can say," explained Lincoln when he and I had exited the store. "People always think I should intercede specially on their behalf. But government can't function that way. Knowing Early, I'm sure he's already treating Owens fairly."

"Before you arrived at Spotswood's last night," I said, "Early was telling me he had some business to discuss with you. Something he's found in the land office files. He didn't say what."

"I'll track him down after I deal with my relations. Let's see if I can't get them to move along out of town and fast. Wish me luck." Lincoln gave a short laugh. "I'll need it."

CHAPTER 5

I saw little of Lincoln for the next few days, and when I did he appeared much more harried than usual. Several evenings later, however, he reported with relief that his father and stepbrother had departed town in search of a rundown gristmill they'd heard might be for sale at a reduced price in Coles County.

"I'm pleased, for your sake," I said as we jostled side by side in front of the looking glass in our bedroom. It was the fourth day of July and we were getting ready for the annual grand summer gala at the home of Ninian and Elizabeth Edwards on Quality Hill.

"Will Miss Sarah Butler be present this evening?" Lincoln asked. He fidgeted with the knot of his tie, which seemed to be either lopsided to the left or lopsided to the right, depending on which way he tugged. "I know you've been walking with her regularly."

"I hope so. I haven't seen her for a few days. I stopped by her house yesterday, but she was out. Her brother said she'd been spending time at the tent meeting of revival."

I contemplated my reflection in the glass: oblong face, strong brows, vaguely aquiline nose, and unruly black hair, which I ran a comb through now in a vain attempt to impose some order. Billy the Barber had given me a cut last month, but already the black curls were falling nearly to my shoulders.

"Have you been out to the tent meeting?" I added.

Lincoln frowned and shook his head. "A folly, if you ask me. And from what I've heard, there aren't many voters lurking about in the forest either. If you have your sights set on eternal salvation, earthly concerns like which party is best able to fix the internal improvements mess seem blessedly inconsequential.

"This blasted thing is never going to sit right," he added, staring at his necktie in the mirror as if it were a mortal enemy and throwing up his hands in frustration. He settled his stovepipe hat on his head and frowned at his reflection. "This is as good as it gets, I'm afraid. Shall we go?"

We took the stairs two at a time. "I have it on good authority," I said as we reached the storeroom on the ground floor, "that Miss Owens's interest is inversely related to your sartorial skills."

"It better be."

With Lincoln a half step behind me, we burst through the door. The warm glow of a sunny summer's day lingered on the streets. The sun had just dipped below the horizon and the azure sky was streaked with clouds glowing a soft yellow. I took in the beauty of the scene and breathed deeply of the fresh, pure air.

"Come," I said, slapping my friend on the back. "There are women to woo."

We headed across town to collect my sister. When Martha had arrived in Springfield last summer, it had been clear at once she couldn't stay with me in the crowded second-floor room above my store. Instead, she'd arranged to lodge with Molly Hutchason, an old schoolgirl friend of hers from Louisville and now the wife of Springfield's sheriff. We soon reached the modest, one-story home of Sheriff Hutchason, and I knocked on the front door.

The door opened and Martha stood before us. She was wearing a white silk dress with a rectangular neckline and wide sleeves. A shiny white sash encircled the dress high above her waist. Draped around her shoulders and arms was a woven red scarf decorated with a stitched pattern. Like me, she had a black silk band wrapped around her arm.

"Lovely," I said, as Martha twirled around and came down the stoop to take my outstretched hand.

Behind Martha I saw Molly Hutchason, her infant son swaddled in her arms. "Have fun for the both of us," Molly called.

Martha gave me a kiss on the cheek, stared, then pulled out her handkerchief and wiped something off my face. "Honestly, Joshua— do you even look in the glass? I don't know how you managed before I arrived in town. Now, let's hurry. I've heard so much about this party. I don't want to be late."

Quality Hill loomed over the rest of Springfield, both literally and figuratively. There were six mansions set upon it, and the men who owned them were the most renowned citizens of the town. But no name, and no mansion, loomed larger than those of Ninian Edwards.

The first Ninian Edwards had been the territorial governor of Illinois before it achieved statehood. He'd then served as senator and governor of the newly admitted state. His son, the second Ninian Edwards, had been the state's attorney general, and he now served with Lincoln in the state legislature. Along the way, the younger Edwards had married a savvy, well-to-do woman from Lexington, Kentucky, named Elizabeth Todd.

Lincoln, Martha, and I walked up the side of Quality Hill toward the Edwards mansion. It glowed above us in the darkening evening, and as we neared we smelled and then saw a dozen whale-oil torches ablaze, lighting up the lawns in front of the house. It was a grand home, two stories tall and large enough to swallow a dozen prairie-farmer cabins. Seven columns created a stately entrance portico. Cannons that had served the United States in the late war with Great Britain flanked either side of the curved drive.

The master and mistress of the house stood at the front door. Ninian Edwards, with a sharp beak nose and receding hairline, greeted us warmly. "It's about time the younger Lincoln arrived," he said, winking at me.

"The *younger*?" asked Lincoln sharply.

"We were chatting with your father and brother earlier," Edwards replied. "Most amusing fellows. I think they may have been the first guests to arrive."

"We could readily see that your sense of humor and gift for storytelling run in the family, Mr. Lincoln," added Mrs. Edwards. She was an attractive woman with straight brown hair pulled back and a soft feminine jaw. She wore an expensive blue lace dress and matching cap.

"They're—*here*?" Lincoln looked dumbfounded.

"Somewhere about, no doubt," said Edwards, waving generally toward the extensive house and grounds.

"Oh dear," murmured Lincoln, and he stalked away in search of his relations.

"An unwelcome surprise?" Edwards asked me, his eyebrows arched.

"He didn't expect them back in town so soon is all," I said, deciding Lincoln would probably think the less said about his father and stepbrother, the better.

"Either way, I'm glad all of you could join us," said Edwards, indicating that we should proceed inside. "I've arranged for a special entertainment at the end of the night. A memorable way to commemorate the anniversary of our nation's founding."

"You go ahead," I murmured to Martha. "I want to see if Lincoln needs help."

I started with the grounds, wandering among the trees and hedges in search of Lincoln's stovepipe hat. I saw many familiar faces, including Jacob Early and Henry Owens standing together and conversing intently, but not Lincoln. I was about to head inside when I heard a hoarse voice call out from behind me, "Why, it's Mr. Fry Speed, ain't it?"

I swung around to find Thomas Lincoln and his stepson slouched beside a gooseberry bush. Each of them held a pork chop, which they were attacking as if they hadn't eaten in some time. I touched my hat in greeting.

"If you're looking for Abe, you just missed him," said Thomas Lincoln.

"He ain't too happy to see us," John Johnston added with a grin. He belched.

"I believe he was under the impression you were headed to Coles County," I said.

"We was until we met a fella on the road who told us the mill we was after didn't exist no more," said the elder Lincoln. "So we come to have a pint at a grog shop, by the by, considering our options, when we met one of the hands of this Edwards fella"—he gestured toward the great house behind us—"who said they was preparing to have a big old party—"

"—'a *grand soiree*,' he called it," said Johnston, pronouncing it "swarry" in what he imagined to be an elevated accent.

"—and that he was sure his gov'nor wouldn't mind the two extra guests, specially not when he heard we was related to Abe. So we showed up, told the mister and missus who we was, and they was most welcoming to us. Most '*enchanted*,' even."

"And generous," added Johnston with a chortle, raising his chop in the air.

"In that case, it's very nice to see you both again," I said. "It looks like you've found a comfortable spot—perhaps you should stay here. I did want a word with Lincoln. I'll see if I can't find him inside."

CHAPTER 6

As I walked back toward the house, I noticed a number of guests had come attired in patriotic costumes. Among the men, powdered wigs and black velvet suits reminiscent of Washington and the waistcoat, breeches, fur cap, and spectacles of Franklin were the most common outfits. Among the women, flowing silk taffeta gowns made popular by Lady Washington were a frequent choice. Several guests of both sexes wore masks in their revelry.

Inside, the Edwards parlor overflowed with people. The room, wide and double-long and covered with light pink wallpaper, was the largest private space in Springfield. Mrs. Edwards had decorated the walls with black silhouette profiles that an artist had executed at last summer's party. I noted with amusement how many guests stood, wittingly or not, beneath their cutout likenesses.

"There you are, Mr. Speed," came a feminine voice from beside me.

I turned to find Miss Sarah Butler, the young woman with whom I'd lately been walking. She was wearing an all-black dress with a deep-purple sash over her shoulder. She had short, dark hair, curled and parted in the middle, a straight nose, an enigmatic smile, and coal-black eyes.

She offered her hand to me and I pressed it lightly as I bowed.

"My brother told me you called," she said.

"I understand you were out at the camp meeting?"

Miss Butler must have noticed a certain skepticism in my voice, because she wrinkled her nose. "Camp is a revelation. I hope you'll join me next time."

"Perhaps," I said without enthusiasm.

"Preacher Crews has been traveling around the county, but he's decided to stay in Springfield for the rest of the summer. There are so many souls waiting to be saved here."

"I'm not sure mine is among them."

Miss Butler gave me a peculiar glance. "Preacher Crews says it takes some people longer than others to hear the Word. Some people might never hear it. But the door's always open for salvation, right up until your last breath. Oh, I see another exhorter from camp," she added, indicating a young woman on the other side of the room. "I must have a word. But do save a turn around the floor for me, Mr. Speed."

Puzzled, I watched her walk away. Miss Butler had been gay and carefree when I'd first made her acquaintance. I didn't think I'd ever heard her utter a religious sentiment. Before I could decide what to make of the change, a strong hand gripped my shoulder from behind.

"Ahoy, Speed," shouted a familiar reedy voice.

Lincoln was standing next to a young woman with long, straight hair. She was wearing a peach-hued satin dress. My first thought was that she was too short to be a proper match for my friend.

"Joshua Speed, I believe you're already acquainted with Miss Margaret Owens," said Lincoln. He shifted his weight from one foot to the other and, unusual for him, carried a nervous expression on his face.

"How do you do?" I bowed deeply.

"Very well, thank you," said the lady.

The three of us looked at each other in silence. After one beat too many, I hastened to add, "I had the pleasure of seeing your brother earlier," at the very same moment Miss Owens blurted out, "I understand you recently lost your sister, Ann. I am so very sorry."

Miss Owens and I nodded at each other and made agreeable noises. We each turned back to Lincoln.

"Well then," said the man, nodding vigorously. He opened his mouth again and then closed it, bobbing all the while.

"If you'll excuse me . . ." I began a moment later.

"Yes, of course, Speed. You go about your business."

"It was very nice to make your acquaintance, formally I mean," I said to Miss Owens.

"And yours as well."

I bowed and she curtsied, and I pushed through the crowd of Washingtons and Franklins and masked men and women, looking for my sister. As far as I could tell, every politician and office-holder in Springfield was present tonight. And so was the press, for looming in front of me was the distinctive figure of Simeon Francis.

"Evening, Speed," he said.

"What's the good word, Simeon?" I asked, still scanning the room for Martha.

"Bloviation."

"That's a new one for me. Meaning?"

"What you get when you have a roomful of politicians competing to see who spews the greatest number of falsehoods for the fewest breaths taken."

"Hah! You haven't seen my sister, have you? I've lost track of her."

"Over in the corner." Simeon indicated behind me.

I looked over but couldn't spot Martha through the forest of hats. I did recognize, however, a highly distinctive silhouette pasted high on the wall where the newspaperman had pointed. "Don't tell me she's talking to . . ."

Simeon snorted and patted me on the back. I hurried toward the silhouette and came upon its subject and my sister in close, almost confidential, conversation. Stephen Douglas looked up suspiciously.

"He's the enemy, Martha," I said without preamble.

"Don't be ridiculous," returned my sister. "He's perfectly charming and perfectly harmless. Aren't you, Mr. Douglas?"

"I will accept the first of those designations with pleasure," said Douglas in a gravelly voice. "As for the second, Miss Speed, I suggest you wait until you know me better before forming a definite opinion."

Martha's eyes widened and she giggled. I glared down at Douglas. He was thickset and barely five feet tall, several inches shorter than my sister. His massive head, covered by dark, curly hair, appeared to have been chiseled out of the craggy granite of his native New England. His blue eyes met mine with the alert, remorseless gaze of a hawk.

"How's the campaign?" I asked Douglas. "I hear Stuart's going to trounce you."

"Don't be rude, Joshua," said Martha.

Douglas allowed himself a brief smile at my sister's intercession on his behalf. Then he said, "I've found in politics that a surplus of confidence is invariably correlated with a deficit of votes. I'm glad to hear confirmation my opponent has the former."

Two loud, argumentative voices rose above the noise of the crowded parlor. Turning, we saw Truett and Early, face to face, in animated discussion. Fortunately, neither appeared to be armed.

"Not these two again," said Douglas.

"I witnessed their brawl at Spotswood's the other day," I said.

"So I heard." He blew out his breath. "Let me see if I can take care of this." Douglas bowed very formally to Martha, gave me a curt handshake, and strode toward the two antagonists. My sister sighed audibly in his wake.

"Are you *trying* to provoke me?" I asked.

"What do you have against Mr. Douglas?"

"He's our political opponent, for one. Against Stuart this time, and perhaps against Lincoln next. And I don't trust him. It's obvious he's out for himself and no one else. He's highly unsuitable for you to speak with, even in public like this."

"Don't be silly. He's a charming man. Very handsome, too."

"I don't see it."

"I think there're a good number of things you don't see," said Martha. She tossed her head and marched away. I caught sight of

Douglas's haughty silhouette likeness, still looming on the wall above me. Looking around to make sure no one was watching, I took a pencil from my pocket and added two horns to Douglas's head.

There was dancing, accompanied by a pianoforte, and I made good on my promise to take Miss Butler around. It was a pleasant turn, during which the subject of eternal salvation mercifully did not arise. The lady's coal-black eyes, I realized as I had ample opportunity to gaze into them, harbored quite a sparkle.

Meanwhile, the party bubbled all around us, fueled by three dozen bottles of champagne lined on a sideboard. All these were soon consumed, and Mrs. Edwards called for their boy to bring up another dozen from the cellar. The table was piled with eatables, including huge mounds of almonds and raisins, trays of oysters that seemed to replenish themselves, and bushels full of apples.

Late in the evening there was a tinkling of glass and we looked around to see Ninian Edwards standing on a chair in the middle of the room. "If I can have your attention, ladies and gentlemen," he called out. "Ladies and gentlemen!" The roar of conversation gradually faded.

"It has been the Edwards duty since the days of my late father to welcome the distinguished residents of this state on occasions of great import. Mrs. Edwards and I thank you, one and all, for joining us for this celebration of the glorious birthday of American independence as well as of our town's rebirth as the new state capital."

"Hear! Hear!" went up a cheer that was accompanied by much clinking of glass.

"My original conception," continued Edwards, "was to let each of the politicians present say a word of their own greeting. But Mrs. Edwards advised that as we've got so many in attendance, and as our species has been known to have a great fondness for the sound of its own voice, the sun would be rising and we wouldn't be through with the speechmaking." The crowd chuckled good-naturedly.

"So, instead of making speeches, we propose to make . . . fireworks."

A great cheer went up. The practice of lighting off fireworks at Independence Day celebrations had been much discussed in the New York papers in recent years, but to my knowledge they had never been seen this far West. Certainly they were a novelty in Springfield.

"Please process out onto the hillside," continued Edwards. "They're being sent off from below, so everyone should have a good view. Only I warn you—don't stand too near the cannons."

I joined the crush of people filing out of the drawing room toward the front of the house. The Edwardses' servants had blanketed the whale-oil torches, and as the crowd left the house they put out the candles inside, too. The lawns were pitch black. The vista looking out toward town was completely dark as well, save for the faint glow of a few hearth fires smoldering in houses below us. The crowd chattered with excitement; I looked around for my sister or Miss Butler but could find neither woman. Finally I spotted Lincoln's distinctive silhouette and went up to him.

"How's your evening been?" I asked.

"I've managed to keep my father and John away from Miss Owens and she from them," he replied. "Judged on those grounds—and those grounds alone—it's been a success. Her brother took her home an hour ago, so I'm in the clear for tonight. Tomorrow?" He grimaced.

Another figure walked toward the little knoll on which we were standing, and when he'd gotten within a foot or two I recognized him as Jacob Early. We greeted each other.

"I was hoping to find a moment with you, Lincoln," said Early. "Perhaps Speed told you—there's a matter concerning the land office I need to bring to your attention."

In the darkness I could just make out the strained expression on Lincoln's face. "Speed did mention it, but I've been busy with the campaign," said Lincoln, glancing swiftly at me and back at Early. The campaign and his relations, I thought to myself. "I'm sorry for the delay. I'll stop by the land office in the morning."

"Very well," said Early. "I've discovered something irregular in the books."

"Irregular?"

"I was looking over the office records, and I noticed a few things that didn't make sense. So then I started to make some inquiries, and I think I've discovered—"

Whoosh! Early's words were negated by the air-sucking sound of a rocket taking flight. There was a large explosion and white drops of fire fell from the sky. A great cheer went up from the assembled guests. Early started up again, but again his words were drowned out by the explosive launch of a rocket, and he had no choice but to close his mouth and watch in amazement with the rest of us.

One after another, heaven-defying messengers flew into the black vault of the night sky, the furious scream of the deadly shell mounting higher and higher like a soaring eagle until it burst with a terrific explosion that spilled out a profusion of bright stars of the most intense brilliancy. The burning stars lingered and slowly started to fall back toward the earth, fading and flickering in wavering scintillations, beautiful to the very last dying spark.

It was apparent Edwards had spared no expense for his pyrotechnic display. *Whoosh, bang! Whoosh, bang! Whoosh, bang!* It was everything I had read about and more. There were serpents and wheels, table rockets, cherry trees, and sunflowers. Orange and white flashes lit up a huge arc of the night sky.

"The grandest is coming!" shouted Edwards above the noise of the blasts and the screams of the delighted crowd.

The rockets were shot up with greater and greater frequency, so that the explosions eventually knit together in one long stream of noise, smoke, and flashing lights. In their midst—*boom! boom!*— came the deep concussive sound of both cannons being discharged. The noise and smoke were absolute and all-encompassing.

Suddenly, I heard and then felt a whistling noise hurtling toward me. I dove to the ground. I lay there for a moment, breathing deeply, but there was only silence. Everything was obscured by a great haze of smoke. I'd been frightened by the final volley of shells, I thought as I picked myself up. Smiling ruefully, I hoped no one else had witnessed my lack of courage.

The smoke started to clear. Men and women all around were cheering and shouting out their approval at the remarkable display.

"Bravo!" I called, clapping my hands.

"Spectacular!" came Lincoln's voice in agreement, although I could hardly make out his figure through the haze.

I looked around to see Early's reaction. He was oddly taciturn, and as the smoke continued to drift away, I gradually perceived that he was lying on the ground, having likewise flung himself out of the way of the hurtling shadows.

"I see they got you, too, Early," I shouted. "No shame in that, I warrant. Not when it's the first display of fireworks we've ever seen. Here, I'll help you up."

I reached out my arm, but Early did not grasp it. In fact, he did not reply at all.

"Early?" I tried again. And then, more insistently, "Early!"

I knelt beside his prone figure, now fully visible, and, a second later, I swore loudly. Early's arms and legs were splayed out and his eyes and mouth were open wide in wonder—or perhaps horror. There was a round hole directly in the center of his forehead. Other than a thin trickle of blood oozing from the wound, Early was motionless.

CHAPTER 7

Lincoln stooped beside the fallen man. "Go find a doctor!" he shouted at me, his face stricken. He added quietly, more to himself, "Though I fear there's no hope."

I pressed through the crowd, frantically scanning faces in search of a doctor. Everyone was in high spirits from the excitement of the fireworks, and few persons noticed me as I passed. After several moments, I ran headlong into Martha.

"Wasn't that . . . what's wrong?" she said, seeing the expression on my face.

I told her what had happened and she put her hand to her mouth in horror. At that instant, I glimpsed the long face and flowing gray beard of Weymouth Warren, one of the senior physics in town. I grabbed his arm, explained the circumstances, and pointed him in the direction of the hillock on which we'd been standing. The Edwardses' servants were relighting the whale-oil torches, and a crowd of people was starting to cluster around Early's body.

"We should go help," said Martha, taking my arm.

"Right at the end of the fireworks," I said, "I felt something whizz close by. It seemed like part of the display, or perhaps a blank from the cannons, but now I wonder if it was the bullet that struck Early."

Martha gaped at me, her face stricken again. "Perhaps it was." She gave me a tight embrace. "You're lucky it missed you, Joshua."

"So is Lincoln that it missed him."

The crowd surrounding the fallen man had grown large, and we had to push our way toward the center. Lincoln and Doctor Warren were conversing in low tones. Early lay motionless at their feet. Someone had folded his arms across his body and closed his mouth. Warren bent down to lower his eyelids, but they were stuck open and refused to move. After a few attempts Warren gave up. Even in death, Early was intent on running contrary to prevailing wishes.

I looked again at where Early had fallen, which was not more than five feet from where Lincoln and I had been standing. We *had* been lucky the fatal bullet hadn't hit us instead.

The jostling crowd was alive with fervid speculation about who or what had caused Early's death. A number of men conjectured that the "devil's fire" had proven fatal, perhaps as a result of a misdirected rocket shell. Several hurried off in search of Edwards to demand an explanation of the wizardry that had produced the spectacular display.

The greater part of the crowd ringing Early's body, however, quickly concluded that his rival Henry Truett was to blame. A group of men deputized themselves and headed off in search of the man. Three minutes later they returned, dragging their quarry along the grass like a squealing hog being led to slaughter.

"I didn't do it!" Truett proclaimed shrilly as he was dumped in a heap next to Early's body. Truett took a look at the dead man, shivered, and scrambled to his feet, but the mob grabbed hold of his arms and legs before he could go anywhere.

There was the sound of approaching hoofbeats and Sheriff Hutchason rode up and dismounted. He was a large, stocky man with broad shoulders and close-cropped hair.

"I came as soon as I heard," he said to no one in particular. "Ah, Lincoln. You're here. What happened?"

Lincoln drew Hutchason aside and talked into his ear. Meanwhile, a tug-of-war was developing among the men holding Truett. It seemed that one faction wanted to string him up from a tree at once, while the other sought to march him off to jail. The suspect himself, being simultaneously pulled in two opposite directions, began calling piteously to attract the sheriff's attention.

Hutchason waded into the mob and seized Truett by the scruff of his neck. "I'm taking you to jail," he said. "For your own protection if nothing else."

Hutchason tied Truett's hands behind his back, hoisted him up onto his horse, and without further ceremony set off down the hill for town. Soon afterward, Higgins the cabinetmaker drove up in his cart. Higgins also served as the town's undertaker, and he infallibly arrived on the scene of any death shortly after Death himself had departed with his grim harvest, almost as if he and the reaper were connected by some direct, though unseen, means of communication.

I helped lift Early's body into the back of Higgins's box cart—it took four men to hoist the large corpse—and Higgins covered the body with a blanket. Higgins resumed the driver's seat and gave a shake of his reins, and slowly they bounced away down Quality Hill.

The sheriff and the cabinetmaker left a trail of men in their wake, all grumbling about an anticlimactic ending to a spectacular evening. The only thing that could have topped the fireworks, several noted with disappointment, would have been a hanging right there on the spot.

Soon Lincoln, Martha, and I were alone on the hillside.

"You're shaking," I said, looking over at Lincoln.

"He was a good man and a loyal supporter," said Lincoln, his face creased with sorrow. "And I can't stop thinking about our last conversation, right before the display started."

"What conversation?" asked Martha.

As Lincoln related it, Martha's eyes grew wider. "What irregularity do you suppose he'd found in the land office?" she asked.

"I doubt we'll ever know now," I said.

"Unless Truett's defense lawyer unearths it," said Lincoln. "After all, it stands to reason it's one possible motive for whoever did this, if something seriously wrong was going on and Early had found out about it."

"But isn't it obvious Truett's guilty?" said Martha. We'd begun to walk down the hill toward town. "Everyone knows about their feud. And their fight the other night."

"That'll be up to the courts to sort out in due time," said Lincoln. "Not that it will bring back Early." He looked down, and I saw that his pants were stained with grass and dirt from kneeling beside the dead man.

"Perhaps Mr. Truett will hire you," said Martha.

"I've no time for a murder case, not right before the election," said Lincoln. "Besides, as a Democrat accused of killing a Whig, he'll want a Democratic lawyer representing him. There're plenty in town, plenty who would be happy for the assignment. One politician accused of killing another—the trial will be on everybody's lips."

"Maybe you could suggest Douglas," I said. "I doubt he could help himself but to take on such a high-profile trial. And it would occupy *his* time right before the election."

Lincoln grinned in the darkness while Martha started to protest. "Settle down," I said, linking arms with her. "I'm joking. I'm sure your Stephen won't do anything to impair his precious political future."

CHAPTER 8

An hour later, Lincoln and I were in our bedroom, stripping off our clothes and preparing for bed. The room contained space only for the two double beds and a rickety dressing table. A single candle flickered on the table now. Since Lincoln's arrival in Springfield last year, he and I had shared one of the beds. Hurst and Herndon shared the other, although, as both were intemperate men, there were many evenings when neither had materialized before we turned in.

"I feel responsible in some way for Early's death," said Lincoln, his face still tinged with sadness.

"You? Why?"

"If only I'd gone to see him earlier. Heard what it was he'd discovered. Perhaps this fate would have been avoided."

"There's no reason to think that."

Lincoln sighed. He was wearing his linen nightshirt, a faded, striped affair that would have reached to the ankles of a normal-sized man. On Lincoln, it did not even cover his knobby, hairy knees. I was in my nightshirt as well. From opposite sides of the bed we clambered in, then tugged the summer blanket back and forth until it covered us more or less equally.

"Did Early have any family nearby?" I asked.

"Only his sister, Lilliana. She's the one Prickett just married."

"That's right." David Prickett was the state's attorney, in charge of prosecuting all criminal cases in Sangamon County. He had lost his wife in childbirth the prior year but had married anew a few months ago.

Lincoln wrestled his pillow into a more comfortable position. "I saw you taking a turn with Miss Butler this evening," he said. "An *extended* turn. The two of you looked a natural pairing."

"Maybe." I thought again about Miss Butler's newfound interest in pursuing the Word and then about her sparkling eyes. "And I enjoyed meeting Miss Owens formally as well."

"She lacks Ann's spirit," said my friend. "That was obvious from the first moment I spoke with her. Still, I'm certain I'll never meet another woman who has *that*."

As I'd gotten to know Lincoln over the past year, I'd come to understand that the loss of Ann Rutledge still weighed heavily on him—even more heavily than the deaths of his brother in infancy, of his mother from the milk sickness when he'd been nine, and of his elder sister Sarah, who had been like a mother to him after their angel mother passed and who died in childbirth a few days short of her twenty-first birthday. Ann was the great love of Lincoln's life. Lincoln had, in his own telling, never been the same since she died of brain fever before they could solemnize their relationship.

"Again, I proffer I'm the last person in the world from whom you should be taking advice on this topic," I said, "but don't you think it right that, at some point, you move on from Miss Rutledge's memory?"

Lincoln did not reply. His brow was wrinkled, his jaw clenched, and his large hands curled tightly around the top edge of our blanket. He stared straight up at the ceiling.

"What made Miss Rutledge so remarkable?" I tried.

"She was as good a mate for the soul as a man could ever hope to find," he said quietly. "Sweet-spirited . . . patient . . . industrious. Quite intellectual, though not highly educated. Shared my love of the poetry of Burns. Kind to all manner of persons, whether highborn or low. And she was beautiful, too. Blond in complexion with golden hair, cherry-red lips, and bonny blue eyes."

"I wish I could have known her."

"As do I." Lincoln's jaw unclenched and he let out a long breath. "But it was not to be."

"Ann sounds like a remarkable young woman, Lincoln, but she's gone. And there's nothing you can do about it except move forward. Quite possibly with Miss Owens."

Lincoln managed a small smile. "I do take your point," he said. He yawned and burrowed into the bedclothes.

"Miss Owens seems like a perfectly pleasant young woman," I said as I turned over myself. "I approve of her wholeheartedly. And besides, her brother can always remedy your toothaches."

Lincoln laughed. I stretched out toward the dressing table and blew out the candle. Darkness descended upon us.

Sometime later I felt Lincoln shaking me awake. "What is it?" I muttered groggily. I managed to open one eye and saw that it was still pitch-dark outside.

"I need you to come with me. I'm heading over to the jail cell."

This woke me quickly, and I swung my legs out of bed and started searching for where I'd discarded my clothes. "Why are you going there?"

"Truett sent for me."

"Why?"

"Dunno. We'll have to hear it from him ourselves."

"Then why do you want me along?" I was fully dressed now, and, buttoning a final button, I followed Lincoln out the door and down the stairs.

"Because I can't help thinking it's a political trick of some sort. It doesn't make sense. I want you there as a witness."

"Didn't you once say Truett was an old acquaintance of yours?" I asked when we were outside in the deserted, silent town. The dirt and gravel of the streets crunched under our boots. The moon had set long ago and our path was lit by a dome of twinkling stars.

"We have a history," said Lincoln, nodding. "Back in New Salem, after I purchased my store from Blankenship, I took Truett on as an assistant shopkeeper. Hired him away from a decent job about a month before my store winked out. I never paid him a cent, couldn't afford to, and he couldn't get his old job back when mine disappeared. I felt awful about the whole situation, but there wasn't much I could do. I still carry a veritable national debt around with me from the failed store."

"From the little I've seen he's a very disagreeable fellow."

"More gormless than disagreeable. He's never seen a deficient situation he didn't find attractive. If it weren't for bad luck, he'd have no luck at all. And there's no poor situation he can't make worse with the way he carries himself. The few times I've tried to help him, it hasn't ended well." Lincoln shook his head. "Let's see what he has to say for himself tonight."

Springfield's lone jail cell consisted of a wood-and-metal enclosure in the backyard of Sheriff Hutchason's house adjacent to the sheriff's barn. As we let ourselves through the gate, we could see a trim figure pacing back and forth inside the cell.

"Who's there?" he called out.

"It's I," said Lincoln in a flat voice.

Truett had worn to the Edwardses' party the same dandified costume he'd had on at Spotswood's the other day, but his appearance was changed in every other respect. His eyes were hooded and his face was smeared with dirt, through which traced the unmistakable lines of tears.

"And who's this?" he said, pointing at me.

Lincoln introduced us. I extended my hand through the iron bars of the cell and Truett shook it hesitantly. Despite the warm summer night, his hands were ice-cold.

"You sent for me and I came," said Lincoln. "What do you want?"

Truett swallowed and looked up at Lincoln with his head cocked to the side. "For you to represent me in court. If I'm charged with murder—which the sheriff tells me I will be."

"Yes, I think you will be," said Lincoln. "By why not a Democratic lawyer? I'd be happy to suggest the names of a few men who are fully qualified to—"

"I don't want anyone else," said Truett. "I want you."

"I think you should know I considered myself close to Early," said Lincoln. "He was a political ally and a personal friend. I'm not sure I could do justice to the defense of the man accused of killing him."

"I know all that. I still want you. I'd like to think, with what we've been through together, Lincoln, you'd feel an obligation to help me in this time of peril."

"That was a long time ago," said Lincoln. His face was blank and I had a hard time guessing at his thoughts.

"It was a long time ago," agreed Truett. "But I remember it like yesterday."

"So do I." Both men looked at each other and then away.

"So you'll do it?"

Lincoln shifted his weight from one foot to another. "I'll think about it. I need to consider how it will fit with my other obligations. *If* it will fit."

"I haven't got any time," said Truett. "The sheriff"—he gestured at the Hutchason house, dark and slumbering, behind us— "says the judge will consider my case at ten in the morning."

"I'll give you my answer before the hearing," Lincoln replied. "The judge will let you have time to hire a lawyer if you need it. And your trial won't be for another week or two, at the earliest."

Truett's face had regained its animation, and he started to bounce back and forth on the balls of his feet like a fighting bantam ready to strike. "I want you to know, Lincoln, I'm not going alone. If I'm going down, I'm taking him with me."

"Who?"

There was the faintest hint of alarm in Lincoln's voice, and Truett noticed it too. He was silent for a few seconds, and then his lips gradually curled into a sneer. "Why—your father, of course."

"What's my father got to do with your case?" asked Lincoln, not bothering to hide his alarm this time.

"I didn't kill Early," said Truett. "Something was going on at the land office. Something crooked, that got Early killed. You know your father, Lincoln, and I know him, too. When have you known Thomas Lincoln to avoid a crooked situation?"

CHAPTER 9

Martha and I set off together for court the following morning shortly before ten. But as soon as we turned the corner onto Fifth Street, we could tell from the crowd spilling out in front of Hoffman's Row that we'd have to stand outside on the street for the hearing.

The old, decrepit courthouse on the corner of the town square had finally been torn down the previous month, a blessing for all the lawyers in town because it was threatening to collapse on their heads without warning. There was to be a modern courtroom included within the grand new state capitol building. However, construction of the new capitol had been delayed by last year's economic Panic; stone walls outlining the ground floor of the building had only recently begun to sprout in the middle of the town square.

It was only after he'd given the order to tear down his old professional home that the judge of the Sangamon County Circuit Court, Jesse B. Thomas Jr., had fully considered the fact that his new home was far from ready. After a frenzy of negotiations, the landlord Hoffman had agreed to host the court in a vacant, first-floor office in one of the series of handsome, two-story red brick buildings he had built a block north of the square. By coincidence, the temporary courtroom was located at No. 3, Hoffman's Row, directly underneath Lincoln's law offices at No. 4.

The location was convenient for Lincoln and the other lawyers in town, and the sturdy walls erected by Hoffman were greatly preferable to the crumbling facade of the old courthouse. Yet the court's new accommodations were far smaller than the prior ones. When, as today, a case of great public interest was being heard, there was not nearly enough space at the back of the courtroom for the spectators who wished to attend. So Martha and I joined the crowd on the dirt street in front of Hoffman's Row and strained to hear the proceedings through the open windows of No. 3.

Fortunately, though half a foot shorter than my roommate, I was taller than most men in town, and by peering over and around the top hats of the men in front of us I was able to get a fair view of the proceedings. I related a running narrative to my sister, who stood by my side and stared with frustration at the backs of the frockcoats of the men around us.

When we arrived, I could see two other lawyers on their feet in front of Judge Thomas's bench, which was located along the back wall of the temporary courtroom, while Lincoln sat on a chair to the side of the room, his legs crossed and his case on his lap. "The judge is hearing some other case," I related to Martha.

"Replevin for a cow," said the fellow next to us, "not that any-one cares who owns Molly the Milk Cow." Indeed, the crowd around us was speculating enthusiastically about Truett's fate and the proceedings inside the courtroom were inaudible over the rib-ald swells of conversation.

While we waited for the main event, my attention was drawn by two young women who were threading through the crowd and pass-ing out handbills. With a start, I realized one of them was Miss Butler. She recognized me, came over, and handed me one of her bills. It read:

SINNERS COME
EVERYBODY COME
Meetings Every Weekend
at the
Big Tent in the Grove
Preacher Crews teaching—many exhorting—
all voices raised in song
All can be SAVED

"An evening of fire and brimstone?" I said. "As though men were to be frightened into heaven, rather than reasoned there. I don't think it's my kettle."

"That's not at all what camp's about," said Miss Butler seriously. "It's a congregation of singing and joy. You'd like it, particularly, Miss Speed," she added, handing a bill to my sister. "A good number of your sisters in town have come."

To my surprise, Martha studied the handbill with interest. "Will you gather this weekend?" she asked Miss Butler.

"You're not seriously thinking—" I began, before being silenced by the looks on the faces of the two young women.

"Every weekend," said Miss Butler. "I'd be most pleased to walk out with you. Truly, I don't think you'll be disappointed if you try it."

We watched as Miss Butler moved away, continuing to pass out her bills to the crowd.

"I think this preacher fellow is almost certainly a charlatan," I said to Martha as I crumpled up the bill.

Before she could respond, a violent "Hush!" raced through the crowd. Lincoln was on his feet in front of Judge Thomas. Prickett, the state's attorney, was standing next to him. Men rustled around and stood on tiptoe to garner a view. After a few shouts of "Quiet!" and "If you please!" the crowd on the street came to a kind of order and the sound of the proceedings inside finally reached us.

". . . not guilty," Lincoln was saying.

"Are you sure that's your plea?" asked the judge. "A slaying in the heat of a political dispute seems an 'irresistible passion' if ever there was one. A case of voluntary manslaughter taken directly from the statute books. If Mr. Truett spares the Court and the People the need for trial, I imagine the prison sentence would be eighteen months at most, perhaps closer to fifteen. Otherwise, the charge is murder and the sentence upon conviction is death."

Lincoln bent over and whispered to Truett, who was seated at his side. Truett looked even more frightened than he had last night when the mob on Quality Hill sought to string him up without delay.

"What's happening?" asked Martha, tugging on my coat.

"Lincoln's seeing if Truett will agree to plead guilty to voluntary manslaughter in exchange for a reduced term in prison."

"But if he's truly innocent, he's got to have Mr. Lincoln fight for his freedom," protested Martha.

"If he's innocent, I'm Molly the Milk Cow's father," said the fellow next to us.

"Moooooo!" bellowed the man on the other side of us.

Lincoln straightened up. "We maintain our plea of not guilty, Your Honor. Mr. Truett played no role in Early's death." Lincoln was interrupted by jeers coming from both inside and outside the courtroom. Undeterred, he continued: "The two men had their share of disagreements; that's common knowledge. But Mr. Truett had no wish to see Early dead and has no explanation for it."

"If I may be heard, Your Honor," began Prickett. As usual, the prosecutor was resplendent in a high-collared, stiff-necked white shirt beneath his shiny black frockcoat.

"I'm coming to you next," said Judge Thomas.

The judge made a show of pulling an unlit cigar from his pocket, striking a match to light it, and taking a deep pull. "Ah," he said, blowing out a large cloud of smoke. Judge Jesse B. Thomas Jr. was a hale, hearty man who looked as though he was fond of his dinner. Having taken another long pull from his cigar, he nodded almost imperceptibly toward Prickett.

"Your Honor, the People seek an immediate trial on the charge of murder—"

"You purport to stand for the People, Mr. Prickett?"

"Of course, Your Honor. It is my statutory duty as state's attorney—"

"And what of your familial duty?" The men around us on the street murmured with interest.

"Because he was Early's brother-in-law," I explained to Martha, who had given me a questioning look. "Recently married to his sister."

"I assure the Court," Prickett was saying, "that my familial connection to the victim, indirect though it is, shall play no role in my zealous prosecution of—"

" '*Indirect?*' " repeated the judge, his eyebrows raised. The crowd chuckled. Prickett turned around and looked out at the overflowing gallery.

"Yes, Your Honor. Indirect. Meaning by the contract of marriage. Not blood. And a recent contract at that. As I was saying, my indirect relationship with the victim shall not affect my actions here, just as any other personal feelings I may have about the defendant or any witness shall play no role. That's my sworn obligation to the People of the State of Illinois."

The judge took several pulls on his cigar and asked, "And what does the new Mrs. Prickett think?"

"My wife's views, whatever they are, are immaterial to my obligations to the People."

"Do you care to comment, Mr. Lincoln?" the judge asked.

Lincoln took a few moments to gather his thoughts. I knew he considered Prickett a formidable adversary, so the prospect of having him removed from the case would hold some appeal.

"I have no doubt of Mr. Prickett's good faith," said Lincoln at last. "If he says the situation won't affect him, I believe we should take him at his word."

"No, no, no!" shouted the judge, cutting through the excited whispering of the crowd. "I know you don't genuinely believe that, Lincoln. You're playing the odds, and that makes my decision clear. You are excused, Mr. Prickett. It's no reflection on you. A state's attorney can't choose the victims of crimes committed on his watch, and a man certainly can't choose his brother-in-law. But I can't let you prosecute this case."

Prickett began to argue, but Judge Thomas waved him off. "Anyway, you're not nearly as irreplaceable as you think. I'm going to appoint another lawyer to act as prosecutor *pro tempore* and present the People's case against the defendant Truett."

The judge scanned the front row of the audience, where other members of the Springfield bar awaited their turn to argue their own cases. The judge looked down the row and his face lit up in a broad grin.

"You there!" he fairly shouted, gesturing with his smoldering cigar.

"Who is it?" asked my sister. Several men around me voiced the same question.

"I don't know," I said. "I can't see who he's talking to." Then I saw the back of a massive head of curly hair rise slightly above the seated crowd. "Oh! Hah! No wonder I couldn't see him." I turned to my sister. "It's Douglas."

CHAPTER 10

"I would be pleased to accept the appointment, Your Honor," came Stephen Douglas's distinctive baritone voice.

There was a pause as this new development was collectively digested, and then a *whoosh* of excitement streaked through the crowd. Men began talking in a frenzy, and the proceedings inside Hoffman's Row were rendered inaudible once again.

Stephen Douglas's stature was the only thing small about the man. His biography was well known to the excited throng on Fifth Street; the man himself had made sure of that. Douglas had been born in Vermont and, after his father died, apprenticed to a local cabinetmaker. But his ambitions, and skills, soon outgrew this humble lot, and so he migrated to the West. Eventually he alighted in central Illinois, where, despite having but a few years of formal schooling himself, he opened a school and passed himself off as an itinerant teacher.

At the same time, Douglas read law, and by the age of twenty-one he was not only a member of the bar but had been elected the state's attorney for Morgan County, Sangamon's neighboring county. Shortly thereafter he'd won election to the state legislature. Along the way he'd acquired the nickname "the Little Giant," an appellation that even his most ardent enemies conceded fit the man. And now, as the Democratic candidate for the U.S. Congress at the age of twenty-five, Douglas was giving the much more experienced Stuart the run of his life.

But the crowd's thrill, I thought as I listened to their chitter-chatter, came primarily from the prospect of a courtroom battle between Douglas and Lincoln. Douglas was the unmistakable rising star of the Democrats in the state; despite his much slower start in public life, Lincoln now seemed a future leader of the Illinois Whigs. Men who knew politics claimed that one day Lincoln and Douglas would meet on the political field in a great debate about the future of the state and—some asserted, however improbably—the nation itself.

A routine dispute between two patronage rivals had suddenly begotten a courtroom contest between two leading political adversaries. In a remote frontier town where courthouse trials were the only form of theater, amid the frenzied atmosphere of an election season, there could not be a more perfect public entertainment.

Gradually the crowd's tumult simmered away and the courtroom discussion in front of Judge Thomas again came to the fore.

". . . need to prepare the case?" the judge was asking.

"I expect Mr. Douglas will want some time to study his new file," said Lincoln. From the tight look on his face, I had a pretty good guess Lincoln thought his task of defending Truett had just become more difficult with the appointment of Douglas.

"We can try it today, if Your Honor pleases," Douglas replied. Another rush of enthusiasm passed through the crowd. Many Democrats could be heard assuring their Whig neighbors of Douglas's superiority to Lincoln.

"I am, of course, familiar with the dispute between the accused and Mr. Early," continued Douglas, gesturing toward where the defendant sat, "as I expect most men in town are. I don't think much study is required."

"He's trying to chuff Lincoln," I said to Martha. "Prevent him from having adequate time to prepare Truett's defense. I told you he's the sort of man to be avoided."

"I think it's quite smart Mr. Douglas is so prepared and ready for his assignment," my sister replied.

"Remember whose side you're on," I shot back. Martha glowered.

". . . more time to investigate," Lincoln was saying inside the courtroom. "Though not overlong. Why not try the case during the last week of July? I have it on good authority that my brother Douglas has no cases on his docket that week." I could see his innocent grin as he turned toward Douglas.

"It is generous of brother Lincoln to offer to occupy my time in that week," returned Douglas's booming voice, "coming, as it does, right before the election. I imagine his law partner brother Stuart would concur in the suggestion." The crowd around us tittered.

"But while Mr. Lincoln may not be worried about *his* election, I freely concede I'm concerned about mine. I'll be busy seeking the vote of each and every man with the franchise in the Third District until the day votes are cast."

"You're saying you care more about your personal political prospects than the course of justice?" said the judge, pulling on his cigar and quite evidently enjoying more and more the drama he had created by his selection of Douglas.

"I'm saying the two are not in opposition," replied Douglas smoothly, "and I readily admit to being greatly interested in each. If the Court determines it must try the case during the last week of July, as brother Lincoln suggests, then I'll respectfully decline the *pro tem* appointment and the case will have to proceed without me—"

The collective sigh of disappointment that escaped the crowd at this was unmistakable. Douglas half-turned toward the gallery, and I could see a confident grin on his broad face. The judge furrowed his brows and sucked on his cigar.

"—but if the Court is set upon the appointment, then, as I said, I would be honored to accept it. And to try the case after the election."

"Your Honor—" began Lincoln.

"The election's Monday, the sixth of August?" asked the judge, waving Lincoln aside.

"Correct."

"We'll empanel the jury on August eighth. That'll give the jury pool twenty-four hours to sober up from election day. You, too,

Mr. Douglas. And you as well, Mr. Lincoln, if the poll results drive you to drink." The crowd chuckled.

"Can I ask the Court for a few additional days, just in case—" began Douglas.

"No." The judge took two long pulls on his cigar. "The defendant is remanded to the jail cell until trial, and I'll not keep him there without a verdict any longer than necessary. If you feel the schedule will interfere with your *political aspirations*, Mr. Douglas"—the crowd laughed at the judge's good-naturedly mocking tone—"I've no doubt I can persuade one of your brother counsel to stand for the People. But tell me now. Once I've set the circumstances for this man's reckoning, I'll not change them."

Douglas looked around and took in the gallery crammed into Hoffman's office and the much larger crowd out on the street beyond. He sneaked a quick sideways glance at Lincoln. Then he turned back to the judge.

"I'll be ready for trial on the eighth," said Douglas. "The defendant had better hope Mr. Lincoln is as well."

CHAPTER 11

As the crowd on the street started filtering away, talking excitedly about the coming entertainment of the murder trial, I felt a hand on my elbow. I turned to see Thomas Lincoln's shabby, worn coat and hangdog face.

I introduced the elder Lincoln to Martha.

"So you're the lass my Abe's been keeping company with," he said, looking her over thoroughly.

"No, Mr. Lincoln—that's a Miss Owens," I said, as Martha blushed a very deep crimson. "Miss Martha Speed is my sister. Well acquainted with Abraham, to be sure. But just my sister."

"Hardly 'just,'" said Martha indignantly, hands on her hips.

Thomas Lincoln squinted at my sister with confusion and turned back to me. "How'd we think Abe did today? He won, didn't he?"

"The thing about these legal cases, Mr. Lincoln, is they tend to be drawn-out affairs," I said. "One day goes well, the next not so much. You don't know how it's gone until the jury has its final say. The interesting thing today is Douglas getting appointed as prosecutor for the case. I'm sure Lincoln wasn't expecting that."

"That midget? I saw him strutting around the grounds last night. He won't last a minute in the ring with my Abe."

"I wouldn't underestimate him," I said, checking Martha, who looked as if she wanted to punch the elder Lincoln in the nose.

"How did you and John enjoy last night?" I continued. "Did you stay to see the fireworks?"

"We was there until we wasn't. Lot of noise and flash for nothing, if you ask me."

"Where is—" Martha began, but at that moment I stuck out my arm and said, "Here's another train coming. We'd better step aside."

A huge cloud of dust was advancing steadily upon us, accompanied by the deep rumble of hooves and the occasional crack of a whip. As the cloud neared, it dissolved into its constituent parts. A long queue of oxen, a team of twelve, was harnessed two-by-two and driven by men walking on either side and carrying whips. At the back of the slow-moving beasts was a huge, open box-cart laden with heavy blocks of buff yellow limestone.

All summer long these ox trains had been rumbling from the quarry near Cotton Hill to the town square, where the stone blocks were being used to construct the foundation of the new capitol building. After many delays, the outline of the building had finally begun to take tangible form on the sunbaked grass field; the foundation had reached shoulder-height in most places just in the past week. The original plan had been to cover the stone foundation with a brick superstructure, but the stone possessed a lovely warm, soft color, especially as it absorbed the setting sun, and popular sentiment in town was rapidly coming to the view that the stone should be left exposed.

We stood back from the rumbling oxen, hands to our noses and mouths to avoid breathing in the dust, and watched them lurch past. I counted ten rectangular blocks of limestone on the back of the cart.

As we waited, I considered whether to raise Truett's allegations from last night with Thomas Lincoln. I hated to think that my friend might be in jeopardy because of something nefarious his father had done. For his part, Lincoln hadn't said anything about Truett's words after we left the jail cell. Instead, we'd walked back to our lodgings in silence, Lincoln's head bowed and his hands clasped behind his back.

Eventually the oxen and their load passed our position and enough of the dust drifted back down to the street that we could breathe again.

"Did you ever have dealings with Mr. Early at the land office?" I asked.

"Me?" said Thomas Lincoln. He swatted at the air to disperse the final remnants of dust and coughed into his fist several times. "What would I want with the land office? Unless they was giving it away for free, that is."

He turned and tipped his worn cap to Martha. "Till next time, my dear." As he shuffled off down the street, there was a hitch in his step, as if one leg was slightly shorter than the other.

"No wonder our Mr. Lincoln is the way he is," Martha said quietly in the old man's wake.

"Meaning?"

"Just imagine that was your father, carrying himself around in public like that, as you tried to make a name for yourself." She made a noise of pity, but whether aimed at the father or the son I could not tell.

As we were getting ready for bed that evening, I asked Lincoln if he wanted any help with his new case.

"You didn't read law with Judge Speed during your time back home, did you?" he replied.

"No, of course not. I merely was thinking about what Truett told us. About your father having something to do with—"

"Thank you, no. It's my case, Speed. My cross to bear. Now, good night." Lincoln blew out the candle and turned over in bed. The topic was officially closed.

Both the *Journal* and the *Democrat* published new editions in the next few days. It was no surprise that Early's murder was the lead story in each one. It was a surprise, however, that each story focused unrelentingly on Truett's guilt. Even Simeon Francis's *Journal*, usually friendly territory for Lincoln, carried a long report claiming Truett had been overheard at a tavern in New Salem the week before the shooting bragging about how he was going to make Early get down on his knees and beg for his life.

The morning this edition hit the streets, Lincoln barged into my store, slamming the door in his wake. His jutting jaw was clenched with anger. He took a copy of the *Journal* from under his arm and threw it onto the counter.

"We're getting killed in the sheets!" he exclaimed.

"I know it," I said as I looked up from sorting a new shipment of ready-made shoes.

"The *Democrat*, I can understand. Everyone knows its publisher, Weber, practically lives in Douglas's pocket. But now Simeon's in on the game as well." Lincoln picked the *Journal* up from the counter, waved it around wildly, then tossed it onto the floor.

"Surely it doesn't matter what the papers say today," I said. "The trial's not for another month. And everyone's going to be focused on the election between now and then."

"If they spend that month reading about how Truett had been looking for an opportunity to kill Early, it'll matter for sure. By the time the jury's selected, they'll be predisposed against my defense."

"Can't you keep men with fixed opinions off the jury?"

"There'll be no one left, not if these stories keep up."

Several hours later, none other than Simeon Francis came through the same doors. "I'll take a sack of flour for the wife," he said.

"Lincoln was in here earlier, complaining about you," I said as I went to my shelves behind the counter to plump up a sack for him.

"I'll bet he was." Simeon grinned. I knew from long experience that irritating his friends was quite nearly as much fun in Simeon's calculus as was irritating his enemies. "I told you attempted murder would sell a lot of papers. And a successful attempt is even better . . . not that I wished for it, of course," he added as an unconvincing postscript.

"Make your readers interested in Lincoln's side of things next time," I said. "I think you owe him after what you printed this week."

"He knows my columns are always open to him. And they're

open to you, too, Speed." Simeon rubbed his stubbly chin with a freckled hand. "I realize I was hard on Truett this week. But I had to keep pace with the competition."

Two days later, the next edition of the *Illinois Democrat* landed on my doorstep. I took it with me when I went to meet Martha for breakfast at the Globe.

"Nothing of interest," I said, discarding the paper onto the table between us when I finished skimming the four pages of small-font type. "Just another regurgitation of Early's shooting. At least it's more neutral toward Truett this time. Ah, Saunders, at last!"

The innkeeper set down between us two steaming mugs of coffee and a single metal plate containing hard-cooked eggs, potatoes, and boiled ham. I dug in greedily.

"Oh my word," exclaimed Martha from across the table.

"What?" I did not look up from my breakfast.

"You must have missed it. Bottom of the back page. There's another letter from S.G."

I took the paper from her and read:

July 8, 1838
Lost Township, Ill.

To the Editor of the Democrat:
    The voters must have the sense to elect the Democrats next month. A trail of ruin follows the party of the rail-splitter of great height and low intellect. They claim to serve their fellow man but, in reality, serve only themselves. Early's fate is a warning to all who would be tricked by their insincere words. Do not follow a False Prophet.

S.G.

" 'Early's fate,' " murmured Martha, reading the letter again over my shoulder. "I wonder if S.G. knows who the real killer is."

"Or if he *is* the real killer." I pushed away from the table, leaving the plate of half-eaten food behind. "Come—let's find out the identity of this blackguard."

Martha stared at me, uncomprehending. "How do you plan on doing that?"

"Both of S.G.'s letters were sent to the editor of the *Democrat*. That's this fellow George Weber. He should know who's writing in his pages."

CHAPTER 12

Other than owning the two printing presses in town, George Weber and Simeon Francis were each other's opposite in nearly every respect. Weber was a serious man with prominent cheekbones, a square jaw, and piercing black eyes. His face was clean-shaven, his hair cut short, his dress always fastidious. He was sober in his habits and opinionated and outspoken in his political views. This last was another point of convergence with Simeon, although the direction of their views was diametrically opposed.

As one might imagine, the two publishers despised one another. Always alert to the opportunity for such mischief, Fate had landed them next door to each other in matching one-story, wood-frame buildings on the dilapidated north side of the town square, an area known as Chicken Row. The side-by-side buildings were visible through the windows from my usual perch behind the counter of my store, and on many afternoons I could see Francis and Weber standing in front of their respective buildings shouting insults at each other.

We pushed open Weber's front door without knocking. The publisher was at his composing table, dressed in a full suit of black silk: coat, vest, and bow tie. He looked up with the conquering expression of a fox who'd been asked to guard the henhouse.

"Wrong door, Speed," he said in a drawn-out drawl reflecting his South Carolinian roots. "Francis is the next one."

"I'm looking for you. Who's S.G.?"

Weber pretended not to understand my question and, when I put it him again, said, "S.D.? Why, that would be Stephen Douglas, don't you think? The next representative from the Third District."

I sensed Martha coloring beside me. "No, *G*," I insisted. "S.G. The author of the two letters you've printed, the ones insulting Lincoln."

Weber's upper lip curled into an unpleasant smile. "I'm delighted to learn you're such a dedicated reader of the *Democrat* that you make it all the way through the bottom of the last page. But I haven't any idea. The letters arrived at the Post Office Department for me and I set them in type. For today's edition in particular I was trying to figure out how to fill out those final column inches, so I was glad to receive it."

"But you must know who's writing to you," broke in Martha, expelling her breath in frustration.

"And you are?" Weber asked, turning to her with a blank stare that nonetheless managed to convey a certain contempt.

"My sister Martha Speed," I said.

Weber gave the most perfunctory of bows. "In that event, Miss Speed, I can do nothing but repeat what I said to your brother. The letters arrived and I printed them."

"And you have no idea who they're from?"

"No idea—and no interest."

"Do you still have the original letters?" asked Martha. "Or even the envelopes they arrived in?" When I looked at her questioningly, she added, "Because we could examine the handwriting and possibly recognize it."

Weber contemplated this, sucking in his cheeks. "There were no envelopes," he said. "Just a single sheet of foolscap, folded into a packet, with my address written on the outside next to the postmaster's notation of the postage due."

"Will you please let us see the sheets of foolscap, then?"

"I burned them."

I stared at Weber and tried to discern whether he was lying. And why. To protect a political ally, was the obvious answer to the second question. But whom?

"If you receive another one," Martha was saying, "will you please save it? We'd like to examine it."

"If I think of it, perhaps I shall," said Weber with a shrug.

He looked back down at his composing table and began searching for some type. I took Martha's arm and we departed. She was muttering unladylike sentiments about Weber as we reached the square.

"Let's go see Lincoln," I said. "He may not want our help in defending Truett, but I think he needs it."

When we reached Hoffman's Row, court was in session in No. 3. It was a routine hearing, however, as we could see through the closed windows only a few spectators watching the goings-on in front of Judge Thomas. We climbed the rickety stairs to Lincoln's law office at No. 4.

The fading white lettering on the door announced, "Stuart and Lincoln, Attorneys and Counselors at Law." I pushed it open and we found Lincoln seated at the square table in the center of the room, hunched over a legal document, his quill pen working furiously. Listing stacks of documents and undone packets of papers were strewn about the table and every other horizontal surface of the room, as if a violent whirlwind had swept through.

A moment later, Lincoln signed the document on which he'd been working with a demonstrative flourish and rose to his feet. "Two Speeds at once," he said. "To what do I owe this honor?"

I handed him the copy of the *Democrat* and pointed to the new letter, but he merely nodded. "I've seen it already. Simeon was by earlier, ranting and raving about Weber's scurrilous publication practices. Of course, we both know Simeon would publish the same sort of thing about a Democratic politician if given half the chance."

"Joshua took us by the *Democrat*'s offices on the way over," said Martha.

"I imagine Weber was as welcoming as a mother rattlesnake guarding her nest."

"Less so," Martha said with a laugh.

"When I said 'S.G.' to Weber," I said, "he thought I'd said 'S.D.,' and he suggested Douglas was the logical S.D."

"That's an interesting slip of the tongue," said Lincoln, his gray eyes alive with thought. "I wouldn't put it past Douglas. Nothing to do with the killing, of course. But the taunting, too-clever letters? That's right up his alley. Just look at the slanted press coverage he's inspired against Truett."

"It's *S.G.*, not *S.D.*, and anyway I'm certain it's not Mr. Douglas," said Martha with passion.

Both Lincoln and I stared at her. "*How* are you sure it's not him?" Lincoln asked, voicing the question on my lips as well.

"It's not important—I just am."

"Martha, I told you to keep away from him," I said sharply.

My sister's temples were flushed and her cheeks flamed. "You have no right to tell me anything of the sort!" she shouted.

"I most certainly do! You're here under my protection—"

At that moment, there was a sharp pounding on the floorboards underneath us. Without a word Lincoln dropped to his knees and started digging away at the floor with his fingernails. I came around the table and saw he was fumbling with a latch set into the boards. Then Lincoln gave a push and a three-foot-square section of the floor swung away, and suddenly we were staring down into Judge Thomas's courtroom through its ceiling. Directly below us, the court clerk Matheny stood with a broomstick in his hands.

"You're making quite a racket," said Matheny crossly.

"Is it too much to ask, Lincoln," called the judge from his end of the courtroom, "that we may proceed with the business of the circuit court without hearing every word of the varied and sundry troubles of your visitors?"

Standing directly above the opening, I had a disconcerting view, from a bird's eye as it were, of the judge, several attorneys, and the few spectators present for the morning's court session, all of them looking skyward with craned necks.

"My apologies, Your Honor," returned Lincoln. He was lying prone on the floor, his waist even with the edge of the opening and his upper torso dangling down into the courtroom below. So much of his body projected through the opening that I feared he might topple in, but then I saw he had taken the precaution of wrapping his feet around one of the table legs to anchor himself.

"Who's in the box this morning, anyway? Oh, it's Prickett. Stop up after you're through, would you, David? I have a new thought about the Thorpe brothers case—our favorite chicken snatchers. Perhaps we can come to an arrangement after all."

"Very well," said the prosecutor, his head tipped far back.

"Carry on, Your Honor," said Lincoln. "We'll do our best to contain our enthusiasms."

Before Judge Thomas could respond, Lincoln wriggled back from the opening and swung the trapdoor shut with a *thud*. Then he bounced to his feet, a broad smile spread across his face, and said, in a more moderate voice, "When Hoffman came 'round to inform me he'd let the ground floor to the judge for the temporary court-room, he pointed the door out. It was specially installed by the original tenant of Nos. 3 and 4. Actually, it's come in handy for the judge a few times. When he's got a jury up here, you see."

"A jury?"

"They had their own special room over at the old courthouse, but there's nowhere at Hoffman's Row for Judge Thomas to put his jury while they're deliberating. So the county commissioners approached me and Stuart with a proposition. When the court holds a jury trial, they come up here to deliberate—Stuart and I clear out, of course—and when they've got a question for the judge, or when they've reached their verdict, they just open the trapdoor and shout down. It works surprisingly well, and the commissioners have agreed to pay us thirty-six dollars each term for the occasional use of the place." He smiled. "I'll be the only attorney in town who's sorry to see the court move to permanent quarters, whenever that day comes."

Martha clapped her hands together and Lincoln gave her a toothy grin. "Let's start over," I proposed, "only, in quieter voices." Both of my companions nodded.

"We've come by because we want to help you with your defense of Mr. Truett," said Martha. "I've got a couple of ideas, and perhaps Joshua does as well. What's your plan for the case?"

"As always, I admire your enthusiasm, Miss Speed," said Lincoln with a twinkling look. "But as I've told your brother, this is one case I can handle myself."

"I talked to your client the other night," Martha pressed on. "The baby was fussing and Molly asked if I would mind carrying their prisoner's dinner out to the cell so she could nurse the little man. Mr. Truett was desperate to tell me he's been wrongly accused. He wouldn't let me leave until he'd told me all about the night of the shooting, how he was on the other side of the grounds on Quality Hill when the cannons went off, so he can't have been the one who killed Early—"

"But he doesn't have any witnesses who can affirm he was where he says he was at that moment," broke in Lincoln. "I've been through this with him as well, Miss Speed."

"What about your father?" I blurted, unable to suppress the question any longer.

"Your father, Mr. Lincoln?" said Martha, her eyes wide. "Don't tell me he's caught up in this somehow?"

Lincoln gave me a long, unfriendly stare, which I returned without blinking. Then he sighed and, pointedly turning his back toward me, related to Martha what Truett had said about Thomas Lincoln out at the jail cell that night.

"Surely you don't believe him," said Martha when Lincoln had finished.

"There's a lot I would believe about my father," he replied. "But land fraud? No, I don't believe that of him." Lincoln swallowed, then continued, "Now, my stepbrother? I'd believe pretty much anything anyone says about John. And about his ability to steer my father into situations in which he's got no business being."

"How did Mr. Johnston first come to live with you?" asked Martha in a soft, sympathetic voice.

"Six months after my angel mother passed, my father realized he had no hope of running the household by himself. We were living in Indiana by then, but he knew of a widow back in Kentucky with three children of her own. They agreed to combine their families. My stepmother Sarah moved into our house with two daughters and a son. That's John."

"Were the two of you close growing up?"

Lincoln frowned. "We tolerated one another. Slept next to each other in the loft in our cabin. Grumbled together when our father ordered us to do the grubbing or hired us out to work in the neighbors' fields. But we are very different, as you can see."

"I imagine he means well."

"I don't think so at all. He needs to get a job. He's been living off my father's resources, meager as they are, for far too long." Lincoln's voice cracked with emotion. "And the schemes I've seen John dream up . . . he's got no sense but a sense for self-preservation. At whatever cost to those around him."

Martha's brows were knit together with concentration. "Who's running the land office," she asked, "now that Mr. Early is gone?"

"For the time being, it's Pollard Simmons, the clerk," said Lincoln. "A few of us got together and agreed we'd wait until after the election before a new registrar is appointed. It'd hardly do to put a new man in place and then have to take him out a few weeks later if the opposite party wins instead."

"Have you been there to see if you can figure out what Early was looking into?" I asked. "And whether there's any truth to the suggestion your father was bound up in it somehow?"

Lincoln expelled his breath and shook his head. "I've been hesitant to draw attention to the issue. The clerk Simmons is close with a few of the lower-level Democrats. If I go in there, asking for any records involving my father, or John for that matter, it'll be as good as letting the entire Springfield Democratic Party know there's something to pursue. But I've resolved I must do it anyway, at the end of next week, when I'm back in Springfield."

"I didn't know you were traveling," I said, turning to him in surprise. "I thought you were staying put, now that we've entered the campaign season in earnest."

"It's the campaign that has me on the road. I'm leaving tomorrow. There's to be a series of meetings around the county for the voters to hear each of the candidates for the state legislature speak for themselves. There are seventeen of us, running for a total of seven seats."

From the clutter on the table in front of him, Lincoln pulled out a sheet with several columns of writing. "We'll be gathering at Bartell's on Sugar Creek on Saturday. The following week we'll all be at Colburn's Mill on Lick Creek, in the southwestern part of the county. There's another meeting in Berlin the day after. And the final one's at Walter's Camp Ground on Spring Creek, two days later.

"At every meeting, each of the candidates will stand up on a tree stump in turn and say his piece—his position on the internal improvements, how he proposes to resolve the banking panic, and so on. With that many men wanting their say, the meetings will last all day. Some might even go into a second."

"That's a lot of talking," said Martha with a laugh. "And we'll work on your case while you're gone. Starting with the land office." Turning to me, she added, "We can say Daddy is considering investing in property here. People will believe that, and it will avoid any suggestion that our questions are related to Mr. Lincoln."

When Lincoln hesitated, I said, "It seems to me you've got nothing to lose by having us poke around. Maybe we'll find something that helps exonerate Truett. Or, at the least, gives you peace of mind about your father."

Lincoln's face relaxed into a smile. "Very well. I guess the Speeds are on the case after all."

My sister gave a small cheer. A few minutes later we made ready to depart. As we reached the door, Lincoln called out, "One favor to ask of you, Miss Speed."

"Anything."

"Don't share our thinking, or the results of your investigations— or certainly this rumor about my father—with your friend Mr. Douglas."

Martha blushed. "No. Of course not."

"He's our adversary," said Lincoln. "It's his job to keep Truett in jail, or worse. It's our job to prevent it. At all events, you must keep that in mind."

CHAPTER 13

The land office consisted of a one-room log cabin over on Second Street. Nailed to the logs beside the entrance was a tattered notice from the national government setting forth the terms of the Land Act of 1820 and the Relief Act of 1821. Across the top of the notice someone had scrawled, "No man's property is safe while the Legislature is in session." I suspected there were a great many in town who concurred with the sentiment.

On the morning after our meeting with Lincoln, Martha and I pushed open the door and came upon Pollard Simmons, seated on an ancient chair behind an even older desk. The clerk was a heavyset, elderly man with thick glasses pressed against the bridge of his nose, who squinted at us as we entered. The office was windowless and lit by two lonely candles. Boxes overflowing with loose papers and bound books cluttered the floor.

"Good morning," I began, "we've come to buy land."

Simmons looked up at us and mournfully shook his head. "You cannot do that, sir."

"This is still the land office, is it not? And you are running the office at present? So I demand the opportunity to purchase land."

"It is, I am, and you cannot."

I rocked back on my heels and thought. Then I made a show of reaching into my pocket. "Perhaps if we offer you something for your, er, troubles?"

The man recoiled. "I certainly hope you're not offering to bribe me," he said, "for I shall send for Sheriff Hutchason at once."

"Oh no, I didn't mean to—"

I was interrupted by the sound of the church bell from down the street. Nine sonorous tones flitted through the small office.

The clerk cocked his head, wordlessly counting the bells. When they ended, he reached beneath his desk and pulled out a small sign, which he fastidiously arranged on the surface in front of him.

"Land Office Open," read the sign.

"Now, sir, how many acres are you interested in?" he asked.

"We've come as agents for our father," interposed Martha. "Judge John Speed of Louisville. He's hoping to purchase a large plot. One thousand acres."

The clerk did not turn to Martha but rather kept his intense stare focused on me. "A thousand acres, you say? We've got some remaining tracts in the southwestern corner of the old Military Tract that are that large. All at the federal price of a dollar twenty-five an acre."

I shook my head. "We were hoping to purchase something a little closer to Springfield. My father shares our optimism about the prospects for Sangamon County, now that the state capital is coming. Perhaps out by New Salem." It was a guess, based on the little we knew, but we had to start somewhere.

"That area's all in private hands already," said Simmons. "You'd have to deal with the landowners directly. And then come register the transaction with me, once you've got it surveyed and the price agreed upon. But I doubt you'll find any one parcel as large as your father's interested in."

"Do all those books show the current owners?" asked Martha, gesturing to the volumes scattered across the floor.

"Take a look at the land entry books if you want," the clerk said to me, again ignoring Martha. "They'll show the entrymen who own each parcel."

"I'm standing right here," Martha hissed into my ear in a not-very-quiet whisper as I took her by the arm and led her toward the disorderly pile of records.

"Of course you are," I said. "Let's take a look."

The monumental nature of our task soon became apparent. The thick, bound books contained a running log of land transactions, including the date, seller, purchaser, amount of cash paid as a deposit, and amount promised on account. Most entries also included the name of the surveyor, a crucial detail, as the jumble of conflicting title claims that characterized the West meant that the surveyor was often a key witness for proving ownership of a given piece of land.

Soon we were awash in a sea of names and figures, dates and dollars. By the time the church bells struck noon, my eyes were weary from staring at tiny, uneven handwriting on page after page. Martha and I went outside to have lunch and reconsider our plan.

"There's almost too much information," I said, squinting into the bright sun after so long in the dimly lit office. "It's hard to make sense of any of it."

"Maybe we should make a list of the names that appear most often," suggested Martha. "If there was some sort of fraud going on, wouldn't you think it would involve particularly frequent buyers?"

"Or frequent sellers," I said. "Or false names. Or faked surveys. There could be almost anything hidden inside those books."

"I saw Lincoln's name frequently listed as the surveyor," said Martha.

I nodded. "He once told me he'd been one of the most prolific surveyors in the area, and now I believe him."

Lincoln had related that surveying had been his favorite of the many assorted jobs he'd held in New Salem, in the time before he read law and moved to Springfield. His surveying career had been interrupted unceremoniously when his surveying instruments were seized by the sheriff because of his failure to make payments on the debt he'd incurred from his failed New Salem store.

"Perhaps Lincoln would be able to make more sense of these records," I said.

"Perhaps he would," agreed Martha. "But we told him we'd go through them in his absence. I don't want to let him down."

Replenished by a pair of ham sandwiches procured from the Globe, we returned to the office. Martha took out a pencil and a blank sheet of paper and started making notes of the names listed in the transaction logs. I decided to proceed more loosely and flipped from page to page and often back again, hoping some spark of inspiration would kindle and show me the pattern we were meant to see. I soon tired of this and returned to the clerk's desk. Simmons had been scratching away at a piece of parchment throughout our visit.

"How long have you been the clerk?" I asked.

Simmons peered up, his eyes grotesquely magnified by his thick glasses. "Ever since the Springfield land office opened in '23. We've had seven registrars in that time but only one clerk. I've outlasted 'em all."

"And how did Early compare, would you say, to his predecessors?"

"I shan't speak ill of the dead."

"Of course not. Would you say he paid more or less attention to the business of the office than the men before him?"

"Most of them was interested in the fees above everything else, and Early was no different," Simmons said with a shrug. "As long as I opened the desk at nine bells and closed them at four, he left me alone."

"In the past few months, did you notice anything changed in the way Early was behaving?"

Simmons put down his pen and gave me his full attention. "For a man who says he's interested in buying property, you sure have a lot of questions about someone who don't work here anymore. What's your real interest?"

At that moment, I felt Martha at my side. She held one of the land entry books in her arms. "I've noticed, Mr. Simmons," she said, "that the entries in these books have been made by several different hands. Can you help me tell them apart?"

Simmons's stare remained fixed on me and his mien was distinctly unfriendly. "It don't matter who wrote what," he said. "The records are the records."

"I've seen black ink and sepia ink," continued Martha, unflinch-ingly. "I'm thinking one color is the one you used and the other was Mr. Early's. Ah, I see you're partial to the black," she added, looking down at the parchment in front of Simmons. "So Early must have been sepia. I've answered my own question."

"You have."

"Come along, Joshua." Martha took my arm, giving it a quick squeeze. "We've taken more than enough of Mr. Simmons's time." She steered me through the door, her hands gripping my arm tightly.

Martha marched me down the block and around the corner. The excitement on her face was unmistakable. "What is it?" I demanded when she finally allowed us to come to a stop.

"I found notes that Early must have made while looking into the scheme, whatever it was. They were tucked in between the pages of a land entry book from 1835, one that isn't being used anymore. I figured they were his, but I wanted to confirm it was his writing, so that's why I asked about the ink color."

"Well done! We can go back tomorrow and you can show them to me."

"Don't be silly," Martha replied with a laugh. She reached into the folds of her dress and pulled out two sheets of paper, creased together into thirds and crisscrossed by tiny notations in sepia ink.

CHAPTER 14

We decided to ask Truett about the notes Martha had found. The next morning, I met Martha at the Hutchason house, and we walked to the jail cell in the backyard.

I was shocked by Truett's appearance when we came upon him. Captivity was taking a great toll. His dandified clothes were gone, replaced by coarse trousers and a sweat-stained work shirt. His hair was disheveled and his face was unshaved and haggard. Slight to begin with, he appeared to be losing weight.

"You must get me out of here," he cried when he saw us approaching, his filthy hands wrapped around the bars of the cell. "I keep telling the sheriff, I'm not made to survive in conditions like this."

"Lincoln's hard at work preparing for your trial," I said, thinking it best not to mention the political stump tour, "and we're doing what we can to help. That's why we've come this morning. Take a look at these."

I handed Early's notes through the bars and explained where we'd found them. Truett examined the pages carefully, turning them this way and that. After a few minutes, he nodded and handed them back to me.

"You say these were made by Early?" he said.

"We think so."

"I always knew he was doing an incompetent job at the land office and these are proof of it. The registrar position should have been mine from the start. In fact—"

"*Please*, Mr. Truett," Martha broke in earnestly, "we're trying to help get you freed. Surely the land office job is secondary right now."

Truett took a step back and exhaled. Gradually his grimy face relaxed into a faint smile. "I suppose you're right, Miss Speed. I can't help myself sometimes, but you're right. Here's what I think he was doing."

Truett led us methodically through Early's densely packed notations. When he had finished, we understood that Early had constructed in effect a grid in three dimensions, tracking the number of land plots bought and sold by different individuals, for every half year since the start of 1834, in each case along with the named surveyors of each plot. Nearly two dozen different men had purchased or sold at least ten properties in the time period in question, and Early's investigation seemed to focus on them. Then Martha had a brainstorm.

"We should match up these names with the list of persons who attended the Edwardses' party," she said, snapping her fingers with excitement. "If Mr. Early was killed to conceal some misconduct in the land office, then the killer's likely to have been someone on this list who was also at the party."

Her logic seemed undeniable. We sent a note to Mrs. Edwards advising her of our desire to call, and shortly after noon we received word back that we were welcome to come at once.

As we climbed toward the Edwards mansion, Martha hummed happily. Despite our long exertions of the previous few days, I had rarely seen her looking so serene. After a while, I asked her to identify the tune.

"'Devote your sacred head for one such as I.'"

"Never heard of it. Where'd you pick it up?"

"At the meeting last weekend." Martha stared resolutely ahead, placing one foot in front of the other, and it took me a minute to comprehend her meaning.

"You went to the *camp meeting*? I thought I told you it was a crock."

"I don't recall asking your opinion on the matter," she said, "and I'm quite glad I didn't. Your friend Miss Butler was right. It was a joyous congregation. And an agreeable place for young women, I should add."

"Whatever do you mean?"

"After the sermon, two of the exhorters gathered a group of us in a circle. Other young women, all. We started talking about the path to enlightenment, but before long we were discussing our common condition. I've never participated in such a conversation, certainly not in public like that. It was really quite amazing."

"Condition? What condition?" I asked, not bothering to hide my skepticism.

"The condition of being a woman in this society," she said, her cheeks glowing with passion. "To have your intellect confined, your morals crushed, your health ruined, your weaknesses encouraged, your strength punished. Of being treated as second-class. Without rights *or* status."

"You can't be serious," I said. "You have rights *and* status. A common farmer's wife, I suppose I could understand your point. Not agree with it, but at least understand it. But not Miss Martha Speed of Louisville, daughter of Judge Speed, proprietor of Farmington."

Martha stopped and turned to face me. Her eyes glistened. "If only you, of all people, understood, Joshua."

"When have you ever been treated as second-class?" I said, resuming my march up the slope.

"When haven't I? Why, look no further than yesterday. Remember how that odious clerk talked to us? Whenever I said anything, he responded to you. It was as if I didn't exist."

"He's old and nearsighted. He probably didn't even see you."

"Exactly!" cried Martha, and when I looked to her for further explanation, she thrust her head back and marched ahead, leaving me in her wake.

Soon the Edwards house loomed in front of us, radiant in the afternoon sun, the cream-colored walls of the mansion giving off the shimmer of pale gold. The front door was opened by a Negro boy of about fourteen years. We asked for the mistress of the house.

"Thank you, Joseph," said Elizabeth Todd Edwards, dismissing her servant as she approached us from the far end of the long entrance hall. "Mr. and Miss Speed. Your note said you're interested in something relating to that dreadful business on the night of our party?"

"Mr. Lincoln's been hired by Mr. Truett," Martha began eagerly, "the man charged with the murder—"

"I know all about Henry Truett," interrupted Mrs. Edwards.

"What do you know?" I asked.

She glanced around to make sure no one else was within earshot. "Ninian always says I shouldn't talk about the other politicians in town, but he can't expect me not to form opinions. We always know the truth about men before the men themselves realize it— isn't that so, dear?"

Martha favored her with a broad smile.

"Henry Truett is the little terrier who thinks he should have been born a Great Dane," continued Mrs. Edwards. "What God didn't give him in stature, He gave him in orneriness. I've never had a five-minute conversation with him that didn't end in a quarrel, even if he's in perfect agreement with me and every other person present. He can't help himself."

"I imagine you saw the argument between him and Mr. Early earlier that evening," I said.

"It was the worst fear of every hostess. I was trying to find Ninian to help extinguish it when Stephen intervened. Thank heaven for Stephen."

Martha sighed audibly. I glared at her.

"Unfortunately," continued Mrs. Edwards, "he couldn't prevent the calamity at the end of the evening. And now Truett's been charged with the killing and Lincoln's representing him. I understand. I'm a lawyer's wife as well as a politician's. I learned more about the law than I ever wanted to know back when Ninian was attorney general. What does Lincoln need?"

"We have two favors to ask," said Martha. "First, we're hoping you have a list of the guests who were present. It stands to reason one of them has to be the killer, as distasteful as that sounds. And second, we want to walk around your grounds. If we can make a map of the area where Mr. Early was standing at the moment he was shot, we might be able to figure out where the shot came from."

Mrs. Edwards nodded. "I think I still have the list I used to send out invitations. You're welcome to copy it. And after that, help yourself to the grounds. Just do me a favor and don't trample on the dahlias. They've just started opening and I do love them."

We assured Mrs. Edwards we would take care to avoid her flowers, and she led us into the drawing room and pointed to two chairs beside a small desk. "I'll have Joseph bring you the list," she said, turning to leave.

"Before you go," I said, "may I inquire of the health of your sister Mary?" Mary Todd had lodged with her elder sister in Springfield the previous summer, and I'd found myself beguiled by her clear blue eyes and serious wit. "She performed a favor for me at the end of her visit last year, for which I am grateful. I found her a most capable and handsome young woman."

"She's doing quite well, thank you," replied Mrs. Edwards. "Indeed, she talks of leaving Lexington to return to Springfield permanently, perhaps as soon as next year. I think she prefers the openness of the frontier to the structure of our father's house."

"In that event, she and I see eye to eye," said Martha with a laugh. "Having lived here for a few seasons myself, I can't imagine ever going back to *my* father's dungeon."

Elizabeth Edwards gave Martha an indulgent look and departed. A few minutes later, her servant came in with two creased, well-handled sheets. He also folded down the desktop to show us the location of a bottle of ink, a quill pen, and writing and blotting papers.

"Why don't you read off the names and I'll write them down," said Martha. "My penmanship's far superior, you have to admit."

I did not argue. I squinted at the pages; they were covered by cramped scribbles, juxtaposed at assorted angles.

"It looks like some of the names have a single check mark next to them and others have two," I said, examining the pages. "I'm not sure what they mean."

"Invitations sent out and replies received," suggested Martha.

"Or persons attending. Maybe you got two check marks if you said you were coming."

"You and I got two marks," I said, "but I see Simeon Francis here with only one, and he was assuredly present as well."

"Do you think he would have sent back a reply note?"

"Almost certainly not. I think we're better off writing down all the names."

Martha agreed, and she copied down the names on a clean sheet of paper as I read them off. At the bottom of the first page, wedged into a corner at an angle, I came upon the notation "Father Lincoln + son," followed by two check marks.

"So she included people who showed up uninvited," I said as I read the names aloud for Martha. "She was certainly a meticulous hostess." Martha nodded, running her finger absently along the ridge of her quill.

When we were finished, we had a list of 129 persons, including virtually every politician, lawyer, and member of the other learned professions in Springfield, along with their wives and some unmarried sisters. Both of us agreed that total seemed about right for what we remembered of the size of the party. Comparing it to Early's list of land purchasers, we found a half dozen names on both lists, including Ninian Edwards himself, the publisher George Weber, Truett, Douglas, and Henry Owens, the apothecary. I pointed at Douglas's name and raised my eyebrows.

"Don't be ridiculous," said Martha. "I think Henry Owens is the interesting one. We should investigate him."

"I did see him having an animated discussion with Early during the party," I said, thinking back. "I wasn't close enough to hear what they were talking about. But I don't think Lincoln would want us to interrogate his beau's brother in his absence."

Martha thought about this. "You're probably right. Let's go walk the grounds."

We stepped into the hallway and nearly collided with the servant Joseph, who was coming in the opposite direction. He was of medium build and dark-skinned, with a scar on his nose and wide-spaced eyes.

"Is your mistress about?" I asked.

"No, sir. She went down into town sometime back. Can I deliver a message?"

"We merely wanted to thank her for her help. We'll be going outside to look around for a spell. Your mistress said that was fine."

Martha had finished blotting her list of names and was beside me now, her shawl around her head and shoulders. "How long have you been the Edwardses' servant, Joseph?" she asked.

"Not their servant, ma'am. Their bondsman."

"How long have you been in bond to them, then?" asked Martha, glancing at me with surprise.

"Since the day I was born, ma'am. My momma was their bondsman before me. She's not with us anymore." He gave a brief nod, then stood with his hands clasped behind his back and his eyes averted as we walked down the entrance hall.

"Can that be true?" Martha asked as soon as the front door closed behind us.

I gave a rueful nod. "Under the Illinois constitution, Negro children can be held in contracts of indentured servitude until they reach a particular age. It's slavery in everything but name. I imagine his mother agreed to indenture him to Edwards upon his birth."

Martha gasped, her hand over her mouth.

"Anyway," I continued, nodding, "you know as well as I do that he's much better off being held to his bond as a house servant on Quality Hill than in the fields of a sugarcane plantation in Louisiana." I did not add, *or the fields of a hemp plantation in Kentucky,* though both my sister and I knew that perfectly well, too. "Now let's see if we can map the grounds."

Martha murmured something under her breath. I thought I heard the phrase "another unseen person," but when I asked her what she'd said, her back stiffened and she replied, "Nothing you need concern yourself with."

We walked away from the house toward the lip of the rise overlooking town. I wandered around a bit, trying to judge the angle we'd had for viewing the fireworks. "About here," I said, coming to rest at last.

"And where was Early standing?"

"He fell right there," I said, pointing to the ground a few paces away. "Presumably that's where he was standing when he was shot."

Martha took out a pencil and a large sheet of card paper and began sketching the immediate landscape with considerable skill.

"Which direction was he shot from?" she asked.

"That's a good question. He was shot from the front. The wound was in the direct center of his forehead. Whoever shot him was staring straight at him, and vice versa. So it depends which way Early was turned at that moment."

"Surely he would have been looking out toward the fireworks."

But when we gazed forward from the spot where Early had been, we immediately saw the problem. The Edwards yard extended for another five feet, then quickly gave way to the sloping hillside. "I don't see . . ." began Martha, before trailing off.

"You're right. If he was shot while looking out, the killer would have been right there in front of him. Surely Early would have seen him and called out or tried to get out of the way."

"And you would have seen him too," said Martha.

I looked around at where I'd been standing and then back to the presumed spot of the assassin. "Probably," I said. I took in the undulations of the grounds again. "Unless he was down the hill."

"But in that case, I don't think he would have had a shot. The crest of the hill would have obscured the line of sight. Here—I'll stand on Early's spot and you go over the ledge and see if you can still see me."

I did as Martha suggested. As soon as I went over the lip of the hill and took two steps down, she disappeared from view. I kept backing away. The slope of the hillside undulated as it fell away toward town. But at no point during my descent was even the top of Martha's shawl visible. I hurried up the hill to rejoin my sister.

"There's no shot from down below," I reported as I reached her position.

"He was taller than me," murmured Martha, chewing on the end of her pencil and lost in thought.

"But not enough to make a difference," I said. "I tried jumping up when I was down there, but I couldn't ever see you. The slope prevented it."

"Which means," said Martha, "he had to have been facing the other direction, back toward the house, at the moment he was shot." She paused. "What would have made Mr. Early turn *away* from what was likely the first fireworks exhibition he'd ever seen in his life?"

It was a very good question.

Chapter 15

On the way back to town we detoured by the offices of the *Journal*, where I told Simeon that Lincoln planned to argue at trial that someone involved in questionable dealings with the land office had been Early's actual killer. The newspaperman readily agreed to run it as the lead story in his next edition, and we left satisfied that the press coverage of the impending trial would finally change for Truett's benefit.

After I'd finished with Simeon, I went next door to the *Democrat*. "Nothing new from S.G.?" I asked Weber when he looked up from his composing table. Lincoln's anonymous antagonist had seemingly gone quiet.

"You sound disappointed," the publisher sneered. "I thought the Speed family position on his letters was outrage. I wish you'd make up your minds."

"Why don't you let me know directly the next time you hear from him," I said. "I'll pass along to Lincoln whatever it is he has to say. That way you can save the column inches and printer's ink."

Weber smiled at this and said, "No wonder you're a damned Whig, Speed. You've got no sense of fun."

The next day was Friday, and that evening my roommates Hurst and Herndon and I decided it was time for a good drunk. There was only one place in Springfield where such lofty aspirations were guaranteed to meet with success: Torrey's Temperance Hotel. So, as darkness fell, we headed to Torrey's.

Torrey's was the shabbiest public accommodation in town. The sign above the door featured a golden eagle, badly faded, and the name of the establishment. Long ago some wag had defaced the final two words such that the sign appeared to read "Torrey's Temper Hot." It was an accurate enough description of the sour, moon-faced proprietor of the place that no one bothered to restore the sign to its original condition.

We pushed our way into the seething public room and Hurst set off to obtain supplies from the open barrel of busthead whiskey, which sat on the bar beside the scowling Torrey. Herndon and I located a comparatively empty corner in which to set up shop. Hurst returned with three brimming glasses and we threw them down, wincing from the harshness of the liquor. There was no question but that it would do the trick, and sooner rather than later, too.

Several draughts later we heard a great roar of laughter coming from the other side of the tavern. I thought I detected a familiar hoarse voice amid the shouting. I stood, teetered, and headed toward the noise, and soon I spied Thomas Lincoln, his face glowing red, surrounded by a half dozen townsmen.

At once I realized the group comprised men who were not friends of Abraham, either Democratic office-seekers or local malcontents always happy to take a successful man down a peg. I forswore my original plans for the evening and attempted to shake off the effects of the liquor I'd already drunk.

Before I could reach this boisterous, dangerous group, however, I felt my arm being grabbed.

"Why, ain't it Speed?" said John Johnston. He was carrying himself carefully in the manner of a man struggling to hold his drink. "I saw you over there with your fellows—I was wondering whether you'd be coming to pay your respects."

"I trust you and your stepfather are still enjoying our precincts," I said, wondering if it could be a coincidence that they had surfaced again after Lincoln himself had left town.

"It's as good a town as any, I suppose," he replied, "though our plans ain't come to pass yet. Soon, we can only hope."

We both looked over at Thomas Lincoln, who'd just been handed a fresh glass of ale by one of his companions. "Perhaps your stepfather would do well to slow down," I said.

"Ain't doing him no harm," replied Johnston. "Besides, what's it to you?"

"Abraham's gone for a few days, but he asked me to keep an eye out for his father—and you, too, of course. I know those men he's drinking with. They don't have Abraham's interests at heart. Especially not at this season."

"What season is that?"

"I mean with the election coming up. Every one of those men would like nothing better than to spoil your brother's chances with the voters."

"Abe has no idea how easy he's got it," said Johnston, the color rising in his cheeks. "He ran through our parents' door so fast after he reached majority it's a wonder it weren't knocked clear off its hinges. He ran out and left me behind with him." He jerked his head toward his stepfather, who was holding a nearly empty glass in one hand while gesturing wildly to his audience with the other.

Another shout of laughter erupted from the men congregated around Thomas Lincoln, and I pushed past Johnston toward the group. As I got within range, I heard one man call out, "Tell us another one, Father Lincoln."

"You really want to know about Abe?" asked Lincoln. The heads of his listeners bobbed eagerly.

"The truth is—and maybe this'll surprise you—the truth is Abe was a goddamn lazy boy. I doubt there was any lazier than him. I'll tell you a story from when he was a youngster that proves it." He drained the dregs of his glass.

"Shall I fetch you another slug?" asked one of his listeners.

"Don't mind if you do," said Thomas, succeeding on his second try at handing his empty glass to the man. "Thank you kindly. You tell the barkeep to keep putting them on the 'Lincoln' account. I'm sure Abe'll be most happy to pay it, eh?"

The men laughed appreciatively. One of them patted Thomas Lincoln on the back and the old man fell into a coughing fit, violently retching, his fist held up to his mouth as he tried to stop the convulsions. Eventually he caught his breath and looked around, waiting for someone to say something.

"You were about to tell us a story," prompted one of the men. "About when Abraham was a boy."

"That's right," said Lincoln. He cleared his throat with difficulty. "When we was living in Pigeon Creek, there was this fella named Baldwin who lived nearby, a rich fella, and he had a big field in need of tilling. This fella Baldwin had seen Abe 'round the area, of course, and he knew what a big, strapping fella he'd become. This must of been when Abe was of fifteen or sixteen years, and he was already six foot and some inches tall if he was a foot. So Baldwin asked me if Abe would be willing to plow his fields for one dollar a day. I said he sure would. He *sure* would. Cuz the money's going straight into my pocket, right? At sixteen those broad shoulders of Abe's was still mine to hire out as I pleased. Ain't they, fellas?"

Thomas Lincoln winked broadly and his audience chuckled. Someone handed Thomas a new glass, filled to the rim, and he drank half of it down before continuing.

"Anyway, the next morning, right as the sun's coming up, I go up to the loft where Abe's sleeping and I shake his shoulder and I tell him it's time to get up and start turning over Baldwin's fields. And he just rolls over and falls back asleep. So I do it again and he does it again. Finally, 'bout the fourth time, I get him up out of bed—I nearly have to drag him down the ladder—and I get him out to those fields and I strap the harness for the plow around his shoulders and I tell him to start walking. 'Get going, boy!' "

As I listened to Thomas Lincoln talk about his son, my temper rising, I thought back to one of the last conversations I'd had with my own father at Farmington, shortly after Ann's funeral.

"I suppose you're making a tolerable go of it with your little store," Judge Speed had said as we sat together in his library, a fire cackling in the fireplace against the nighttime chill. He was paging through one of his account books, as he always did during our talks, though I doubted he could make out the figures anymore.

"It's one of the finest establishments in Springfield," I'd shot back, "and I've managed to grow our sales every year, even during the depression. Through hard work and determination."

"Hard work and determination are the keys to success in life, my son. Have I ever told you that?"

My anger broke and I laughed out loud. "Only about a hundred times." A thousand was more like it; it had been his constant refrain for as long as I could remember.

"Hard work and determination," he repeated. "Hard work and determination. You've got that, you say? That's . . . that's . . ." He drifted off, stared into the fire, and did not continue. A minute later he was snoring.

I felt, in that moment, an acute sense of loss. Because I realized Judge Speed would never be able to comprehend just how well I had learned his lessons. Just how well I'd followed his example.

"Now, about an hour later I comes back," Thomas Lincoln was saying, "and what do I find? Abe ain't plowing. Abe's sitting against one of them stonewalls marking out Baldwin's fields and he's reading a book. Reading! I ain't never do such a thing. And neither did my father, nor his father before him. I tell you, my son is meant to be working, not reading for . . . for what? *Amusement? Pleasure?* Ain't never been a Lincoln in all the generations, I tell you, who's so lazy as to be *readin'* when he should be *workin'*.

"So I grabbed my rod and I walked up to him and I slashed that book right out of his hands. And then I slashed him over the head for good measure. And I held my stick over him and I told him I was going to keep on slashing him till he put that yoke back on and got back to work. Back to work like a man!"

Thomas Lincoln took in the startled faces of his listeners. He nodded with satisfaction. "I'm telling you, fellas, that's exactly the way it happened. And if you ain't believe me, you can ask Johnnie and he'll tell you it was so. He'll tell you what a lazy tramp Abe was."

This was more than I could take. I waded into the group and called out, as if I had just recognized him, "Hello, Mr. Lincoln!"

Thomas squinted at me for a few seconds and said, "Oh, it's

Mr. Fry Speed. Hello, yourself. Did you see Johnnie, too? He's around here somewhere."

"I'm right here, Papa," said Johnston from beside me.

"There you are, Johnnie. Care to join us, Mr. Fry Speed?"

"No, thank you. I was going to see—"

"Cuz I was just about to tell these boys," continued Thomas, as if he hadn't heard me, " 'bout the scheme we're fixing to run down at the camp with that crazy preacher."

"What scheme's that?" asked one of the Democrats surrounding him.

"We was down there cuz they give out free food and drink to anyone who'll come. Anyone who listens to the nonsense of that preacher, telling folks God'll show 'em the path to heaven on the day of judgment if they agree to do this and thus. 'Do this, do thus, and the gates of heaven will be open to you.' It ain't nothing but hogwash, but some folks are too fool to know it. So we figure, if they got their heads caught up in the next world, they'll forget to pay attention to the earthly one. And maybe they'll be willing to part with their earthly goods for a price to our liking. Cuz it's the earthly world we're concerned with, ain't it, Johnnie?"

"Yes, Papa."

"It's a pretty fair scheme, I'd say. We'll see if we can make a go of it, but I wager we can."

There was a general shaking and nodding of heads. How Thomas Lincoln's scheme was supposed to work was anybody's guess. Finally, the group recalled the business at hand. "Got any more stories about Abraham, Father Lincoln?" one of the men asked.

I reached over and touched Thomas on the shoulder. "Me and some of Abraham's friends have an extra chair on the other side of the room. Will you take a social glass with us?"

"These fellas here are making things nice and comfortable for me, Mr. Fry Speed. Ain't you, boys?"

The men who had been hanging on the elder Lincoln's every word grunted in agreement. "Leave him alone, Speed," growled one of them, a longtime Democratic functionary with a particularly nasty disposition.

I took Thomas Lincoln by the elbow. "I really think you'd be more comfortable sitting down over with us, Mr. Lincoln." But the old man resisted. Suddenly, John Johnston grabbed a fistful of my coat and pushed me several steps away from his stepfather.

"Papa said he's comfortable," growled Johnston. His back to the group, so they couldn't see what he was doing, he reached into his pocket and pulled out a small knife. The blade shone in the candlelight of the dim taproom. "The old man's got few enough pleasures in life. Leave him be."

I gazed at Johnston's knife with interest, not fear. Lincoln had said he thought his stepbrother capable of nearly anything. Did that include murder? I wondered.

I shook loose of Johnston's grip. "You and I aren't enemies," I said. "At least, we don't have to be. I want what's best for your stepfather. And for Lincoln."

"You leave my stepfather alone," he growled, his knife still clenched in his right hand. "He ain't none of your concern. And as for Abe, next time you see him, you give him a message from me."

"What's that?"

"You tell Abe he's getting what's coming. Nothing more, and nothing less."

CHAPTER 16

I described my encounter with Thomas Lincoln and John Johnston to my sister the following day. When I came to the part about Johnston drawing his knife, Martha's eyes grew wide.

"Do you think he really intended to hurt you?" she asked.

"More of a warning, I think, to stay away."

"Away from what?"

"I've been trying to figure that out." I paused, then continued, "Thomas mentioned that the two of them have visited the camp meeting. Have you seen them there?"

Martha frowned. "They weren't there last weekend, which was my first time in camp. I'm going again tonight. Why don't you come along?"

When I hesitated, Martha added, "Oh good! I knew you'd keep an open mind. I'll send word to Miss Butler. She'll be happy to see you there."

The camp meeting was a novelty in Springfield that summer, a phenomenon that had seemingly come from nowhere and quickly affected many people in the community—though whether for good or ill was a matter hotly debated. Since I'd moved to Springfield several years ago, life in the frontier town had been oriented around three nearly universal public institutions: Politics, Commerce, and Liquor. The camp meeting had unexpectedly added a fourth—the Revival—and the people of the town were still adjusting to its presence in their midst.

So it was that after taking our supper that evening, we saddled up my horse, Hickory, and a rented mare for Martha in the stables behind the Globe Tavern.

It was a warm, cloudless night. We rode through the streets until they petered away and were replaced by a single carriage track cutting through the nearby farms and then out into the open prairie. A glittering vault of stars illuminated our path. The field insects were in full throat, a concert of crickets, katydids, and grasshoppers whose competing and overlapping cries called to mind a chaotic woodwind ensemble of oboes, clarinets, and bassoons jousting for the principal chair.

The first hint we were nearing the camp was the glow of fires that gradually emerged, flickering, from beyond the trees. As we came closer, we saw dozens of persons moving to and fro in the forest, many holding candles or torches. It was a sea of human beings, agitated into perpetual motion as if by a storm. We dismounted a few yards away from the edge of the encampment and tied our horses to a pine tree.

Several dozen white, triangular tents had been staked out beneath the tree canopy. Inside the open flaps of the tents I could see bedclothes and cooking supplies and a sleeping small child or two. Beyond, the tents melted away into the woods, where fireflies flitted about in the gloaming.

In a clearing beside the tents, a two-story speakers' platform had been erected. Several men stood on the upper story now, exhorting the crowd to gather around for the coming evening sermon. In front of the platform were ten rows of simple wooden benches. These were full of men and women and older children in formal, churchgoing attire. Many in the crowd were singing hymns. I noted that the women in the audience far outnumbered the men. I looked over the crowd but did not see either Thomas Lincoln or John Johnston.

"Over here," shouted a voice. Sarah Butler waved and pointed to several empty spots next to her at the end of a bench. We approached, and Martha and she shared a warm embrace and sisterly kisses.

"I was pleased to get Miss Speed's note," Miss Butler said when she turned to me. "I don't think you'll be disappointed you came."

"I decided it was as good a time as any to see what it was about. How long have you been coming for?"

"I discovered the meeting two months ago, shortly after the camp was first pitched, and I've attended every weekend since. The more I listen to Preacher Crews, the more the true path reveals itself to my soul."

A look of doubt must have crossed my face because she added, in an earnest tone, "You'll see for yourself. The preacher knows the way."

Before we could converse further, a hush fell over the assemblage. A new man, tall and striking, mounted the platform. All eyes were riveted upon him. Cries of "Teach us, Preacher!" and "How wonderful God's word!" rang out. Miss Butler beamed up at the preacher, her face radiant. And then all were expectant and silent.

Preacher Crews looked as if he had stepped from the pages of the Old Testament. He had a long face with a narrow nose, arched eyebrows, and a fiery mouth. His forehead was very high and very pale. His hair had retreated just past the crown of his head but he kept it long in back, dangling on his shoulders, and though having no mustache he wore a magnificent, fierce brown beard, coarse and bristling, that extended several inches from his jawline.

"Brothers, sisters," began Crews, in a thunderous voice, "whether this is your first time in camp or your tenth, I welcome you. Today you join in something larger than yourselves. Today you join the Almighty. I'm here to tell you that your spiritual destiny resides in your own hands, just as your earthly circumstances reside in your hands on every other day of the week. The Lord God is omnipotent and He is merciful. Let Him reign in your hearts, submit to His will, and everlasting salvation shall be yours."

Crews continued to illuminate the path to righteousness, his voice rising and falling like a squall, but my attention was diverted by the audience. All around me, people fell to the Word like corn before the wind of an approaching storm. Men slid off their benches and thudded to the earth, lying motionless and apparently breathless on the ground. Women jerked their heads back suddenly, yelping involuntarily, their heads flying back and forth so quickly that their long hair cracked like a carriage whip. Others, with divine glory shining on their faces, sang, shouted, and clapped, hugged and kissed their neighbors, cried for mercy, rejoiced in forgiveness.

For her part, Miss Butler shouted responsively to the exhortations of the preacher. My sister, sneaking a glance at me periodically, was more restrained, but eventually she linked arms with Miss Butler and joined in her responsive calls. A few seats over on our bench, a young girl was sitting on her father's shoulders, listening in rapt attention to the sermon and declaring in a small, high-pitched voice how wonderful were the works of God.

I had never seen a religious observance remotely like this, and I was shocked. My presence at the Methodist church in Louisville had been, frankly, sporadic, and my church attendance since moving to the frontier even less regular. But I strongly associated the practice of religion with a stolid minister leading a proper prayer service in a formal setting. Nothing had prepared me for the wild, ecstatic ritual at the outdoor campground.

Toward the close of the sermon, the cries of the distressed and the saved rose almost as loud as Crews's thundering voice. He spread out his arms and pleaded for quiet, that his final words of benediction might be heard by all.

"You see the great battlefield before us," the preacher said, gesturing to the many persons who now lay on the ground, felled by ecstasy. "You see the wounded. You feel the wounds inside of yourself. All can be healed. All can be saved.

"I ask you, brothers and sisters, every one of you, give what you can to help our crusade. If you can give love, then give love. If you can give material aid"—the preacher gestured to several young women, dressed in long priestly robes and holding straw baskets, who had begun to circulate among the crowd—"then by all means give us your money too.

"Tonight, you must tend to your wounds and the wounds of the ones you love. Tomorrow, we shall share Communion. Tomorrow, you shall be closer to the Lord God."

Two women appeared beside Preacher Crews on the raised platform, and he kissed them in turn on the tops of their heads. The women began their own testimonies, exhorting the audience to follow their journeys to salvation. Meanwhile, Crews climbed down from the platform and stood off to the side, alone. He took a long drink from a water jug; his pale forehead glistened with sweat.

I turned to Miss Butler. Her face was streaked with tears, yet her expression was one of radiant joy. "Wasn't it wonderful?" she said. "Did you feel the awesome power of the Word?"

"Perhaps not quite as strongly as you, but it was an enlightening experience." I gestured at Preacher Crews. "Do you suppose the preacher would speak with me now that he's finished?"

Miss Butler nodded enthusiastically. "He's always eager to minister to the willing. Come, we'll introduce you."

The three of us rose and walked over to Crews. "Sister Butler," he said, still breathing deeply from his performance. "And Sister Speed, isn't it? How is the Word within you both?"

"Stronger than ever," Miss Butler replied with a beaming expression. "We've been studying every day, just as you instructed last weekend." Gesturing toward me, she added, "This is Mr. Speed, Preacher. It's his first time at the meeting."

Crews gave me a concentrated stare and I felt a chill shoot through me. For an instant I feared he was able to see through any artifice into my real reason for being here this evening, but then I put aside such nonsense. Still, the force of his presence was impossible to ignore.

"Is the power of God strong upon you, Brother?" he asked.

"I hope so, though I come tonight in service of an earthly concern."

Preacher Crews took another long swig from his jug. "Earthly concerns are temporary and fleeting," he said, his searching stare now replaced by a beneficent smile. Up close I realized the preacher was not much more than thirty years of age, notably younger than he had seemed on stage in full cry.

The gowned women who had been collecting money from the crowd came up to the preacher and, after a whispered consultation, slipped several clinking bags into Crews's hands. The bags disappeared silently into the folds of his garment. He turned back to us with an undimmed smile, as if the monetary transaction had been merely a figment of our imaginations.

"For tonight, Brother Speed," he said, "put aside your earthy concerns and glory in the divine."

"I shall try my best," I said, figuring I should pretend to meet the preacher on his terms. "I did feel my spirit moved by your words."

"No living soul could remain unmoved by them," said Miss Butler.

"I felt the glories of divine friendship all around," added Martha, giving Miss Butler's arm a squeeze. The preacher smiled at the two women.

I was struck by a sudden inspiration, and so I blurted out a guess. "I believe we've encountered each other before, Preacher, at the home of Ninian Edwards on Quality Hill, on the evening of the Independence Day party."

Martha shot a glance at me, which I ignored. Crews appeared not to notice. Instead, he shook his head and said, without artifice, "I fear you are mistaken, Brother. I make it my practice to be here at camp every evening, even when no meetings are scheduled. A person in need of God's mercy may appear at any time."

The testimonies of the female exhorters on the platform had finally come to an end, and the crowd—or at least the part of it not still in the grip of a cataleptic fit—began filtering toward the tents in the woods. The father with his little daughter on his shoulders walked past us, nodding at the preacher as he did. The girl had closed her eyes and rested her head on her father's.

A woman passing nearby smiled at the father and said, "I think the poor thing needs to be laid down to sleep."

At this, the girl suddenly sat straight upright. "Do not call me 'poor,'" she said, in a determined, small voice just barely audible over the general commotion, "for Christ is my brother, God my father, and I have a kingdom to inherit. I am not poor but rather rich in the blood of the Lamb."

"So you are, my child," said Preacher Crews, reaching out to pat her small head. "So you are."

I decided to try another tack. "I was speaking recently with two men who are often in your midst, Preacher. A father and his stepson. Thomas Lincoln and John Johnston."

Crews frowned. "Those names aren't familiar to me, I fear."

"Johnston's about my age, slight, with a wispy blond beard. And his stepfather's older, solid, with a large nose."

"Ah, yes. 'The watchers.' That's what some at the camp call those two. Because they are always watching our revival from afar. They are hesitant to give themselves up to it. They will do so yet, I am certain."

The scavengers was more like it, I thought. Aloud I said, "Did you minister to them?"

"To the son, yes. He has a troubled soul. A destitute soul, even. He was interested in learning the paths to forgiveness."

"Why was he troubled?" I asked, feeling my heart starting to beat faster.

"It is not my place to examine his heart," said the preacher. "It is for him alone. People are not born sinners. They choose to sin, and equally they can choose to repent and renounce sin."

"Did Johnston repent and renounce sin?"

"I suggest, Mr. Speed, you examine not the heart of another but rather your own. Repentance, forgiveness, grace, salvation. Each of us is capable of it, if we choose the path of the righteous. It's all up to you."

Preacher Crews's words stuck with me as Martha and I saddled up our horses and rode off into the dark night.

CHAPTER 17

A few days later, Lincoln finally returned from his political stump tour. He materialized one evening in a state of disquiet, for which, it soon appeared, there were multiple causes.

"You're back early," I said as he barged through the door of my store just as dusk was beginning to close in. "I didn't expect you back until tomorrow at the earliest."

Lincoln dropped his saddlebags onto the floor with a great sigh and slumped against the wall. His eyes closed, he murmured, "That was exhausting. Only sixteen days left."

"Until what?"

"The election."

"Then it's eighteen until Truett's trial."

He slid down the wall until his backside came to rest on the plank floor, his long legs splayed outward. His boots and trousers were splattered with mud. "I can't even . . ." he began, before trailing off. He took off his stovepipe hat, ran his fingers through his hair, and gave a great yawn.

"How was the journey?" I asked.

"Saunders loaned me Old Charley for the ride. 'A dependable fellow,' he said, 'a *true* hero of the Black Hawk War.'" Looking up at me, Lincoln gave a weary smile and added, "In contradistinction to me, you understand. Saunders can't help but try to be clever. Anyway, Old Charley may have been a true hero of the war, for all I know, but that was a long time ago, especially in equine years. He had one grievous fault. As we were riding along the trail he would go to sleep occasionally, fall on his nose, and pitch me over his head in the process. Other than that, nary a complaint."

I laughed. "And your speeches?"

"If I have to explain my position on state support for the internal improvements scheme one more time, I think I'll throw myself into the unfinished canal. Hand me a bottle of soda water, will you? I don't think I can move."

I took a sage-green, eight-sided bottle from my shelves, broke the seal, and brought it over to Lincoln. "That'll be half a cent."

"Put it on my account," he said between gulps. "I'm good for it."

"That's what they all say."

Lincoln grinned. "Did you and Miss Speed make any progress on the Truett case? You were going to look into the land office."

"We did," I said eagerly, but as I started to launch into a detailed discussion of our activities, Lincoln yawned and held up his hand. "Can the two of you come by Hoffman's Row tomorrow? I'm going upstairs to get a good night's sleep. I haven't had one in days. Do me a favor and stick to your side of the bed tonight."

When Martha and I showed up at Hoffman's Row the next afternoon, we found Lincoln greatly agitated.

"At last," he said as he heard us push through the door. He was kneeling in front of the decrepit bookcase at the far side of the room, rapidly sifting through the stacks of books and papers balanced on its listing shelves. "Did either of you enter this office in my absence?"

I looked over at Martha, who shook her head. "No. Why do you ask?"

"Someone's been in here. My files have been disturbed."

Doubtfully, we looked around the office. To my eye it appeared the same as it always did, a disorderly mess of papers and parchment and legal books strewn about on every surface.

"How could you possibly tell—"

"I know the difference. My notes relating to the Truett case have been moved. They used to be over there"—Lincoln pointed to one area of the cluttered worktable in the center of the room—"but when I returned they were over here." He pointed to another area, seemingly indistinguishable from the first.

"Is anything missing?" Martha asked.

"Not that I've found yet. I'm still taking an inventory of my cases."

"Could it have been Stuart?" Lincoln's law partner was rarely to be found in their shared chambers, but he seemed the obvious culprit.

Lincoln shook his head violently. "He's been campaigning in the northern part of the state for the past two weeks."

"Did the judge have a jury up here?"

"I asked Matheny straightaway when I realized someone had been in here, and he said no." Lincoln pushed a few volumes into the bookcase, grunted, and rose to his feet. He moved over to Stuart's reclining lounge and started furiously sorting through the papers spread across it. "There's no question in my mind," he said, more to himself than either of us. "Someone's been here."

A few minutes later Lincoln threw his hands up in frustration and flung himself onto his chair. "Nothing to be done about it now, I suppose. Now, what have the two of you been up to?"

We told him about the land office visit, the notes Martha had found, the discussion with Truett, and our visit to the Edwards estate. I decided not to mention my encounter at Torrey's with Thomas Lincoln and John Johnston. I knew Lincoln would demand to know every detail, and I didn't see the good that would come of relating his father's storytelling. As for Johnston, I didn't want to share my suspicions with Lincoln until I had something more concrete.

Lincoln listened to our narrative carefully, nodding occasionally and asking a clarifying question or two. When we had finished, he said, "Did you bring Early's notes?"

"Here they are," said Martha, passing them to him with a satisfied smile. "We think they show—"

Lincoln held up his hand and she stopped short. He studied the two pages for a long time in silence, looking at each, front and back, and then flipping back and forth between them. Then he laid the pages on the table in front of him, pressed his index fingers together, brought them to his chin, and exhaled.

"Well?" I asked.

"Now I understand what Truett meant, that night, about taking my father down with him."

"You do?" Martha and I had studied the notes in vain for such a meaning.

"Does it have something to do with the plots you surveyed?" asked Martha.

Lincoln nodded. "In a way it does. In my time, I was pretty prolific with the compass and chain. Enos and Neale each did a fair number themselves, and you can see them listed in these notes, too, but I did probably as many as anyone in this area. In fact, I've heard it said my name became associated with surveys that a buyer or seller could rely upon."

I leaned over and looked at Early's notes. "That's exactly what the notes reflect."

"Except that I stopped surveying around the start of 1836," continued Lincoln. "That's when I determined to study Blackstone's *Commentaries on the Laws* seriously, to read law and get admitted to the bar. I no longer had time to tramp around through the brambles. Now look."

I studied Early's notes again, and Martha came up beside me to do the same. I swore under my breath and Lincoln nodded.

"The 'Lincoln survey' numbers don't tail off. Well, they dip a little at the start of 1836 but then they pick up again, and by 1837 it's like nothing happened."

"Someone is falsifying surveys?" asked Martha. "Why would someone want to buy land that wasn't surveyed properly?"

"They wouldn't," I said. "But someone might want to *sell* land that wasn't properly surveyed. In fact, I imagine they could use that strategy to sell the same plot of land, over and over again, to different buyers. And they could make quite a profit doing so."

Lincoln bobbed his head. "Though some buyers might be savvy enough to want to see the surveyor with their own eyes. I suppose they could have paraded my father out in front of them." He considered for a moment. "Or they could have—"

"Paraded John Johnston and introduced him as your brother, 'John Lincoln,'" I said. Lincoln nodded.

"Let me see that list of the principal sellers again," said Lincoln. He leaned forward to scrutinize Early's notes. Martha also handed him our list of the persons who'd been present at the Quality Hill party.

"The one I'm interested in is Henry Owens, the apothecary," I said, pointing to his name on the list.

"What about him?" Lincoln asked sharply.

"We know he was cross with Early, and I saw the two of them having a vigorous discussion earlier that evening. I think he's as likely a suspect as any of these men."

"You didn't talk to him about this, did you?" asked Lincoln. I shook my head. "Good. Leave him for me. It seems unlikely. And I don't want Margaret getting upset about it, either." Lincoln looked at me with intense eyes, seeking understanding, and I nodded.

He looked back at Early's list. "There's another interesting name on here, although he wasn't at the party."

"Who's that?"

"John McNamar." Lincoln pointed to several of Early's entries. McNamar was associated with a good number of transactions in 1834, and then again from 1836 to the present. "He was Ann Rutledge's original beau."

A distant bell of recognition went off in my head. "Didn't your stepbrother mention something, that first night they arrived, about Ann having an understanding with someone who'd gone missing, someone with two different names?"

Lincoln was staring through the window of his office at the sky outside. He nodded. "I'd forgotten I'd ever mentioned it to John. Not sure what would have caused me to do so. But his recollection is correct. McNamar's father had gone deeply into debt in his native New York, and so as a young man he'd left home, determined to make his own way and earn enough to pay off his family's debts and restore their standing. To avoid any stigma tracing to his father's failures, he traveled west as 'John McNeil' and settled in New Salem as such. McNeil and Ann met there, before I arrived in town, and they formed an understanding."

"How did you learn his real name?" I asked.

"He turned out to be an industrious fellow. Succeeded very quickly in business and ended up quite a landowner. While I was employed as a surveyor in New Salem, I was called upon to attest to a few of his land purchases, and he signed them under his real name, 'John McNamar.' As these records reflect." Lincoln waved at Early's notes.

"This is all before I'd ever met Ann. Then one day McNeil rode off to New York to relieve his family of their embarrassments. He was gone a year when I first made Ann's acquaintance, and gone two—with no word whatsoever sent back to his intended—when she and I first discussed marriage ourselves. All I knew was that she'd had an alliance with a fellow named John McNeil, who had disappeared without a trace. She insisted we wait with our arrangement until she could tell him of her change of heart. But the fever stole upon her before she could." Lincoln looked down at the floorboards.

"Did you ever see McNamar again?"

"He returned to New Salem with his parents that fall, not long after she succumbed. It was only then I realized her McNeil was one and the same as my McNamar. I wasn't happy to see him, nor he, when he learned what had transpired in his absence, to see me."

"What did he do?"

"What could either of us do? She was gone." His face was pale.

"When was the last time you spoke with Mr. McNamar?" asked Martha quietly.

Lincoln shook his head. "Sometime before I moved here from New Salem. Likely more than two years ago. I haven't been back to New Salem once since I moved away. Not even for politicking."

"I didn't know that," I said, turning to him with surprise. "Why not?"

There was a faraway look in Lincoln's eyes. "Sometimes the past," he said, "is best left in the past."

CHAPTER 18

As we were dressing the next morning, Lincoln asked if I would accompany him and Miss Margaret Owens on an evening walk to Watson Grove, a stand of white birch that stood just outside of town.

"Surely you need me as much as a cart does a third wheel," I protested.

Lincoln shook his head. "I know the two of you didn't get much of a chance to visit at the Edwardses' party, and I'd like you to know her better. Truly, I think her a substantial woman, but I'd value your honest opinion of the matter."

"In that case, there's only one answer. I assent."

Twilight had begun to nestle in when Lincoln rapped on the window of my store. By the time I had finished closing up and headed outside, Lincoln and Miss Owens were talking with great engagement. I greeted Miss Owens with a bow. Though her emerald evening coat was unadorned, I could tell at once it had been stitched from expensive French cloth.

"Thank you for permitting me to join your stroll," I said as I fell into step with them.

"We've been discussing the opening of the play *King Richard the Third*," said Lincoln. "I wonder if you have an opinion, Speed, of how Gloucester should mount the stage."

Adopting a triumphant tone, I recited, waving my arms with

a grand flourish: "'Now is the winter of our discontent / Made glorious summer by this sun of York.'"

Lincoln and Miss Owens looked at each other and burst into laughter.

"Have you invited me along only to mock my line readings of Shakespeare?" I asked, not bothering to cover my irritation.

"I assure you it wasn't our intent," said Lincoln, "but you've demonstrated precisely how those lines *shouldn't* be read. Think of it, Speed. Richard appears on stage just after the crowning of Edward. He is burning with repressed hate and jealousy."

"He's already plotting the destruction of his brothers to make way for himself," added Miss Owens.

"Exactly!" said Lincoln. "He can barely contain his impatience at the remaining obstacles to his own ascension. His prologue must be pronounced with the most intense bitterness and satire."

Lincoln stopped in the middle of the street. He raised his forearm in front of his face, hunched over his back, and assumed the character. He recited the first dozen lines of the famous soliloquy, rendering it with a force and power that made it seem like a new creation to me.

When he finished, Miss Owens smiled broadly—I noticed how beautiful and even her teeth were—and clapped her gloved hands together. "I think you have it perfectly, Mr. Lincoln," she exclaimed. "It's precisely that bitterness that leads Richard to imprison his brother in the Tower and then send the two murderers to stab him."

We were a few blocks away from the town square by now, and the darkening streets were alive with other groups of walkers conversing in quiet tones. Some were other sets of three, like ours, but most consisted of one man and one woman. Evening strolls were the principal way in which the young men and women of Springfield visited. And, not incidentally, courted.

Here and there we passed houses with a single candle alight in a first-floor window. The burning candle signified the presence of a young woman available to be escorted around town. In fact, the frontier town on the edge of the prairie was characterized by a sharp overbalance of unmarried men as compared to the number of unmarried women. Especially on fine summer evenings such as tonight, the women of Springfield did their best to address this disproportion by hurrying home at the conclusion of one walk and relighting their candles in order to accommodate an additional male walker. For their part, as-yet-unaccompanied men tended to hover around homes of eligible women, trying not to appear over-eager while waiting to pounce upon the first flicker of a newly lit flame.

As it happened, we were approaching Miss Butler's home. As we rounded the corner I looked expectantly. But the front window was dark.

"Speaking of King Richard," Lincoln was saying, "makes me recollect the situation in my prior home of New Salem. This is back in '31 or perhaps '32, shortly after I left my father's house and moved there to begin my own life in earnest. There were not many books in the region at the time. I had a copy of Shakespeare that I kept locked in a trunk along with my other prized possessions, including several packs of cards.

"One night, I came back to my room and realized my trunk had been broken into. Frantically, I took inventory. To my relief, Shakespeare was not disturbed, and I have him to this day. But the cards"—Lincoln paused for dramatic effect—"the cards had been stolen." He grinned at us and added, "You can infer which was the more popular."

Both Miss Owens and I laughed out loud. Turning to the woman, I said, "Where did you take your education, Miss Owens? I recall you are Kentucky born and bred, as am I."

"In Beardstown, at—"

"Don't tell me you studied with the Sisters of Nazareth?" I interjected. She nodded. "I learned at Bishop Reynolds's hand at St. Joe's, or through his rod, more precisely."

"You did not!" she exclaimed, her eyes flashing. "What a funny coincidence." To Lincoln, she explained, "They're twinned academies, Nazareth and St. Joseph's College, where Mr. Speed did his studies. Buildings at either end of the same grounds. All the girls I knew growing up went to Nazareth, and all the boys to St. Joseph's."

"I knew plenty of girls and boys who went to neither," said Lincoln, unable to keep an edge out of his voice. "Nor to any organized schoolhouse at all, for that matter."

The three of us were silent, and the hard dirt under my boots crunched with a sound hollow and desiccated.

"Of course you did," I said, trying to prevent Miss Owens from feeling any embarrassment. "As did each of us, in truth. I believe Miss Owens only meant to observe that, from a certain element of Kentucky society, those parents seeking a true English education sent their offspring to the Beardstown academies."

Lincoln looked only somewhat mollified. Despite his substantial accomplishments in recent years, his impoverished childhood still niggled at him. The old resentments had reared themselves with the arrival in town of his father and stepbrother.

"You yourself are proof positive, Mr. Lincoln," said Miss Owens, "that graduates of the academies don't have a monopoly on Shakespeare or the other arts." She made no further apology. Turning back to me, she added, "What year did you matriculate? I doubt our periods of residence coincided. I venture I had a substantial head start on you."

"Perhaps a year or two," I said with a casual wave of my hand. Having observed her up close during the walk, I had realized Miss Owens was much older than I'd previously thought, a few years on the far side of thirty, even. "But as it happens, I didn't graduate. I attended from '28 to '30, then left, never to return."

"Why not?"

I found myself liking Miss Owens's boldness. "Grave illness, at first. I was brought home to Louisville to die in my own bedroom." She gave a little gasp and covered her mouth. "And then, when I cheated death, I felt—you'll pardon me for being so direct, I hope—I felt there were greater things out there for me than St. Joseph's Academy."

The lady had opened her mouth to reply when the sound of a loud *crack* made all of us jump.

"What was that?" I exclaimed. Miss Owens wrapped her hands around Lincoln's arm.

The noise seemed to have come from behind a row of bushes that paralleled our path. I took several steps toward the bushes and peered into the dark, but I couldn't see anything.

"Probably just the wind," said Lincoln, shooting a quick glance at me before giving Miss Owens a reassuring pat on the arm. For another minute we stood there, in silence, waiting and listening. A cool breeze blew through. But there were no other sounds.

"Probably just the wind," I repeated. We started walking again. Gradually, my heart stopped racing. The quarter moon made its appearance, providing some light.

We came upon a flowering bottlebrush buckeye plant, and Miss Owens stopped to admire it. I thought the cones of small white blossoms set into the towering dark bush looked like clusters of steeples on a mountaintop, and I remarked on the similarity to my companions.

"The path to heaven," murmured Miss Owens.

"What?"

"It's something Preacher Crews often says at the camp meeting. The path to heaven leads equally up the side of the mountain and down into the depths of the valley. Whether you're going up or down, you can be on the road to salvation as long as you proceed with purpose." She turned to Lincoln and added, "I wish you'd come with me sometime."

Lincoln straightened his shoulders stiffly. "I've told you before," he said, a little harshly, "I doubt my views on the subject and this preacher of yours would mix easily. It seems to me more likely that all men and women will be saved than that there's an omniscient God somewhere—omniscient and *extremely* busy—making judgments one by one."

"He's not my preacher; he's there for all of us. Many have been saved by him already this season." The lady turned to me. "What about you, Mr. Speed? Have you had occasion to attend the camp meeting?"

"I was present last weekend, with my sister. In candor, I'm not sure I'll return. I fear my views regarding salvation are closer to Lincoln's than to yours." I put my arm around Lincoln's shoulders and added, "Perhaps the two of us will have the opportunity to discuss our error together someday in Hell."

Lincoln laughed heartily. Miss Owens frowned and looked as if she had more to say on the topic, but with a quick shake of her head she kept her tongue.

We resumed our stroll and I searched for a neutral topic. "What brought you to Springfield, Miss Owens?" I asked.

"My brother suggested it. He thought the change of scenery might benefit my health, and it has. I believe you know Henry?"

"Your brother's a fine man," I said. "I saw him talking to Mr. Early at the Edwardses' party, as a matter of fact." Lincoln shot me a warning glance, which I ignored. "Did your brother know the registrar well?"

"He was an occasional customer at the apothecary, and of course Henry had business at the land office. Mr. Early had been over for supper at our house once or twice. Both Henry and I were devastated by what happened."

"Were there any disputes in the business dealings between your brother and Early?"

"I certainly don't know of any," replied Miss Owens, a small frown forming on her lips.

"Did you—"

"Now, Speed, you must give Miss Owens a rest," broke in Lincoln. "She signed up for a stroll, not an interrogation. Leave the interrogating to me." He added a pointed glance to underscore his seriousness.

"Yes, of course. I didn't mean to cause offense. Like everyone else in town, I merely hope we get to the bottom of who committed the murder. But I'm sure you will, Lincoln." I patted his shoulder and left it at that.

Ten minutes later we reached our destination. The grove of birch trees stood in a vale through which a small stream, a tributary of the Sangamon River, cut. Stray moonbeams filtered through the trees and provided a dim light. There were a few sizable boulders bordering the stream, and I leaned against one of these while Lincoln helped Miss Owens settle herself beside its neighbor. We watched the stream gurgle past, making eddies around squat stones that stuck up from the streambed. The shadows cast by the tree canopy danced back and forth in the evening breeze.

In repose, my thoughts turned to my departed little sister Ann. The stream in front of us reminded me of the one cutting through Farmington, along which Ann and I had played on many afternoons. I could almost smell the aromatic mint and pungent cress that grew on the steep banks of our stream back home. I thought about the time I'd dreamed of Ann after her funeral, and I reached over and ran my fingertips along my mourning band.

"Lincoln . . ." I began.

"Hmm?" The man had his eyes closed and was reclining in peace.

"In *King Richard the Third*, when the shades of dead men appear to Gloucester on the night before the final battle, do you suppose we're to think they are actual ghosts, or merely figments of his dreams?"

"They must be actual, tangible ghosts, mustn't they?" said Miss Owens. Both Lincoln and I turned to her. "Think of it," she continued. "They are seen that same night by the Earl of Richmond, Gloucester's opponent in the battle to come, and foretell Richmond's victory. 'Live and flourish' and all that. They can hardly appear to Richmond if they exist only in Gloucester's dreams."

"That's an excellent—"

Crack! This time the sound was much closer and much louder. There was a *thud* close behind, and a section of a tree trunk along the riverbank opposite us exploded into splinters. *Someone's shooting at the tree,* I thought, but I immediately corrected myself. *Someone's shooting at us.*

Without thinking, I raced in the direction of the shot, scrambling up the edge of the shallow ravine and into the dark forest. Inside the thicket, away from the river, there was near total darkness. I stopped and listened: for the sound of footsteps, a man breathing, anything.

But it was silent and the only breathing I heard was my own. I struck a match from my pocket and held it up. There was nothing to see—and then a sudden breeze blew out the flame. I swore and lit another one, cupping it with my hand this time.

I advanced slowly through the forest, weaving around the graceful, slender trunks of the birch trees. I stopped and listened. Again, nothing. I headed in the direction I thought the shot might have come from, treading silently over the springy grass carpeting the floor of the grove. But I heard no new sounds and saw nothing. I lit a new match and walked in one last arc, peering intently through the dark woods. Suddenly, I tripped and was sent sprawling to the ground.

"Hello?" I called out.

No one answered back.

Lighting a new match and looking around, I saw a rotting stump behind me—evidently the culprit in bringing me to my knees. I was rising to my feet again when I spotted something lying on top of the stump. I went over and picked up the object and saw, in the shifting light of my flame, a single, right-handed woman's kidskin glove: ready-made, medium size, with a lace ribbon threaded around the wrist. On the back of the hand there was an ink drawing of a man and woman courting. I had a number of models of ready-made gloves in my own inventory, but none so fine or elaborately decorated. The glove was worn but in good condition; it couldn't have been lying in the woods for long.

I made my way back toward the boulders by the stream. Before long, I could hear the voices of Lincoln and Miss Owens. On impulse, I slid the glove into my pocket as I approached them.

"Is that you, Mr. Speed?" came Miss Owens's voice as I walked through the final layer of trees.

"It is. I didn't catch them."

As I came out into the clearing beside them, I saw Miss Owens had a small muff pistol in her hand, her index finger resting not far from the trigger. I nodded toward the firearm approvingly.

"My brother taught me how to fire the first month I moved to

Springfield," she said. "Told me any woman living on the frontier needed to be able to handle a gun to protect herself."

"I'm glad he did," I said, curling my hand around the glove in my pocket. "I couldn't find anyone. I must have chased them away." I turned to Lincoln. "Who do you think it could have been?"

Lincoln looked back warily. I could see his hands trembling faintly. "I wish I knew," he said in a voice that lacked his usual confidence.

CHAPTER 19

The next morning, I was behind the counter of my store when Lincoln's office boy Milton Hay burst in. Hay, fifteen, slight, and pimple-faced, was even more disheveled than usual.

"Where's Lincoln?" he shouted before the door had closed behind him.

"I've no idea. As we were dressing this morning he said he was heading to Hoffman's Row. Have you checked his office?"

"It's Hoffman's Row I've come from," said Hay, panting. "He ain't there, but he's needed there. He's needed there at once."

"Why?"

"Because the judge, he's havin' a hearing on Mr. Truett's case. He's havin' a hearing *right now*! I told him I didn't know where Lincoln was, and he said if Lincoln didn't care enough about his case to show up on time that was his problem."

"A hearing on the case without Lincoln?" I repeated, my pulse racing. "You damn well better track him down. Get going! In the meantime, I'll go to court myself."

I was out the door on Hay's heels and rushed up the street to Hoffman's Row. When I entered the temporary courtroom on the ground floor, Stephen Douglas was on his feet making a presentation to Judge Thomas, who was caressing an unlit cigar with a particularly nasty expression on his face.

"As I told Your Honor's clerk when I requested this hearing," Douglas was saying, "the issue is the body of the decedent in the

People against Truett murder case. We seek the Court's permission to retrieve the body to examine it for additional evidence relating to our prosecution."

"Retrieve the body?" said Judge Thomas. "From where?"

"Four feet underground. Early's remains are reposing in Higgins Burying Ground, end of Adams Street."

"And what evidence do you expect to find on the corpse of a dead man?"

"I believe the fatal ball is still lodged inside him. We've recently discovered what we believe to be the murder weapon. It's a pistol we can connect to the defendant Truett, and we seek to recover the ball to match it with the weapon."

Judge Thomas struck a match and held it in front of his cigar. He inhaled deeply to get the tobacco smoldering. "Makes sense to me," he said, "though I suspect it may not to your brother Lincoln. Which raises the question—where is he?"

I looked frantically around the courtroom, willing Lincoln to materialize from the ether. But the gallery was dotted with only a few courtroom regulars at the early hour. I didn't even see any other lawyers present.

"I sent word to his office this morning noticing this hearing and received a note back in his hand acknowledging the same," said Douglas with apparent sincerity. He turned around and took in the courtroom, an innocent look on his face. "I cannot account for his absence. Perhaps he does not consider this case worthy of his attention."

"You're certain you noticed him, Mr. Douglas?"

"Absolutely. I affirm it as an officer of the court."

"In that case, I'm surprised and disappointed by Mr. Lincoln's absence, but I do not intend to delay the course of justice. On the People's request to exhume the body of the decedent Early, the Court rules—"

"Wait, Your Honor!" I shouted, rushing to the front of the courtroom.

Both the judge and Douglas turned to me with surprise. "Do you know where Lincoln is, Mr. Speed?" the judge asked.

"No, but—"

"Then stand back. You know full well I'll only hear from members of the bar, and I've listened to you recount on more occasions than I care to remember how pleased you are that you decided *not* to follow your father and older brother into our learned profession. The Court grants—"

"I'm certain Mr. Lincoln would like to be heard on this matter, Your Honor."

Judge Thomas glared down at me. "I imagine he might, but he should have appeared for a duly noticed hearing if he did. You are out of order, Mr. Speed. One more word and I'll hold you in contempt."

"Give me five minutes to find him, Your Honor."

Without waiting for a response, I sprinted from the courtroom. I clattered upstairs to No. 4 and pushed open the door. Nothing but the usual clutter greeted me. Scanning the top surface of the mess, I couldn't see anything that suggested Lincoln's destination this morning. So I raced back out onto the street and toward the square. Simeon might know something, I thought, as I headed for the *Journal*'s offices.

"Lincoln's missing?" the rotund newspaperman asked after I hurriedly explained my mission. "I haven't seen him in days. I trust nothing bad's happened."

A shock of cold terror jolted through my body. "I don't think . . . I certainly hope not. Probably he's gotten tied up with something and lost track of the time. But to miss a court hearing . . ."

"It's not at all like him," agreed Simeon.

"Let me know if you see him," I called, taking my leave and racing back into the town square.

I stopped and gazed about. It was another hot summer day, and the desultory business of the town carried on all around, ignorant of the turmoil swirling inside of me. Two elderly ladies, shielded by faded parasols, walked arm in arm along the far side of the square. A stonemason chiseled away at the corner of a block of limestone meant for the capitol foundation. Not far from him, a few horses stood languidly, grazing on limp brown grass. On the south side of the square, the postmaster Clark talked to the driver of the mail-stage, who had driven up with a team of four. Opposite me, Ninian Edwards walked out of the apothecary, a package in hand.

At least he's a lawyer, I thought as I hurried up to Edwards. "Do you know where Lincoln is this morning?" I called.

Edwards fumbled with his package, jamming it into his pocket. "No idea," he said. "Now if you'll excuse me, I'm late for something, Speed."

"He's missing and Judge Thomas is having a hearing on the Truett case right this minute. The judge wouldn't hear from me. I'm sure Lincoln would be ever grateful if you'd step in and speak to his client's interests."

"But I have to . . . oh, very well," said Edwards, grabbing his lapels and staring down the edge of his beak nose. "You be sure to tell Lincoln he owes me a favor—a big one—when he gets reelected."

"I'll ensure he knows," I said, putting my hand on Edwards's back and steering him toward Hoffman's Row. As we neared, however, we saw a tall, gangly figure striding toward us in great haste from the opposite direction. Edwards and I arrived at the door to the courtroom at the very same moment as Lincoln. He was out of breath and his face shone bright red.

"You've missed—" I began.

"I know. Hay found me. Let me see if I can undo the damage."

Leaving Edwards, who was muttering about having his day interrupted, I followed Lincoln inside. As soon as he saw us enter, Judge Thomas stood up on his platform at the far end of the room.

"Tell me why I shouldn't hold both you and Mr. Speed in contempt," the judge thundered, shaking his smoldering cigar. Douglas was sitting on the other side of the room, his legs crossed and his short arms folded across his thick chest, smiling serenely.

"My profound apologies, Your Honor," said Lincoln. "I assure the Court it won't happen again."

"What's your explanation for your tardiness?"

"I don't have one, Your Honor." Lincoln sneaked a glance at

me; I could tell at once from his eyes that his true meaning was that he didn't have one he cared to share with the court—or perhaps with Douglas.

"That's not good enough."

"As for Mr. Speed," continued Lincoln, "whatever he did in my absence, he did on my behalf. If you intend to pronounce any punishment on him, I ask you to visit it on me instead." He paused, but when the judge did not immediately continue his scolding, Lincoln continued, "With the Court's leave, and yours as well, brother Douglas, I'd ask that the issue of the day be restated."

Douglas did not bother to stand. "I want to have Early's remains dug up so we can retrieve the fatal ball, in order to match it to a weapon we've found. The Court has already granted my request. The gravediggers may already be on their way to the cemetery."

"What weapon?" asked Lincoln sharply.

Douglas was taken aback. He looked at the judge and said, "I don't have to answer that question, do I? Since the hearing has already concluded and the Court has already given me the relief I sought."

"If you wanted the hearing to be over, you shouldn't have lingered," said Lincoln. Turning to me he added, in a not-very-quiet whisper, "He couldn't resist waiting around to see me humiliated." To the judge: "If it's the basis for the Court's order, I think I'm entitled to know."

"I expect this will never happen again," said the judge, looking at Lincoln sternly. Then he trained the same unsparing gaze on Douglas. "Enlighten us," he ordered.

Douglas sighed, uncrossed his arms and legs, and rose. "We found a pistol under some shrubbery at the back of the Edwards property. It stands to reason it's the weapon that killed Early, but of course we want confirmation of the same."

"What type of pistol?" asked Lincoln.

Douglas held his hands about six inches apart. "It appeared to be a standard gentleman's belt pistol. Walnut stock. Percussion cap."

My heart sank. Douglas's description matched precisely Truett's pistol, which I had seen that evening at Spotswood's. That it had been found on Quality Hill was very bad news for Lincoln and his client.

"I'd like to inspect the weapon at your convenience, Mr. Douglas," Lincoln was saying. "And see exactly where you found it. In the meantime, I have no objection to your retrieving the ball from Early's remains. You expect the exhumation to take place this very afternoon?"

"Indeed," said Douglas, looking sour.

"Very well." To the court, Lincoln added, "If there is nothing else, Your Honor, I apologize again most humbly and bid you a good day." Lincoln turned on his heels and departed, with me in tow.

As we reached the door, he whispered, "Let's not repeat Douglas's mistake. We've achieved victory—the relative victory of not being cited for contempt, at least. We shouldn't tarry at the scene."

Outside on the street, Lincoln gestured that we should continue walking away from Hoffman's Row. Finally, a few blocks away from the courtroom, he came to a halt.

"Where were you?" I asked.

Lincoln looked around to make sure we were alone. Then he said, "When I got to my office this morning, there was a note, on my chair, telling me to come to the streambed north of town. I found something nailed to a tree there. This."

He handed me a piece of foolscap, folded in two. Written in crude capital letters, like those of a small child just learning to write his name, was the following:

I KNOW
I KNOW WHAT YOU DID
I KNOW WHERE YOU SLEEP
I KNOW WHERE YOU WORK
I KNOW WHERE YOU EAT
I KNOW WHO YOU LIVE WITH
I KNOW WHO YOU WALK WITH
I KNOW I KNOW I KNOW

I read it over twice, my eyes lingering the second time through on the phrases "who you live with" and "who you walk with." I gulped.

"The note telling me to come to the streambed was written in the same hand," said Lincoln quietly. "It's bad business."

"It certainly is. Come with me." I took his arm and walked quickly toward the square.

"Where are we going?" Lincoln asked.

I didn't answer. Instead, I led him into my store, through the opening in the counter, and to the back of one of my rows of shelving. Reaching up to the very top shelf, I felt around and grabbed two new pistols, one after the other. Then I took down a box of balls and a flask of powder and, working silently, loaded both weapons. I put one pistol in my pocket and handed the other to Lincoln.

"Don't go anywhere without this."

He nodded.

"Are you going to tell Miss Owens?" I asked.

"I don't think so. I don't want to alarm her. Besides, it's clear I'm the target, not her."

"I suppose you're right. Any idea who it could be?"

Lincoln shook his head. "Hopefully just an overeager Democrat, trying to make me lose my nerve right before the election."

"Maybe it was Douglas," I said, "trying to get you out of the way for the court hearing so he could exhume Early in secret."

Lincoln laughed. "That, I know, is a joke. A duly sworn member of the bar wouldn't resort to such trickery. But I am surprised the judge started the hearing this morning in my absence. It's highly unusual procedure."

"Douglas said in court he'd sent you a notice of the hearing and received back a confirmation in your hand."

Lincoln looked at me with surprise. "Did he?"

"It's not true?"

"I never saw a notice and I certainly never sent a written acknowledgment back to Douglas. So either he's barefacedly lying, or someone's been forging my hand."

"Ask Douglas to see the confirmation supposedly written in your hand," I suggested. "Maybe the handwriting will tell you something."

"I shall. In the meantime, you'd better hurry."

"Where?"

"Over to the burying grounds."

I gave him a questioning look.

"I need you to watch them dig up poor Early."

CHAPTER 20

A small city cemetery had been established years ago on what had originally been the outskirts of the new frontier village. It had filled up much more rapidly than the founding town fathers had imagined as Springfield's first residents dropped dead of disease, childbirth, violent acts of nature, accidents, and—occasionally—old age. Like the pilgrims of New England, these early citizens sometimes seemed to think that they lived only to die.

Meanwhile, the cabinetmaker John Higgins, not long after establishing his undertaking enterprise, had purchased a large plot of land to serve as a family burying ground. The ever-enterprising Higgins, sensing yet another opportunity to expand his business (this time horizontally), volunteered to throw open his gates, and thus it was that Higgins Burying Ground had become the final resting place for the deceased citizens of Springfield.

By the time I reached the cemetery, the scorching sun was directly overhead. It was the hottest day yet of an already hot summer, the kind of day where you wouldn't be surprised to see whole suits of clothes walking along the streets, the occupants having melted away.

The burying ground was surrounded by a low, wrought-iron fence designed to keep the spirits of the dead from wandering too far from their former corporeal hosts. No other living person was present when I arrived. I wandered among the rows of graves, a few marked by engraved limestone slabs but many more by carved planks of wood or even simple wooden crosses, as the sun beat down and drops of sweat gathered beneath the rim of my hat. Early's grave was as yet unmarked, but a rectangular mound of hard-caked brown earth, with no grass growing on top, readily showed its location.

In the back corner of the burying ground, Higgins had built a modest wooden chapel. I tried the door and found it unlocked. Inside it was dim and cool, with two plain benches and a small altar. I sat on a bench, my hands clasped and my eyes closed, and said a prayer for the soul of my sister Ann. The last time I'd been to a cemetery had been for her burial.

Then I went back outside and stood in the shade of a tall oak tree. Birds twittered from the branches above. Every few minutes I patted my pocket to make sure my weapon was still there. At length two navvies walked up, carrying a single shovel between them and jabbering at each other in an unintelligible Irish dialect. With the state's canal projects ground to a halt by the dire economy, I imagined the men were grateful for any work they could get.

"Are you the doc?" one of them asked me through a thick brogue.

"Excuse me?"

"We was told there'd be a doc to show us where to dig and to pay us. The doc who's gonna cut apart the body, once we dug it up."

"I'm not him, but the grave you want is there," I said, pointing to the fresh patch of earth.

The navvies began attacking the hard, unforgiving earth with their shovel while I sweated in the shade. About half an hour later, the dolorous face and long gray beard of Doctor Weymouth Warren made a steady approach up the street. I waved him over.

"Douglas told me you might be here," he said when he reached my position. He was sweating profusely, and he took out a handkerchief and mopped his forehead.

"It's going to be a long wait yet," I replied, gesturing at the navvies. The pile of excavated dirt beside the grave was still modest. They had spent most of their time arguing with each other about whose turn it was with the shovel.

"Let me have a word," said Warren. He went over to the two men and soon returned to the shade. "They reckon another hour at most, but I have my doubts. I told them there's an extra dollar in it for them if they hurry. Come, let's retire to the Globe. Saunders has a new brew I want to try. We'll come back when they've reached the coffin."

The public room at the Globe proved to be even hotter than the shade provided by the cemetery's oak, which at least afforded an occasional breeze. Warren and I sweated on either side of the common table while drinking eagerly of Saunders's offering.

"Don't know why Truett went and did a foolish thing like shooting Early," said Warren, tugging on his beard.

"We—Lincoln and I—think the killer may have been someone else."

Warren took a long sip and looked at me with a skeptical gaze. "Those of us trained in healing know the most obvious cause is usually the correct one. When a man appears in my examining room complaining of pains in his stomach, I know his humors are out of balance, and I know my leeches will be able to restore his balance. I expect the same principle applies to the so-called legal sciences."

I took a long drink from my own glass, thinking that we needed concrete evidence of Truett's innocence if we were going to counter this widespread assumption of his guilt.

Two hours later we left the Globe and headed back to the burying ground. Warren had taken to Saunders's new brew with enthusiasm, and he wobbled as we walked along the dusty streets. At least, I thought, Early was one patient to whom he could do no harm. The falling sun was still hot in our faces.

The navvies, now covered with dirt and grime from head to toe, were sprawled out in the shade of the oak tree.

"We was about to give up," said one as we approached. "Give us our pay. And have at him."

"You'll have your money when I have the body," replied Warren. "That was your agreement with Mr. Douglas."

"He's right there." The navvy pointed to the mound of dirt, which had grown large in our absence. Warren and I walked over and stared down into the hole. The top of a fine wooden coffin, painted bright red, was indeed visible about three feet beneath ground level. Two handles were affixed to each of the long sides of the box.

"We'll need their help to get it out," I murmured.

Warren grunted. He approached the men and an argument ensued, with many angry gestures and strong remonstrations on both sides. After a bit, Warren rejoined me.

"Do you have a golden eagle on you?" he asked. "They say they'll only take hard currency, no notes, not even bills, and I'm a little short. Those Paddies may not have come off the boat long ago, but they've learned quickly the value of specie in the New World."

I fished a coin out of my pocket and Warren held it high above his head. The navvies ambled over and one of them grabbed the coin. Each of us knelt and leaned down to grab one of the handles. We pulled. Nothing.

"We need to be in unison," the doctor grunted. "One, two . . ." We all pulled on "three," and slowly, reluctantly, the earth loosened its grasp on Jacob Early's lonely bed. As soon as we had the coffin clear of the earth, the laborers set down their end roughly and stalked off, wiping their hands on their filthy blouses and grumbling unintelligibly to each other.

"Come on, then," Warren said, suddenly cheerful, rubbing his hands together. "Let's have at him." The doctor produced a crowbar and started to pry off the coffin's lid. After the third nail had been loosed, I was struck full in the face by a noxious scent suggestive of rotting meat, human waste, and decayed leaves. I turned away, bent over at the knees, and gagged. The doctor continued his task, humming a child's lullaby as he worked.

"There, that about does it," he said, as I heard him tossing the crowbar aside. "Come now, Speed, it's not that bad. Help me remove the cover, won't you?"

Hesitantly, I turned and helped Warren lift the cover away from the casing of the coffin. Then I forced myself to look down. Early's body was dressed in dark, formal clothes, but it was horribly misshapen. The belly swelled unnaturally; the legs pressed against the seams of the trousers. I studied what had been his face. It was grotesque—the eyelids swollen and tightly closed, a distended tongue protruding between pouting lips, the cheeks puffed out. Two lines of a sort of bloody froth ran from the nostrils down the sides of the cheeks, through the thicket of the muttonchop whiskers, and curled around the neck.

But the worst of it was the insects. Dozens of blue, green, and copper-colored flies, shaped like tiny bottles, crawled in and out of the corpse's nostrils and rested on its whiskers, rubbing their forelegs together greedily. Hunchbacked black flies infested the forehead and neck area, scuttling back and forth as if engaged in a frantic dance. A thick tangle of maggots surrounded the ears, nose, and tongue, wriggling and writhing like piglets feeding at a trough. What had been the bullet wound in the center of his forehead was now invisible beneath a seething frenzy of tiny scavengers. I turned away and gagged again.

"Hmm," the doctor said behind me. "Very interesting. Fascinating! Let's have a closer look."

"Out here in the open?" I asked, nodding around the graveyard. The sun was low now, and tombstones cast long, brooding shadows over Early's uncovered coffin. "Don't you think we ought to proceed somewhere more . . . formal, or private at least?"

"I hate to have any delay at all," said the doctor as he fidgeted with his flowing beard. "But I suppose you're right." His eyes alit on the chapel to the rear. "No one'll bother us in there. Here— let's lift up old Early and lay him on the inside of the coffin cover. Then we can carry him in. I'll take the legs if you can grab his shoulders."

I took a deep breath and positioned myself near the top of the casket. But when the doctor gave the word and I reached in to pull the torso up by its shoulders, I found myself not bearing the corpse's weight but rather pulling the dead man's topcoat toward me, almost as if the corpse's skin was sliding off along with its clothing. I gave a yell and dropped the body back into its box; Warren had apparently experienced a similar sensation when trying to lift the dead man's legs.

"Very interesting!" Warren exclaimed. "How very, very interesting. I've always wondered . . . but of course, yes. In this state of decomposition, buried for several weeks, it does make sense. I think we'd better try something different."

"We could leave him lying on the bottom board, as a sort of litter," I suggested. "If you knock off the sides . . ."

Before I could finish my sentence, Warren had retrieved his crowbar and was swinging away enthusiastically at the joints holding the four side panels in position. He quickly succeeded, and soon all that was left of the coffin was its bottom panel, on which Early's inert remains lay.

"Right, let's bring him on in," the doctor said. Together we lifted the base of the coffin and carried Early into the small chapel, where we balanced the board between the two benches. The flies buzzed around us, angry to have been disturbed. Little slivers of the fading light of the day filtered in through narrow windows.

Warren went up to the altar and used a flint to light the devotional candles. There were about a dozen in all, and when he was finished the dancing little lights brightened the room in a sufficient manner. Warren nodded in evident satisfaction, pushed up his sleeves, and drew out of the pocket of his pantaloons a long hunting knife.

"Do you want to do the honors, Speed?" he asked.

I blanched. "There was a reason I never considered medicine."

Warren shrugged. "You're missing the fun part. Let's see, where is that ball?"

I tried to avoid watching too closely as the doctor shooed the flies away and started digging around in the corpse's forehead with his knife. But it was impossible to avoid *hearing* the doctor's search, which filled the small chapel with a sawing sound, steel on bone, intermixed with slurping and squishing.

"Must have gone in deep," the doctor murmured to himself. "I'm going in after it."

The still air inside the chapel rapidly filled with the stench of the dead man. I was about to leave for some fresh breaths when Warren exclaimed, "Ah! There it is!" And after a final few decisive thrusts of his knife, he stuck three fingers into the corpse.

"Got it!" he shouted.

Warren lifted up a small mass from inside the corpse's head. He took his handkerchief and cleaned something—decaying brain matter, I supposed with a shudder—off the ball. Then he handed it to me.

I took the projectile reluctantly and held it next to the devotional candles to have a good view. The black sphere of lead was intact, although one side had been flattened, presumably from its impact with Early's skull. I rotated it around in my fingers. And, right away, I realized the great importance of what Warren had found.

"Are you taking this to Douglas?" I asked, trying to hide my excitement.

Doctor Warren remained bent over the corpse. "Not yet," he said without looking up. "Now that we've gone to all this trouble of digging him up—well, we might as well see what else there is to learn." He was hovering above the corpse's torso, and he made several sharp incisions with his knife. "Good luck for me when Douglas came calling."

"I think perhaps—"

"This reminds me of the times back when I was at the College of Physicians and Surgeons," he continued, heedless of my interruption. "We'd head off to the local plot quite a few nights. Have a poke or two around, underground. I daresay we learned more there than in the lecture room. Though the less said about that, the better, I suppose. Anyway, let's see . . . Hoy! What now?"

"How about I take the ball then? I'll show it to Lincoln—and Douglas too, of course."

"What? Oh. That'd be fine," Warren said distractedly. "Whatever you think best, Speed. What's this? You don't say . . . you don't say! Fascinating . . ."

I left Warren to his corpse. The graveyard was nearly dark now, only the faintest hints of midsummer twilight lingering in the corners of the sky. I paused on the steps of the chapel and breathed deeply of the fresh night air. Then I weaved my way around the dark, still graves toward the exit and the town beyond.

When I reached the iron fence, I stopped short. The gate was standing wide open. The navvies must have forgotten to shut it in their wake.

Hopefully, I thought, no restless spirits had followed them out.

CHAPTER 21

I found Lincoln at Hoffman's Row, scratching away on a piece of parchment in the candlelight. Unusually for the late hour, he was still dressed in the suit he'd worn to court earlier in the day.

"It's not from Truett's gun," I shouted as I pushed through the office door and flung myself onto Stuart's lounge.

Lincoln looked up, squinting. "What?"

"The lead ball that felled Early. Doctor Warren dug it out. Here." I handed it to Lincoln. "But it didn't come from Truett's gun."

Lincoln held the misshapen ball in front of the flame. "How do you know?" he asked.

"Truett pulled his pistol at Spotswood's, remember? It's a small belt pistol, not more than six inches from butt to muzzle. Takes a .37-caliber ball, I'm certain. That's the same type Douglas described in court this morning as having been discovered on Quality Hill. I have no doubt the gun they found on the Edwards grounds is Truett's. But this ball didn't get fired from that gun."

"You're sure?"

"Absolutely. This is for a dueling pistol. I don't sell those, obviously, at my store"—dueling was nominally illegal in Illinois—"but I do carry balls fitting them. For anyone passing through town who might be in need. That's going to be hard to measure precisely, with its deformation, but I'd wager anything it's a .42-caliber. I've matched plenty of ammunition to gun barrels in my time."

Dueling pistols were much larger than belt pistols like Truett's. A typical one was close to a foot and a half in length, with a ten-inch octagonal barrel, fitted with a single, hair trigger. All designed, of course, to be as accurate as possible at twenty paces.

"If this wasn't fired from Truett's gun," Lincoln was saying, "I wonder how Truett's gun came to be in Edwards's bushes?"

"We'll have to ask him. But that's for another time. Shouldn't you go show the ball to Douglas right now and tell him to set Truett free?"

Lincoln held up the ball to the flame again. "I'll pass the ball along to Douglas first thing tomorrow." He glanced at his pocket watch, which he had laid on the table next to him. "But I'm going to keep your expert observations about its size to ourselves for now. There'll be a time to use your detective work—later on."

"But Truett's suffering in jail right now, and this new evidence should be enough to get him out." I recalled Truett's desperate state the last time I'd seen him.

"Knowing Douglas, it won't be. He's not going to abandon his prosecution without a fight. And knowing a thing or two about trials, I judge the best time to use the evidence you've uncovered is further along in the legal process. That's when it will have maximum effect."

"But—"

"You've got to trust me on this, Speed."

"Very well. Have you had a chance to ask your father or step-brother about the land office records? Did either of them admit to being the false surveyor?"

"I did, and they didn't," said Lincoln, a frown on his face. "Claimed, both of them, to know nothing about it. I'm not sure I believe them—especially John—but there you have it." He glanced at his watch again. "Now, if you don't mind, I have some work to do before I turn in. I'll see you back at the room."

"You're still carrying the pistol I gave you?"

"I am," said Lincoln, patting his pocket.

"Good." I started to rise but then remembered the other unresolved issue from earlier in the day. "Did Douglas show you the note you'd supposedly sent acknowledging the hearing?"

Lincoln pursed his lips. "It was a pretty poor imitation of my handwriting, but Douglas pretended surprise when I told him it was a fake. Someone was trying to impersonate me."

"Or Douglas did it himself. To ensure you missed the court hearing so he could get Early dug up without your interference." *And make you look bad in front of the judge*, I added silently to myself.

"Doubtful. He was going to get the order anyway. I think whoever sent the note asking me to come to the clearing is the culprit."

"But why would *he* care if you missed the court hearing? That person is trying to frighten you, from the looks of it."

Lincoln shrugged. "I told Douglas that, in the future, he was to tell me or my office boy in person about any court hearing in Truett's case." Lincoln turned his attention back to the parchment in front of him.

"What are you working on?" I asked. I didn't think Lincoln had any other active legal cases between now and the election.

"That's the other thing Douglas and I discussed." There was a hint of impatience in his voice now. "We agreed to hold one last debate of the campaign, on this coming Sunday, here in Springfield at the old market house. One last chance for the voters to hear from representatives of the two parties—two men a side. I imagine I'll be one of those chosen for our party. And Douglas, I expect, for his."

"Is that wise? What do you have to gain, if the Whigs are already ahead, by holding an event so close to the election?"

"It's the course we've settled upon. Now, if you don't mind, I want to prepare some remarks for the debate while the subject's fresh in my mind."

"I'll leave you to it."

As I turned to depart, there was a soft knock on Lincoln's office door. I looked over at him in surprise and he flushed.

"Come in," he called, in a voice an octave deeper than his usual register.

Miss Margaret Owens walked into the office. She was wearing the same dress she'd worn for our nighttime stroll the prior week. As soon as she saw me, her face turned a similar shade to Lincoln's.

"Oh—Mr. Speed . . . I didn't . . ." the lady began.

"Speed was leaving," said Lincoln.

"I was leaving," I affirmed. I bowed hastily to Miss Owens, shot a glance at Lincoln that he did not return, and retreated from the office.

CHAPTER 22

The old market house was decorated in patriotic bunting for the occasion of the final debate of the campaign. Red, white, and blue streamers fluttered in the breeze from the second-floor balcony of the building. A squat, newly cut tree stump, emblazoned with red, white, and blue paint, had been set up in the grassy field in front.

A crowd of close to a thousand persons—roughly half the entire population of Springfield—formed a wide semicircle facing the stump, talking excitedly and jostling for the best view. Lincoln and I stood with a group of Whig men who were sharing a jug of whiskey and preparing to support our champions with much enthusiasm. My sister stood a little ways away in a cluster of women that included Mrs. Edwards, Miss Owens, and Miss Butler.

Sheriff Hutchason, as close to a nonpartisan figure as could be found in town at election season, flipped a sparkling new gold dollar coin. Douglas, for the Democrats, called "heads" and was rewarded when the crown-wearing profile of Lady Liberty landed face up on the grass. Following standard debate tactics, Douglas deferred to the second position.

The first two speakers were Ninian Edwards for the Whigs followed by David Prickett for the Democrats. Each man did a creditable job, sketching out the benefits of his party's positions and the terrible faults of their opposition. The crowd, filled with partisans on both sides, cheered and hooted lustily as each verbal punch landed or was missed, a scoring system that depended entirely on the stripes of the person conducting the tally.

Each of the opening speeches lasted the better part of an hour. When they had finished, a break was taken, and local innkeepers pulled around carts loaded with beer for the men, lemonade for the ladies, and ice creams for the children, who ran around on the field with bipartisan enthusiasm. Our cluster of Whigs all agreed Edwards had acquitted himself well and had been the decisive victor of the opening round.

Prickett was standing nearby, still sweating from the vigor of his performance. He was dressed with his usual haughty grandeur, with a white ruffled shirt beneath his elegant black frockcoat, though in his oratorical exertions he had come untucked, a fact he had not yet noticed.

Two small boys, not more than seven or eight years of age, walked past, each holding a hokey-pokey paper wrapper. Between the ice cream remains still on the hokey-pokeys and the streaks smeared across their noses, cheeks, and chins, it was an open question how much of the frozen treat the boys had actually managed to consume.

"What'd you think of that feller, Bill?" said one of the boys, gesturing to Prickett, who stood not five feet away. The prosecutor lifted his eyebrows with amusement and waited for the answer.

"I think," said Bill wisely, "if he knowed his shirttail was sticking out of a hole in his britches, maybe he wouldn't of been so high-falutin'."

Our group of Whig fellows roared with laughter as Prickett, his face suddenly crimson, turned away from the crowd and hurriedly tucked his shirt back inside his trousers.

On the other side of the crowd I glimpsed John Johnston, loosely attached to a cluster of Democrats who were drinking from an open keg. The apothecary Henry Owens walked past, and Johnston grabbed at his arm and seemed to have a word with him before Owens shook loose and continued on his way. I wondered what Johnston could have wanted with him. In the trees beyond, I could just make out the distinctive beard of Preacher Crews, watching the political proceedings with his arms folded in front of his chest.

A gong sounded the time for the rebuttal round. It was Lincoln's turn. He was already a head taller than every other man in the crowd, and when he climbed atop the stump he towered over the assemblage like Moses preaching to the Israelites from the mount.

"I have three words for the Democratic nonsense you heard coming out of Mr. Prickett's Democratic mouth," began Lincoln in his high-pitched, reedy voice. He paused dramatically.

"You'll never win," shouted one voice from the crowd.

"Go to hell," shouted another.

A ripple of laughter spread through the audience. Men and women tried out three-word put-downs on each other. Lincoln grinned and flapped his long, wing-like arms, gesturing for quiet.

"*Pooh . . . pish . . . p'shaw,*" he said at last.

The Whigs let out a great cheer at this pithy insult. I heard some Democrats grumbling about such nonsense words being the best Lincoln could offer, but by their deflated posture they seemed to concede he had effectively diminished Prickett.

Lincoln proceeded to build a sustained argument against the Democratic positions on the issues of the day and in favor of the Whigs. His principal thrust was one of conviction and constancy. The Whigs, Lincoln argued, had always stood for the policies in the best, long-term interests of the country and would continue to do so, while the views of the Democrats in general, and Prickett in particular, had vacillated wildly based on changing popular sentiment.

At one point in his extended discussion of the charge, Lincoln invoked the Barbary pirates, whose infamous, marauding attacks along the southern coast of the Mediterranean had not long ago been extinguished by the Second Barbary War. "Prickett and the Democrats," said Lincoln, "have changed their flags as often as a sea-pirate changes his."

Shouts of protest rang out from Democrats in the audience, but Lincoln met these with a stern shake of his head.

"You have," he insisted, pointing directly at Prickett, who stood near the front of the crowd with his hands on his hips. "You have. And for the same purpose, too. For both the Democrats and the pirates alike hope by their new flags to decoy the unwary."

The laughter and great cheers arising from the Whigs in the crowd drowned out the catcalls of the Democrats.

In delivering his oratory, Lincoln's manner was the same I had witnessed many times in the courtroom. At first his air was modest, almost embarrassed, as he laid out his party's positions. He stood on the stump uneasily, a little stooped in the shoulders, and his hands played fretfully with the buttons of his coat.

But as he warmed to his subject, he became physically warmer as well. His bearing became more erect and commanding. His voice deepened. His speech became more fluent and his manner easier. From beginning to end he was frequently interrupted by loud bursts of applause.

When Lincoln finished his assault on the Democrats' most recent set of positions, he paused, and I thought perhaps he was finished. But then he sought out my face in the crowd, and I knew at once what was coming. *The lightning rod.* We'd discussed this the previous night, and I had encouraged him to use it to conclude with a rhetorical flourish if he believed the crowd was with him.

"I was informed a few days ago," said Lincoln, "that Mr. Prickett has installed on the very top of the roof of his house a new device. An invention claiming almost magical properties. A metal stick—what some are calling a 'lightning rod'—purported to be able to absorb the deadly force of the heavens' electrical bolts and divert them away from the inhabitants of the abode."

As the crowd began to murmur with skepticism, Lincoln insisted, his large head bobbing with excitement, "Prickett has placed one of these lightning rods atop his house. I swear it is so. I invite all of you to walk over to Mr. Prickett's house on Jefferson after this afternoon's festivities have completed and have a look for yourselves."

All of this was indeed true—and genuinely useful. Lightning storms were a serious threat on the frontier, and the vast prairie encompassing Springfield was especially prone to spawning such calamities. Just the other month, a deadly bolt had struck the house of Mr. Otho Carr in Peoria. The house itself had been little injured, but the bolt had struck down Mrs. Carr and four of her children. Prickett's rod was the first to appear in Springfield, and if it operated as promised I'd be able to sell every last one I could stock in my store.

"But I've come to wonder," continued Lincoln, motioning again for the crowd to settle down, "why it was that Mr. Prickett decided to install this new device. Why is it that my opponent chooses to try to alter the course of Nature, much as he has altered the nature of his political positions with the shifting winds of popular sentiment? While we've been alive on this Earth for about the same number of years, I freely concede Mr. Prickett is substantially more practiced than me in the tricks and the trades of the politician."

Lincoln was in full cry now. "Last night I hit upon the answer and I will share it. It is to my credit and my opponent's shame. I declare honestly to all of you listening as follows. Hear me out! Live long or die young, I would rather die now than, like Mr. Prickett, change my politics, and simultaneous with the change, receive an office worth three thousand dollars per year, and then . . . *have to erect a lightning rod over my house to protect a guilty conscience from an offended God.*"

This last phrase was said at a shout, and the crowd—Whig and Democrat alike—was sent into a frenzy. The Whigs shouted with joy and derision, clapping each other vigorously on the back. Many blew tin horns or bugles. One of my excited fellows belted me with such enthusiasm that I was sent sprawling and nearly landed face-first on the ground. Meanwhile, the Democrats shouted foul and cried that Lincoln was a blasphemer for claiming the Almighty's allegiance to his cause. Prickett himself had gone white as a ghost, his pallid color matching his carefully laundered shirt.

The tumult continuing all around, Lincoln stepped down from the stump, his arms raised high above his head in triumph. He was surrounded by a group of jubilant Whigs, who offered their congratulations on his *tour de force.*

At length, the boiling crowd reduced to a simmer. Stephen Douglas detached himself from a gaggle of Democrats, walked to the front of the arena, and mounted the stump.

"Stand up!" yelled some wag from the audience.

The crowd laughed, and Douglas smiled good-naturedly and bowed.

"My friend Mr. Lincoln—" began Douglas, only to be drowned out by a chorus of Whigs shouting "*Huzzah!*" and blowing their horns one last time to celebrate the speech of their champion. Douglas waited until they quieted down.

"My friend Mr. Lincoln is never one to let the facts get in the way of a clever argument," he began again. Douglas's deep, rumbling voice, studded with hard New England vowels, was an immediate contrast to the high-pitched tone of Lincoln's, and I'm sure I wasn't the only man present struck by the incongruity of the deep voice emanating from the little man, while the high-pitched one came from the large man.

"And Mr. Lincoln does like his clever arguments. A lightning rod, eh?" Douglas found Prickett in the front rank of the crowd and pointed at him. "That will teach you to try to protect your wife and little ones, David." Douglas shook his massive head, a sardonic smile playing on his lips, and then turned serious.

"But those of us who mean to govern, and govern seriously, must do more than stretch for metaphors or cast fishing lines for jokes. We must find the facts and face them. Face them straight up and without flinching."

Douglas proceeded to lay out the Democrats' position on the issues of the day with articulateness and fluency. The Little Giant explained where he stood, attacked where he could, and conceded where he must, all the while chopping the air with his arms to emphasize his points. If his speech lacked Lincoln's homespun charm, it was, I was forced to admit, at least his equal in terms of both rhetorical flair and substance. The Whigs standing near me gradually lost the elation that had filled them at the rousing conclusion of Lincoln's address.

After he had been talking for about an hour, Douglas hopped down from the stump and took a tankard of beer from the cart of the nearest merchant. This he downed in one long swig to the approving shouts of the assembled Democrats. I thought perhaps he was finished, but it turned out he was just getting started.

"The Whigs appear to have anointed Mr. Lincoln their future standard-bearer," said Douglas after he resumed his position on top of the stump, "and so I think it only fair that I direct a few remarks to the gentleman. To the *character* of the gentleman, to be precise about my intentions."

Lincoln was standing next to me and I saw him stiffen. He gazed out at the crowd jostling behind him. I turned toward the clutch of women spectators and saw Miss Owens looking very tense. Mrs. Edwards leaned over, said something into her ear, and patted her on the arm. My sister stood next to them, listening to Douglas with her head half-cocked to the side.

"Now I freely admit," continued Douglas, "that I've not been a citizen of Illinois for my entire life—"

"There's still Vermont mud on your boots!" called out one Whig.

Douglas made a show of examining the underside of his boots, one after the other. "Perhaps there is," he said. "I would not swear an oath against it. But I think each of you can agree Vermont mud is to be much preferred to Illinois horse sh—" The crowd took in its collective breath as Douglas paused before continuing. "Horse-shoes," he finished, with a grin. The Democrats cheered.

"But even during my residency in this state," Douglas continued, when the noise had died down, "I have learned a few facts about the tall gentleman in the stovepipe hat that give me pause. A few facts about his past. His *history*. A history he has perhaps tried to dispatch by his move to Springfield several years ago, but a history that remains nonetheless.

"Now, I don't mean the fact he comes from humble origins. I do as well, and so do many of our new leaders rising here in the West. Such self-reliance is to be celebrated. Not all of us were swaddled by ruffled shirts in our cradles, Prickett," Douglas added with a grin, unable to resist the dig at his fellow Democrat. Prickett managed a wan smile in return.

"But it is fair, I think, to wonder about the gentleman's grasp of financial affairs, when I am told reliably that he still carries in his pocket the unpaid notes he incurred by the failure of his store in New Salem. It is no wonder the internal improvements scheme, which he has championed in the legislature, now sits in shambles and ruin. The gentleman purports to tell the people of our state he will be a responsible superintendent of their money, yet he has proven by his actions that he cannot be trusted with his own."

The swell of the crowd had a different character now. Good-natured call and response had been replaced by unfiltered expressions of condemnation and anger. This type of direct, personal attack on the opposing candidate was unheard of at stump debates. I did not look at Lincoln but saw many in the crowd doing so without pretension.

"And it is fair to wonder," continued Douglas, jabbing the air for emphasis, "about his judgment of his fellow man, when I understand he has been taken in by a confidence man. Indeed, I understand the gentleman pursued a failed courtship with a lady already betrothed—betrothed to a confidence man gone missing. He aspires for a position where he may direct the affairs of the state, but it is plain he has trouble keeping his own affairs in order."

The crowd was roiling. This time I did look at Lincoln. His eyes were bulging, his jaw straining, his face burning bright. My own blood was boiling; I felt it pounding in my head. It was far beyond the bounds of fair play to dredge up the memory of Lincoln's failed romance with Ann Rutledge. If Douglas kept at it, there would be violence. And I would be in the front rank of the advancing army.

Douglas affected not to notice the turmoil caused by his words. "And it is fair to wonder," he continued, "about his temperance and sobriety, when his own relations are seen by all stumbling about town in the lowest state of—"

That did it. I broke free of the crowd and sprinted toward Douglas. I thought I heard my sister scream my name. In a few long strides I was nearly to him, leaning forward with outstretched arms. I was going to wrap my hands around his thick neck and throttle him. But in the instant before I reached him, it struck me there was one sensation Douglas feared even more than physical pain. Ridicule.

I flew at Douglas, but instead of knocking him over and choking him, at full speed I picked the little man up underneath both armpits. I lifted him off the stump, bearing his considerable weight, and hurtled away with him. One lap around the market house should do it, I thought, and so I raced a broad circle around the structure.

"Let me go!" Douglas screamed as he tried to wriggle out of my grasp.

"No!" I had locked my fingers together around his midsection and had a good hold on him.

"Put me down!"

"Not after what you said about Lincoln."

"It's politics!"

"That was personal."

By now my energy was flagging from carrying such a heavy load, and as I looped around the final corner of the market house and approached the stump again, I slowed. The crowd in front of us was in utter tumult, raging and screaming and shouting. Several fistfights had broken out. I noted, with a cruel satisfaction, that more than a few men were pointing at Douglas in my arms and laughing.

At that moment Douglas bit down, hard, on my thumb. I screamed in pain and dropped him. Blood gushed from my hand and I fell to my knees.

Before I knew it, twin phalanxes of Whigs and Democrats poured toward me. The Whigs shouted my name jubilantly and pounded me on the back. The Democrats arrived with equal frenzy but considerably less friendship. One of them carried a metal beer tankard in his hand. And I noticed, much too late, that it was arcing toward my head.

CHAPTER 23

When I began to wake, the world was dark. As I lay in a semiconscious state, I realized gradually that I was in my own bed. I used my left hand to feel its mate and discovered a heavy bandage wrapped around my injured thumb. At least it was still attached. Slowly, I began to push myself up into a sitting position.

"He's awake!" came my sister's voice.

In an instant, Martha and Lincoln were above me. Martha was holding a flickering candle in her hand.

"Did we win?" I asked weakly.

"You behaved very badly," said my sister. "I can't tell you how relieved I am to see you conscious again, but still—you behaved very badly."

"He behaved like a loyal friend," said Lincoln, "though perhaps some perspective was called for."

"I didn't have a plan for what to do after I'd completed our loop," I said. "And I didn't think about Douglas's teeth. Or about his confederates."

"That lack of foresight is the one thing I fault you for," said Lincoln with a lopsided grin. "Anyone who's witnessed any Western fighting—and I know you've seen your share—should have realized a well-timed and well-executed thumb bite is the one surefire way to make your opponent lose his grip."

I laughed.

"It's not funny," protested my sister. "You could have gotten seriously hurt. And Stephen . . . Stephen didn't deserve that."

"What he said was outrageous," I said. I tried sitting up completely, but a sharp pain flashed through my head and I lowered myself down again.

"I deserved every word," Lincoln said quietly.

"No, you didn't!" I shouted, feeling indignant enough for the both of us.

"Yes, I did," replied Lincoln. I could see in the candlelight that the skin around his eyes was drawn tight. "Every word he said was true. Or close enough, anyway. I'm not sure which of us was most humiliated by today, but it wasn't Douglas." He paused. "If it wasn't so near election day I'd withdraw from my race."

"You cannot be serious! You can't let that little man intimidate you."

Lincoln sighed. "The thing is, he spoke a truth. I have been running from certain aspects of my past. I suppose the long view is that Douglas did me a favor. From now on I needn't worry, for I have nothing left to hide."

"But . . . but . . ." I was flummoxed.

"Lie still, Joshua," commanded Martha. "You're not well. You need to rest. Deserving or not, Stephen shouldn't have bitten you. You're lucky you still have your thumb."

I put my head back on my pillow and took several slow breaths. "I'll go back to sleep," I said, "once both of you finally admit I've been right about Douglas all along."

"What do you mean?"

"*Douglas* is the one who's been tormenting Lincoln. Following us on our walk, writing threatening notes, authoring the S.G. letters for the newspaper. What more proof do we need than the debate today? Which, more than likely, means he's the one who killed Early. Everyone in town saw today he's capable of violence. And now, to top it all off, he's prosecuting Truett. Which means he's in charge of trying to put an innocent man in jail to cover up his own crime."

My words hung in the air. Both Martha and Lincoln were silent. I'd made the accusation out of anger, but as I played it back in my head it seemed pretty convincing.

It was Martha who spoke first.

"You're wrong! Surely you're wrong." She turned to Lincoln, pleading. "Tell him he's wrong."

The flame of Martha's candle cast Lincoln's lantern jaw in sharp relief. His gray eyes were deep in thought. "Why don't you go talk to him," he said at last. "Tomorrow, assuming you feel better. You owe him an apology anyway."

"He owes me one," I protested, raising my bandaged hand with difficulty.

"You both owe the other," said Lincoln. "And if you want to keep selling your goods to the Democrats in town as well as the Whigs, as you always say, I venture you want Douglas spreading the word to his allies that he harbors no hard feelings against you." I hadn't considered this; it was a good point.

"Ask him about S.G.," continued Lincoln. "To be clear, I don't for a moment think it's him. If I truly thought him capable of murder, I wouldn't be suggesting you meet with him. But it's indisputable that his ally Weber is the one who's been printing the letters, and it stands to reason Douglas gains from attacks on me."

"I'm going with you, Joshua," said Martha.

I began to raise myself up again to argue, but she urged me down. "Don't bother to speak. It's settled. Besides, if it's just the two of you, someone's thumb might get bitten clear off."

So it was that Martha and I set off to find Douglas the next morning after we'd finished breakfast at the Globe. Our fellow diners at the common table that morning were eager to hear my account of the confrontation with Douglas, even though each of them had been there to witness it in person, but under Martha's stern gaze I contented myself with telling them it had been a regrettable moment of emotion and one that wouldn't be repeated.

"Doesn't it make you feel better to be benevolent about it?" said Martha as we walked along the streets.

"No—much worse."

Douglas was an enthusiastic Freemason and could often be found in the Masonic Hall, which was located in the upper part of a two-story wooden building on the south side of Jefferson. The lodge consisted of a single long room running the length of the building; several images of the Masons' square and compass, in varying sizes and configurations, decorated the walls. Douglas was alone in the hall when we arrived, working away at a desk positioned in front of one of the few windows cut into the sloping eaves. A folded copy of the *Illinois Democrat* lay at his side.

Douglas smiled as soon as he saw Martha, and he was in the middle of rising to greet her when he saw me walk in behind. His expression turned sour and he gazed back down at his papers and continued to scratch away. I waited for him to speak first, while Martha looked back and forth between us with growing frustration.

Presently he asked, in a brusque manner, "How's your thumb, then?"

"Fine. Takes more than the nibble of a mouse to do me serious harm." Martha began to remonstrate against me, but she stopped when she saw a smile forming on Douglas's lips. "How's your— well, pride?" I added.

"Never better. Takes more than the opprobrium of a second-rate shopkeeper to make me question my stature."

"Honestly, is that the best either of you can do?" exclaimed Martha. When she saw the expressions on each of our faces, she sighed. "I suppose it is."

"I assume, Speed, that if you came intent on trying to do me harm this morning, you wouldn't have brought along Miss Speed, whom I find as delightful as I find you tiresome. It's quite amazing you're blood relations."

"I came to ask about those anonymous letters about Lincoln that have appeared in the *Democrat*," I said. "The ones signed 'S.G.' I'm making it my mission to figure out who the author is."

Douglas's eyes flickered. "What about them?"

"You and S.G. have the same goals—to undermine Lincoln's credibility and with it his political aspirations. It seems to me there are two and only two possibilities. The first is you know full well who S.G. is. And the second—"

"Is that I am him." Douglas looked up at us, perfectly composed.

"No, you're not," said Martha indignantly, her hands on her hips.

I ignored her and took in the remorseless gaze of Douglas's steely blue eyes. "You admit it?" I said.

"I admit nothing."

"Do you deny you're S.G.?"

"I deny everything." When my skeptical glare did not abate, he added, "I have no need for fictitious signatures. I'm perfectly capable of attacking Lincoln under my own name. I'd think, after yesterday, you would know that better than anyone."

"Of course it's so," said Martha. "I told you, Joshua, the notion that Stephen—Mr. Douglas—was involved with the letters is absurd."

Douglas smirked.

I clenched my good fist and shook it near his face. "Stay away from my sister," I said, "or there will be another murder trial on the docket."

"Miss Speed," Douglas said without removing his eyes from me, "have I at all times conducted myself in your presence with the decorum and bearing of a gentleman?"

"You have," she said with an enthusiasm that made my teeth clench.

He nodded. "You have my word, Speed, that I shall continue to do so. You're entitled to that word—and nothing more."

"Come along, Martha," I said, taking my sister's arm with a firm grip. "Let's see if we can't make productive use of the rest of the day." We had taken several steps toward the door when I had one final thought. "By the way," I said, turning to face Douglas again, "do you have any idea what the initials 'S.G.' stand for?"

"Yes, I do."

I thought I hadn't heard him clearly. "You—what?"

"I believe they stand for 'Salem's Ghost.'"

"There's a Salem in the Bible, isn't there?" said Martha. "It's another term for Jerusalem. So, 'Jerusalem's Ghost' . . ."

"I don't think that's what's intended here," said Douglas, "but that's very good, Miss Speed. Your classical education does you credit." Martha smiled brightly at him.

The man was impossible. "It seems like quite a stretch, Douglas," I said. "The 'S' could be practically anything. Why do you think 'Salem'?"

Douglas smiled an infernal smile. He picked up the copy of today's *Democrat*, which had been lying beside him this whole time. "Because," he said, "the man himself has told us so."

I rushed over and snatched the sheet from his hands. With Martha reading over my shoulder, I located the new letter on the last page:

July 29, 1838
Lost Township, Ill.

To the Editor of the Democrat:
    Today's stump debate destroyed any hollow pretense which the man of great height and low intellect carries himself with. Now the whole world knows what I know. He is a Fraud, a Fake, a Fiction. Not even the exertions of his trained monkey can save him. Judgment Day is almost here.

Salem's Ghost

" 'Trained monkey?' " I murmured as I read the letter for a second time. Turning to Douglas, I added, angrily, "And you still maintain you have nothing to do with the letters?"

"Surely you must have some idea who's writing them, Mr. Douglas," said Martha with great earnestness. Her cheeks were even rosier than usual and her eyes brimmed with barely restrained tears. "I'm worried for the safety of our friend Mr. Lincoln, and I know under your bluster you must be as well."

Douglas softened, and he reached out a hand and placed it on Martha's arm. "I assure you there's no need for worry, Miss Speed. When he says 'Judgment Day,' he only means the election next week—nothing more serious than that. We politicians tend to puff up the importance of our trade this near to voting."

"Do you have *any* idea who he could be?"

"Truly I don't. Beyond the fact it's clear he's a Democratic politician of some stripe. I'd tell you if I knew his name. At the least, I'd tell him to level his charges out in the open. But your Mr. Lincoln needn't worry about anything greater than his chances at the polls. About those, I hope, he and his fellow Whigs have a great deal to worry."

Martha looked mollified, though I wondered whether the flame in her cheeks was brighter because of the touch of Douglas's hand, which had lingered longer than necessary. Staring at the man, I felt certain he couldn't be trusted.

"Let's go," I said, taking Martha's arm again and steering her toward the door. "We've gotten everything we can out of him."

"But what do we do now?" she asked.

Douglas made a noise and we turned back to him. "Really," he said, "I should be the last person in the world volunteering to help you on this fool's errand, but it *is* obvious, isn't it?"

"What?"

"Go to New Salem. Your answer must be there."

CHAPTER 24

New Salem was located on a bluff overlooking the swirling waters of the Sangamon River, some twenty miles downstream from Springfield. Lincoln had told me he'd first visited the town as a young man of twenty-two years when a flatboat he piloted down the river toward New Orleans got stuck in a snag at the town's milldam. He later made the town his first permanent home after leaving his father's house, hoping like many others he could rise along with the town's fortunes.

But the alchemy of the frontier was an inscrutable magic. For every new town, like Springfield, whose combination of location, natural resources, and business interests produced rapid growth, there was another that failed to ignite. When Lincoln arrived in New Salem, it had been a vibrant, growing outpost, with several hundred persons calling it home at its peak. Today it was barely half that size, and I had heard that the only persons who remained were those too poor or infirm to move on to more promising pastures.

Martha and I made one stop in Springfield before heading to New Salem. Weber had promised Martha he would save S.G.'s next letter.

Weber looked up at us expectantly as we barged into the *Democrat*'s offices on Chicken Row. "I'm surprised it took you this long," he drawled. "But then, Speed, I wasn't sure you'd show your face in town today, not after the way you embarrassed yourself yesterday."

He looked down at my bandaged hand, and without thinking I tucked it behind my back.

"You know what we've come for," said Martha. "May we see the new letter, if you please?" She held out her hand.

Weber reached underneath his composing table. But when he withdrew his hand, it was empty. He rolled his shoulders and straightened his immaculate black frockcoat. The publisher seemed consumed by an internal debate about how unhelpful propriety allowed him to be. After a long pause, he reached down again and this time came up with a folded sheet of foolscap, which he reluctantly handed to Martha.

"*Weber—The Democrat*" was printed on the outside fold in child-like block letters.

"How was it delivered?" I demanded as I looked over the letter from Salem's Ghost that had appeared in the sheet this morning. "And when?" I could see immediately that the letter had been written by the same hand that had produced the threatening "I know" note tacked on the tree for Lincoln to find.

"It was on my doorstep, pinned under a stone, when I arrived early this morning to set the final type for today's edition."

"Who do you think wrote it?" asked Martha. "And what do you think this means—'Salem's Ghost'?"

"No thanks for saving the letter for you? No gratitude? Miss Speed, I don't care what Douglas says, I declare you are nearly as tiresome as your brother. Which is a status to which no one should aspire." Weber's sharp black eyes glinted. "Figure it out yourselves."

"What an awful man!" exclaimed Martha, for about the fourth time, an hour later. We were riding side by side through parched summer grasslands, following the course of the Sangamon toward New Salem. The fierce sun was high overhead. I held Hickory's reins in my left hand, my right held stiffly by my side.

"I'm surprised he showed us the letter at all."

"He must have figured there was no value for us in seeing the original. But he's wrong. Based on the handwriting, we now have confirmation S.G. is the same person who's been harassing Lincoln."

"Hopefully we'll learn more in New Salem," I said. "Lincoln didn't want to go back to his past, but—much as I hate to credit him with any good idea—I think Douglas is right that we must."

It was for this reason that we'd decided not to tell Lincoln about our trip before setting off. We were afraid he'd try to talk us out of the expedition. But the connection of Salem's Ghost to New Salem appeared inescapable.

We made good time on horseback, and we soon arrived in the environs of New Salem. In truth, all the little village had were environs. There was a mill on the banks of the river, the very same one, I supposed, that had snagged Lincoln's flatboat all those years ago. The waterwheel turned lazily in the low summer current, but the mill building itself had begun to fall apart and several boards were missing. Near the mill, about a dozen other structures clung to two dusty roads. They were more like cow paths than proper roads a buggy could travel, one beside the river and another perpendicular to it and ending at the mill.

There was not a single tree in sight. In fact, it had been several miles since we'd seen anything taller or more substantial than prairie grass. Presumably, the residents of the struggling village had cut down everything within easy walking distance for use as firewood.

There was a building directly at the crossroads, a squat one-story log cabin giving the appearance of a general store. It had a porch out front, with two wooden chairs occupied by large bundles wrapped in checkered cloth. As we rode up I realized the bundles were actually men, both over sixty years if they were a day, sitting so motionless they barely appeared alive. Each of them had a weather-beaten face and wispy, graying hair.

"Afternoon," I called, tipping my straw hat.

One of the men shifted slightly in his chair.

"I'm looking for a man named Lincoln," I said. "Ever heard of him?"

"You've come to the wrong place," said one of the men. "Used to live here, long time ago, but he left."

"And's been too prideful to return," said the other.

"Where does he live now?" I asked, curious to see whether word of Lincoln's prominence in Springfield had traveled back to his old home. But apparently it hadn't, as the two men looked at one another and then back to me. One of them shrugged.

"What about a Henry Truett?" I tried.

"Used to live here, too," said one of the men.

"Worked for Lincoln," said his companion.

"Till he didn't have a store no more," said the first.

"Would you know where we could find Truett now?" I asked. Again, I was met only by blank stares.

I tried to think of the other persons from New Salem whom Lincoln had mentioned. The two men rocked back and forth in their chairs and watched me, but seemingly without any real interest.

"What about John McNamar, or John McNeil?" I tried, thinking of Ann Rutledge's other suitor.

"Gone, too," replied one of the men on the porch. His companion nodded.

Who else? Lincoln had once mentioned the name of the man he'd bought his store from, the one where he'd briefly employed Truett. Blanket or . . . "Blankenship," I said aloud, pleasantly surprised the name had come to my tongue.

"Eli Blankenship?" said one of the men.

"I assume so. Is he still around?"

The two men slowly exchanged glances. One of them said, "Sure is."

"Owns a tavern in these parts," said the other.

"Whereabouts, if you please?"

"Down the road a ways." The man pointed to a structure two doors down. "Over yonder."

I tipped my hat again and indicated to Martha that we should dismount and lead our horses to the building in question.

"It's no wonder Mr. Lincoln left here for Springfield," Martha whispered to me as we walked along, holding the horses' reins. "It's hard to imagine a more deadening place."

Blankenship's tavern was the only framed structure in the village, with a stone chimney protruding from the rear. There were no hitching posts in sight, so we tied the horses up to one of the vertical struts of the porch.

Inside, I gazed around with interest. It was a combined general store, tavern, and inn, with goods for sale as well as signs indicating the cost of board and overnight stays. We were greeted, from behind the counter, by a portly man of about forty years, with a blunt nose and narrow eyes beneath bushy brows. He wore a faded apron atop a dusty jeans suit. The man looked my sister up and down before saying to me, in a nasal voice, "Yes?"

"Eli Blankenship?" I said.

"Who's asking?"

"My name's Prickett." I felt my sister swing around to stare at me, but I squeezed her hand and kept my gaze focused on the tavernkeeper. "And this is my sister. We're in need of a meal, and we were told Blankenship cooked the best one in New Salem. Now if you'll direct us to him, we'll be off."

"You've found him," said Blankenship in a somewhat friendlier manner. "You and the lass can have a seat." He indicated a table made of a slab of timber, roughly hewn, surrounded by half a dozen three-legged stools. "I'll get to cooking you up that meal."

"I've an idea for getting the information we want out of him," I whispered to my sister when we were seated across from each other. "Follow my lead when he comes back."

"Why are we 'Prickett'?" asked Martha.

"He was the first Democrat who came to mind. You'll see."

Blankenship had disappeared into his kitchen, and we could hear the sounds of pots and pans being banged about. I pulled the kidskin glove I'd found in the woods out of my pocket and laid it on the table in front of my sister. "What do you think?"

Martha scrutinized the glove. She tugged at the lace ribbon gently and studied the ink drawing on the backside. Then she slipped off her own glove and pulled the found glove onto her hand. It fit snugly.

"It's stunning," she said. "Are you thinking of carrying it in your inventory? I'd buy several pairs, and I'm sure my girlfriends would, too."

"I don't know the source. I was hoping you could help me. French manufacture, I'm guessing."

Martha studied the glove again and shook her head. "Definitely Spanish. If you look at the costume of the woman in the courting pair, it's obvious her dress is meant to suggest a famous one Maria Christina wore on the day of her wedding to King Ferdinand in 1829. A French glove manufacturer would never honor the Spanish Queen Consort, but a Spanish one certainly would."

I gazed at Martha with astonishment. "How do you know all that?"

Martha tossed her head with impatience. "Seriously, Joshua—the things you don't know could fill volumes." She paused. "If you don't know the source, how did you come to have it?"

"A passing merchant gave it to me," I said vaguely. I didn't fully trust that anything I shared with Martha wouldn't make its way to Douglas. "I'll take it back, thank you."

A few minutes later, the tavernkeeper brought us a groaning board of young pork, good bread, potatoes, preserves, and tea. I dove in and found the food unexpectedly delicious. Martha agreed and said as much to the man, who nodded at the compliment.

"If we tell you something, Blankenship, can you keep it a secret?"

He looked me over with interest and then sneaked a quick glance at Martha before responding, "I'm sure I can."

I gestured to the stool next to me and the man sat. The hot, still air clung to the ceiling, floor, and everything in between. "The thing is," I began, "there's an election going on now, and our brother is running against a fellow named Lincoln—perhaps you've heard of him?"

Blankenship's face showed no reaction. He said, slowly, "I may have."

I nodded enthusiastically. "Our brother has sent us to find out everything we can about Lincoln. Something we can use *against* Lincoln in the election. To hurt his chances and help our brother's, if you follow my meaning. Is there anything you can tell us?"

Blankenship considered this. After a few moments, he said, "Lincoln owes me money."

"He does?" I shouted out with a combination of surprise and excitement, while Martha played her part by opening her eyes wide. "How much?"

"I don't make it a habit of revealing my business," replied Blankenship, "but I don't mind telling you the debt was near on one thousand dollars at the start."

"You don't say!" This time my surprise was genuine. It was an enormous sum to be owed by one man, a sum I imagined it could take Lincoln a decade or more of law practice to pay off. No wonder he referred to it as his "national debt."

"Is Lincoln the one who did that to you?" Blankenship asked, gesturing at my bandaged hand.

"In a way, I suppose he did." I stepped on Martha's foot to stop her from contradicting me.

"Figures," said Blankenship. He thought for a bit. "Since Lincoln owes me money, if I help your brother defeat him, don't that come back and hurt me?"

"No, it *helps* you," said Martha quickly. "Lawyers are better paid than politicians, aren't they? If Lincoln's out of office, he'll have more time for lawyering. More time to earn back the money he owes you."

Blankenship nodded slowly, stroking his chin.

"Is Lincoln paying down his debt to you?" I asked.

"A bit each month. I tell him surely he can afford more, but he cries poverty and says I'm getting all he can spare. I reckon there was one time, a few months back, when he was late by a day. Does that help you?"

"It might," I said without enthusiasm. "Lincoln's tied up in defending a man named Henry Truett. Some sort of political dispute. I don't know the details. Are you familiar with Truett?"

Blankenship nodded. "After I sold him my store, I think Lincoln hired that Truett fellow at one point."

"What do you remember about Truett? Did he have any enemies here in New Salem? People who wished him ill?"

Blankenship thought for a moment but shook his head. "Nothing that's coming to mind."

"What about Lincoln?" asked my sister. "Did he have enemies here?"

"He was a friendly enough fellow," replied Blankenship. "At least, he was if he didn't go into debt to you."

"How about the phrase, or the name, 'Salem's Ghost'? Does that mean anything to you?"

I was watching his face closely, but he did not give any special reaction. "'Salem's Ghost?' I don't think so. The ghosts of New Salem, perhaps? Only spirits will be living here in a few years if things don't turn around soon."

We had finished eating our food. Martha turned to me and said, "I know Mr. Blankenship's doing his best, but we're not making much progress. Perhaps we should go try to find someone who knew Ann Rut—"

Blankenship clapped his hand to his forehead. "The cooper!" he shouted. "Why didn't I think of him earlier? Follow me."

He rushed out the door and down the street as we trailed in his wake. At the far end of the little village was a shed with a wisp of smoke rising up from its peaked roof. We followed the tavern-keeper inside and saw the telltale signs of a cooperage: wooden staves of various lengths stacked against the wall, the floor covered with sawdust, and a glowing hearth in the center of the room for bending iron bands into hoops. A cooper wearing a leather vest full of tools was sitting next to the fire. I saw at once his left ankle had been put out, as it bent unnaturally and his left foot dangled uselessly to the side.

"John!" shouted Blankenship. "These two were asking about Ann and Abe Lincoln. This is her brother," he added, turning to us.

"Are you friends or enemies of Lincoln?" John Rutledge asked.

"Enemies," I said emphatically.

Rutledge took a flat strip of iron and thrust it into the fire. After a bit it began to glow, a cool orange at first, but then a progressively hotter and angrier red. He looked up.

"I've been waiting for you for a long time."

CHAPTER 25

"Abe Lincoln killed my sister."

"What?" Martha exclaimed, as I said, "I'd heard she died of brain fever."

"It was the brain fever that brought her to death's doorstep," said John Rutledge. "But it was Lincoln that handed her to the Reaper. And soon afterwards he handed my dear old pa to the Reaper, too."

Blankenship must have seen our confused expressions because he said, "Slow down, John. You're going too fast for them."

The cooper plucked the iron strip from the fire with a pair of tongs and examined it. He placed it on an anvil and, taking a hammer from a loop on his vest, gave it a few exploratory whacks. Then he thrust it back into the flames. I guessed he was close to thirty years, broad-shouldered, with close-cropped brown hair and large ears. But for his disjointed ankle he seemed a vigorous man.

"We Rutledges was in New Salem long before Lincoln ever floated by," he said, poking the embers to raise the flame higher. "There was nine of us—I'm the oldest boy—and my ma and pa. My pa's the one who laid out the town, back in '29. First time I recall Lincoln was when he and I were mustered up at Beardstown, awaiting our orders to march against Black Hawk and his Injun warriors."

"You and he fought in the Black Hawk War together?" asked Martha.

"Yes, ma'am. Lincoln was my captain, matter of fact. Not that it proved much of a war, mind you. Black Hawk and them ran away faster than we could run after 'em. Anyway, at Beardstown, we was wrestling, to pass the hours waiting for the call, and I remember there was a time when Lo Thompson and Lincoln faced off, because they was the two biggest, strongest men in the company. Lincoln wasn't looking and Lo grabbed him by the foreleg and yanked and he took Lincoln down. Hard." Rutledge gave a shout of laughter and stirred the fire again. "That's the only time I ever seen Lincoln brought to the ground in a wrestle."

"He was a *scientific* wrestler," said Blankenship from behind us. "He throwed every man I ever saw him wrestle. Even Jack Armstrong. Nobody but Lincoln could throw Jack Armstrong."

"Your sister Ann and Lincoln eventually came to an understanding?" I said, hoping to keep Rutledge focused.

"That ain't what happened." Rutledge shook his head vigorously. "My sister Ann . . . there's never been a gentler or more amiable maiden created by the Almighty. I miss her every day." He paused, and for a moment I thought he might be on the verge of tears, but then he collected himself.

"Ann made the acquaintance of a man called John McNeil. He was a proper fellow, a businessman, from somewheres back East. A friendship grew between them, which ripened apace, and soon they was engaged to marry. McNeil had to make one trip home and then he was going to make Ann his wife."

"I heard McNeil was a confidence man, a swindler," I said.

"No, sir," said Rutledge. "His conduct with my sister was strictly high-toned, moral, and honest."

"But wasn't his real name John McNamar?"

Rutledge took his iron out of the fire and tested it again. This time he found it sufficiently pliable, and we watched as he pounded it into a hoop, expertly manipulating the iron around the anvil with his tongs in one hand while he wielded the hammer with his other. When he was finished he had a perfect circular hoop, which he tested and then tossed onto a pile of similar hoops at the side of the shed.

"McNeil and McNamar were one and the same, but there was no deception. My sister knew the truth all along. And while Mr. McNeil was visiting his kinfolk out East, she was preparing for the rest of their lives. She was a smart one, was Ann. She even had plans to enter the Female Academy, in Jacksonville, and get a proper education.

"But Lincoln came along and took advantage of McNeil's absence. He paid attention to Ann, courted her, even though she was engaged to another. She remained firm. She was passing through another fire. I told him myself she was already spoken for, but he wouldn't listen. He persisted. And persisted. He had just about overcome her womanly defenses when the illness stole upon her."

It was a very different version of these events than the one Lincoln had told me. Looking at John Rutledge's earnest expression, I had no reason to doubt him, though I equally had no reason to doubt Lincoln's narrative. One thing was beyond dispute: both men, in their own way, had loved Ann Rutledge dearly.

"And then she died," said Martha softly, "which I'm sure was a great tragedy for your family and all who loved her."

Rutledge looked up at Martha and nodded.

"But why do you blame Mr. Lincoln for that terrible misfortune?" she went on.

"Cuz he's the one who caused it," the cooper insisted. "After Ann had laid on her sickbed for a week, my pa sent for a doctor, and he came and sat with Ann for a spell and he told us she'd get better but that she had to lie still, not move, and not talk to anyone. We spread the word all over town she needed absolute quiet. I told Lincoln myself. But Lincoln, he didn't listen to me or no one else. He pretended to be a common folk, but deep down he thought he always knew best. He stole into Ann's sickroom one evening and he held her hand and he talked to her. He did exactly what the doctor said not to do. Three days later she was taken from us."

John Rutledge appeared on the brink of tears again. "And losing Ann killed my pa, too. He couldn't bear to be without her, especially not after the doctor told us she'd survive. His heart was done and broke. We buried Ann in August, and we buried my pa not three months later."

A single tear escaped Martha's eyes and rolled down her cheek.

"Come," said Rutledge. He struggled to his feet and grabbed at a crutch leaning against the wall. "I'll take you to her grave, if you'd like. She's buried on Concord Ridge. Ain't too far away."

"I don't think we have time—" I began, but my sister interrupted me, saying, "Of course we'd like to see it. That would be very kind of you." She shot me a glare full of daggers and I put up my hands in defeat. It was useless to argue.

Blankenship said he needed to get back to his tavern, so Martha and I followed Rutledge as he hobbled out of his shed and down the road away from the cluster of cabins that made up the village. His progress was slow, as his ruined limb could not bear any weight.

"Did you ever meet Lincoln's stepbrother?" I asked him as we walked. "Came to visit him here once or twice, I think. Fellow named John Johnston?"

"Johnnie and I had some good times together," Rutledge said as his face brightened. "He wasn't anything like his stepbrother. I remember one time, before my accident"—he gestured vaguely toward his ankle—"he and I went turkey hunting together. I tell you, that fellow's a good shot with his hunting rifle. Don't think he missed a bird all day, and we bagged a goodly number. Other times we just lazed on the porch. Sittin' and sippin' and spittin'."

"How about McNeil—or McNamar—whatever he's called? What happened to him?"

"He got back to town just a couple of weeks after Ann passed. He was all broke up about it. His true love, gone forever. He lingered about for a few months, but then he up and disappeared one day. I don't think he could bear to be here no more, not without Ann by his side."

Rutledge continued limping along, but he was silent, as if trying to puzzle something out. "It's a funny thing," he said at last, "you two showing up and asking these questions about Lincoln and such. Not a month ago there was another fellow who did just the same."

"What other fellow?" I asked, trying to conceal my interest.

"Never met him before, but he told me his name three times. Said he wanted to make sure I remembered it. The fellow's name was . . . Simeon Francis."

Martha and I exchanged wide-eyed glances. In our discussions of what had appeared in the papers, Simeon hadn't said a word. What business could the Whig publisher have seeking out such an avowed enemy of Lincoln's in the midst of the election season? We'd been suspicious all this time about his rival publisher, Weber. But was it possible that *Simeon* had been the one tormenting Lincoln? That he was S.G.? Even the initials matched almost perfectly.

I dropped back to where Martha was walking and voiced my suspicions to her under my breath. "I can't believe it," she whispered. "Simeon a turncoat?"

"I agree, but what other reason could he have for coming to talk to Rutledge?"

"I don't . . . wait a minute!"

Martha took a few quick steps and caught up with Rutledge. "The burying ground is just up there, over that ridge," he said, indicating in front of us.

"Very well. This man who came to visit you, Simeon Francis. Did you get a good look at him?"

"Yes, ma'am. He must of been standing in my cooperage, right where you were, for an hour or more."

"What did he look like?"

"Don't know. Average build. Smartly dressed, clean-shaven, black eyes."

"Was his shirt covered with printer ink stains?" Martha asked.

"Was he shaped a bit like an egg, round in the middle, with a weak chin and an irregular growth of whiskers?" I added.

Rutledge came to a halt and looked back and forth between us in confusion. "I just told you," he said. "Average build and clean-shaven. Definitely a printer, though, because of his hands. His shirt was laundered clean, but his hands were dotted with ink. In my line you always notice a man's hands."

"I imagine you do," said Martha. Her eyes were sparkling. She pulled me back as Rutledge continued to lead the way toward the cemetery.

"It was George Weber," Martha hissed into my ear.

"What?"

"Weber coming to New Salem to ask about Lincoln's past. And giving his name as 'Simeon Francis'—and repeating it three times to make sure Mr. Rutledge here remembered."

I laughed out loud. Plainly we hadn't been the first people from Springfield with the idea of coming to New Salem to poke around under the name of our opponents.

A few minutes later Rutledge reached the top of the ridge and stopped. We gazed down on a windswept hillside, the long grasses swaying in the breeze. The vibrant prairie, full of muted greens, yellows, and browns, spread out in the distance. About two dozen wooden markers of various sizes stuck up irregularly from the grass immediately in front of us.

Rutledge crutched down the hill a ways and came to a stop in front of a large rectangular slab of wood. It was carved:

James Rutledge
1771–1835

Stuck into the ground next to this marker was a simple wooden cross, about eighteen inches high. It had originally been painted white, but the paint was chipped and peeling.

"Couldn't nobody afford a proper headboard for Ann," said John Rutledge quietly, his head bowed. "But I know she's there. And the Good Lord does, too."

"What a beautiful resting place," murmured Martha. Rutledge nodded.

A few minutes later I cleared my throat.

"I'm afraid we should be going," Martha said. "Thank you for sharing Ann's story, Mr. Rutledge. We had a sister pass recently, as well." She fingered the black mourning band on her arm. "Her name was Ann, too, by chance. We know how painful it is."

"Yes, ma'am," said Rutledge. He looked down to the ground.

"I wish I could tell you otherwise, but the pain . . . it don't ever go away."

As we cantered back toward Springfield, Martha and I talked over what it all meant—Ann Rutledge's tragic death, John Rutledge's grudge, Lincoln's debt, Weber's prying, and everything else we'd learned. There seemed to be plenty of aspects of his former life in New Salem that could be haunting Lincoln. But, the signature notwithstanding, a ghost wasn't writing those letters threatening Lincoln. And a ghost hadn't shot Early on Quality Hill, or menaced us on our walk, or written the taunting note. A man was responsible, and somehow we were closer to figuring out who.

The daylight started to fade. As we neared Springfield, we saw a speck on the road ahead. The speck was advancing on us, and as we rode forward it waved its arms helter-skelter.

"Isn't that Hay?" asked Martha, when the speck had gotten to within a hundred yards and slowly resolved into Lincoln's bedraggled office boy.

"Where have you been?" Hay shouted, running up to us. "Lincoln's been looking frantically for you. For hours."

"Why ever?"

"It's terrible. He's devastated." Hay gulped. "Margaret Owens is dead."

CHAPTER 26

Hay led us to Henry Owens's apothecary on the square. He and his sister lived on the second floor, above the store. The street in front of the apothecary was full of men and women conversing in low tones. We spotted the hulking form of Sheriff Hutchason and went up to him.

"Horrible business," he said, nodding at us.

"What happened?" I asked. "Martha and I just returned from a ride."

Hutchason motioned for us to follow him away from the mass of people toward the capitol construction site in the center of the square. "Her brother found her body in bed shortly after noon," he began in a low rumble. Martha put her hand to her mouth. "It's a mystery how it happened. Owens said she hadn't been ill recently."

"I saw her a couple of days ago," I said, "with Lincoln at Hoffman's Row. She looked glowing—never better, actually."

Hutchason nodded somberly. "That's just what Owens told me. Apparently when she woke this morning, she complained of a headache and he mixed a compound for her to take with a glass of brandy. A normal remedy, he says, a tonic he's dispensed to her many times in the past. The poor fellow was beside himself. He's sleeping now. Doctor Warren forced enough whiskey down his throat to knock out five men."

Martha and I locked eyes and I could tell we had the same thought. Salem's Ghost had warned Lincoln this very morning that judgment day was at hand. "Have you considered the possibility of foul play?" I asked the sheriff.

"Are you saying Owens killed his sister?"

Was I? I had no reason to suspect ill feeling between brother and sister. On the other hand, several circumstances fingered Owens as a potential suspect in the killing of Early. And here he was again in close proximity to an unexplained death.

To Hutchason, I said, "Surely it's possible something in the compound he gave her proved fatal. How did it get there? The most likely explanation is that the apothecary himself put it in."

"I suppose he might have added a deadly ingredient by mistake," said Hutchason. "These are cloudy, mysterious compounds we're talking about."

"He's been practicing his art for many years," said Martha. "Would he really have added a fatal ingredient by accident?"

"I'd like to examine the bedroom where she died," I said.

Hutchason looked uncomfortable. "The, er, corpse is still there. Higgins isn't able to collect it until tomorrow. And as for Lincoln, have you seen him yet?"

"We came straight here when we heard the news from Hay."

"I think you should find him, talk to him, before you do anything else. The last I saw him . . . He's in a bad way."

"Let's go," said Martha.

"I'd better go alone," I said. "I'll escort Martha back to your house first. But later, after I've talked to Lincoln, I want to examine the bedroom."

Hutchason and Martha reluctantly agreed to this plan. After depositing Martha at the Hutchason house and ensuring she locked the door behind her, I began to search for Lincoln. I started with our lodgings and clambered up the back stairs from my storeroom, calling out his name. But our bed was empty, and Hurst, lounging in his, said he hadn't seen Lincoln all day. Next I tried Hoffman's Row. It was dark outside now, but no candle burned in the window of No. 4. Nonetheless, I mounted the stairs and, finding the office door unlocked, pushed it open.

"Lincoln?" I called out.

The room was silent and inky. The still air tasted stale. Nothing moved. I was about to head out, wondering where to search for Lincoln next, when my eye caught the faintest hint of movement from the far, dark corner of the room.

"Lincoln?" I shouted again.

There was still no answer, but as I took a few steps in that direction I realized it was him, or at least his form. He was sitting in the corner, his arms hugging his knobby knees to his chest. His buffalo robe was gathered around his shoulders and cinched in front. His jaw was clenched and the skin covering his cheekbones was drawn so tight it looked like a hole might be ripped in his skin at any moment. His eyes, open but lifeless, stared straight ahead.

He did not move or react in any way as I approached, and for an awful moment I thought he, too, might be dead. But then I perceived his chest rising and falling with shallow breaths.

I took a seat on the floor beside him. Still he did not acknowledge my presence.

"I've come from the apothecary," I said quietly. "I talked to Hutchason. I . . . oh, Lincoln, I'm ever so sorry."

Nothing.

"She was a good person, Lincoln. A kind person. She's in heaven now." I didn't know if I believed this last part, but what else was there to say? What else was there to say to a man who'd lost his mother, brother, sister, first love, and now another woman he had thought could make him happy?

Nothing.

"I'm going to stay with you for a spell. I don't think you should be alone, not at a time like this."

I sat with my back against the wall, about five feet over from Lincoln. I breathed slowly and deeply, trying to convey to my friend, I suppose, the importance of continuing to breathe. I'd seen Lincoln laid low before; the nervous burdens of daily life sometimes weighed on him more heavily than they weighed on the normal man. But I'd never seen him in such an enervated state.

Some amount of time passed. In the darkened, motionless room, it was impossible to tell how much.

Eventually he spoke, in a low monotone. "What's the purpose of it all, Joshua?"

I thought about this, a dozen different answers parading though my mind. Finally, I offered: " 'The great object of life is sensation—to feel that we exist, even though in pain.' "

He expelled his breath, something like a weak laugh. "Byron? You chose Byron? Better than *Macbeth*, I suppose."

"Life's a tale told by an idiot, as well," I said. "Certainly it is today."

He nodded in the darkness. "Where were you this afternoon?"

"Martha and I went for a ride." I'd thought about how to answer this question while waiting beside him; I couldn't imagine telling him we'd been to New Salem, not in these circumstances. "It was a fine day and we went further than we intended. Hay said you'd been looking for me. I'm sorry I wasn't here."

"It wouldn't have mattered."

"Perhaps not. Still, I wish I'd been here."

Lincoln shrugged.

I wanted to keep him talking, but I struggled with what to say next. *I know you'll miss her? There'll be another one? Death comes when Death wants?* It all seemed inadequate.

"It's my fault," he said suddenly.

"*Yours?* How can you think that?"

"On our last walk—that evening you were here—the question of our future arose and I . . . hesitated. I wasn't sure. I think she took it as rejection."

"You think she took her own life?" I hadn't considered this possibility.

"It's obvious, isn't it? What other explanation could there be?"

"I talked to Sheriff Hutchason. He's planning a full investigation. Maybe it was the man who shot over our heads the other day. The man who left the threatening letter." *I know who you walk with.*

"Then it's certainly my fault," he said in a low, agonized voice.

"It's not your fault, Lincoln. Whatever happened, it's not your fault."

Lincoln was silent for several minutes. Then he mumbled, "It doesn't matter. Nothing does," and pulled himself into an even tighter ball. He lapsed back into silence. More time passed.

"Will you come back to our room with me now?" I said at last.

"No."

"Will you come back later this evening?"

He paused. "I suppose so. At some point."

"Promise me you will," I said earnestly. "Promise me, or I'll start reciting everything Byron and Shakespeare ever said about life and death. And Wordsworth, too, for good measure."

Lincoln gave a short cry, a mixture of anguish and laughter. "That's quite a threat."

"I know it is. So promise me."

He paused again and sighed. "I promise."

"Good. I'll leave you, then. If there's truly nothing I can do for you . . ."

"There's not."

I put my hand on his shoulder and rested it there. His shirt was clammy. After a while he nodded and I climbed to my feet. As I walked toward the door, I spied a small letter-opening knife lying on his table in the center of the room. Without breaking stride, I slid the knife into my pocket.

Outside on the dark streets I breathed deeply, glad for fresh air after several hours spent inside the close office. I strode across the green to the apothecary. The crowd outside had dispersed and now only Hutchason remained, standing guard beside the door.

"I was about to give up on you," he said. "Did you find Lincoln?"

I nodded and gestured we should proceed inside.

"It's pretty gruesome. You sure you want to see it?"

"I need to do something that might help figure out what happened. For Lincoln's sake."

Hutchason led me through the apothecary and up the stairs. I struck a candle and followed behind him. On the second floor was a small landing with two closed doors leading off. "Owens is asleep in there," Hutchason whispered, pointing at one of the doors before heading toward the other. "Steel yourself."

In truth, nothing could have prepared me for the horror waiting behind the other door. Miss Owens's corpse lay atop her bedclothes. She was dressed all in white, with a long, linen nightgown, adorned with a few ruffles and a frilled neck, and a simple white nightcap covering her hair and tied around her neck.

But if the clothing on the corpse was commonplace, her person was anything but. Miss Owens's body was arched horribly, such that only the back of her head and her two heels touched the bed; the rest of the body formed a long, frozen arc. Her arms were rigid at her side. Her face was bright red. The muscles of her face were contorted, her lips were fixed in what seemed like a wild grin, and her eyes bulged out of their sockets.

"Dear God!" I shouted.

Hutchason nodded somberly. "The body's been frozen in this pose from the moment I first saw her. Her face was even redder originally."

"What could have caused it? Did Owens have any ideas?"

"I couldn't get two words of sense out of him after he showed me the body. Not that you can blame him."

"Have you ever seen a corpse like this?"

Hutchason shook his head. "Owens told me he gave her a glass of brandy and the normal draught he's always dispensed to her for her bouts of illness."

"She must have ingested some foreign substance, some poison, to cause these symptoms. That's not a natural way to die. Have you examined the drinking glass?"

Both of us looked at the small wooden table beside Miss Owens's bed. It was bare.

"I haven't seen it," said the sheriff. "I assumed Owens took it back after she drank it down."

I walked up to the bed and, without touching the dead body, felt around in the bedclothes. Nothing. Then I lowered my candle and looked on either side of the bed. Finally, on my knees, and taking care that the candle didn't set the bed on fire, I peered beneath the bedframe. I saw the glint of a small wine glass that had rolled partway under and reached for it.

I scrambled to my feet and handed the glass to Hutchason, who examined it with interest. There was a tiny residue of brown liquid clinging to the bottom of the glass. Hutchason sniffed it carefully, considered, then put his little finger inside the glass and brought it to his tongue. He winced and handed the glass to me. I repeated the examination and put a tiny drop of the liquid on my tongue.

"Bitter!" I exclaimed, and Hutchason nodded.

"The lady was poisoned," announced Hutchason. "Whether accidentally or on purpose—that's the unanswered question."

"And by whom," I added, thinking of Lincoln's suggestion she had done the deed herself. But who in their right mind would choose such a horrible way to die? "Owens, surely, is the most likely suspect," I continued. "He's admitted he gave her the draught. But why would he kill his own sister—and in such a horrendous way?"

Hutchason just shook his head.

When I returned to our lodgings, Hurst and Herndon were already snoring in their bed. Our bed was empty. I lay down, my body tense, waiting for Lincoln's return. I tried without success to drift off.

So I lay wide awake and listened to the summer insects outside our open window cry and sing through the night. Well after midnight, I finally heard heavy, familiar footsteps ascending the back stairs. When, at last, Lincoln lowered his body into bed next to me, I exhaled a long, low breath.

CHAPTER 27

The following days were at once dreamlike and altogether too real.

Lincoln was plunged into a deep melancholy from which there seemed no hope of rescue. He spent his days trudging silently up and down the street, his head down, his back bent nearly in half, his hands fidgeting pensively behind his back. He wore all black, from his stovepipe hat to his scuffed leather shoes. He was a study in sadness, a slow-moving shuffle of mourning. The citizenry of Springfield took to scattering from his path, mumbling excuses and condolences, for they could not bear to witness up close the fresh, searing pain etched on his features.

Lincoln spent his nights next to me in bed, tossing and turning, and often calling out in wrenching sadness from the depths of his sleep. I had not the heart to ask what he saw in his dreams. Every morning when he awoke, his pillow was drenched with sweat.

Together with Herndon, Hay, and Martha, I organized an informal watch on Lincoln to try to prevent him from doing harm to himself. Especially in the first few days, when his distress was at its greatest depth, I worried he might take his own life. I removed the ball from the pistol I'd given him, and I confiscated all sharp objects from any place I thought he might frequent. We set up a rotating schedule of persons to follow him each day, at an unobtrusive distance. But the arrangement proved unnecessary, as Lincoln never seemed to wander very far from the town square, returning always to gaze forlornly at the apothecary where Miss Owens had breathed her last.

Lincoln's suffering was confined, held tight within his breast, and shared with no one, not even me. After that first night at Hoffman's Row, he had not said more than a dozen words to me and none, as far as I knew, to anyone else. He had not once spoken Miss Owens's name aloud.

Meanwhile, the election campaign entered its final sprint, as voting was to take place exactly one week after Miss Owens's death. Out of respect for the grieving Lincoln, all of the candidates reached an unspoken agreement not to discuss politics within his presence. Lincoln—and Lincoln alone—wrapped in his profound thoughts and indifferent to transpiring events, was ignorant of the ongoing banality and brutality of politics.

But in all other places in town, indeed all around the county, the raucous campaign careened toward its uncertain conclusion. Dinners were thrown, rallies were staged, speeches made, debates held, parades organized. Candidates schemed and connived. Voters gladly accepted favors and asked for more. Inducements flowed as freely as whiskey and quite often in the *form* of whiskey. The vote of every last man with the franchise was courted—propositioned, even—with a lascivious wantonness, a naked lust, which would have made a New Orleans madam blush.

Lincoln's own reelection to the state legislature had seemed a foregone conclusion before Miss Owens's death, and I figured that, if anything, the natural sympathy his current condition engendered would help his cause at the polls. As for Stuart's campaign against the detested Douglas for Congress, Stuart's side made do without the aid of their principal speechmaker. Ninian Edwards and other Whigs pitched in with their own efforts, and the popular consensus was that the race remained on the knife's edge, with Stuart perhaps carrying a slight advantage.

Sheriff Hutchason kept me apprised of the investigation into the bitter substance that had felled Miss Owens.

"Strychnine," Hutchason told me confidently one morning on the green, several days after Miss Owens died.

"How do you know?"

"We found four substances in the apothecary having a similar taste, and Warren tried them out one by one on stray dogs he found around town. The doc was quite eager to do so, in point of fact. The progress of medical knowledge and all that.

"Anyway, Warren said when he fed a good quantity of strychnine to a dog, it reacted just the way Miss Owens must have. About fifteen minutes after ingesting the substance, the poor beast started having muscle spasms in waves. Eventually it threw the whole body into convulsion. The dog's face went red as it gasped for breath. The lips peeled back, the eyes bulged. Finally, after three or four waves of attack, the dog expired from asphyxiation, with its body arched frozen from head to toe. Just as we found Miss Owens."

I felt sick to my stomach. "What a horrible way to die."

"I know it," agreed Hutchason, looking very grave.

"And Owens actually carries strychnine in his apothecary?" I said.

"He tells me he dispenses it for persons under physical strain. He says it can have the effect of calming them. But in low doses only. Never more than a fiftieth of a grain per dispensation. He says he thinks two full grains are missing from his vial."

"Could he have put them into her brandy by accident?"

"He swears up and down it would have been impossible. He says he didn't give her any strychnine that morning. His standard female remedy is different. Something involving extract of elderflower seeds."

"Then how did the strychnine get in her drink?" I asked. "I tell you, I never trusted Owens, what with all his potions and incantations."

"If you'd seen his horror upon discovering her body," said Hutchason, "you'd know it wasn't him. Owens says he left his shop at midmorning that day to make a delivery. Perhaps someone slipped in while he was gone and poisoned the drink. Though that doesn't tell us why she didn't notice the bitter taste as she was drinking it."

Unless she drank the poison intentionally, I thought. Aloud I said, "Have you found anyone who saw anything that morning?"

Hutchason shook his head.

On a typical day, I would have had a good view of the front of the apothecary from behind the counter of my store. But it hadn't been a typical day, and I hadn't been behind my counter.

Two men were responsible for my absence: George Weber, for printing Salem's Ghost's letter that very morning, and Stephen Douglas, for urging Martha and me to travel to New Salem. I started with Weber.

"What do you want this time?" the newspaperman barked when I barged through his door.

"Why did you print that letter on Monday?" I demanded.

"We've been through this. It was placed on my doorstep that morning. My practice, as a newsman, is to deliver the news as quickly as possible. Verily, that is the essence of the vocation."

"Did you know Miss Owens was going to be attacked that very day?"

Weber recoiled. "Miss Owens? Of course not. You can't seriously believe I had something to do with that."

"I'd believe anything about you, Weber. For example, I'd believe you pretended to be Simeon Francis and traveled to New Salem, trying to dig around in Lincoln's past."

The accusation caught Weber short. He swallowed and considered his words before responding. A smile crossed his face. "I'm a newsman. I make no apologies for seeking the news."

"By lying about your identity? By publishing unfounded accusations under false names like 'Salem's Ghost'?"

"By whatever means I find expedient. You ask your friend Francis about his methods sometime."

My encounter with Douglas was no more satisfactory. I grabbed at his arm as he was leaving a rally of Democrats and demanded he explain why he had directed us to New Salem on the morning of Miss Owens's death.

"Why would I possibly want to harm Lincoln's belle right before the election? I know you think me motivated by self-interest, Speed. How would it be in my interest to provoke popular sympathy for my opponent, this week of all weeks?"

Typical for Douglas, the argument was coldhearted but persuasive. I did not have a good reply.

I was still ruminating on this circumstance that afternoon when my store door opened and Sarah Butler walked in. "Good afternoon, Miss Butler," I said, giving a half-bow.

"Good afternoon, Mr. Speed. We haven't had the chance to talk since the evening you came to the tent meeting. I hope it didn't disappoint you."

"To the contrary, I found it most enlightening." In fact, my interest in Miss Butler had dimmed in proportion to the fervor she'd displayed at the wild, ecstatic gathering. "And I've been busy. Most recently, in looking after my friend Mr. Lincoln. I'm sure you heard what happened to Miss Owens."

Miss Butler's eyes turned moist. "Such a tragedy. Preacher Crews held a special meeting last night for us to pray for her soul."

"That was a nice gesture."

"She was a regular at the camp. Very popular. She preached from the platform on several occasions. One time, she and I led the exhortations together."

"Do you have any idea how it could have happened?"

Miss Butler started to speak, then put her hand over her mouth and shook her head. "I can't . . ." she began, but did not continue.

"If you know anything at all, please tell me. I want to get to the bottom of what happened."

"I can't speak ill of the departed," Miss Butler said slowly. "But the last few times I saw Miss Owens, her manner was . . . different. She was quieter, more reserved—and quicker to temper, too. Like she'd experienced some private disappointment she didn't want to share."

I was silent in response. For Lincoln's sake, I found myself not wanting to give any credence to the idea that the lady had been driven to harm herself.

"I need a sack of flour for my mother," added Miss Butler, her voice colder now, "and then I'll be off. I'm afraid I can't tarry today, Mr. Speed." We completed the commercial transaction at arm's length; the special flame, if it had ever burned, had seemingly gone out of our relationship.

On Friday morning, glancing at the glass on my way down to the counter, I decided I needed a trim to look presentable for the following Monday's election day festivities. So when Herndon arrived for his shift at the counter, I headed toward a two-room shack in the run-down part of town, the formal establishment of a free Negro named William de Fleurville. Or, as he was known to all, Billy the Barber.

Billy nodded wisely as I knocked on his door. "Thought I'd be seeing you about now, Mr. Speed," he said in his singsong lilt. "You'll be next, after I finish this one up. I understand you two folks are the best of friends these days."

Billy smiled as he turned back to his barbering chair, and I saw it was occupied by none other than Stephen Douglas.

"A hog in a silk waistcoat is still a hog," I murmured as I took a seat along the wall. "Or, in this case, a piglet."

His scissors in hand, Billy was hovering around Douglas's over-large head, trying to make some sense of his mass of brown curls, and whistling a tune while he worked. Without moving his head, Douglas said, "Speed's still sore from our encounter last weekend, Billy. I think my teeth shed more blood than your blade ever has."

"Someone was telling me about your dispute," said the barber. "White folks sure do like to see blood spill out on the ground, don't they?"

"It does provide a certain thrill," said Douglas with a grin.

"Prepared to lose on Monday?" I asked him.

"It's not going to turn out your way, Speed. I've secured all the votes I need. I'm here because I want to look my best at our victory celebration. What about you, Billy? If you had the vote, who'd you cast for? Myself or Stuart? Democrat or Whig?"

Billy's scissors continued to fly around Douglas's head. "Don't rightly know," he said seriously. "Which of you is most interested in the lot of the Negro?"

Douglas and I exchanged glances. "I'm not sure either one . . ."

"That's the way I figured it," said Billy. "I'll stick to barbering."

Douglas looked back at me and said, with a smirk spread across his face, "Even men without the franchise care first and foremost about what's in it for them. I tell you, Speed, it's all self-interest. The world runs on it, from the highest rank to the lowest. And it's the key to success at the polls, as you'll see next week."

A few moments later Billy finished with Douglas. As the Little Giant climbed down from the chair, he said, "Win or lose on Monday, Speed, the Truett murder trial begins on Wednesday. Will your man be ready?"

"I have no reason to doubt it."

In reality, I had every reason to doubt it, given what I'd seen of Lincoln's condition. His deep melancholy was showing no sign of abating. I wondered whether Judge Thomas would agree to delay the trial.

As if reading my mind, Douglas said, "He'd better be. I was talking to the judge at a Democratic party gathering the other day, and he reminded me of the trial date. He's determined to resolve the case on time. And I stopped by the jail yesterday afternoon to give Truett an update on some Democratic matters. With the wretched condition he's in, I'm sure he won't brook any delay either, even if he has to represent himself in court."

"Miserable little man," I muttered in his wake as I reclined into Billy's chair.

Billy's scissors started to fly around my locks. "When the Almighty gives you such a small bite, like He gave Mr. Douglas," said Billy, "you need a large bark to go with it, or you ain't going nowhere."

"I hesitate to give him credit on any account," I said, "but even Douglas's bite can prove lethal, or nearly so." I held up my bandaged hand.

Billy smiled. "I reckon he was merely marking his territory."

"I wonder how much more he's capable of, though."

"What're you saying?"

"I've been thinking about whether Douglas is capable of murder. We've had two murders in the past month here in town, both unexplained. Both of the victims were associated with Lincoln, which makes Lincoln's biggest enemy the likeliest suspect, in my view."

Billy did not respond to this, instead working away at my hair and whistling contentedly. But when the barber finished twenty minutes later and accepted a half-dime as payment, he looked me up and down and dispensed a final piece of wisdom.

"You truly think Mr. Douglas is Mr. Lincoln's biggest enemy?" asked Billy.

"I do."

"Then you'd better be thinking a whole lot harder."

CHAPTER 28

E lection day arrived.

Unlike most neighboring states, Illinois allotted only a single day for voting. In addition, the paucity of men who could be depended on to display the neutrality and sobriety required for the position of election clerk reduced the number of polling places to no more than a handful in each county. A single location on the Springfield green would be open to register the votes of the free, white, male residents of our town and the surrounding farms. It was guaranteed to be thronged the entire day.

All of this put great emphasis on party organization, and the Whigs had arranged to muster on Ninian Edwards's lawn on Quality Hill at seven AM sharp. I gave no thought to the store. No establishment other than the taverns would be open today; no business would be conducted. Every man was consumed with the election and nothing else.

Every man but one, that is. I woke Lincoln on my way out the door to remind him of the day and ask if he wanted to join me. He blinked once, shook his head, and turned over in bed.

It was a hot, sweltering morning, and my shirt was clinging to my chest by the time I'd climbed to the top of Quality Hill. Already several dozen Whigs were milling around on the manicured lawns, enjoying the breakfast Mrs. Edwards had laid out and the open busthead cask of whiskey Mr. Edwards had seen fit to provide. Another few men came up every minute. The broad stars and stripes, displayed with pride, fluttered in the breeze from a tall flag-pole. Meanwhile, a five-piece brass band played up some lively airs, among them "Yankee Doodle Dandy," with great spirit.

When the crowd was fully mustered and well watered, Edwards climbed atop a chair and shouted out final instructions. Then our parade formed up: banner carriers up front; followed by the band; followed by Edwards and Stuart, two of our principal standard-bearers, on horseback; followed by the veterans of the several Indian wars who retained military uniforms into which they could still fit; followed by the Whig regulars. I was in this last group, and I estimated our overall strength at 150 men or more.

Edwards gave the signal and the two cannons flanking his grand house exploded with concussive *booms*. The Whig army gave a great cheer and began streaming down the hillside.

"Hurrah for the Whigs!" we chanted as we marched. "Hurrah for the Whigs! Down with the damned Democrats! Lick them! Kick them! Drive them away! Democrats to hell! Whigs do well! Hurrah for the Whigs! Hurrah for Stuart! Hurrah for Edwards! Hurrah for Lincoln!" And so on, as we *hurrah*ed every Whig on the ballot.

As we approached the polling place on the town green, a sign of serious trouble with our finely wrought plan emerged.

"The goddamn Democrats have beaten us to it!" exclaimed the man next to me.

They had. A motley collection of Democrats had taken up residence at the sole entrance to the sole polling station. The Democratic banner was held high, the Democratic band played loudly, and several hundred Democratic men in matching straw boater hats swarmed tightly around, forming a stout human barrier against any and all Whig voters.

Undaunted, we continued our march toward the poll. The Democrats brayed and jeered as we approached. "Stick to your positions, boys!" yelled the Democratic organizers. "Don't give them a foot! Don't give them an inch! Don't let the Whigs humbug the people of Springfield. Don't let a single, damned Whig anywhere near the poll."

The Whigs marched straight into the battle, crying loudly. The bands came face to face, trumpet to trumpet, flute to flute, each playing at the top of their instruments to try to drown out the other. Men from the warring camps yelled back and forth. The noise and confusion became intense. Some men imitated the barking of dogs, others the roaring of bulls, all making as much noise as they could. It was a raucous, cacophonous medley.

Whigs pushed against Democrats, trying to reach the polls; Democrats pushed back, defending their territory. The crowd swayed back and forth in ecstatic waves of emotion. Then, suddenly—I couldn't see which side was the *casus belli*—a pitched battle broke out.

The town green was soon covered by some of the bloodiest fighting I have ever seen. Beneath their coats, men were armed with dirks, Bowie knives, clubs, and all other kinds of tools the occasion might require. I laid hands on several Democrats, then barely dodged another Democrat swinging a handkerchief with a large stone nestled inside. The fighting continued all around me. It was a screaming, shouting, punching, kicking melee. Not a few eyes were blackened and not a few noses bloodied.

Eventually the combatants tired of fighting their neighbors and, one by one, flung themselves down on the ground in exhaustion. The active battle sputtered, flickered, and winked out. Sweat and blood mingled on many faces. A relative quiet prevailed, although the competing bands continued to play on. Each side tended to their wounded. Eventually most men were back up on their feet, staggering around to regain their equilibrium, a number chugging whiskey to aid their recovery. Many men had their coats torn off, and several were minus their hats as well.

The poll had not yet opened.

On the sound of the church bells pealing nine, it did. All at once, the two sides formed up again and rushed forward, desperately seeking to claim the battlefield position of prime strategic importance: the single set of steps leading up to the voting platform.

All votes were recorded *viva voce*—that is, by voice. Illinois had used the "ballot" system in years past, but it had proven to be too susceptible to fraud and abuse, most notably by party men who adopted the practice of handing out preprinted ballots featuring only their side's candidates to men unable to read. After some partisan controversy—it was not immediately clear which side had more illiterate voters susceptible to being tricked by sharp ballot tactics—the legislature had repealed the ballot and reverted to *viva voce*, the system used by most Western states and the one generally considered to be most appropriate for Western elections.

Jones, the elections clerk, had erected a raised wooden platform in the middle of the town green adjacent to the rising walls of the new capitol building. Voters waited, wrestling for position, at the bottom of the platform until Jones called them up one by one. When a new voter arrived, Jones recorded in turn the voter's choice of candidates for each of the positions being voted upon. In addition to U.S. representative and state legislature, a slew of other county and city positions were at stake today. It was a slow, tedious process and the line of waiting voters soon stretched across the green and far down the street.

Poll watchers from each party lingered at the edge of the platform to hear how each man voted. Some voters tried to avoid accountability by whispering their selections to Jones, but the clerk adopted a practice—whether from being hard of hearing or merely pretending to be, it was never clear—of repeating in a loud voice any vote conveyed to him by whisper. By this method, the parties' poll watchers were able to keep an accurate running tally of where the Springfield vote stood. They could also ensure that men who had accepted favors in exchange for their votes did not cheat them.

By midmorning, the thermometer surely registered ninety degrees in the shade. Every man who waited to vote took a full sweat for it.

Stephen Douglas and George Weber periodically materialized to confer in conspiratorial whispers with the Democratic poll watcher. If Douglas felt an ounce less than certain about his election by the people, his proud face gave no hint of it. At one point when Douglas stood at the base of the platform, Sheriff Hutchason arrived with his prisoner. Douglas affected to have his back turned as

Truett, his hands bound together by rope, ascended the stage to cast his vote.

As the voting proceeded, one contingent of Whigs remained near the entrance to the platform, trying to hustle as many of our partisans as possible up the steps. Others manned the nearby Whig barbecue. A bonfire had been built, and a whole ox was roasting on a thick iron spit. Everyone who could certify he'd voted the straight Whig ticket was welcome to as much roast beef as he could eat and as much whiskey and hard cider as he could drink.

In the event any voters remained undecided, the Whigs had also set up a tall stump not far from the election clerk's stand. Throughout the day, a rotating cast of Whigs raised our candidates above the most superior class of mankind and sunk the Democratic candidates below the lowest of humankind, to whom the Devil himself would be virtuous, all at a pitch approximating an Indian war cry.

I myself took a shift on the stump at three o'clock in the afternoon, immediately after I managed to fight my way through the crowd and cast my own vote. When I climbed down from the stump an hour later, I found myself hoarse of voice and drenched through with sweat. My fellow Whigs clustered near the bottom of the stump, offering me much-needed refreshment and congratulating me for having persevered through one of the hottest parts of the day.

From the top of the stump I saw Preacher Crews arrive, surrounded by a coterie of female exhorters in long gowns. The women waited patiently at the bottom of the stage as he strode up to cast his vote. One of the women with the preacher was Miss Butler, and I kept my eyes trained on her back to see if she would turn around and acknowledge me. But she never did.

A little while later I saw Thomas Lincoln and John Johnston creeping tentatively along the edge of the green like ants arriving late at a picnic. They approached the Democratic barbecue, and I could read from the hand gestures each made that the man turning three suckling pigs on the spit indicated they needed to vote first before partaking in the feast. Johnston and Lincoln huddled together and evidently decided that expressing a civic opinion was too high a price to pay for a solid meal, and they slunk away, unvoted and unfed.

As I looked around the field, now littered with men in various stages of exhaustion and intoxication, I wondered if *he* was out there. *Salem's Ghost.* Was he, even at this very minute, staring at me, marking me as his next victim? I reached, involuntarily, for my pocket to check that my pistol was still close at hand. Was he haunting the front of A.Y. Ellis & Co., or perhaps Hoffman's Row, waiting for Lincoln to make his next public appearance, so that he could bring down the biggest target of all? *Where was he? Who was he?* I had no answers, and the questions swirled around inside my head with such a frenzy that I began to feel dizzy.

Around seven o'clock in the evening I checked the tallies being maintained by the Whig and Democratic vote counters at the foot of the stage. Their numbers were in close agreement, and Lincoln's reelection seemed assured. The contest in Springfield between Douglas and Stuart was just as close as predicted. And since the Third District stretched all the way up to Chicago and was being conducted at several dozen polling stations in that vast territory, it would be several days until the final tally in that contest was known.

I had not seen Lincoln all day. I found him at Hoffman's Row, dressed in his court clothes, reading over some legal papers. It was the first time since Miss Owens's death he had done either.

"Well?" he asked when I entered.

"It's been quite a battle."

"I've heard as much through the windows."

"You're doing well. Stuart and Douglas are neck and neck."

Lincoln nodded but continued reading his papers.

After a few moments of silence, I asked, "What are you doing?"

"Getting ready for Truett's trial."

"Good. I wasn't sure . . ."

Lincoln looked up. On his face I saw a clear manifestation of the pain he'd held within his breast over the past week.

"I made a commitment to Truett," he said, "which I'm obliged to keep." He seemed as if he were going to say more, about Miss

Owens perhaps, but instead he shut his mouth and looked down again.

"If you're going to vote, now's probably a good time."

Lincoln got to the end of a page and put his papers down. He rose and settled his stovepipe hat atop his head. As we left Hoffman's Row and headed for the election platform, I tried to stick closely to his left side, in order that he not glance across at the quiet apothecary on the other side of the square. But his eyes remained straight ahead and focused on the poll.

The town green was quieter now than it had been this morning, in the midst of the pitched battle, but the parties' banners still flew and their bands still played. All at once people started to notice Lincoln's distinctive presence striding across the green, and they fell silent. Several took off their hats as we walked by. By the time we reached the platform, an eerie quiet had descended upon the entire scene.

Several dozen men still waited their turn at the bottom of the steps, but to a man they stood aside as Lincoln approached. He touched the brim of his hat in silent thanks.

"Next!" cried Jones hoarsely from atop the stage.

"Abraham Lincoln," said Lincoln as he ascended.

Jones showed no reaction but rather carefully scrawled Lincoln's name in his book. "Your vote for the Third Congressional District? The candidates are Mr. Douglas and Mr. Stuart."

"Stuart," said Lincoln in a loud, clear voice. Earlier in the day this would have unleashed a great swell of cheers, but in the suddenly subdued crowd it produced only a small ripple of scattered applause.

"Your vote for representative to the Illinois Legislature from Sangamon County? The candidates are—"

"I believe I know the candidates," said Lincoln. A faint smile played on his lips. "I vote for the man of great height and low intellect. I reckon he's worth returning for another term. Lincoln."

CHAPTER 29

The next morning Lincoln reached across and stopped me as I was rolling out of our bed. "How did Margaret die?" he asked.

I looked at him with surprise. "You don't know?"

"I asked the sheriff that day, right after he'd given me the awful news, and he said it was too soon to know anything. Just that she was gone forever. After that . . . well, after that I fell into an abyss."

"Are you sure you want to know?"

"Tell me."

I explained the sheriff's conclusion that Miss Owens had swallowed a fatal dose of strychnine in the restorative concoction Owens had prepared for her. Lincoln looked very grave, and for a moment I thought he was going to fall back into his abyss. But then he gathered himself.

"Someone ingesting strychnine," he said, "would suffer seizures before they died, wouldn't they?"

"The sheriff said they would, yes." I hoped mightily Lincoln wouldn't ask about the condition of Miss Owens's body in death; the horrible image of her arched, frozen body was burned into my memory, and I was afraid of what it would do to his.

Lincoln was out of bed now, and he shook his head sorrowfully. "The same thing happened to Ann Rutledge," he said quietly.

"I don't understand—I thought it was brain fever that killed her."

"It was, but she also suffered seizures. Caused by the fever. She had a particularly violent one the last time I visited her bedside. It was terrible to see—her body writhing on top of her bedclothes, without any control. And it was exhausting for her as well. Death almost came as a relief, after how she suffered."

Lincoln reached into the pocket of his coat, still lying on the floor from last night, and pulled out a slender volume. "And then there's this."

I took the book from his hands and saw that it was a book of poetry by Robert Burns. "It was on my table at Hoffman's Row when I returned for the first time, yesterday," he explained.

"What was it doing there?"

Lincoln's eyes were hooded and his face was drawn. "All I know is that I didn't leave it there. He's my favorite poet, but I don't own this particular volume. So someone had broken into my office again."

"Was anything else disturbed?"

"Not that I could find."

"Why would someone break into your office and leave that book?"

Lincoln shook his head, wordlessly. But an explanation immediately occurred to me. It was a message of some sort.

I thought some more. "Didn't you once tell me that Miss Rutledge enjoyed Burns as well?"

Lincoln nodded.

"What are you going to do?" I asked.

"What can I do? Prepare for Truett's trial, as best I can. Nothing's going to bring back Miss Owens—or Miss Rutledge." He sighed. "If you want to be of help, will you talk to Truett at the jail cell? I'm going to be busy at Hoffman's Row all day, writing out my opening speech and preparing my witness examinations."

"Certainly. About what?"

"Ask him about Miss Owens. Whether they knew each other well, or had any other connection—beyond both knowing me, that is. It stands to reason that Early's death and Miss Owens's may be connected in some way. Also, see if Truett has any explanation for his gun being found by the sheriff on Quality Hill. I've never gotten a straight answer from him on that."

We agreed to meet at Hoffman's Row later in the day. While I dressed, Lincoln dug through his clothes chest. At the bottom he found an old frockcoat. He ripped out the black silk lining and tore it into several strips. Finally he got the size he wanted and carefully tied it around his right forearm. Then he nodded somberly and, without a word to me, walked from the room.

When I got out to the square a half hour later, I was confronted with the sorry remains of election day. The town green was littered with whiskey bottles, torn campaign placards, and discarded hats. A workman had just shown up to hammer apart Jones's polling platform. Several men had been too intoxicated to make it home at the end of the long, hot day of electioneering and drinking (not necessarily in that order) and their sleeping forms were scattered about the green, their clothes covered with dirt and grime.

One misbegotten Democrat—his straw hat gave away his affiliation—was sitting with his back leaned against the low capitol walls. He had a whiskey bottle in one hand, which was held not far from his partially opened mouth, and he was snoring loudly. Evidently he had fallen asleep mid-drink.

I passed few conscious men on my way over to the jail. The town was quiet, subdued, still recovering from the turmoil of election day. But when I let myself through the gate into Hutchason's backyard, I found two men in intense discussion. Truett was standing inside his cell by the door, his hands clinging to the bars, talking with animation to Doctor Warren, who stood outside the jail in a defiant posture.

"What's all this?" I asked as I approached.

"We're trying to fix the terms of my insurance policy," said Truett. His physical appearance was, if anything, even worse than the last time I'd seen him. His face, hands, and clothes were streaked with dirt, and I sensed at once an unpleasant odor that got stronger as I approached the cell.

"I don't understand."

"That's because your life isn't in jeopardy this week," he retorted. "I know you'll say I can trust Lincoln to save it by proving my innocence, but you'll pardon me if I'm not prepared to rest on your assurance. Hence Doctor Warren." He gestured toward the medical man.

"You have legal skills as well, Doctor?" I asked.

Warren gave me a sour expression and tugged on his long white beard. "No. Medical ones, of course."

"And how will those help you," I said, turning back to the prisoner, "in the event, however unlikely, you're convicted and sentenced to death?"

It was Warren who answered. "Because I intend to cut him down from the gallows and bring him back to life. If he agrees to my price, that is."

I started to laugh until, looking back and forth between the two men, I realized both were deadly serious.

"How ever?" I asked.

Warren glanced at the Hutchason house, which still appeared to be slumbering. "If I tell you," he said, in a quieter voice, "will you promise most profoundly not to tell the sheriff or the judge or anyone?"

My curiosity won the battle with my common sense. "I suppose."

"I have been experimenting, these past few months, with the effects of galvanic batteries. With the amazing effects of such batteries, I should say. These batteries harness the *electrical* force, including the force of life operating inside your body to move your limbs, power your thoughts, and so on. Through my study and experimentation, I've discovered galvanic batteries possess the power to give life where another has taken it away."

"Impossible!"

"I have been lately experimenting with my batteries on several dogs," continued Warren, his face glowing with excitement as he rose to his subject. "When I began each experiment, the dogs were, I assure you, very much dead. But when I attached two electrical leads to the dog's body and connected the other end of the leads to my battery, the bodies started moving around. They became reanimated. Once, a dog even started getting back on its feet." He spread out his arms with a flourish. "As I said, I have harnessed the electrical force that powers life."

Listening to Warren, I thought back to Sheriff Hutchason's discussion of the doctor's eagerness to conduct his strychnine experiments on the town's stray dogs. Evidently Warren had been trying to mimic the role of the Almighty in both directions on the unfortunate strays—taking life and trying to restore it.

Turning to Truett, I said, "And you actually believe this might work?"

"Right now I believe in anything having the potential to prolong my life," he said. "You and Lincoln tell me Lincoln's words in the courtroom will do the trick. Doctor Warren here says his scientific knowledge will do so." Truett shrugged. "I don't know which of you is correct. When you're in my position, you want to pick as many tickets as you can." He turned back to Warren. "I'll give you seventy-five dollars in hard currency to perform your procedure, if the need arises."

"Five hundred," replied Warren.

"Five hundred? Outrageous! One hundred dollars. That's my best offer."

"You don't think your own life is worth five hundred dollars, Truett? If you don't think yourself that valuable, I'm not going to waste my skills on you. Four-fifty."

The men haggled back and forth for another few minutes before coming to a bargain at 275 dollars in gold coins, payable by Truett after his resuscitation by Warren. "But remember," said Warren, "when the hangman slips the noose around your neck and prepares to open the trapdoor, *lean forward*. This is very important. Lean forward, so your neck is not broken when you fall. My battery can restore life, but I'm afraid it can do nothing for a broken neck."

"What happens," I asked, "if your effort at resuscitation fails?"

"Impossible," said Warren. "It will not fail."

"So you take nothing if you don't bring him back from the dead?"

"That seems fair," said Truett.

"Certainly not." Warren pulled on his beard. "But I do agree I shouldn't receive my full fee in the unlikely event of failure. If it fails, you shall pay me one hundred dollars in gold coins."

Truett beat me to it. "If it fails, I shall be in no condition to pay you any amount," he said, a perverse grin lighting up his dirt-encrusted face.

"Ah." The doctor paused. "I suppose you are correct. Then these shall be the terms. If, despite my earnest efforts, I fail to bring you back to life, I shall have your permission to dissect your body. Such opportunities are, these days, all too rare." He looked at me with a glint of hunger in his eyes and then quickly away, and I recalled his enthusiasm for spending time with Early's corpse at the burying ground, even after he had extracted the fatal ball.

"We have an agreed bargain," said Truett, sticking his hand through the bars. Warren shook it enthusiastically before taking his leave.

"Probably best if you don't breathe a word of our arrangement to Lincoln," Truett said as we watched Warren walk away through Hutchason's gate. "I don't want him to slacken his efforts, even though my long life is now guaranteed one way or the other."

I assured Truett that, notwithstanding his agreement with Warren, I was confident Lincoln would work tirelessly for his acquittal. "That's why I've come this morning. Have you heard about Miss Owens's death in town last week?"

Truett nodded. "Mrs. Hutchason mentioned it when bringing me my supper on the day her body was discovered. Further proof of my innocence—make sure Lincoln realizes that."

"What do you mean?"

"Two mysterious deaths in town must be connected. The same killer. But, obviously, not me." He rattled the bars of his cell. "I was locked up in here when she was killed."

"Did you know Miss Owens?"

"Only from a distance. I never trusted the apothecary. Too clever by half. And underhanded in his business dealings. I don't doubt he might have been the killer all along."

"Can you think of any person you and she had in common?"

I asked. "A common acquaintance—or a common enemy, perhaps? Or any connection between her and Early, for that matter?"

"It seems to me the only commonality," said Truett, "is that both of them were killed in a public fashion. Early in the midst of a grand celebration, and Miss Owens in her bedroom, to be sure, but on the town square in the middle of the day. The killer must be someone who's well known to the townspeople, someone who can come and go without attracting attention."

It was, I thought, a good observation. "I'll pass it along to Lincoln, see if it gets us anywhere. One more question: what was your gun doing under the bushes on Quality Hill after the shooting? The sheriff found it there."

Truett's countenance, which had brightened during the discussion of galvanic batteries with the doctor, fell again. He swallowed and said, "Hutchason asked me the same question."

"Well? What's the answer?"

"I brought it with me that night, but I never used it. I swear I didn't. When the mob came to find me, I chucked it away. I was going to go back and retrieve it, but I've been in custody ever since."

This hardly seemed credible. My expression must have revealed my skepticism because he added, plaintively, "You tell Lincoln I've known him a long time. I'm depending on him to do his best for me."

"He knows that. I'm sure he will."

I turned to leave, but Truett called out, "What about the election—did Douglas prevail?"

"It was close here in town. I don't think the results have come in yet from the rest of the district."

"Do me a favor and send a messenger as soon as you learn the final tallies," said Truett. "I need to know whether I have the registrar's job in hand when Lincoln gets me out. Or when the doctor brings me back to life."

I assured him I would and headed for the square. It was only after I'd gone several blocks that I realized I'd failed to ask Doctor Warren an obvious question: if he truly had the power to bring the dead back to life, why hadn't he used it on Miss Owens?

I found myself in front of the offices of the *Sangamo Journal* on Chicken Row. "Who won, Simeon?" I asked the newspaperman as I pushed through the door.

Unlike most men in town, Simeon Francis appeared no more disheveled today than he did on every other day. "Lincoln was returned by a comfortable margin," he said. "He'll likely end up with more votes than any other candidate for the legislature."

"And Stuart against Douglas?"

The newspaperman gave a gravelly cough. "That one doesn't look good. Stuart was ahead by a handful of votes here in Springfield, but from what I've been hearing Douglas ran up big margins in the northern reaches of the district. A fellow on the Peoria stagecoach this morning told me Douglas was ahead by more than a hundred in Knox County and that he'd heard the margins for him were even larger up near Chicago. All those Irish navvies fell for the Democratic fiction about restarting the improvements scheme. A real shame. Douglas will be even more insufferable as congressman-elect."

A few hours later, I returned to No. 4, Hoffman's Row. To my surprise, Martha was present. She and Lincoln were hovering above the table, and when I came over I saw they were staring at a white woman's glove. The glove I'd found in the woods the night Lincoln, Miss Owens, and I had gone strolling.

"Where'd you get that?" I exclaimed.

"Henry Owens found it in his sister's room, when he was cleaning it out this morning. It was wedged beneath her mattress."

"But how did he—or she—get it back from me?"

Lincoln looked at me with confusion. I picked up the glove from the table, and I realized it was left-handed.

"Wait a minute!" I shouted as I ran from the room. I burst into my storeroom, rushed past Herndon as he looked up from the counter, and raced up the stairs to our lodgings. I located the glove I'd found during our walk tucked into the recesses of my trunk. Two minutes later I was charging through Lincoln's office door again, panting, the glove I'd found in my outstretched hand.

"Where did that come from?" demanded Lincoln, when he realized I had the glove's mate.

"A passing merchant—" began Martha.

"No, that's not right," I said. I explained about finding the glove atop the stump in the woods.

Martha shot me a wounded glare—for lying to her, I supposed—and turned her attention back to the gloves. There was no doubt they were a set; they featured the identical ink design of the courting couple. They even had similar amounts of wear in the palms and fingertips.

"I wonder how Miss Owens's glove ended up in the woods," said Martha.

"They weren't Miss Owens's," said Lincoln. "Her brother told me he'd never seen her wearing them."

"He probably didn't realize it," said Martha. "Men never look carefully at women's fashions. Especially not brothers at their sisters."

"No, he was very sure of it. His sister never wore this glove—these gloves," said Lincoln, correcting himself as he stared at the two together. For a moment, his eyes widened and I thought I saw a tremor run across his face, but when I looked again it had vanished.

"Then whose are they?" asked Martha.

"And could it be a coincidence one was left in the woods, near where a shot was fired at us, and the other in Miss Owens's bedroom?" I said.

"It was no coincidence," said Martha. "Whoever shot at you is the same person who killed Miss Owens. These gloves link the two together."

Lincoln suddenly pushed himself away from the table and walked around in a tight circle. When he turned back to us, his jaw was set.

"I don't have time for any more speculation. I need to finish preparing for trial, and I'm quite sure these gloves have nothing to do with getting Truett acquitted. I must ask both of you to leave. And take the gloves with you, if you please."

His tone brooked no discussion, and Martha and I were soon on the street. A block down, Martha put her hand on my arm and came to a halt.

"What is it?" I asked.

"There was something about . . . Lincoln was looking at the gloves in a most peculiar fashion. Did you see?"

"I'm not sure. Perhaps?"

"I'm certain of it," said Martha. She looked down at the gloves, which were dangling from her hand. "I think he recognized them." She gave a little gasp, and she turned to face me. "In fact, I think he recognized them as belonging to *Miss Rutledge*."

"Miss Rutledge? But she died three years ago. When did she lose her glove in the woods? And how did its mate get into Miss Owens's bedroom? There are dozens of other young women, several hundred probably, in Springfield, to say nothing of the rest of Sangamon County. They could be any of theirs."

"I think I'm right," said Martha, shaking her head with conviction. "I know I am."

"But how—"

"Perhaps it was Miss Rutledge's ghost. Watching over you on your walk. And watching over Miss Owens on her deathbed."

CHAPTER 30

The following day, trial arrived. In what we could only hope was not an omen of more bad things to come, the morning started dismally. The tallies for the Third Congressional District had finally been collected from all parts of the far-flung district, and Douglas had garnered nearly a thousand more votes than Stuart.

"Douglas is Elected," conceded the headline in the *Sangamo Journal*. The only part of Simeon's accompanying story that was enjoyable to read was his not-so-private joke of using the adjective "short" a dozen times in his narrative: "the short victory," the concession from Stuart expected "in short order," and so on.

But the effect on Douglas as he strode through the throng of people gathered on the street in front of Hoffman's Row was anything but small. His chest puffed out, his face glowed, and he even seemed to have grown several inches in physical stature overnight. The crowd surged toward him, men offering outstretched hands and hearty congratulations and women offering becoming smiles and curtsies. I heard four separate men inquire of Douglas about being appointed to government positions within the span of a single block.

"Some of these same men are going to be on our jury," said Lincoln as he stood next to me and watched the scene with a sour look on his face. "Do you think they'll be prepared to judge my client fairly as against *him*?"

"Truett was hoping Douglas would win so he'd be granted the land office position," I said.

"That was foolhardy. As he should know better than anyone, dead men are ineligible for government service."

"I think you're overly concerned about Douglas. You've just prevailed in your election as well. Both sides' counsel in the trial will be victorious politicians."

"There's quite a difference," said Lincoln as he stalked off, and in truth there was no doubting he was right. No men surged toward Lincoln as he walked up the street toward the courtroom, and no women curtsied. Almost a hundred men served in the Illinois General Assembly, and the patronage each could distribute on behalf of the bankrupt government of our frontier state was comparatively limited. Meanwhile, Douglas would now be one of only three Illinois representatives to the national government, with its huge natural resources and immense number of offices. The gulf in prestige and power was vast.

The disagreeable fawning continued inside the courtroom. Judge Thomas nearly tripped over himself in his effort to rush forward to offer Douglas his congratulations. Thomas wrapped his arm around the victor's shoulders and whispered at length into his ear. Douglas listened intently, his arms crossed in front of his chest, giving a sober nod at regular intervals as if to signal his newfound gravity. I guessed Thomas had his sights set on the federal district court judgeship for Illinois, a position with a generous salary and lifetime tenure.

Sheriff Hutchason brought Truett into the courtroom. I was glad to see that Truett had managed to scrub the dirt off his face and hands and that his normal set of clothes had been restored to him. But he still wore a haunted look, and his clothes hung uncertainly from his withered frame.

Seeing the defendant enter the courtroom, Judge Thomas recollected himself and, reluctantly detaching himself from his would-be patron, went to assume the bench.

"Call the case, Clerk," directed the judge with one last, longing look toward Douglas.

My friend Matheny, the court clerk, shouted at the top of his lungs, "The People against Henry Truett on the charge of murder with malice aforethought."

"Is the defense prepared, Mr. Lincoln?"

"We are, Your Honor," said Lincoln, swelling up to his full height, the top of his stovepipe hat seemingly close to the ceiling.

"And Mr. Douglas, notwithstanding your recent increase in national responsibilities, you are still willing to undertake the People's burden in this matter?"

"I am, Your Honor," announced Douglas in his deep, sonorous voice. "My sense of duty and patriotism demands it."

An appreciative murmur spread throughout the crowd, which filled the small courtroom and spilled far down the street outside, listening through the open windows. From the seats Lincoln had secured for us on the end of the front row, Martha and I turned around to survey it.

"I think I'm going to be ill," I said in a not-very-quiet whisper.

My sister elbowed me in the ribs. "Don't be a sore loser."

"We'll proceed to select the jury," Judge Thomas was saying. "In light of the notoriety of the crime under consideration, I've asked the clerk to draw up a list of forty-eight potential veniremen, double the usual number. Pull the first name, Clerk."

Matheny reached his hand into a square wooden box containing the names of the potential jurors and drew out a single slip of paper. "William Stearns," he shouted.

It soon became apparent that even forty-eight potential jurors was too shallow a pool from which to assemble an impartial panel of twelve. Every man selected for questioning knew about Early's murder, and many admitted to having formed an opinion on the question of Truett's guilt. Judge Thomas summarily dismissed these men from service.

Then there was the ever-looming issue of politics. Because of the presence of the poll watchers at the base of the voting stage on election day, the votes cast by each potential juror were public knowledge. As Matheny drew the names from his box one by one, Lincoln and Douglas wrangled in front of the judge over whether the candidate's Democratic or Whiggish tendencies rendered him unable to consider the evidence fairly. Because Truett was a Democrat being defended by a Whig, who was being prosecuted by a Democrat for killing a Whig, the attorneys not infrequently tied themselves up in knots while attempting to put forward arguments of political bias. On consecutive names late in the morning, Lincoln seemed to argue one potential juror was unacceptable for being biased against Democrats and the next was unacceptable for being biased in favor of Democrats. Douglas's positions were equally muddled. In the middle of one such tussle, the judge tossed his hands with impatience and called for an early lunch break. Only three jurors had been selected.

"Which is it?" I asked Lincoln after he, Martha, and I had filed out of the courtroom and found a comparatively quiet spot on the street. "Are Democrats biased in favor of your case or against it?"

"Both and neither," he returned, his eyes twinkling.

"Surely you must have a position," said Martha, blowing out her breath with frustration.

"My position is that only certain jurors can be counted on to give Mr. Truett a fair hearing. Anyone else I'm doing my best to keep off the panel. The rules let me strike twenty jurors peremptorily, for any reason at all, so for anyone else drawn whom I don't want, I need to come up with a reason they should be struck for cause. All the excitement about the election gives me a handy basis to try to find cause. Your friend Mr. Douglas is trying the same tactic, and he's got half the number of peremptory challenges to work with as me. Inconsistency is an occupational hazard, I'm afraid. Besides, this is nothing compared to the Adkin cases last year."

"The Adkin cases?" asked Martha, not satisfied.

"I think you'll remember this one, Speed," Lincoln said, with a sly grin. "It takes the prize. Old Mr. Macon called a fellow named David Adkin a 'hog stealer.' Adkin sued Macon, claiming slander—a false statement—and Macon hired me. I defended Macon, proved the accusation wasn't slander because it wasn't false, and Macon was let free by the jury.

"Wouldn't you know it, but Adkin was indicted by the prosecutor a few weeks later for stealing a hog. He hadn't any money for counsel, and the judge, having a well-developed sense of humor, appointed me for the defense. What could I do but try my best? A trial was held, and lo and behold I succeeded in obtaining a verdict of not guilty. So within the span of a few weeks, I was charged with proving before a jury that Adkin was and was not a hog stealer."

"And succeeded each time," I added.

Martha laughed while Lincoln gave a modest shrug. "All in a day's work," he said. "I have a few things to prepare for the afternoon. I asked Hay to set up my lunch—only for one, I'm afraid."

I told Lincoln we'd manage on our own, and we watched as he pushed through the crowd. The spectators from the trial filled the street and spilled into the town square. Several young women walked about, passing out handbills for the tent meeting and collecting donations no doubt destined for Preacher Crews's pocket. Over near the unfinished capitol walls I saw Douglas talking in close consultation to a familiar figure: Henry Owens.

"I wonder if he's here somewhere," said Martha, interrupting me before I could figure out what business Douglas could have with the apothecary. "Would he be bold enough?"

"Who?"

"The real murderer. Salem's Ghost."

"I doubt you'll be hearing from him again," came a nasal voice from behind us. Turning quickly, we saw the haughty figure of the *Democrat* publisher George Weber.

"Why do you say that?" asked Martha, her hands on her hips, as I wondered how long Weber had been hovering near us.

"The fellow, whoever he was, seemed obsessed with judgment day, wouldn't you say? Well, the election's come and gone, and the voters have rendered their judgment. And a very good one it was."

Weber held up a copy of his new sheet, which carried the headline in large, bold letters:

Douglas Wins!

and beneath that, in somewhat smaller letters:

Whigs, Stuart Fall Short

"We think 'Judgment Day' referred to something else," I said before I could check myself.

Weber looked at me with interest. "Do you now? And what, exactly, is that?"

"You're the newspaperman," I replied, "or claim to be, at least. Figure it out for yourself."

Weber stared at me for a moment, but when I did not elaborate, he gave an imperious toss of his head and moved away. Martha muttered an epithet in his wake.

"What do you make of Weber's remark?" I whispered. In the large, swirling crowd, I realized we didn't know who else might be within earshot.

"You think he's bluffing?"

"I think it's very interesting he would tell us S.G. isn't going to write any more letters. One obvious question is how can he know that, if he claims not to know S.G.'s identity."

"And another," added Martha quietly, "is if he's merely trying to put us off the scent. Perhaps he realizes we're getting close to figuring out the identity of his Ghost."

"Perhaps." I paused. "I only wish we knew what he thinks we know."

Martha laughed. "Now you're sounding as confused as Lincoln and Douglas."

We located a sandwich hawker with a comparatively short line and joined the queue. Just as we neared the front, I felt a heavy hand fall on my shoulder and a grizzled voice called out, "Lookee here, it's Mr. Fry Speed."

"Good day, Mr. Lincoln," I said. I saw his stepson lingering behind him. John Johnston's eyes were averted, and he was busy searching for stones in the dirt-and-gravel street to kick.

"There's quite a line," Thomas Lincoln said, gesturing to the persons formed up behind us. "Would you mind greatly . . ."

"Four ham sandwiches and three beers," I told the vendor as I handed over several coins.

The two men accepted their food and drink greedily and started wolfing them down as if they had not eaten in some time. Halfway through his sandwich, the elder Lincoln finally paused and gave me a nod of thanks.

"Think nothing of it," I said. "You son Abraham has done me numberless favors in our time living together. The Lincoln name goes a long way in my book."

"We've been finding that to be true here, haven't we, Johnnie?" said Thomas Lincoln, in between bites. "Most welcoming of us, your local citizens have been."

"Sure enough," said Johnston. "Some people are fool enough to pay you just to write your name."

I had almost missed the import of what he'd said until Martha stepped on my foot and nodded portentously at Johnston. I played his statement back in my mind.

"Is that so?" I said casually to Thomas. "People paying for your autograph, are they?"

"Yessir, Mr. Fry Speed," Thomas agreed. He'd finished his sandwich and was working on draining his mug of beer.

"Do they usually ask you to sign your full name, or just 'Lincoln'?"

"Just 'Lincoln.' 'Thomas' ain't nothing special, at least it don't appear to be so to the folks around here. But some men seem mighty happy to have 'Lincoln' wrote down on a piece of paper." He bent toward us and whispered, confidentially, "Some folks'll give me a dime just to put my 'Lincoln' down. A dime for each one I do. Hah! Like you say, Mr. Fry Speed, my name goes a long way around here."

Martha and I exchanged glances, thinking the same thought. We had seemingly stumbled onto the explanation for the forged real estate surveys.

"These pieces of paper you're signing," I asked, "are they blank, or do they have lots of legal writing on them?"

Thomas Lincoln shrugged. "I don't pay much attention to that. See, it's the dimes that hold my interest. Far as I'm concerned, if they want to pay me a dime to sign my name, I'll sign whatever they put in front of me. I'd sign the belly of a fish if that's what they wanted." He finished his beer and set it down. "Not much of interest in there this morning, eh?" he added, gesturing to the courtroom behind us.

"I expect Abraham would disagree," I said. "I've often heard him say that without an impartial jury, it's pointless for him to argue his client's brief."

"Have either of you seen Abraham in court before?" asked Martha.

Thomas shook his head. Johnston gulped down his last bite and said, "I don't see what the fuss is about."

"What do you mean, Johnnie?" asked his stepfather.

"You and Ma always go on about how impressive Abe is for reading about the law. As near as I can tell from this morning, all that reading has done is give him the right to stand in front of the judge and dance a jig while spouting some jibber-jabber." Johnston took a swig of beer and spit onto the ground. "Shoot, I can do all that myself, if anyone'd be interested in watching."

"Don't be a fool," said Thomas Lincoln. "There's a lot more to it. Like it or not, there's plenty Abe's learned that you ain't cut out for."

Johnston tried not to flinch at this blow. But it was impossible to miss the sag of his shoulders as he turned, kicked at a stone in the street, and slunk away.

CHAPTER 31

Lincoln and Douglas, both, had a lot more dancing and jibber-jabbering to do before jury selection was complete.

The venire process lasted all day Wednesday and into Thursday morning. With intense thrusts and parries, the two lawyers battled over the fitness of would-be jurors one by one. Both men seemed to be following some sort of complex internal logic in choosing when to advance and when to retreat. Along with the rest of the spectators, I found it impossible to divine what that logic was, but it was hard not to be impressed by their determined efforts in front of the increasingly belligerent judge. It was like watching two masters play a game whose rules remained obscure and whose score was unknown: you could readily admire the skill of the players without understanding the full dimensions of their art.

By midday on Thursday, a jury of twelve men was seated. I knew all of them, at least by sight. They comprised a mixture of farmers and merchants along with a single professional, a doctor from a neighboring village. Six were Democrats, five Whigs, and the twelfth had, as far as I knew, never cast a vote nor expressed a political preference of any sort. Lincoln seemed satisfied enough with the lot, although looking at Douglas I perceived an infernal smile on his lips as well. All twelve jurors would have to agree on the verdict.

After opening statements, Douglas called his first witness: Sheriff Hutchason. The hulking lawman made his way toward the front of the room. With the seating of the jury, the small courtroom had contracted even further. The judge's bench had been pushed to the right-hand corner of the room, and twelve chairs for the jury had been squeezed into the left-hand corner. Lincoln and Truett sat immediately in front of these, their knees almost touching the knees of the closest juror, while Douglas sat in similar proximity to the judge's bench on the other side of the room. A single chair for the witness was placed between them.

Those few portions of the yellow-pine planked floor that remained visible were covered by the stains of expectorated tobacco juice.

The judge had ordered Matheny to open the windows all the way, and he now directed Hutchason to keep up his voice such that the swollen crowd outside on the street would not miss his testimony.

"Yes, Your Honor," replied the sheriff in his booming voice.

"I believe the jury are familiar with the basic facts," began Douglas abruptly, before Hutchason fully settled himself upon the witness chair, "so let's get straight to the heart of the matter."

The sheriff gestured for the lawyer to proceed.

"Jacob Early was killed on the night of July fourth while standing on the Edwards estate on Quality Hill."

"Correct."

"What was the cause of death?"

"Early was hit by a single shot, directly in the forehead. Death was immediate."

"At what time, during the evening, was Early shot?"

"It was during the display of fireworks Edwards arranged. About eleven o'clock at night, I'd judge. And I find the timing of the shooting significant."

"Why is that?"

"It's apparent the shooter used the noise of the exploding works to cover the sound of his gun's discharge. So the timing shows intention. It shows malice aforethought, as you lawyers like to say. Someone *planned* to shoot Mr. Early and planned it carefully."

The large crowd murmured with satisfaction. The story thus far possessed the appealing qualities of a good yarn, one they'd be pleased to retell around their hearths next winter.

"Now, did anyone see the person who fired the fatal shot?" asked Douglas.

"Not to my knowledge."

"Then tell the jury how you went about determining who did it."

Hutchason shifted on his chair to face the jury, who were only a few feet away. Each man on the panel listened attentively.

"The first thing I looked into," said Hutchason, "was motive. Who wished Early ill? I considered business associates, neighbors, tenant farmers—everyone. But I kept coming back to Mr. Truett." The sheriff nodded toward the defendant, who was sitting directly opposite him. "Every man in town knows about their feud over the land office position, I suppose."

"Had that feud already turned violent prior to the night of July fourth?" asked Douglas.

Hutchason nodded. "At Spotswood's smoking room, about a week before the shooting, Mr. Truett confronted—"

"Objection, Your Honor!" called Lincoln, springing to his feet. "My brother Douglas has not established the sheriff was present at Spotswood's on the night of this incident, and the evidence would show he was not. Sheriff Hutchason lacks any foundation for the testimony he was about to give."

"Don't you have another witness to put this in through, Douglas?" asked the judge.

"I think it's common knowledge what transpired that night," protested Douglas. "Mr. Lincoln was there, as was his confederate Mr. Speed"—I startled upon hearing my name—"and any number of other men. Does Mr. Lincoln genuinely want me to process all of them in here to testify?"

"How about *one* of them?" replied Lincoln with an edge to his voice. The crowd on the street outside started to chatter. I heard one or two indistinct shouts. The excitement the gallery had been waiting for these past two days had finally begun to materialize.

Douglas spread out his stubby arms impatiently. "Your Honor," he began, "I hardly think an experienced, *national* judge would find such witnesses necessary for the common ground we're talking about here."

Judge Thomas took a long pull on his cigar and nodded. "I see your point. The objection's overruled."

"But, Your Honor—" began Lincoln.

"The objection's been overruled. Please proceed, Mr. Douglas."

Lincoln shot a concerned glance at me, and I grimaced in response. It was going to be an uphill climb at every step for Lincoln, facing the combined forces of the judge and Representative-elect Douglas.

"Remind the jury about the confrontation at Spotswood's," Douglas was saying to Hutchason, "and, as a service to my brother Lincoln, please confine yourself to undisputed facts regarding the incident."

Douglas gave Lincoln a particularly unctuous smile while Hutchason recounted Truett's arrival at Spotswood's that night, the verbal confrontation with Early, and the fight that ensued.

"Did Truett draw a pistol on Early that evening?" asked Douglas.

"He did."

"Was it discharged?"

"Not that evening, it wasn't."

"Are you, Sheriff, familiar with the pistol owned by Mr. Truett?"

The sheriff nodded. "I've seen Mr. Truett pull it on more than one occasion. There was a time—"

"Objection," called Lincoln. "We shouldn't have testimony here about other, unrelated events."

"That wasn't my intention," said Douglas smoothly, before the judge could respond. "Let me redirect the witness." To Hutchason: "You say you're familiar with Mr. Truett's pistol. Please describe it."

"It's a belt pistol. Silver barrel, walnut stock, about yay long." Hutchason held his hands six inches apart.

"After Mr. Early was shot on the night of July fourth, did you search the grounds of the Edwards estate for the weapon that fired the fatal ball?"

"I did."

"And?"

"And I found Mr. Truett's belt pistol under a mulberry bush. At the side of Edwards's house. He must have discarded it there—an attempt to hide it, I suspect."

The crowd buzzed with excitement at this testimony. Douglas opened a leather pouch and carefully took out a silver-barreled pistol. "Is this the weapon you found, Sheriff?" he asked.

Hutchason made a show of inspecting the piece and nodded. "You see, I scratched 'H.H.' and '7/7' with my knife into the butt, right there." He indicated with the tip of his little finger.

"Is this the same weapon you know to be owned by the defendant, Mr. Truett?" asked Douglas.

"I believe it to be so, yes."

Douglas took the gun and handed it to the nearest juror. "While the jury has a look," he continued, "let me put a new query: after you found the gun, did you ask Mr. Truett if it was his?"

"I did. When I showed it to him, he tried to grab it from my hand and said, 'Where'd you find that?' Something like that, if not exactly those words. I repeated my question, 'Is this yours?' but he refused to answer. Wouldn't open his mouth again. Just stood there, his arms folded, staring at the gun."

"Thank you, Sheriff Hutchason. That's all I have, Your Honor."

Douglas retreated as Lincoln rose to his feet. But instead of resuming his seat, Douglas wandered back to the gallery, greeting a few men with firm handshakes as he walked past them. Douglas proceeded to where the usual prosecutor, the Democrat David Prickett, was watching the proceedings from a chair in the back corner. The Little Giant gave a small hop and settled himself comfortably onto Prickett's lap, his feet dangling several inches above the floor, like an oversize child seeking out the comfort of his father. He even threw his arm around Prickett's neck, from time to time whispering in his ear.

No one present batted an eye at this, as Douglas habitually watched the testimony in court from the lap of another man. Perhaps he merely sought a better view, given his short stature. Regardless, the behavior would have seemed odd in the extreme if practiced by anyone else. Coming from Douglas, it was merely one more eccentricity of a thoroughly peculiar man. Given the force of his personality and his ever-greater political successes, people weren't about to start questioning his habits now.

"Afternoon, Sheriff," began Lincoln casually. I knew Lincoln considered Hutchason a friend and a good man, and I suspected Lincoln hoped to score some points on Truett's behalf without badgering the sheriff unduly.

"Mr. Lincoln," replied Hutchason with an assured nod.

"You described for Mr. Douglas the steps you say you followed in trying to determine who fired the shot that killed Mr. Early."

"Correct."

"You say you considered motive. Then you considered the weapon. Then you went looking for a weapon and found it. And then, based on all of your investigations, you concluded Mr. Truett was the murderer. Do I have that right?"

Hutchason weighed this in his mind before replying, "Just about."

Lincoln nodded. "In reality, Sheriff, you first took Mr. Truett into custody on the very night of July fourth, indeed, very shortly after you yourself first arrived at Quality Hill. Isn't that the case?"

Hutchason shifted slightly in his chair. "That's true."

"And that was before you found the pistol in the bushes?"

"Correct."

"According to the date you scratched into the gun, you didn't recover the gun until three days later, on the seventh of July, is that correct?"

"It is."

"In fact, you arrested Mr. Truett before you conducted any part of this investigation you described to Mr. Douglas—isn't that the case?"

"I did it for his own good," said Hutchason. "A mob had grabbed ahold of him. I didn't want them to string him up before he could be tried through the regular legal process."

"It was a mob of men who first decided Mr. Truett must be the guilty party. Is that what you're saying?"

"Yes."

"And this mob were the ones who first took Mr. Truett into custody?"

"You could look at it that way, yes."

"And you decided to accept, uncritically, the passions of the mob in charging Mr. Truett rather than conducting your own independent investigation."

"Objection!" called out Douglas from his perch on Prickett's lap.

"Sustained."

"I don't agree with the way you're putting it," insisted the sheriff. "I took possession of Mr. Truett in the first place to protect him from the mob. But I was convinced then and remain convinced now that he killed Mr. Early."

"You mean . . ." Lincoln began, but he cut himself off and looked down at the sheaf of papers in his hands. Truett stared at him. Several members of the jury whispered to each other. Lincoln had scored a partial point about the sheriff's investigation, I thought, but Hutchason's steady demeanor had prevented him from advancing very far.

"Let's talk about the gathering on Quality Hill," Lincoln began again. "It's well known Early was shot in the midst of a large gathering, a party Ninian and Mrs. Edwards threw to mark the Day of Independence."

"Correct."

"And how many persons in total attended the party, do you know?"

"I believe the number was in excess of one hundred."

"And since the fireworks were held as the culmination of the evening's festivities, would you agree it's a fair assumption that most if not all of those one hundred persons remained on Quality Hill at the time of the shooting?"

Sheriff Hutchason thought about this for a moment before answering. "That's probably fair."

"And, at least in theory," continued Lincoln, "any one of those hundred or more persons could have been the assailant who shot Early, correct?"

"But my job wasn't to investigate theory," protested Hutchason. "I was interested in the actual facts."

"Did you question each and every one of those one hundred persons in the course of your investigation?"

"Not all of them. But—"

"Did you consider the motivation each and every one of those hundred persons might have for wishing Early dead?"

"I didn't consider it necessary."

"How many of those hundred persons had business dealings with Early, dealings that might have gone awry?"

Hutchason pondered this question, looking, I thought, for some way to limit the damage Lincoln was inflicting. "I don't know the exact number," said the sheriff eventually. "If there were any at all."

"Any at all? But surely many of the men present would have dealt with Early at the land office."

"I'd probably agree with that," said Hutchason, frowning.

Lincoln nodded to himself and strode around the small open space in the front of the courtroom, giving time for the concessions to sink in. Several jurors were whispering to each other. Turning to the back of the room, I saw Douglas and Prickett doing the same, looks of consternation on each man's face.

"Let's talk about the pistol," said Lincoln, after he had let as much time pass as possible. "As I understand your testimony, you're certain this is the one you found at the Edwards estate, because you scratched your initials and the date into it?"

"Yes."

"But you're not certain this pistol was actually owned by Mr. Truett. All you can say is that you've seen Truett with a similar gun at some point in the past, correct?"

"I'm not sure I follow you," said the sheriff, his eyes darting over to Douglas before returning to rest on Lincoln.

"That's a common sort of belt pistol, wouldn't you agree?"

"I'm not sure I would."

"If I told you my friend Mr. Speed sells an average of two or three models just like this every month at his store to the citizens of Springfield, would you have any reason to doubt it?"

Lincoln indicated toward me as he put this question, and nearly everyone in the courtroom turned to stare. I heard some of the persons outside on the street jockeying for a view as well. I felt my ears reddening. In fact, I had never said anything of the sort to Lincoln, and I doubted I sold that many similar belt pistols in the course of an entire year.

"If Mr. Speed said that, then I'd have no reason to disbelieve him, I suppose," the sheriff was saying through an upturned mouth.

"Now, am I right you arranged for the fatal ball to be retrieved from Mr. Early's remains so it could be examined?"

Sheriff Hutchason looked at Lincoln with surprise. "No, that's not right."

"And—what? You didn't order the extraction of the ball?"

"No."

"Well, have you subsequently examined the ball that was removed from the remains?"

"No, I haven't," replied Hutchason with evident sincerity.

"Who did, then?"

Hutchason shrugged helplessly. Lincoln glanced at me and then back at Douglas, who was looking on serenely. I thought I understood what was happening. Lincoln couldn't make his point—my discovery—that the ball didn't fit the pistol without a witness who was knowledgeable about both the pistol and the ball. Hutchason had testified about the pistol, but since he had no knowledge of the ball, Lincoln couldn't cross-examine him about it. I wondered whether Douglas had purposely kept the ball away from Hutchason, precisely in order to thwart Lincoln's examination.

"Anything further for the witness, Mr. Lincoln?" prompted the judge. Lincoln was standing in the middle of the room, his right hand supporting his left elbow, staring at the ceiling in frustration.

Casting one last, suspicious glance at Douglas, Lincoln replied, "Not for this witness, no."

After a short recess for the judge to replenish his supply of cigars, Douglas called his next witness. Doctor Weymouth Warren slowly made his way to the witness chair. Lincoln would surely be able to spring his trap regarding the mismatched ball with him, I thought.

Douglas led Warren through a brisk direct examination. Warren described coming upon Early's dead body on the Edwards lawn and his determination that Early had expired from a single gunshot. Douglas then asked Warren about his posthumous examination of Early's remains and his recovery of the ball. Warren described his procedure in the graveyard, though he left out both my presence at the autopsy and whatever other bodily investigations he had undertaken on the corpse after I'd departed the scene.

Douglas produced the ball, the same misshapen object I'd seen Warren extract from the corpse. From outside on the street arose a great clamoring from spectators eager to see for themselves the agent of death. Several yelled for Douglas to hold it up higher or, better still, to bring it outside where the crowd could have a closer look themselves. Indeed, the clamor got so loud that the judge was forced to announce that the clerk would take possession of the ball after the testimony ended for the day and that persons wishing to examine the evidence could do so that evening at the clerk's office. This quieted the masses enough for Douglas to proceed with his examination of Warren.

"This is the ball that caused Early's death?" asked Douglas, holding the object up in front of the jury, which looked on with great interest.

"It is. I found it deep inside his brain cage." An enthusiastic smile creased Warren's long face. "This surface right there, the one that's flat, it was caused by the ball crashing into his skull. The explosive collision of ball against bone was so powerful it caused the ball to flatten. And, I can tell you, what it did to the brain was a lot worse."

An ecstatic gasp arose from the crowd outside. Through the open windows I heard several men ask their companions where the clerk's office was, and it sounded as if a few departed for it at once in order to secure a prime spot at the front of the viewing line.

"And the injury the ball would have caused, upon its entry into Early's skull?"

"Catastrophic," said Warren. "And instantaneously fatal."

"No further questions, Your Honor." Douglas left his witness and wandered back to Prickett, where he hopped up into his lap again.

Truett leaned over to Lincoln and whispered something. Lincoln nodded, but when he rose there was a distinct frown on his face.

"Doctor Warren," began my friend, "your testimony is that ball caused Early's death."

"Correct."

"But to know what *person* is responsible for the death, we need to know whose gun fired the ball, would you agree?"

"Most certainly. The ball didn't enter Early's skull on its own whim." Warren evidently meant this as a joke, and he began to laugh until he saw only serious faces around him and regained his composure.

"And you, yourself, don't have any testimony on that point, correct?"

"I was standing outside earlier, listening to the sheriff's testimony. It sounds like he found Mr. Truett's gun in the bushes, so that's your answer."

Lincoln turned back to Douglas. "Do you still have the belt pistol?"

Douglas pointed to a package beneath his counsel seat. Lincoln bent over, retrieved the gun, and handed it butt first to the witness.

"Do you recognize this as the gun the People allege was the murder weapon?"

Doctor Warren rotated the belt pistol in his hands. "Do I recognize this? No. I've never seen it before in my life."

"So you've seen the ball but not the gun, and the sheriff has seen the gun but not the ball." Lincoln threw up his arms in frustration. The witness looked back at him with confusion, and Douglas called out from the back of the room, "Your Honor, could my brother Lincoln be directed to ask questions of the witness, if he has any, and not merely to regale us with his observations on life."

Judge Thomas nodded while blowing out a large cloud of smoke.

"Let me ask you this," said Lincoln, taking an aggressive step forward so he was nearly on top of the seated witness. "Isn't it the case that this ball couldn't possibly fit in this gun?"

The doctor took his time examining both objects, one held in each hand. "I think you may be right—"

"So—"

"Because the ball has been deformed, as I explained earlier," the witness continued, ignoring Lincoln's interruption. "Let's try for ourselves." Doctor Warren took the ball and tried to push it down the barrel of the belt pistol, but the flattened side of the ball was much wider than the opening of the barrel. "Yes, you're right," the doctor continued, "although that doesn't tell us whether it would have fit originally, before it was fired."

"Exactly!" said Douglas to his companion Prickett, loudly enough that the jury and everyone else in the courtroom could hear.

Lincoln's temples had turned red. "The truth, Doctor Warren," he insisted, "is that ball wouldn't have fit down the barrel of that gun even if it were in pristine condition, right out of the box. It's the wrong size ball, isn't it?"

Douglas slid off Prickett's lap and strode forward with smart, aggressive steps. "Objection! Objection, Your Honor! Mr. Lincoln can't ask this witness that question. The witness has already said he's never seen the gun before in his life."

"Sustained."

"But, Your Honor—"

"The objection is sustained, Mr. Lincoln."

"I need to be able to ask the question of some witness, Your Honor."

Judge Thomas took two long pulls on his cigar. He let smoke drift out through his lips, which curled into a gleeful smirk. "That, Mr. Lincoln," he said, as the final remnants of smoke leaked from his mouth, "is your problem."

CHAPTER 32

I had never seen Lincoln so angry. He was pacing up and down the length of his office on the second floor of Hoffman's Row, grumbling loudly to himself, aiming kicks at the papers and parchment scattered about. For good measure he kicked his chair, which toppled over with a clatter. Martha and I stood to the side, trying to stay out of the way of his fury.

"Douglas had to have known," Lincoln said for about the third time.

Martha and I murmured in agreement.

"He had to have known about the ball not fitting the pistol. He prevented the cross I was entitled to, on the evidence. He pulled the sting, dammit!"

Lincoln rounded on me. "You didn't tell him they were a mismatch, did you?"

"I wouldn't have—"

"No, of course not. So how could he have known?"

"Don't you think he could have figured it out on his own?" asked Martha. Her voice was unusually timid, and I swung around to stare at her.

"Certainly not," said Lincoln, his rage unabated. He didn't appear to have noticed Martha's tone. "Stephen knows a good deal, I'll admit, but he doesn't know a thing about guns. I doubt he's handled one in his life before this case arose."

"Martha," I said, "if there's something you should tell us . . ."

Martha bit her lip; then her face crumpled and she hid it in both hands. She started to sob.

"You didn't!" shouted Lincoln. He clapped his hand to his forehead in disbelief.

"I . . . I didn't mean to," she managed through her sobs. "I thought you'd told him already. I thought you'd tell him and he'd understand there'd been a mistake and he'd let Mr. Truett go free. Truly I did. I'm . . . I'm so sorry. So very, very sorry." She threw herself down onto Stuart's lounge, buried her head in her arms, and sobbed. After a moment, I came to sit beside her and put my arm around her trembling shoulders.

Lincoln took several steadying breaths. He righted his chair, picked up the buffalo cloak he'd sent flying, and sat down at his worktable. He took out a fresh piece of foolscap, dipped his pen, and started making notes.

For a minute, the room was silent save for Martha's sobs and Lincoln's scratching.

"Couldn't *I* testify the ball must have been fired from a different gun?" I said at last. It was a possibility I'd been thinking about since court that afternoon.

"You didn't sell the pistol to Truett, did you?" Lincoln asked without looking up.

"No."

"Then the judge wouldn't allow the testimony. Even if you had, he probably wouldn't. You can only testify to things you have historical knowledge of, and you don't have historical knowledge that the gun and the ball don't match. It's a limit the law places on any factual witness."

Martha had been slowly regaining her composure. She wiped her eyes on her sleeve. "Can you ever forgive me?" she asked Lincoln.

His features softened, but only a little. "I'm sure I will. Someday. For right now, it would be best if you left us alone."

Martha started to protest, but I touched her arm and she thought better of it. "I'll escort you home," I said, "and be right back." Lincoln did not look up from his table as we departed.

Outside on the darkening streets, Martha clutched my arm. We walked in silence for several blocks. "I never would have said anything to Stephen if I'd thought it'd hurt our case," she said.

"Lincoln knows that. And so do I."

"Not that it matters now, I know."

"No."

We walked the rest of the way to the Hutchason house without talking, and Martha took her leave and let herself inside. I didn't think I'd ever seen her so subdued. I was about to head back to Hoffman's Row when I heard two voices coming from Hutchason's backyard. I walked to the edge of the picket fence and listened.

". . . appoint me to the land office when this is over," said the first voice, which I immediately recognized as Truett's.

"You know I can't do that," replied a second voice.

"No one deserves the position more."

There was a harsh bark of laughter. "I wouldn't be sure."

"Why not? No one worked harder to get our party leaders elected. Including you."

"Plenty of people worked harder, Truett. And longer. Don't forget—you spent the last month of the campaign locked up here." With the suddenness of a thunderbolt, I realized the second voice belonged to Stephen Douglas. Ducking down, I crept as close as I could to the jail cell without risking being seen.

"But back when I was charged, you agreed—"

"I did no such thing."

"We had a two-way agreement," insisted Truett. "You told me to be patient and to hire Lincoln to fight the charges. You even suggested how to make sure he'd say yes. In exchange, you promised that after the election you'd make the trial go my way and give me a suitable job. Meaning the land office."

My blood had gone cold. *Douglas* had told Truett to hire Lincoln? And Douglas had told Truett to suggest that Thomas Lincoln might have played a role in the events leading to Early's death? Perhaps Lincoln's political opponent was even more devious than I had thought possible.

"I'm afraid you've misunderstood." Douglas's tone was flat and unemotional.

"Misunderstood what?"

"I said I'd help you if I could. As it turns out, I can't."

"That's not what—"

"You're not thinking, Truett. We talked before the judge appointed me prosecutor. Since then I've been duty-bound to try to convict you of the crime for which you've been charged. And I still am. I don't know how you could have thought otherwise."

"But . . . but you never should have taken the assignment, in that case."

"That was never an option. Not for me."

"You can't . . . but . . ." Truett was lost for words. Though I couldn't see him, I could easily imagine the fury on his features. "I'll tell the whole world you promised to take care of me and now you're welching!"

Douglas snorted. "No one will believe you. The word of a criminal—a convicted murderer, within a day or two—against the word of a United States congressman? Hah! Besides, as I've told you, there was no agreement."

"Even if people don't believe me, it will tarnish you. It will end your career in politics."

"I find that most unlikely. Good night, Truett." I heard the sound of footsteps approaching and dove out of the way seconds before Douglas came striding through the gate. Lying in the grass, I watched as the Little Giant marched away down the street, his chest thrust out and his head held as high as his stature permitted. If he felt the slightest bit of remorse, his carriage gave no sign of it.

When I returned to Hoffman's Row, I found Lincoln reclining in his chair, reading. I watched him silently, and after a moment he put down the volume. It was the book of Burns poetry.

"I miss her," he said quietly.

"I know you do."

"First Ann and now Margaret . . ."

"I know. I feel awful for you, Lincoln."

At length, he shook his head to rouse himself and reached out for the legal papers on the table in front of him. "I have more work to do tonight," he said, as if to dismiss me.

"First, let me tell you what I just overheard."

Lincoln listened attentively while I related the conversation between Douglas and Truett, but when I finished he turned back to his table and continued to write out his lines of argument.

"Can't you use it against Douglas?" I said. "Surely he's committed some type of misconduct. The judge would never stand for it."

"It sounds like he gave a general offer of assistance to a political ally," said Lincoln, "*before* he was appointed *pro tem*. Since he's been appointed, he's certainly been trying his hardest to send Truett to the gallows. I have no ability to contest that."

"But what about this business that it was he who convinced Truett to hire you?" This part, in particular, rankled me. "Isn't that . . . improper, somehow?"

"I consider it a compliment, coming from Stephen."

I was at a loss for words. Lincoln was missing the larger point. Douglas had been conniving against him from the start, planning to use this case to undermine Lincoln, in both the legal and the political arena. But perhaps because of his grief, Lincoln couldn't see it, and I was failing to make him understand.

"What's your strategy for getting Truett acquitted, then?" I asked.

Lincoln put down his pen. "Douglas's case is far from open-and-shut. My examination of the sheriff established all the other people who were present on Quality Hill, persons with an equivalent opportunity to fire the shot. And I'm planning to call Ninian Edwards in my case to expound on the point. For all that I wish your sister hadn't undermined my argument about the ball and the belt pistol, I think Douglas'll have a hard time establishing Truett's guilt beyond a reasonable doubt."

"And you think the jury's following all that?"

"Ah—now you've put your finger on it. That's the Wellington problem."

"What's the Wellington problem?"

"After the Battle of Waterloo," said Lincoln, his face relaxing into a warm smile for the first time in ages, "the British press asked the Duke of Wellington what had been the toughest part of the fight against Napoleon. And he said, trying to work out what was happening on the other side of the hill.

"Jury trials are a bit like artillery battles. You can unleash a vast expenditure of shot and shell, but how much of the ordnance actually reaches its target? In my case, the jury?"

I shrugged.

Lincoln nodded and said, "There's no way to know until they come back with the verdict."

CHAPTER 33

The next morning began with some unexpected news. Encouraging news, for a change. As I came down the stairs to my storeroom, I saw the distinctive figure of Simeon Francis peering through the windows from the street outside. I threw open the door and he charged in.

"It's not over!" he shouted before I could greet him.

"Of course not. The trial's continuing today, and Lincoln said maybe into tomorrow as well, depending on how long the evidence takes."

"Not the trial—the election. Or the counting of votes, at least. Stuart might have beat Douglas after all."

"What?" I exclaimed. "But you yourself reported that Douglas won. By more than a thousand votes, as I recall."

Simeon shook his head vigorously, and his whole body quivered with enthusiasm. "I was wrong. I just finished interrogating two fellows who arrived on the southbound stage this morning. One coming from Chicago, the other from Peoria. But they both had the same story—that more votes for Stuart have been discovered in their towns. Not enough to bridge the entire gap, not by themselves, but enough to narrow it greatly. I reckon the margin isn't more than a hundred in Douglas's favor at this point. And if only we can find a few more missing votes out there in the district somewhere . . . well, it may be Congressman *Stuart* after all."

"How can more votes be discovered four days after the election?" I said. "Won't the Democrats put up a stink?"

"Oh, they'll raise the biggest stink known to mankind," said Francis. He rubbed his ruddy, freckled hands together in glee at the prospect. "Just let them. They can have their stink, as long as we get the seat in Congress. Is Lincoln still in your bedroom?"

I nodded.

"I've got to go tell him." And Francis charged up the flight, the stairs groaning in protest under his girth.

Over at the courtroom an hour later, it was clear Douglas had received a similar report from the overnight stage. When I arrived, he and Prickett were whispering back and forth vigorously with some fellow Democrats. Judge Thomas looked over their way when he entered the room, though a minimal sense of judicial decorum prevented him from joining their intrigue. Nonetheless, Thomas did not call the court to order until Douglas and his fellows finished their hasty conference and two of the fellows dashed out. No doubt they were on a mission to prevent the discovery of additional Whig votes or, failing that, to gin up some new Democratic ones.

Just as Judge Thomas finally shouted for order in the court, I felt Martha coming in beside me. She greeted me with a tentative squeeze of my arm, which I returned with full force. Her expression was still chastened, and she did not look at Lincoln as she settled into her seat.

The scene inside the small courtroom was the same today as it had been yesterday: the judge, attorneys, defendant, and twelve gentlemen of the jury crammed into the front of the room, while every available inch on the two rows of spectator benches in the back of the room was filled to bursting. Gazing through the open windows, though, it appeared the crowd outside was not quite as large or loud as yesterday. Not for the first time, it seemed, the thrilling promise of courtroom drama had, for some of Springfield's citizens, been dimmed by the prosaic accretion of hard evidence.

Douglas began the day by calling several Democrats, holders of minor offices, who testified to the origins and depth of the feud between Truett and Early over the land office position. It was apparent Douglas had been thrown off his stride by the distressing news that had begun his morning. Or perhaps he was so wrapped up in the intricacies of party politics that he couldn't help himself.

Whatever the cause, his examinations of these witnesses were stuffed with a wealth of minute, irrelevant details about political machinations. The testimony quickly became tedious in the extreme. That was my reaction, at least, and examining the faces of the jurors, confused and peevish in equal measure, I felt sure it was theirs also.

I noted with amusement that every time Douglas referred to the land office position, Truett glared over at him with a particularly aggrieved expression on his face. Even in the midst of the evidence in whose balance his life hung—unless Doctor Warren's resuscitation efforts were to be relied upon—Truett could not help but focus on the patronage spoils to which he thought himself entitled.

Lincoln's cross-examination of these witnesses was to the point and, I felt sure, effective. In each case, Lincoln established that disputes among party men over offices they felt should be theirs was a routine feature of political life. And, in each case, Lincoln established that the witness had no personal knowledge of the events on Quality Hill on the evening of July fourth. With those points he resumed his seat, receiving grateful expressions from the jury for his brevity.

It was late morning by the time the last of these party witnesses was finally dismissed from the courtroom. Douglas stood and announced in his grave tone, "For our next witness, the People call Henry Owens."

Lincoln's head shot around, and spectators both inside and outside the courtroom began chattering with excitement. What could the apothecary know of Early's death, I wondered, and how did Douglas dare call him as a witness with the grief of his sister's loss still fresh on his face?

Owens pushed through the gallery and took the witness chair. He stared straight ahead, acknowledging neither Douglas nor Lincoln, each of whom was not five feet distant.

"You are Henry Owens, the apothecary?" began Douglas.

"I am." Owens sat glumly in his seat. His brow was furrowed, and the skin around his mouth, previously the embodiment of pink good health, was gray and saggy. He wore a thick black armband around his right arm.

"Right off, I should convey, sir, the sympathies I feel, and I know the judge, jury, and Mr. Lincoln share, for the recent passing of your sister."

Owens nodded silently. His scowl did not abate.

"But you understand the course of justice, in this case justice for the departed Mr. Early, can wait for no man, however grief-filled, and to the contrary demands every man's evidence?"

"So you have informed me, Mr. Douglas," replied Owens, not deigning to look at him.

"Did you know Mr. Early?"

"He was an occasional customer at my apothecary."

"A customer of what?"

"Compounds . . . potions . . . whatever he and I thought might help restore his good health."

"What were your relations with him?"

"I hope they were good, just as I would hope my relations are good with every member of the public who chooses to make use of my expertise and the treatments and remedies I offer."

Lincoln frowned at this. Owens might be grieving and might be testifying unwillingly, as he suggested, but plainly he was not going to let a high-profile public appearance pass without advertising his services.

"And how about the defendant in this matter, Henry Truett? Are you familiar with him?"

"Again, Mr. Truett is an occasional customer of my establishment. Less regular than Mr. Early was, I should say."

"Now we come to the night of July fourth," continued Douglas. "Did you attend the gathering at the Edwards house on Quality Hill that evening?"

"I did."

"Did you encounter Early during the gathering?"

"He and I spoke for about ten minutes, early in the evening."

"About what?"

Owens stiffened. "I wouldn't like to reveal his confidences, especially now that he's no longer able to speak for himself. I'll say merely he had a number of questions about a compound I'd lately dispensed to him, and I tried my best to answer him."

I thought back to seeing the two men argue on the Edwards lawn that evening. There had been something intensely personal about their vigorous discussion. Owens's explanation didn't ring true.

"Later the same evening, did you have occasion to speak with the defendant Truett?"

"I did."

"What did you speak about?"

"He said he'd seen me with Early. I believe his words were to the effect of would I please slip some poison into the next compound I gave Early so that he, Truett, could be over and done with him."

The crowd murmured excitedly. Judge Thomas pulled on his cigar. Truett grabbled Lincoln by the arm and hissed into his ear. The words "He lies!" could be heard throughout the cramped courtroom. Lincoln made a halfhearted attempt to get his client to be quiet.

When the commotion died down, Douglas continued, "And how did you respond to him?"

Owens looked discomfited. "What do you mean?"

"When the defendant Truett made the remark you just recounted, about poisoning Early, did you say anything in return?"

"Not that I recall," said Owens. He looked over at Truett and then away. Immediately, Truett began whispering in Lincoln's ear again, but his manner this time seemed more in the nature of excitement. Lincoln bobbed his head as he listened.

Sensing danger, Douglas hurried to move on. "The fireworks, sir. At the end of the evening, were you present for the display of fireworks Edwards arranged?"

"Yes, I was."

"Where, exactly, were you when the fireworks began?"

"All of the guests had been in the drawing room, where Edwards made some brief remarks. He then announced there would be works. This caused quite a stir, and so everyone rushed outside all at once for viewing."

Owens paused, and Douglas said, nodding, "Go on."

"The main door to the room, leading to the entrance hallway and the front of the house, became quite clogged with persons trying to leave. There is a rear door from the room as well, leading through the kitchen to the rear of the house, and a number of us ended up taking that route to the outside."

"You say a number of us. Do you recall any persons in particular who exited to the rear of the Edwards house along with you?"

"Henry Truett was among them," said Owens confidently. "He was a few feet in front of us as we filed out."

Truett did not react. I realized I'd never questioned him about his precise movements leading up to the fireworks display, and I hoped Lincoln had.

"You said 'us.' Who were you with as you left the house at that time?"

"My sister Margaret." Owens dropped his head and ran his fingers along his mourning band.

Douglas paused to give Owens a moment to mourn before asking, "What happened next?"

"We wanted to see the works, of course, and Edwards had indicated they would be shot off from below the front of the house. So we proceeded along the back perimeter of the house and around a clump of bushes, and then we turned the corner, heading toward the front drive."

"What, if anything, happened next?"

Owens opened his mouth but closed it without speaking. His features tensed. He seemed to be having some sort of unspoken argument with himself.

"Mr. Owens?" prompted Douglas.

"I . . . I don't recall."

A sudden change overtook Douglas. He had been meandering about the room during his examination, but he now stomped his foot and charged right up at Owens, his fists clenched, as if he meant to assault him. The gallery took in its breath sharply. Douglas stopped only inches from the witness; the standing Little Giant and the seated witness, sitting up straight with his shoulders thrust back defiantly, were practically nose to nose. Their eyes locked.

"What . . . happened . . . next?" asked Douglas with unmistakable menace. When Owens did not immediately respond, Douglas added, "Mr. Owens, we've discussed this before, outside the courtroom. All I want is for you to repeat for the jury what you've told me previously. What happened next?"

Owens blinked. His shoulders slumped and his belly sagged. "I saw him," he said, in barely a whisper.

"You need to speak up," commanded Douglas. "And explain yourself. You saw whom? Doing what?"

"I saw Truett," said Owens softly. His posture remained deflated. "I saw Truett pulling his pistol from his belt. And—"

A great clamor of excitement arose from the street outside. "String 'im up!" shouted a coarse voice. Inside the courtroom, the gallery started talking all at once. The judge spit out his cigar and pounded his gavel for order. Truett rose from his chair, looking as if he couldn't decide whether to attack Owens or Douglas first. Lincoln, who had the advantage of close to a foot and fifty pounds on his client, grabbed him under the arms and restrained him.

The courtroom was in an uproar. Then, slowly, the judge's pounding and the clerk's shouting for order came to the fore. Sheriff Hutchason, who had been standing guard off to the side, came over to ensure Truett did not leave his seat again.

"Silence!" shouted the judge. "Silence!"

Eventually, silence did prevail. The judge nodded at Douglas and Douglas in turn at Owens.

"Please continue, Mr. Owens," said Douglas.

Owens stared straight ahead. "Like I said, I saw Mr. Truett pulling his pistol and checking it to make sure it was loaded and primed. And then I saw him striding forward toward the front of the house, with the pistol held at his side, like so." Owens demonstrated, using his hand as the would-be pistol. "And then the works began."

Owens took a deep breath. "And then," he continued, "after the works had ended, after all the noise and smoke was gone, I saw Mr. Truett running back to where I'd been. And I saw him taking his pistol and flinging it toward the bushes. There isn't a doubt in my mind that he shot Early."

The courtroom and street exploded again, and this time it was many minutes before order was restored. Through it all, I kept my eyes trained on Lincoln. There was a calm, even confident expression on his face as bedlam raged all around.

CHAPTER 34

Eventually, the judge was able to call for the lunchtime recess. Lincoln beckoned me over. "Didn't your sister make a sketch of the Edwards grounds?" he whispered. I nodded. "Good. Have her bring it to me upstairs as soon as you can. And one more thing: find me a farmer's almanac." And then he vanished.

I relayed Lincoln's first request to Martha, who nodded and, glad for some way to help the cause, hurried off to her room to retrieve her map. For my part, I pushed through the swirling, excited crowds on the streets to my store. We carried several different brands of almanacs, which were always popular sellers with their mixture of weather and astrological forecasts, civic information, and homespun advice for the farm and kitchen. Usually we sold out of them early in the year, but I thought I'd recently seen one on a back shelf.

Sure enough, after digging through several piles of accumulated debris, I found it: a salmon-colored copy of *"Poor Richard's" New Farmer's Almanac for the Year of Our Lord 1838.* An ink drawing of the smiling Benjamin Franklin, bespectacled, calm, and wise, graced the cover. Slipping it into the pocket of my frockcoat, I retraced my journey through the lunchtime crowds to Hoffman's Row and mounted the stairs to No. 4.

Martha had returned before me, and she and Lincoln were standing above her hand-drawn map of the Edwards property, which was spread out on Lincoln's square table. I handed Poor

Richard to Lincoln, who took him eagerly and flipped through the pages until he found one of interest, which he examined briefly, nodding, and then dog-eared.

"It's set," said Lincoln, more to himself than either of us.

"What's set?" asked Martha.

"You'll see in a bit. Now if I can just find the notes I made for the rest of the examination."

Lincoln riffled through the loose papers in his immediate vicinity, looked underneath Martha's map, then walked around the table, bent over at the waist and scanning the cluttered surface, muttering to himself all the while.

"The divan?" I suggested, pointing to the reclining chair where Stuart liked to read his law papers on the rare occasions on which he was in the office.

Lincoln walked over and sorted through the packets of papers that completely obscured the surface of the sofa. "No."

"Your pockets?" said Martha.

Lincoln felt through the pockets of his trousers and then retrieved his frockcoat where he'd discarded it on the floor near the door and felt through those pockets as well. "No . . . Blast it all . . ."

"I know—your hat," I said suddenly.

"Aha!" Lincoln strode over to the bookcase against the far wall, on top of which he'd set his stovepipe hat. He felt inside the band of black velvet running above the brim and pulled out a sheet of foolscap folded over many times. "You know me well, Speed," he murmured as he spread the sheet out and read it over. "Yes . . . all set."

Half an hour later, Judge Thomas called the court back to order. Henry Owens resumed the witness chair, wearing the same insolent expression he'd worn during his direct testimony. As Lincoln stood up, he straightened the black armband on the sleeve of his frockcoat. Owens watched him closely.

"Brother Owens," began Lincoln.

" 'Mister' will do fine, thank you," replied Owens stiffly.

Lincoln nodded and wandered over to one of the open windows, which he gazed out. He took a deep breath. Turning back toward the witness, he said, "You and I have always had cordial relations, Owens. Is that a fair statement?"

"It is."

"How about between you and Mr. Douglas?"

Owens shrugged. "Don't know that I've had any relations with Mr. Douglas, until the question of testifying in court arose."

"And since that question did arise, how would you characterize your relations with Douglas now?"

"Objection, Your Honor," called Douglas from the back of the courtroom. He was watching Lincoln's examination from his perch on Prickett's lap again. "Lack of relevance."

"I'll withdraw the question for now," said Lincoln, "though we may have cause to return to it later." Turning back to the witness, he said, "I want to ask you about your conversation with Mr. Truett on the evening of the Edwardses' party. Your testimony, I believe, was that Truett said in jest to you something to the effect of maybe you should consider poisoning Mr. Early."

"I don't think it was a joke," replied Owens.

"Well, did you?"

"Did I what?"

"Did you consider poisoning Early?"

Owens blanched. "Did I consider . . . of course not. What sort of question is that?"

"Isn't the truth, Mr. Owens," continued Lincoln, "that the joke, if it was a joke, actually went the opposite direction? Which is to say, it was you who suggested to Mr. Truett the idea of poisoning Early?"

"What?"

"You and Early feuded, didn't you? You disagreed with the way he handled your business at the land office."

Owens stared wildly from Lincoln to Truett—who was nodding vigorously—and then back again. The crowd outside began to talk among themselves. "I deny it," Owens said loudly.

Lincoln looked back calmly. "You do admit you talked with Truett and the subject of poisoning Early came up, is that correct?"

"As a joke," sputtered Owens.

"Now you're saying it was a joke?"

"No—Yes—You see . . . if I said anything of the sort it was a joke. If—if he—Truett—said it, then my testimony is he was serious."

Several members of the gallery tittered. Owens glanced at Douglas, who was glowering in the rear of the courtroom, and then back at Lincoln. The jury was looking on with skeptical expressions, and Judge Thomas chewed his cigar with consternation. Lincoln walked about as much as the cramped courtroom permitted, forcing Owens to twist in the wind of his own words.

At length Lincoln returned to his chair and took up the map Martha had drawn. After showing it to Douglas and the judge, he handed it to the witness. "Do you recognize this," Lincoln asked, "as an approximate map of the Edwards house and grounds?"

Owens frowned at the map, turning it this way and that. "I suppose," he said. "A crude one."

"Yes, a crude one," agreed Lincoln. "It's all I have, but I think it will do for our purposes. May I ask my colleague Mr. Speed to come forward, Your Honor, and act as a human chart holder?"

The judge grinned at me and said, "It's about what he's good for. You may."

"Speed," said Lincoln, cocking his head and gesturing me forward. Reluctantly I complied, and Lincoln directed me to hold the map in front of my body, gripping it from both sides, while he angled me such that both the witness and the jury could see Martha's drawing. Lincoln proceeded to take Owens though his direct testimony again, asking him to use the map as a reference, showing the path taken by those persons who exited the drawing room through the front door as well as those who exited out the rear.

"Now, did you actually see Mr. Truett point the gun at Mr. Early?" Lincoln asked Owens.

"No."

"Did you see him pull the trigger?"

"No. As I said to Mr. Douglas, I saw him before and after Early was shot, holding the gun both times."

"Right. So let's explore those two times. As I understand it, your testimony is you saw Mr. Truett with his pistol drawn twice. Once before the fireworks began and once after they'd ended—is that right?"

"Correct."

"Can you please indicate on the map here, where you were located on the first occasion and where Mr. Truett was?" The witness rose from his chair and pointed to two spots on the drawing. "And where the two of you were on the latter occasion?" Again, the witness complied.

"Now, I'm not sure this crude map, as you correctly termed it, is exactly to scale, but based on where you've just pointed, I'd estimate you were about fifty yards from Mr. Truett on the first occasion and seventy-five yards from him on the latter. Does that sound right?"

Owens dropped his head and thought. The courtroom was silent with anticipation. For the first time, I understood Lincoln's request for the almanac. "Sounds about right," said Owens at last.

Lincoln gave a decisive bob of his head.

"Now—oh, we're done with you. No more need for my human chart holder." It took me a moment to realize this comment was directed to me. I folded up the map, handed it to Lincoln, and resumed my place in the gallery next to Martha. When the commotion ended, Lincoln turned back to his witness.

"What time was it when you and everyone else went out into the yard to view the works?"

"After ten o'clock at night, I should think. Perhaps closer to eleven."

"Do you recall, Mr. Owens, that earlier in the evening there had been whale-oil torches ablaze on the Edwards lawn to illuminate the gathering?"

"That's right."

"But when you went out after Edwards's speech, these were blanketed, presumably to allow for better viewing of the works. Isn't that right?"

Owens thought, but only for a moment. "I believe that's correct."

"And the two times you say you saw Truett, one was before the works had begun, and the other was after they'd ended?"

"Yes."

"So the works were not up in the sky, providing any illumination on either occasion?"

Owens nodded. He shifted uncomfortably in his chair.

"Did you have a candle in your hand?" asked Lincoln.

"No. What would I want a candle for?"

"Now, how could you see Mr. Truett, from a distance of fifty or seventy-five yards, in the dark, without a candle, after ten o'clock at night?"

Owens's eyes darted from Lincoln to Douglas and back to Lincoln again. "Why, the moon, of course."

"It was a bright moon that evening, is that what you recall?"

"That's right." Owens nodded eagerly.

"A full moon?"

"Full . . . or close enough to it."

Lincoln strode back to his chair and pulled out Poor Richard, whom he had hidden at the bottom of a pile of papers. After first showing the cover to the judge and the jury, he opened it to the page he'd marked during lunchtime and handed it to the witness.

"Does not the almanac say that on July the fourth the moon was barely past the first quarter instead of being full?"

Owens stared at the page Lincoln had given him, then began riffling through the adjacent pages. He did not answer. The gallery buzzed excitedly.

"Does not the almanac also say," continued Lincoln, "that the moon had disappeared by ten o'clock?"

Again, Owens looked back and forth from the page Lincoln had given him to the surrounding ones. He remained mute.

"Is it not a fact that it was too dark to see anything from a distance of fifty to seventy-five yards?"

Owens closed the almanac, handed it back to Lincoln, and folded his hands in his lap. "What do you want me to say?" he asked quietly.

Lincoln rose to his full height. "I want you to say," he said, his index finger pointed at Owens with accusation, "what business you have coming into this courtroom and making these false claims against my client."

Owens touched his mourning band. "My sister . . ." he began, but he did not continue.

"What about your sister?" asked Lincoln in a softer voice.

Owens's face was drained of all color. He took a deep breath and continued, speaking slowly. "My sister passed recently, as you know all too well, Mr. Lincoln. The cause of her passing, it seems, was the ingesting of an ingredient, strychnine, which I keep on my shelves. In small doses it can be restorative. In large doses it is fatal." Owens swallowed. The crowd was silent.

"I had nothing to do with it, I swear. I have no idea how the strychnine came to be administered to Margaret. But Mr. Douglas . . . he told me if I didn't—"

Douglas had been on his feet, pacing back and forth through the gallery, ever since Lincoln first pulled out the almanac. Now he strode forward toward the judge, shouting, "Objection! Objection, Your Honor! This has nothing to do with the questions presented by this trial."

"It has everything to do with them," returned Lincoln.

"Nothing—nothing at all," insisted Douglas. "Your Honor, I feel confident any *national* judge would immediately see the folly of the path Mr. Lincoln is trying to lead the witness—indeed, lead all of us—down."

Judge Thomas pulled on his cigar and studied Douglas with great care. I felt sure I could see in the judge's gaze a calculation based on Douglas's suddenly narrow and declining lead in the election returns.

"Overruled!" announced the judge. "You may proceed, Mr. Lincoln."

CHAPTER 35

Late that evening we were back where it all began, in the gentlemen's smoking lounge of Colonel Spotswood's hotel, cele-
brating Lincoln's victory. Lincoln, Truett, and I had been there
from the start, as had Martha. Truett had insisted she attend as soon
as he learned she'd been responsible for creating the map that proved
critical for Lincoln's cross-examination of Henry Owens. The smile
on Martha's face, broad all evening, had been no broader than when
Lincoln came up to her and threw a celebratory arm around her
shoulders.

Other townspeople had come and gone, or come and stayed,
drawn by Truett's promise to cover the entire bill in honor of his
vindication. Much of the jury had been by, shaking Truett's hand
and accepting a drink or two, as had many Democratic and Whig
officials. Thomas Lincoln and John Johnston were in the "come
and stayed" category, although both men quickly had their fill of
drink and dozed off in a corner.

The concluding acts of the trial had been rapid after Lincoln's
decisive cross-examination. Douglas promptly rested the People's
case, having been humiliated by Owens's testimony that Douglas had threatened to charge him in connection with his sister's
death if he did not testify against Truett. A string of hisses and
catcalls from the audience greeted Douglas when he stood to
announce he had no further witnesses.

For his part, Lincoln then indicated the defense would rest on its cross-examination of the People's case and did not intend to call any witnesses of its own. Counsel proceeded to closing arguments, Lincoln's first and then Douglas's, and while the Little Giant argued gamely, he was unable to overcome Lincoln's demonstration that many other persons could have fired the fatal shot combined with the stain of Owens's discredited testimony.

After arguments concluded, the judge charged the jury and sent them upstairs to No. 4, Hoffman's Row, to deliberate, after first checking with Lincoln to make sure he'd removed all of his papers from his law office.

"Did you actually clear out everything?" I asked Lincoln now as I accepted Truett's offer of another glass of whiskey from Spotswood's reserve. "It was quite a mess."

"Everything but one item," said Lincoln. "I may have left Poor Richard sitting alone in the middle of my worktable, open to the moon chart for the night of July fourth."

Everyone laughed and toasted Lincoln's artfulness.

Thirty minutes after they retired upstairs to No. 4, the jury returned down to No. 3 with their verdict.

"What say you, in the matter of the People against Henry Truett?" demanded the clerk when everyone resumed their places inside the courtroom and outside on the clamoring street. In truth, little suspense remained in the game at this point.

"Not guilty!" shouted the jury foreman, and it was all over except for the drinking. Doctor Warren would require a different human subject on which to prove the supposed life-restoring capabilities of his galvanic battery.

Late in the evening, accepting yet another glass of liquor from Truett, I looked over at Lincoln. He was slumped on a couch, his chin resting in his hands and his eyes half-closed. The flush of the decisive courtroom victory had faded. Suddenly, he looked very sad.

"Thinking of Miss Owens?" I asked.

He nodded silently.

"I'm glad you won," said Martha from my other side, "but we didn't learn the truth today, did we? About who killed Early? Or Miss Owens? Or who was S.G. and why was he haunting you? I'm pleased Mr. Truett was found innocent, of course, but we haven't *solved* anything."

Lincoln gave a great sigh. "As I've told you before, Miss Speed," he said, "trials are merely meant to determine whether the man in the dock bears legal guilt. They've never been intended as mechanisms to seek the truth. Truett was adjudged not guilty under the law. Not 'innocent'—just 'not guilty.' That's all that happened today."

"Are you saying you think Mr. Truett *could* have done it after all?" asked Martha quietly. All of us glanced over at the man, who was dancing a drunken jig with a few confederates on the other side of the room.

"It's possible," admitted Lincoln, "but I think it more likely there's still some unknown killer out there. First thing tomorrow morning, I'm going to Sheriff Hutchason to see what aid I can lend to his investigations. We'll figure out who did these terrible things. We'll get to the truth and soon. The truth just wasn't in the dock today."

Martha's posture, her arms crossed in front of her chest and her chin thrust forward, made clear her dissatisfaction with Lincoln's answer.

Eventually, the church bells tolled midnight. Only a handful of men remained spread about Spotswood's with us, most in various states of intoxication. A few minutes later, Stephen Douglas walked into the smoking room.

"Ah, they said I'd find you here, Lincoln," said Douglas, marching over to my friend and offering an outstretched hand, which Lincoln took. Douglas was still wearing the formal suit of clothes he'd worn to court earlier, his tie still done up smartly. "I wanted to offer my congratulations on the verdict. The better man for today won. May I have better luck in the future."

Douglas noticed Truett's presence for the first time. Truett was on his feet, swaying a bit, but circling the Little Giant like a predator sizing up his next meal.

"I'm glad for your sake, too, Truett," said Douglas in the same jovial tone. "No hard feelings, I hope." Douglas stuck out his hand. As much as I detested the man, I admired his nerve. It was hard not to.

Truett, however, was focused on more concrete matters. He swatted Douglas's hand away. "You've wronged me, Douglas, in more ways than one," he growled. "I ought to punch you in the mouth. But I'll settle for a more palpable measure of satisfaction."

Douglas faced him squarely and without blinking. "What's that?"

"The land office position, with a guarantee I'll have it for life."

"You know I can't offer that," replied Douglas. "Indeed, if Lincoln and his cronies keep ginning new votes from up north, both of us may be out of a job before long."

Several of the Whigs scattered about the room gave a muffled cheer. Everyone was riveted by the tense confrontation.

"Promise me the land office position for as long as it remains within your gift," said Truett. There was an unmistakable hunger for retribution in his eyes, and I was reminded at once of Truett's ravenous look as he had watched the land auction at the market house months earlier.

"I can't do that either. I won't."

"Why not?"

"Because if I do have the power to recommend an office-holder, I'll be duty-bound to recommend someone I think worthy of the job. You can hardly expect me to consider you as such, not after what we've been through."

Several men around the room took in their breaths sharply. Truett's face went red as a beet. "You . . . you bastard," sputtered Truett. "You no-good goddamned liar."

Douglas calmly glanced over at Lincoln, who was already on his feet and grasping at Truett's arm. "Come now, Truett," said Lincoln, trying to pull his client away. "Let's not let old animosities spoil our evening. There'll be plenty of time in the future to sort out offices among you and Douglas and the rest of the Democrats. There's no call to worry about all that tonight."

But Truett would not budge. "I said," he repeated, his glare still locked on Douglas, "you're a no-good goddamned liar. If you were a true gentleman, there's only one way you'd respond to those words, you scoundrel."

"Go home, Truett," said Douglas, flicking dismissively with

the back of his hand. "You won the trial. You're a free man. Go home, sleep in your own bed, and enjoy your freedom."

"Come along, Truett—" tried Lincoln again, but his client shook him off.

"You're a no-good goddamned liar, Douglas," repeated Truett for a third time. "I demand satisfaction, on the field of honor." A gasp ran all the way around the room. These were words that, once spoken, could not easily be retracted.

"A duel?" asked Douglas, looking at Truett with incredulity. "Are you truly going to challenge me to a duel?"

"I just did," replied Truett. "Now, are you a gentleman, or are you not a gentleman?"

Douglas's broad face gradually hardened. His eyes narrowed and his lips curled into a sneer. "Very well," he said, taking a deep, steadying breath. "It's the only way."

My sister Martha cried out, "No, Stephen. Don't!"

But Douglas did not appear to have heard her, and he continued, his hawk-like eyes narrowing in on Truett. "I accept the challenge. Daybreak Sunday. On the island in the river near Sangamon. Pistols. Prickett shall be my second. Have your second contact him. They can agree on the rest of the details. Oh, and I'll arrange for a minister so there's someone to read you last rites."

Douglas thrust his shoulders back, straightened his coat, and walked from the room.

Truett turned to Lincoln, who had gone pale. "You shall be my second, Lincoln," said Truett. "That bastard has it coming. You know it as well as I. Let's make sure he gets it right between the eyes."

CHAPTER 36

"You're not actually planning to go through with it, are you?" I asked Lincoln the next morning as we lay in bed. "I don't have a choice."

"You could decline to serve as Truett's second. Let someone else have the trouble of trying to corral him."

Lincoln sighed and rolled over to face me. "I can't do that. I feel responsible for the way it got out of hand last night. I should have steered Douglas outside as soon as he arrived. Intended or not, his presence was always going to provoke Truett."

"No one but Truett is responsible," I said. "His pigheadedness caused the original fight with Early, and now this." I shook my head in wonder. "Although I suppose Douglas bears his fair share for last night as well. Can you imagine Douglas going through with the duel? Surely it would be catastrophic for his future, no matter what happens on the field. Look what it did to Burr."

Lincoln nodded. The example of Vice President Aaron Burr, who killed Alexander Hamilton in a duel but forever ended his political career in the process, was well-remembered even several decades after the fact.

Duels remained common in other parts of the Union; one was said to occur nearly every day beneath The Oaks in New Orleans. In Illinois they were outlawed by the state's constitution. The state criminal code likewise proscribed them, with prison sentences running up to five years for anyone remotely involved in a duel, including mere spectators. The seconds, the position Lincoln now found himself in, faced particularly harsh punishment.

But the code of the duel was far too ingrained in American society—especially here in the West—for the nominal legal prohibition to have full effect. Challenges and near challenges were a regular feature of Springfield's brawling political culture. The only real surprise of Truett's challenge was that it hadn't come sooner. But if threats and feints were relatively commonplace, the actual use of weapons on the dueling field was not. Duels in Illinois were often threatened, occasionally agreed upon, and almost never fought.

Thus, as a practical matter, the key figures in duels became the seconds, tasked with coming up with a compromise of sufficient ambiguity as to allow both principals to claim satisfaction and accordingly desist from the main event. In issuing and accepting the duel challenge, as Truett and Douglas had done last night, the main actors demonstrated their *willingness* to defend their honor on the field, as so many generations of gentlemen had done before them. They had assuredly not demonstrated their *intention*—to say nothing of *desire*—to face the business end of a loaded pistol.

"Do you want my help?" I asked Lincoln.

"A second to my second? Or, I suppose, a third?" He laughed. "No, I'll manage on my own. I'll track down Prickett soon enough. Stephen arranged it so that we'd have more than twenty-four hours to resolve matters. That's proof enough he has no interest in going through with the blasted thing."

Douglas had exercised his prerogative last night as the challenged party to set the terms of the duel: time, place, and weapons. As Lincoln noted, the comparatively lengthy time period Douglas had specified before the duel was to take place gave the parties plenty of time to reach a compromise.

But when Lincoln came into the anteroom of my store late that afternoon, his disgruntled expression told me at once that compromise between Truett and Douglas was not proving easy.

"What's happened?" I asked.

He took off his stovepipe hat, ran a hand through his unruly black hair, and shook his head. "Where to begin? Truett's being completely unreasonable. No surprise there. He says he'll accept nothing less than a guarantee of the land office position for life. Doesn't care for an apology and acknowledgment of his merit or anything else. It's land office registrar or 'see you on the field.'"

"*If* the land office is Douglas's to give," I said.

"That's the other problem. As you say, Douglas has the land office job to dispense only if the Democrats hold on to the congressional seat. But reports of more Whig votes for Stuart keep arriving from various northern counties. Every time a new stage pulls up at the Globe, it seems as if Douglas's lead shrinks a little more. Simeon and Weber are each keeping their own running tally, but Douglas's lead is all the way down to single digits, if it exists at all anymore."

"Good news for Stuart, I suppose."

"Great news for Stuart. Under any other circumstance I'd be overjoyed. If we Whigs have actually captured that congressional seat—why, it'll do big things for us here in the state. And set us up well for '40, when we'll need to muster everything we've got to try to get rid of van Buren.

"But now that the trial is over, Douglas is absolutely and completely preoccupied with the election returns. He's convinced some of the Whigs up north are manufacturing new ballots to add into the counting pile. I can't say I blame him—he might be right!" Lincoln gave a short laugh. "Anyway, Prickett can't get him to focus on the duel and how to resolve it, and neither can I."

"Sunrise tomorrow should focus him," I said. "Nothing concentrates the mind like a hanging in the morning, or a duel, in this case."

"But it may be too late by then. If the principals arrive at the field, with their weapons . . . you know as well as I anything can happen at that point."

I voiced aloud the thought I'd been turning over in my mind since the previous night. "Perhaps it wouldn't be the worst thing that could happen for you, Lincoln."

Lincoln jumped as if he'd been struck by an electric shock. "What? No, Joshua, you can't suggest that. It would be a disaster for me, for you, for everyone in Springfield, if Stephen ends up on the dueling field, no matter what happens next."

"Why? He's a blackguard, and your main obstacle in the state. Everyone says so. Even you must know it, even if you'll never admit it. If he draws and shoots Truett, or gets shot himself—"

"Stop!" Lincoln held up both hands in front of my face. "I won't hear another word."

Reluctantly, I let go of the idea. Sometimes, I thought, Lincoln was too upright for his own good. "What's left, then?" I said aloud.

"Prickett and I agreed to talk again after dinner. He's going to push Douglas one more time. At the least he should offer that Truett can be in charge of the land office on the condition that Douglas ends up winning the election. There's nothing but pride keeping Douglas from making that offer. And giving up a bit of pride is a lot better than the alternative. Prickett certainly realizes as much. He just needs to convince Stephen."

"Will that be enough for Truett?"

"It should be. It's all he can hope for. I'm going back out to see if I can't talk some sense into him. Wish me luck."

I did, and Lincoln departed. Several hours later, just as I was about to lock up for the evening, the door opened again. I looked up, expecting Lincoln, but saw Martha instead.

"Did they work out a compromise?" she said. "Oh, tell me they did! I can't bear the thought of Stephen having to fight a duel against that *awful* man."

"They did," I replied. If Martha knew there was to be a duel, she would insist upon coming to the field herself in the morning. At all odds, I needed to make sure that did not happen.

"Oh, good!" Martha collapsed against the counter and breathed great sighs of relief. "I've been so worried all day. I figured you'd let me know as soon as they agreed on something, but when I hadn't heard from you, well, I feared the worst."

"I was going to come tell you once I closed up the store. Lincoln only stopped by recently with the good news."

"What'd they agree upon?" she asked.

"Um . . . Lincoln didn't give me all the details. An acknowl-edgment by each that the other had proceeded in good faith . . . that sort of thing, I imagine."

I convinced Martha to go home and retire for the evening. Thereafter I waited for Lincoln to return with word of the final negotiations. I paced back and forth in the storeroom until I thought I'd worn a path in the floorboards. The moon rose and set again. It was very late, long past midnight. Finally, I clambered up the back stairs, changed into my nightshirt, and lay down in bed. Waiting. Much later, through the fog of a drowsy sleep, I heard Lincoln returning and then felt him lying down beside me.

"Speed, are you awake?" he whispered.

"Mm–hmm."

"The duel is on."

CHAPTER 37

There were two places in central Illinois where duels, on the rare occasions they proved unavoidable, were fought. The first was Bloody Island, an island in the middle of the Mississippi River between the Illinois and Missouri shorelines. Its very name, of course, bespoke its heritage as the place where disputes between gentlemen were resolved. Offshore and out of sight, participants in duels staged on Bloody Island were reasonably assured of escaping prosecution under the laws of Illinois. Whether they could escape with their lives was another matter altogether—a matter for the Almighty God, who alone rendered judgment as to which of the two men facing each other on the field of honor deserved to walk off intact.

The second place used for dueling was the one indicated by Douglas on Friday night, a small, unnamed island in the middle of the Sangamon River, not far from the town also bearing the name Sangamon. Since the island was surrounded by Illinois territory on both sides, duelists and their retinue were more at risk of prosecution than those who availed themselves of Bloody Island. The island was, however, much closer to Springfield, about an hour's ride on horseback rather than the two-day journey Bloody Island required.

It was to the unnamed island in the middle of the Sangamon River that Lincoln and I rode early on Sunday morning. The sky was still pitch black and neither of us had gotten more than an hour of sleep when we left the stables behind the Globe Tavern. But it was safer to leave town before anyone else woke and thought to ask why we were setting off at this hour.

"You left your gun behind?" Lincoln asked me as we rode side by side.

"Reluctantly." The dueling code required that only the two principals could be armed. There was too much chance for mischief otherwise.

"Good. Me too. I still hope to make one last attempt at compromise."

"What will Truett take now that he hasn't taken before?"

"We'll see. I remain of the belief cooler heads will prevail at the last. We just need something we can convince Truett of. And Douglas too, for that matter."

We soon arrived at the riverbank opposite the dueling island. The landing was deserted, but a few minutes later we heard the sound of approaching hooves and Truett materialized out of the inky predawn. He was wearing a military uniform and a tight expression. He swung down off his horse, walked over silently to us, and shook our hands.

"I believe it's still possible to resolve this," said Lincoln.

"My fate is in the hands of the Almighty," said Truett, shaking his head gravely. "And I'm perfectly content to let it rest with Him. I slept the sleep of the innocent last night. Now let's get over to the island. I want to pace out the terrain and find the most advantageous location before Douglas arrives."

Hidden beneath some bushes, we located the old rowboat that was used to access the island, carried it to the riverbank, and stepped in. A faint glow began to nose into the eastern skies. It was about a hundred yards out to the island, and I rowed while Lincoln and Truett looked out, silently. There was no point in further conversation until Douglas and his second, Prickett, arrived on the scene.

Once at the island, I tied up the craft while Lincoln and Truett began to walk about. The outer perimeter of the island was ringed by willow trees, their graceful bows dipping toward the summer waters of the gently flowing river. The middle of the island was a mostly flat hump of land some fifty feet long and twenty feet wide.

It was as if nature herself had thought to provide the local citizens with a patch of earth custom-made for the purpose.

With Lincoln at his side, Truett walked the length of the island, examining every step of ground as he went. He peered down the field from one end, then walked toward the other end and repeated the exercise. It would be his choice of sides and his right to specify the distance apart the two men would march before turning to face each other. Each footfall or tuft of grass could prove decisive. The Lord God might have the final say, but only a fool would not do what he could to increase his odds when he stood before the Almighty.

There was a call from shore. "Ahoy! Anyone out there? Where's the boat?"

"I'll go," I said. "You two keep up your pacing."

I slipped into the boat and rowed back to shore. Three men waited next to the reeds, watching my approach. Douglas, Prickett, and . . . who was that third man? He had a long, clean-shaven face, with a narrow nose, arched eyebrows, and a high, pale forehead. I knew I'd seen him before, but I couldn't for the life of me place him.

"I figured you'd be here, Speed," said Douglas as he leapt aboard. "You'll pass along my regards, and regrets, to your sister, I hope, if it comes to that."

"It won't, Stephen," interposed Prickett, patting his champion's arm.

Prickett must have seen me staring at their companion because he said, "Speed, I believe you know Preacher Crews? Stephen said on Friday night he'd arrange for clergy in case any final blessings must be administered."

"Ah, Preacher. I didn't recognize you at first without your beard."

"Shaved it by candlelight this very morning," Crews replied. "I decided it wasn't right for the occasion." Though his face looked very different without the whiskers, his voice was unmistakable, the same thunderous voice I'd heard at the camp meeting, one sounding as if it belonged to the God of the Old Testament.

The little rowboat bobbed under the weight of the three men as they climbed in beside me. It could barely hold all four of us; any more and it would surely capsize.

I waited until the rocking stopped and rowed toward the island. The river and surrounding woods were starting to get light now. The sun must be close to breaking the horizon. The testing hour had arrived.

"Did anyone see you on the way out of town?" Prickett asked me.

"No. You?"

"I don't think so. Hopefully we'll be able to resolve this quickly and without undue consequences. I wouldn't like to think what'd happen if Sheriff Hutchason were to blunder by."

Each of us was taking a risk by being present this morning, but, I realized, as the chief prosecutor for Sangamon County, Prickett was taking more risk than the rest of us. Preacher Crews stared intently toward the approaching island. He had a look of fierce determination. Perhaps he was recalling his most recent sermon from the platform before the tents.

When the nose of the boat reached the shore, Prickett jumped off and made it fast. I hurried ahead while Prickett waited for his companions to disembark. I broke through the ring of willows and saw that Lincoln and Truett had taken up residence on the eastern end of the field. Truett had decided to make Douglas squint into the rising sun.

"They've arrived," I called as I strode over.

Lincoln looked over my shoulder at the men coming up behind me. His eyes widened and his mouth dropped open. "What's *he* doing here?" he asked.

I followed his gaze. "The third fellow? That's Preacher Crews— the one from the camp meeting. Douglas said he'd be bringing a clergyman."

"That's no preacher," said Lincoln quietly, his eyes still wide. "That's John McNamar. Or John McNeil; take your pick of names." When I did not immediately respond, he added, "My old rival for Ann Rutledge's affection. From New Salem."

I looked again at the preacher, who was standing near Douglas at the opposite end of the field, and my pulse started to race. Lincoln's old rival from New Salem. Someone well-versed with disguises and false names. And one familiar with the language of "false prophets" and "judgment day." It hit me like a thunderbolt: *Salem's Ghost!*

"Lincoln—" I began, grabbing at his arm.

But he was already striding away from me and toward Prickett, who had called out, "Let's meet in the center of the field and discuss terms, Lincoln." The two seconds spoke loudly so everyone could hear what was being said.

"Have you brought the weapons?" asked Lincoln.

Prickett took out two long dueling pistols. One after the other, he cocked each, pointed it at the sky, and pulled the trigger to prove it was unloaded. As Prickett performed his demonstration, I saw Lincoln's gaze avert to Preacher Crews for a moment before returning to rest on Prickett.

"Is there anything more to discuss before we choose pistols and proceed to load?" asked Prickett.

"I want to ask one final time," said Lincoln, "whether your man is willing to guarantee that he'll appoint Truett registrar of the land office on the assumption he ultimately prevails in the election count. I can tell you we'd accept that guarantee, along with mutual apologies for insults unintended, et cetera, as full and complete satisfaction."

Prickett called Douglas over, and Lincoln stepped away to let the two men consult. Lincoln looked down at the ground, up at the sky, anywhere but at the preacher. For his part, the preacher stared straight ahead, his hands clutched behind his back.

Prickett stepped away from Douglas and back toward Lincoln. "We cannot agree," Prickett said. "For reasons previously conveyed." He paused. "So I take it we should load."

Lincoln held up his hand. "There must be some other way." He turned to face Douglas directly. "Stephen," he said in a pleading tone. "Surely there's something you're willing to give that lets Truett keep his pride and his good name."

Douglas's eyes darted around the field like a hawk's. "Perhaps . . . but it's little use to try to reason with that blackguard." He gestured in Truett's direction, and Truett clenched his fists and took a few steps forward before Lincoln restrained him.

"What do you have in mind?" asked Lincoln, holding back his client with a long, powerful forearm.

"Oregon," said Douglas.

"Oregon?" echoed Lincoln. There was a faint light in his eyes.

"More specifically," continued Douglas, "postmaster for all of the Oregon Country."

It took a moment for the suggestion to sink in. "Oregon?" said Truett, when it did. "What would I possibly want with Oregon?"

"It's a vast tract of land," said Douglas. "Said to be larger than ten of the original colonies put together. It's a fresh start—and a huge position. There'll be a tremendous number of routes to survey and depots to staff. And a large fur trade on which to assess duty. In sum, there'll be substantial finances to handle and many jobs to give out. For an enterprising man such as yourself, Truett, I'd think there's plenty you could do with Oregon."

Lincoln had been listening to Douglas with a trace of a smile on his face. "You're proposing, Douglas," he said now, "that you agree to support Truett for Oregon if you're ultimately seated in Congress, and that Stuart agrees to support Truett for the position in the event he's our next representative?"

"That's right," said Douglas. "Do you think you could convince Stuart of it?"

"I'm sure I could," replied Lincoln. A look passed between the two politicians, as if they were sharing a private, unsaid thought.

"So Mr. Truett would be guaranteed this position, with the opportunities I advert to, whatever the outcome of the election?"

"Correct."

"And we'd both agree to apologize to the other for insults unintended and all the rest. Let bygones be bygones."

"Exactly."

Douglas nodded and beckoned Prickett over. They whispered back and forth while Lincoln and Truett conferred. My eyes reverted to the preacher at the far end of the field. Why had he come this morning? I wondered. What was his game?

The two consultations over, Lincoln and Prickett met again in the center of the field and spoke, this time in hushed tones inaudible to the rest of us. I could see them smiling—from relief, I thought—and quickly they shook hands and broke apart.

"We have mutual satisfaction," announced Lincoln. Truett and Douglas approached each other, hesitantly at first, but then Douglas stuck out his hand and Truett shook it without reservation.

"We should be off this island at once," said Prickett. "Best if no one sees us gathered here, even with this happy outcome. Why don't you come with us, Truett? You and Douglas can discuss the terms of your posting to Oregon." Turning to Lincoln, he added, "Once we four have rowed across, I'll come back to pick up you and Speed."

"Very well," said Lincoln, as Truett and Douglas followed Prickett across the field to where the rowboat was tied up.

I stared at Preacher Crews, who had remained at the far end of the field during the entire proceeding. I expected him to make a move toward Lincoln, or at least to say something. Instead, he headed over to join the other three at the rowboat.

"Maybe it's not him," I said under my breath.

"Who's not who?" asked Lincoln, standing next to me now.

"Preacher Crews, who turns out to be your long-lost McNamar. For a moment, I thought he meant to do violence to you."

"To me? Whatever for?" The other four men had just disappeared through the willow trees at the edge of the river.

"I'd made him for Salem's Ghost."

Lincoln opened his mouth to respond but closed it and stood silently for a minute, his brows clenched in concentration and his jaw muscles pulsating. Then he said, "I don't think so. McNamar and I were on friendly enough terms the last time we parted."

"He left New Salem before you?"

Lincoln nodded. "He'd brought his family from back East, but he didn't want to stay around once he learned Ann was gone. Can't say I blame him." It occurred to me that Lincoln, too, had been chased from New Salem by the lingering memory of the departed Ann Rutledge. "So one day he packed up his family and was gone again."

"Had he shown any interest in the ministry during the time you knew him?"

"None. And I doubt he has a true interest today. But then I suspect it's like that for many of these traveling preachers. They show up from nowhere and set up shop and then, once they've converted their share—and been rewarded handsomely by the grateful converts for illuminating the supposed path to heaven—they disappear to nowhere. I don't think anyone's got the time to check their bona fides, to say nothing of the inclination. When eternal salvation is on offer, it makes people forget themselves."

"McNamar always had a talent for making people believe whatever he said. Confidence men and traveling preachers sing from nearby pews—at least they do in my book."

I looked up and saw the sun was high in the sky. "I wonder what's taking Prickett so long. He should have been back with the boat by now." I turned to face Lincoln. "And what's funny about Oregon? You and Douglas seemed to be sharing a laugh about something back as you reached your compromise."

"Do you know who owns the Oregon Country?" he asked.

"It's shared between us and Great Britain, right?"

"It's *disputed* between us and Great Britain. Even the name is disputed. They call it the Columbia District. Do you suppose our former overlords permit the United States Post Office Department to operate in territory they still claim for themselves?"

"You mean . . ."

"Douglas's suggestion was a boodle. Douglas and Stuart can both agree to appoint Truett to oversee the Department's operations in Oregon, but when he gets there he'll discover he's in charge of precisely nothing. Course, it's about a nine-month journey, even with the best conditions. With the snows coming to the Rockies before long, I imagine he won't leave for the Pacific Coast until next spring, and he couldn't possibly get back to confront Douglas until two or three years after that. Or, better still, Truett'll decide to stay in the Far West and make a go of things. I've no doubt there are opportunities to get rich out there—just not the ones Douglas sold him on."

I gave a shout of laughter and Lincoln grinned. It was nice to be on Douglas's side of the joke for once.

We heard the *clunk* of the wooden rowboat arriving back at the landing.

"At last," I said, taking a few steps toward the shore and calling out, "What took you so long, Prickett?"

A few seconds later, John McNamar walked through the gap in the willow trees. He held a dueling pistol in each hand.

Chapter 38

"Do not take a single step, either of you," said McNamar in his booming voice, as if he were commanding Moses at Sinai. "I convinced Prickett to give me the powder and balls for safekeeping, along with the pistols themselves. I assure you, these are very much loaded and primed."

We were about forty feet away, too far to make a run at him without testing his accuracy. Instead, I cupped my hands to my mouth and called out toward the shoreline: "Prickett? Douglas? Truett?"

There was no reply.

"Come back to the island!" I shouted at the top of my lungs. "We need help!"

Silence.

McNamar smiled. "Prickett was in a hurry to get back to town, as were Douglas and Truett—the new best friends—so I told them to go ahead and I'd take care of the two of you. And I waited to make sure they were far clear before rowing back across the river."

"I'm surprised to see you back in Sangamon County, John," said Lincoln. His facial muscles were relaxed, as if he'd been overtaken by a sudden calm.

"You only see what matters to you, Lincoln." McNamar spat onto the ground. "I've never mattered to you. Besides, I never left."

"But I saw you ride off with your family."

"We rode off all right, but I never left. My heart never did. It was always with Ann. It will always be with Ann. And my head never left, either. It's always been fixed on the man who destroyed my life."

He crouched into a shooting stance and aimed one of his pistols directly at Lincoln. Lincoln flinched and I threw myself in front of him and started to pull him to the ground. But then McNamar loosed a vicious laugh and let the pistol dangle from his hand once again.

"There was nothing more I could have done for her," said Lincoln, shaking loose of me. There was no fear in his voice but rather a kind of softness.

"You killed her," said McNamar. "I know you did. Her brother told me so. He told me you visited her bedside when the doctor had prescribed absolute quietude. You didn't care about what was best for her, Lincoln. You only cared for yourself."

"That's not true," said Lincoln. "I cared for her. I loved—"

"Don't say it!" screamed McNamar, raising his pistol again. "Or I'll shoot you right now."

"I cared for her," Lincoln repeated, more quietly now. "I called to look in on her. And it's a good thing I did, because she was in the middle of a seizure when I arrived, and I was able to keep her from harming herself."

"John Rutledge told me about how your visit *caused* Ann to have her seizure," replied McNamar. "He told me everything. From that moment, I knew I'd have my revenge someday. I just didn't expect it to come this way."

"Why did you kill Early?" I asked. We needed to play for more time.

"I had a good thing going at the land office, using false names and surveys to keep on selling the same property, and Early was going to ruin it. When I found Truett to put in his place, I thought I had a solution. I knew I could control Truett. Douglas was all but guaranteed to win and I did everything I could to help him. But then Early kept digging into the records and asking around and I realized I couldn't wait for the election. I needed to make sure there was a new registrar right away. Or, at least, to do away with the old one. So I attended that party, in disguise, and when the fireworks ended I had my shot. And I took it."

"What did that have to do with Lincoln?"

"It had everything to do with Lincoln. Early was Lincoln's man. My land office scheme used his father's signatures on the surveys— I'd always particularly liked that touch. And when Lincoln was appointed to represent Truett, I saw in the papers that he was looking into the land office dealings as a possible explanation for Early's death." McNamar glared at Lincoln again. "You ruined my life once. I wasn't about to let you do it again."

"John, I—"

"I've never forgotten the way you moped around New Salem after Ann's death. It was pathetic. You were indulging in a grief you weren't entitled to."

Lincoln flushed.

"But the memory of it gave me an idea. I know you're weak, Lincoln. I know you have a weak mind. So I decided to prey on that mind. I wanted you to feel the discomfort of being watched by loathing eyes. And to suffer public humiliation, the way I'd questioned my sanity and been humiliated when I returned to New Salem to discover Ann wasn't mine anymore and that she was gone.

"I know all about you, Lincoln. And I wanted to make sure you knew you were being watched by someone who knew all about you. Someone who knew everything."

"And you followed us when Lincoln and I went for an evening stroll with Miss Margaret Owens," I said. "And fired a shot over our heads. And dropped one of Ann Rutledge's gloves in the process."

"Margaret!" cried Lincoln, and he clutched at his heart.

McNamar smirked. "Ann gave me those gloves when I rode off to New York to get my family. They were a token to remember her by, she said. I've done it. I've never forgotten her. But you're wrong, Lincoln, if you think I was responsible for what happened to Miss Owens. *You* were responsible for her fate, with what you did to Ann. I was only the agent of her death."

"You bastard!" Lincoln's face was contorted by a mixture of grief and rage.

"Once I started tormenting him," McNamar said, speaking to me, "I realized how thrilling revenge could be. And when I saw him squiring his Miss Owens around town, it hit me in an instant. He'd taken my love from me. I would take his from him. It's just like Lincoln said here on the field earlier—mutual satisfaction."

"How did you kill her?" asked Lincoln, his face white, through clenched teeth.

"The same way you killed Ann. I sat at her bedside and watched her squirm. Watched her whole body shake and convulse until the very life was wrung out of her. Only I enjoyed it. Thoroughly.

"It was much easier than I thought. I knew from the tent meeting she hadn't been feeling well. So I slipped into the apothecary shop when Owens headed out on a call, took a few grains of strychnine, and went up to her room. She was coming in and out of sleep. I put the grains in the mixture her brother had made and told her to drink up. I told her it was God's will. As it was."

Lincoln fell to one knee, sobbing. I bent down, my arms around his shoulders, and tried to comfort him. McNamar was looking on with a gleeful expression.

As Lincoln shook with sorrow beneath my touch, I considered the situation. Each of McNamar's pistols would be loaded with a single ball. He'd boasted about being a good shot, and there was no reason to doubt him. Two balls and the two of us, alone in the middle of an isolated island. Where no one else knew we were; we'd made sure of that ourselves. There were no good options.

At length, Lincoln stood and carefully straightened the stovepipe hat on his head. His face was dry and his countenance clear, as if he'd managed to reach some internal resolution from the depths of his grief.

"Good speed, Speed," he whispered.

And he started walking directly toward McNamar. He had both hands raised in the air, defenseless.

Lincoln had taken two or three steps forward when McNamar saw him coming and yelled out, "Stop! Stop or I'll shoot!"

"I want you to shoot," said Lincoln, continuing his steady advance. He was thirty-five feet from McNamar, then thirty, then twenty-five. "I want you to rescue me from this woeful existence. I didn't have the courage to do it myself, two weeks ago, when I found out about Miss Owens. But I don't need courage now. I don't need anything. Because I have you.

"You'll get your revenge, John. And I'll get my peace."

I wanted to shout out for Lincoln to stop. To race forward and tackle him before he could get too close to McNamar, before he forced McNamar to use his weapon. Or to dive in front of Lincoln and take the bullet myself. But my shout was frozen in my throat and my feet were glued to the ground.

Lincoln kept up his slow advance. Fifteen feet. Twelve. McNamar had dropped one of his pistols and held the other with both hands. I saw that they were shaking slightly. He was crouched into a shooting position.

Ten feet separated the two men from their destiny. Nine. Eight.

"Stop!" screamed a voice.

At first I thought I'd managed to speak, but as both Lincoln and McNamar turned I realized the command had come from the side of the field, from the direction of the boat landing. John Johnston was striding forward. He was dripping wet, and he held a long-barreled hunting rifle against his shoulder.

A belated sign of recognition flashed across McNamar's face. His finger reached for the trigger.

There was a giant explosion of gunpowder.

CHAPTER 39

On the middle weekend of September, we engaged a large carriage pulled by a double team. I drove from atop the high box, while Lincoln, Martha, Thomas Lincoln, and John Johnston sat in back, facing each other two by two. The package was wrapped in brown paper and resting against the side of the carriage compartment next to Lincoln. He had not let it out of his possession since it had been delivered the previous day. The oppressively hot summer had finally broken, and a tart crispness in the air portended the coming arrival of fall.

"Everyone keeps telling me you saved my Abraham, Missy," Thomas Lincoln was saying to Martha, "but I don't understand how it could be."

"John did it," she replied, blushing.

"But you gave me the chance," said Johnston. "And you, too, Abe." He punched Lincoln good-naturedly in the shoulder. For once Lincoln did not recoil or frown but rather reached out and returned a friendly slap on Johnston's knee.

"I don't understand," repeated Thomas Lincoln. Looking up at me, he called, "I don't understand these young folks, Mr. Fry Speed. Maybe you do, but I don't."

"Tell Mr. Lincoln the story, Martha," I directed. I knew she'd already done so on several occasions, but there was no harm in letting her repeat it.

"When I woke up that Sunday morning," said Martha with a

smile, for I knew she was justly proud of her role in the affair, "I found a note slipped under my door. Written by Mr. Douglas."

"That goddamned midget!" roared Thomas Lincoln. "I knew he'd cause no end of trouble for my Abraham. What'd the note say, Missy?"

"Yeah, what did it say?" I called down from the high box. I'd never gotten a full answer from Martha on this question.

Martha blushed again. "The only part that's relevant to my story, Mr. Lincoln," she said, "is that it ended by Mr. Douglas saying 'good-bye' to me. I didn't know what he meant at first, but it alarmed me, enough that I ran over to the store to ask Joshua. And when I got there and saw he and Abraham were gone from their bed already, well, suddenly I knew exactly what he meant.

"I went back out on the street and I was frantic, because I didn't know how I was going to stop them. How I was going to save his life, because I knew Mr. Douglas's life was very much in danger. I'd just about decided I'd have to wake up the sheriff and send him, even though I knew that might cause trouble for Stephen, as well as Joshua and Abraham and the others."

"She was willing to sacrifice our well-being, Lincoln, just like that," I called down. "All for the sake of her Little Giant."

Lincoln chortled, but Martha said, seriously, "I certainly was. I didn't want *anyone* getting shot at. Everything else could get worked out, I figured. But not gunshot wounds. So, I was striding back and forth next to the capitol walls, trying to figure whether there was any alternative to going to get Humble, when I bumped into John."

Thomas Lincoln squinted at his stepson through his rheumy eyes. "What was you doing out at the early hour, Johnnie?"

"Don't you remember, Papa?" said Johnston. "You sent me to scavenge up some breakfast."

"And it's a good thing you did, Mr. Lincoln," said Martha. "John saw the look on my face and asked me what was wrong, and I told him what was happening and where I thought he could find Abraham and Stephen and the rest."

"Now you're just part of 'the rest,' Speed," said Lincoln, reaching up and poking me in the back.

"I used to be her favorite brother," I said with a sigh.

Martha kicked Lincoln in the shin. "Stop making trouble! That's my part of the story. The rest is John's."

"So I grabbed my hunting rifle," said Johnston, turning to his stepfather, "from the place we'd stashed it in the stables when we first got to town. And I, er, borrowed a horse from the stables. Ain't nobody around to ask, not at that time of morning. And I rode as fast as I could towards where Miss Martha directed me. And when I got to the shoreline, there was no boat, and then I saw a rowboat tied up across the way, on the edge of the island.

"I might have left it at that and turned 'round to come back home, but Miss Martha'd been so insistent I get over to the island. I tested the waters and realized they was low enough, from being late summer, that I could walk all the way across the river to the island if I kept my rifle held up above my head. Which is what I did."

"Most bravely," said Abraham, and Johnston gave him a heart-felt smile.

"And when I got ashore," continued Johnston, "I came into a field and saw a man holding a pistol on Abraham in close range. About to shoot. There wasn't no time to think. All I could do was aim and pull. That was my brother he was threatening."

Thomas Lincoln grinned and reached out both arms, patting Johnston's knee with one hand and Abraham's with the other. Neither man fled from his father's touch.

"It's just like I always told you boys," said the elder Lincoln, "when you was growing up. Ain't nothing stronger than family."

The family Lincoln and Martha shared smiles, while I turned back to the road and drove on. It had been a busy week in Springfield, one filled with departures. On Monday, Henry Truett, eager for his new Oregon posting, had ridden out of town. He planned to winter in Des Moines before pressing west with the melting snows.

On Wednesday, Sarah Butler had departed with the tents and platform of the camp meeting for parts unknown. Along with some of the other female exhorters, Miss Butler vowed to carry on the work of Preacher Crews, who had not been seen or heard from since that fateful Sunday in August. The faithful had concluded that the preacher had been called away for a personal audience with the Almighty, an event that only redoubled their fervor to spread the Word up and down the frontier.

The unnamed dueling island in the middle of the Sangamon River already harbored many secrets. One more would not tip the balance.

On Thursday, Lincoln's law partner John Todd Stuart had left for Washington, where he was to assume the U.S. congressional seat for the Illinois Third District. The local Whigs threw a great party in the shadows of the capitol walls—now rising to a second story—to send him off. In the final, official tally, Stuart had defeated Douglas by a mere thirty-six votes out of 37,000 cast. George Weber published a new article in every edition of the *Illinois Democrat* decrying the supposed fraud that had stolen the seat from Douglas and the Democrats, but the complaints were in vain. Somehow, someway, Stuart had won.

If his ally in the press was still fighting the last war, Stephen Douglas was assuredly preparing for the next one. Douglas was well on to his next scheme for gaining power at Lincoln's expense. There was talk that he had set his sights on the Illinois Supreme Court, where he would have supervisory powers over Lincoln and all the other lawyers in the state. The one thing I could say with complete confidence was that we hadn't heard the last of Douglas.

Consumed with these thoughts, it took me a few moments to realize we had reached our destination: New Salem. I drove toward the mill on the edge of the river.

"There she is," said Lincoln to his father and stepbrother. He pointed at the mill as it came into sight. "Like I told you, that's the very mill that snagged me the first time I ever floated down these waters. It's been abandoned for a couple of years now, but I wager the two of you can get the wheel working in no time. And while I can't promise there're too many folks in the environs, I do know there'll be a consistent demand for a working mill right in the middle of town."

Thomas Lincoln stood up and gazed at the mill and wheel long-ingly. I pulled the reins to slow up our two horses lest the old man pitch over.

"Lookee there, Johnnie," said Thomas, a trembling hand point-ing toward the mill. "Lookee there! Just what we've been hoping for."

"Could be, Papa," said Johnston.

"Why don't you take a closer look," said Lincoln. I pulled up in front of the mill and Johnston jumped out, and he and Lincoln together helped Thomas Lincoln step down slowly from the car-riage. "Take a look and talk to the folks hereabouts. We'll be back to pick you up in about an hour, unless you decide you want to stay and make a go of it."

When the two men were safely clear of the carriage, I gave a shake of the reins and we lurched into motion again.

"That worked out well," I said. "It was a brilliant idea on your part, Lincoln. Gets them gainfully employed and keeps them out of your path for good."

"I think that's *most* unlikely," said Lincoln, watching his father and stepbrother as they faded into the distance.

A few minutes later we reached our other destination: the bur-ying grounds on Concord Ridge. I pulled up the horses at the top of the ridge beneath a clear blue sky. Spread out before us was the sweeping hillside and beyond that the receding prairie, now flecked with the reds and browns of the coming fall.

A cool breeze blew through. Instinctively, I touched the right arm of my coat, but I found it bare. There had been one more departure as well this week. The mourning period for our sister Ann had finally passed. I had taken my black band off my sleeve for good and placed it carefully at the bottom of my trunk. Our youn-gest sister was gone, but she would never be forgotten.

Lincoln, Martha, and I sat in the still carriage and gazed out wordlessly at the decaying prairie, nature's timeless cycle of birth, death, and renewal playing out before our eyes. Then Lincoln sighed, grasped the package by his side with both hands, and climbed out.

He helped Martha down, and she led him over to the head-board for James Rutledge and the simple white cross next to it. Lincoln carefully placed his package on the ground a few feet away and unwrapped it. It was a slab of marble, engraved:

Ann Rutledge
1813–1835
Beloved

Lincoln knelt on the earth next to the white cross. He took a small spade from his pocket, and he started to dig.

HISTORICAL NOTE

Those who think the current political moment is beset by unique coarseness and animosity would do well to study the American political environment of the nineteenth century, especially in the Western states such as Illinois. By comparison to that historical record, the current political class is—to adapt the famous dictum—playing beanbags.

Final Resting Place is a work of imaginative fiction, but it is based directly on the life and times of the young Abraham Lincoln and his roommate and lifelong close friend, Joshua Speed. Lincoln and Speed shared a bed in the room above Speed's general store in Springfield from 1837 until 1841. The only time during that period when Speed returned home to his native Louisville was to attend the funeral of his youngest sister, Ann Speed, who died suddenly in early 1838. For the rest of his life, Speed would recall the vivid dream about Ann he had one night during his return journey to Springfield.

Each of the principal political events of 1838 Springfield depicted in the novel actually did occur that year in Springfield in something very close to the form portrayed. In real life, Jacob Early, an aspirant to the position of federal land office registrar, was shot and killed after a dispute with Henry Truett, the holder of the land office job, in the gentlemen's smoking lounge of Colonel Spotswood's Rural Hotel in central Springfield.

Truett was accused of the crime and hired Lincoln to defend him. After the regular prosecutor was recused from the case,

Stephen Douglas was appointed by Judge Jesse B. Thomas Jr. to handle the prosecution. So, just as in the novel, Lincoln and Douglas tried the *People vs. Truett* murder case against each other in what was the highest-profile trial of the year in Springfield.

Since Springfield's old courthouse had been torn down and the new one was under construction (as part of the new capitol building), the actual trial was held in an office at Hoffman's Row, directly underneath Lincoln and Stuart's law offices. The sessions of the Sangamon County Circuit Court were to take place at Hoffman's Row for several years as the capitol construction slowly progressed, and many contemporaneous accounts report on Lincoln opening the trapdoor in his floor and leaning down precariously into the courtroom below.

Lincoln and Douglas would appear together in the same legal case dozens of times during their largely coextensive legal careers. As depicted in the novel, they were also principal political rivals in Illinois beginning in the 1830s, a contest that would span more than two decades. Speed later recalled that the "two great rivals, Lincoln and Douglas . . . seemed to have been pitted against each other from 1836 till Lincoln reached the Presidency." Their most famous political clash would come much later, of course, when they faced each other in the 1858 campaign for the U.S. Senate seat from Illinois, the campaign featuring the landmark Lincoln–Douglas Debates.

But that's getting ahead of the story. In the most important political races of 1838, again as in the novel, Lincoln ran for reelection to the state legislature while his law partner John T. Stuart faced Douglas in the race for U.S. Congress. The entire political season was nasty and violent, highlighted by a raucous debate at the Springfield market house at which a prominent Whig (in reality it was Stuart, not Speed), enraged by the provocative speechmaking of the diminutive Douglas, picked up the Little Giant and paraded him around the market house to widespread ridicule. In response, Douglas bit Stuart's thumb so hard it became infected, and Stuart was forced to miss the final debate of the campaign. Stuart was said to bear the scar of Douglas's bite for the rest of his life.

As in the book, the actual election took place on August 6, 1838. Lincoln won reelection to his seat in the state legislature easily, capturing the most votes among all seventeen candidates, but the U.S. Congress race was very close and highly contested. The early returns had Douglas ahead decisively. "Douglas is elected," conceded Simeon Francis's Whig organ the *Sangamo Journal* on August 11, 1838. But then additional votes for Stuart continued to trickle in, many from highly suspect sources. Both sides alleged fraud as the votes were counted and recounted. In the end, Stuart was adjudged the winner by thirty-six votes out of 36,472 cast. Douglas and the Democrats protested loudly but to no avail, and it was Stuart who took the seat in Washington.

Unbowed by his loss, the Little Giant continued his meteoric rise in Illinois politics. Douglas was named secretary of state in 1840 and became a justice on the Illinois Supreme Court at the age of twenty-seven in 1841. He was elected U.S. senator in 1846, a position he held until his death in 1861. He was several times a presidential candidate, including in 1860 against Lincoln. As a politician, he was a vocal proponent of "popular sovereignty," which advocated letting the people of each state decide important issues for themselves. In the highly charged politics of the time, this equated to supporting the right of the southern states to maintain slavery.

Throughout his political career, Douglas also continued to practice law. He was a man of great talents and many peculiarities. One in particular, noted by many contemporaries, was his habit of sitting upon the laps of other, larger men in court while he was simultaneously engaged as counsel or even as a judge in the case.

Roving self-styled preachers who set up camp meetings of revival were a common feature of the American frontier in the 1830s, part of the Second Great Awakening of religious fervor that swept the country in the first half of the nineteenth century. Shut out of nearly every other aspect of public life, women often played a large role in these revivals. A controversial tent meeting headed by a Preacher Crews was established near Springfield in the late 1830s, which produced many saved souls and just as many non-believers.

Numerous books have been written on the question of Lincoln's religious beliefs, which is one of the most hotly contested areas of Lincoln scholarship. Speed later wrote that, "in early life, [Lincoln] was a skeptic. He had tried hard to be a believer, but his reason could not grasp and solve the great problem of redemption as taught." It is probably fair to say that Lincoln believed deeply in a God but that his beliefs did not easily align with those of any major religious denomination.

The political wars of the 1830s prominently featured anonymous letters to the editors of local newspapers. Such letters often contained baseless charges that the authors were not comfortable airing over their actual name. In one notable series of letters from 1837, Lincoln, writing as "Sampson's Ghost," criticized the position of a legal and political opponent, one James Adams. Lincoln's efforts to tarnish Adams were largely unsuccessful, and the litigation in question dragged out inconclusively for many years.

It was the mischief caused by another series of anonymous letters that provoked the only duel challenge of Lincoln's public career. In an episode in 1842 that later caused Lincoln much embarrassment, letters signed only "Rebecca" appeared in the *Sangamo Journal*, criticizing the official behavior of state auditor James Shields. Historians generally believe Mary Todd (whom Lincoln was courting at the time) was chiefly responsible for writing the Rebecca letters, but Lincoln gallantly took sole responsibility.

Shields challenged Lincoln to a duel, a challenge Lincoln felt obligated to accept. But, as the challenged party, Lincoln got to choose the duelists' weapons. He famously specified "cavalry broadswords of the largest size," which were much less likely to prove fatal than were pistols. (One imagines Lincoln also hoped to benefit from his much longer reach when employing broadswords against the five-foot-nine-inch Shields.) The two combatants met on Bloody Island, but—happily for the future course of U.S. history—the seconds were able to work out a last-minute compromise and the broadswords were never unsheathed.

Other figures of note in Springfield also had frequent scrapes with dueling. Indeed, according to one source, Jacob Early, the very man whose murder sparked the trial of Henry Truett, "earned the epithet 'the fighting parson' for his habit of resigning his pastorate in order to fight duels that never quite came off." In a perfectly symmetrical ending to the story, Truett himself left Springfield shortly after his trial and headed for the Pacific coast. In San Francisco, he got into an argument with a business associate, challenged him to a duel, and shot and killed him.

Lincoln had strained relations throughout his life with his largely uneducated father Thomas and his stepbrother John Johnston, whom Lincoln condemned for living off of Thomas's meager resources. Thomas and Johnston lived an itinerant life, moving from place to place together in search of money-making schemes. They frequently asked Lincoln for loans (which, invariably, were not repaid), and on at least one occasion Lincoln paid off a large debt the two men had incurred.

In one episode, Johnston wrote to Lincoln that he needed to return home urgently because Thomas Lincoln was on his deathbed. Lincoln abandoned an ongoing legal case and raced home, only to find Thomas in good health and in need of money. Several years later, Johnston again wrote to Lincoln to say that Thomas was on his deathbed. Though Lincoln was only one day's ride away, this time he ignored the plea and did not come to visit. Thomas Lincoln passed away a few weeks later, never seeing his son again. Lincoln did not attend his father's funeral and refused to pay for a gravestone.

Lincoln's early relationships with women were nearly as tumultuous. He fell in love with Ann Rutledge in New Salem, a woman already engaged to another man who alternately went by the names John McNamar and John McNeil. After a long, fitful courtship with Lincoln, Ann agreed to break off her engagement with the missing McNamar and marry Lincoln. But she died suddenly of "brain fever" (probably meningitis) in August 1835. As in the novel, McNamar returned to New Salem shortly thereafter to find out that his intended had forsaken him for Lincoln and then passed away.

The character of Margaret Owens is based on Mary Owens, whom Lincoln courted in Springfield after the death of Ann

Rutledge. By some accounts, Lincoln successfully proposed to Miss Owens and later tried to back out of the engagement; by others, Lincoln proposed to her and was rebuffed. In any event, later in life Lincoln referred with much embarrassment to his haphazard conduct. "Others have been made fools of by the girls," he wrote, "but this can never with truth be said of me. I most emphatically, in this instance, made a fool of myself."

ACKNOWLEDGMENTS

This manuscript benefited greatly from detailed and insightful notes from my sister Lara Putnam, my college roommate Joshua F. Thorpe, and my writing partners Michael Bergmann and Christin Brecher. I am grateful that all four of these treasured early readers have continued to consider my drafts and give me their invaluable thoughts long after most people would have considered the obligations of friendship satisfied.

I conducted substantial original and on-site historical research as part of the development of this story. I want to acknowledge in particular the assistance of the staffs of the Lincoln Presidential Museum, Old State Capitol Historic Site, and Lincoln–Herndon Law Offices State Historic Site, all in Springfield, Illinois, as well as Diane Young of the Farmington Historic Home site in Louisville. Jana Meyer and Jim Holmberg at the Filson Historical Society in Louisville helped me locate original correspondence between Joshua Speed and other members of the Speed family. Dr. Thomas Gest at Texas Tech University and Dr. Dennis C. Dirkmaat at Mercyhurst University educated me about body decomposition for the autopsy scene (any errors are assuredly my own). This book was principally written at the august London Library, founded by Thomas Carlyle in 1841, whose research librarians and other staff provided invaluable assistance.

My editor and publisher, Matt Martz of Crooked Lane Books, provided fantastic support for my project as well as editorial guidance that strengthened the manuscript at every level. I am grateful as well to the rest of the outstanding staff at Crooked Lane, including Sarah Poppe and Jenny Chen. My incomparable agent, Scott Miller, remains an unerring guiding light.

My writing has been greatly aided by the support of family and friends too numerous to list by name. I'll mention here only Shannon Campbell, Joel and Carla Campbell, Steven Everson, Andrew M. Genser, Donna Gest, Marc Goldman, Julie Greenbaum, Atif Khawaja, Laura Kupillas, Laura Lavan, Alice Leader, Brett Olson, Joel Schneider, Mark Stein, David Thorpe, Alina Tugend, Carolyn Waters, and Caroline Werner.

This book is dedicated to my parents, Bob and Rosemary Putnam, who taught *me* the value of hard work and determination. Throughout their lives they have set an exemplary standard for their family and their communities. They are wonderfully loving parents and grandparents. And they have supported my writing career beyond measure, from editorial input to tireless help on the publicity front. Thank you, Mom and Dad.

Finally, I am incredibly grateful for the love of my family. My three sons, Gray, Noah, and Gideon Putnam, continue to be supportive and enthusiastic about my writing career. And nothing would have been possible without my wife, Christin Putnam. She is the first and last reader of every word I write and an endless source of love, encouragement, good cheer, and plot points. I am blessed to have her as my partner and my divine muse.